For Ann D, my excellent friend & tennis cohort! Enjoy Judy H

A Woman of Valor

A Novel about Naomi

Judy Higgins

GOSSART
PUBLICATIONS

Gossart Publications
Washington, D.C

First Gossart Publications Edition, November 2020
Copyright © by Judy Higgins, 2020

Published in the United States in 2020

Photo Credits
Cover: Nat Jones
Map: Nat Jones
Author Photo: Studio Walz
Formatting: Polgarus Studio

First Gossart paperback edition November 2020
First Gossart eBook edition November 2020
Printed in the United States of America

Judy Higgins
A Woman of Valor: a novel/ Judy Higgins

Summary: "A Woman of Valor" tells the story of Naomi's journey, tragedies, and eventual fulfillment as first told in the Book of Ruth in the Old Testament.

ISBN 978-0-578-75738-4

In remembrance of my grandparents,
Mercer Fulton Goss and Julia Tracy Goss

Other Books by Judy Higgins

The Lady
Unringing the Bell
Bride of the Wind

A Woman of Valor

Paraphrased from Proverbs 31: 10-31

Who can find a virtuous woman? Her value is far above that of rubies.

A virtuous woman is not idle. Nor does she allow her servants to be. Before the sun rises, she is up and prepares food for her family and servants. She considers where to cultivate a garden. She plants vegetables and fruit trees, tends the plants, and harvests the produce. And like a merchant's ship, she brings food from wherever she can find it.

She works willingly with her hands, spinning and weaving. When it is cold, her family is comfortable for she has provided them with warm clothes. She weaves tapestry and cushions for her home. What weaving is left after clothing her family, she sells to merchants.

She lights lamps and candles, keeping some burning throughout the night.

Her husband trusts and praises her. Throughout her life, she does him good, never evil. Her goodness is recognized by her husband's peers. She is known by all for her strength and honor. Her children adore her.

She keeps herself strong and healthy, so that she can work until the end of her days. She aids the poor and needy. She is wise and kind. She understands that beauty is vain and does not last, that favor is deceitful. She will be praised for faith, loyalty.

Around 1350 BC, Moishe (Moses) leads the Israelites out of Egypt where they have been slaves for more than two hundred years. The Israelites comprise twelve tribes, each named for one of Jacob's sons. On their way to The Promised Land, they experience many adventures and endure multiple misfortunes, not the least of which occurs when the King of Moab refuses to let them pass through his kingdom. This denial forces the Israelites to detour through the desert, lengthening their journey by many years. Because of this, the Israelites and Moabites are to remain enemies for untold generations.

When the Israelites reach the River Jordan, Moishe delivers the laws to them, climbs Mt. Nebo to view the land he'll never enter, and then dies. Two of the twelve tribes claim land on the eastern side of the Jordan, while the remaining ten tribes cross over into the Promised Land, each tribe settling in an area assigned by the drawing of lots. Only the Levite tribe, whose members will act as priests, receive no land.

The Tribe of Judah occupies the hills which will come to be known as Judea. They claim their fields, build their villages, and set about living. Among these villages rises one known as Bet Lehem. Some two-hundred years after Moishe's death, and eleven-hundred years before the birth of the Messiah, a story that will be known to posterity, and that will affect the course of history begins in this village.

Part I

The Journey

Around 1100 BCE

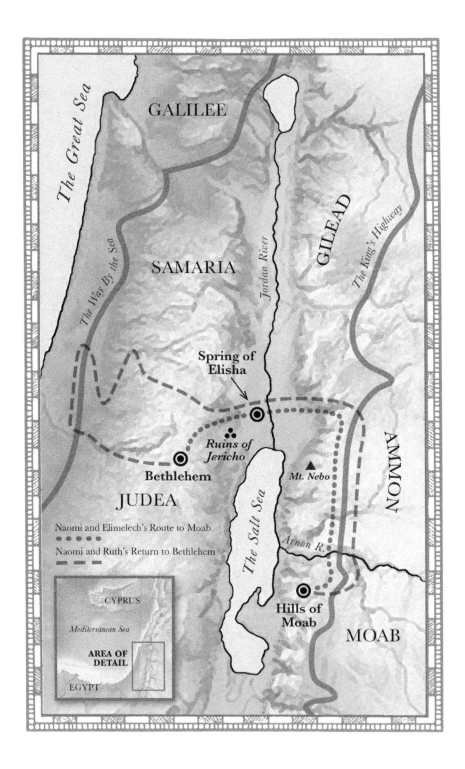

Chapter 1

Come sit beside me, and I'll tell you a story. Hear me, then help me understand what deeds, what thoughts, what failings led Yahweh to inflict on me a curse no woman should have to endure.

Listen . . .. I begin.

On Yom Rishon, the first day of the week, Mighty Samson, my husband's beloved ram died. Like most creatures in Bethlehem, the ram was hungry. Drought scorched the land and, other than small patches of withered forage, there was little for grazing. Shortly before the sun rose, the ram wandered away from the flock, found a growth of poison parsley, and gorged on it. Uri, our shepherd, discovered him bloated and rolling around in pain. The ram died soon after. Uri loaded the carcass onto the back of a donkey, left the flock in the care of the mute who was his helper, and brought the dead sheep to Elimelech.

I say *beloved* when I refer to the ram as he was indeed beloved by my husband. Elimelech loved all his sheep. He took fastidious care of his field, his vineyard, and his orchard, but it was the sheep he cared for most. Only his family came before them in his affections. My heart broke at the sight of his distraught face as he helped Uri lift the animal to the ground. I consoled my husband as best I could and then tried to ease our shepherd's guilt. Uri, still not much more than a boy, had watched our flock since the age of fourteen, and his attachment was nearly equal to Elimelech's.

Elimelech instructed Arioch, one of our bondsmen, to cut away the fleece and prepare the meat for roasting, then, with a look of grim intent, set off to finish his morning's chores. I also returned to mine, not knowing that the ram's death would change our lives.

When my two serving women and I finished our midday meal and were still seated on the upper floor of our dwelling, picking at breadcrumbs and licking olive brine from our fingers, I heard Elimelech talking below. Usually, the men rested wherever they worked, which on this day would have been the vineyard where they'd gone to repair the cistern. I climbed down from the upper floor to see what brought my husband home.

Our sons, Machlon and Killion, leaned on the fence of the rams' stall watching Elimelech examine three lambs chosen to escape the fate of castration. One would be selected as the main breeder and, in two years, take over Mighty Samson's job of seeding the flock. Machlon and Killion had named our unfortunate ram "Mighty Samson" because he'd once broken the ribs of Festus, the town bully, who taunted animals just as he taunted people smaller than he. The sweeper ram, who would be performing Mighty Samson's duties meanwhile, and who hadn't been blessed with a name, stood in the corner eyeing what was going on.

Elimelech, his face drawn, clasped one of the lambs beneath an arm and, with the opposite hand, pried open the animal's mouth and looked inside.

"We're choosing the heir to Mighty Samson," Machlon, my oldest, said when I wedged myself between him and his brother.

"Only Father isn't looking at the right parts." Killion gave me a naughty grin.

I had little patience for the interest seventeen-year-old boys showed in the act of procreation, so I pretended to not hear.

"You've got a bit to learn about sheep," Elimelech said to Killion. There was a forced smile on his lips as he probed the lamb's tongue and gums. "What you see inside the mouth and ears can be as important as the size of his male parts."

"I know, I know," Killion said. "We've heard it before. *To check for parasites, pull down the bottom eyelid. If it's pale, the sheep is sick.*"

"*And the best sheep are long in back.*" Machlon spoke in a deep bass, imitating his father. A year older than Killion, Machlon's voice, though mature and pleasant, hadn't taken on the deep, resonant timbre of my husband's.

Killion reached over to pet one of the young rams. "I'm glad I'm not one of those poor things who has his balls tied so tight they dry up and fall off."

Elimelech shot him a warning look. "Don't talk like that around your mother." He let go of the lamb and caught a second one, imprisoning him under his arm as he had the first. He checked mouth, hooves, ears, genitals. When he finished, he straightened and, his eyes still on the young rams, asked, "So which will it be? Who is to be the next lord of the flock?"

"The one that looks like Mighty Samson," Machlon said.

The lamb Elimelech had been examining when I joined them did look like our unfortunate ram with his dark face but, otherwise, pure white body. My husband ran his hand over the back of each lamb as he reexamined their eyes.

"I agree," he said finally and knelt in front of the first lamb. "You're the chosen one. You shall go forth and multiply as soon as you're big enough."

"You mean as soon as his shofkha is big enough," Killion said.

"Killion!" Elimelech glared at him.

"Sorry, I forgot."

"Shall we call him *Little Samson*, Mother?" Machlon asked.

"Until he gets big."

One of the two remaining lambs pushed between Elimelech and Little Samson.

"I like little Blackfoot," Killion said. "He has spunk. And he's the opposite of Little Samson with a black foot instead of a black face."

Elimelech rose and gave the three lambs a long, intense look. "We have to keep a close watch on these three; it would be catastrophic to lose them." He pushed open the gate and came out. "Go back to the vineyard," he said to our sons. "The damaged cistern awaits you. I'll be there shortly." He watched Machlon and Killion make their way along the corridor between the stalls and storage rooms as they headed for the front gate.

"You sired handsome sons," I said.

"I agree." He waited until the gate creaked shut behind out sons, then turned to me but looked at his feet instead of meeting my eyes. "We're losing too many sheep."

I pushed aside a lock of hair that had fallen across his forehead. "I'm sorry, but what can you do that you're not already doing?"

"The grass in the pastures is nearly gone and, without a harvest, there'll be no stubble." He shifted from foot to foot, still refusing to meet my eyes. "I started with eleven sheep. Only eleven, Naomi." He did look at me then. "That was before we married. Did you know I had so few?"

"Everyone knows how hard you worked."

"I took care of my sheep like they were babies."

"And now you have more than a hundred."

"The grass is disappearing, while over there," he motioned to some indeterminate place as he turned to walk away, ". . . there's plenty of grass."

I knew that wherever *over there* was, Elimelech would send the flock. He might have to pay for grazing rights and hire another shepherd to help Uri and the mute, but what was a bit of silver compared to losing sheep which provided half our sustenance as well as our wealth?

Chapter 2

Abi, one of my two serving women, sat cross-legged on the ground peeling cucumbers, piling the peels beside her to be used as fertilizer in the garden. A sliver of green lodged in her kinky, black curls.

Damaris had lit the bread oven and was kneading dough, her long, large-knuckled fingers strong and supple despite her age. She and her husband Zacharias, our vineyard keeper, had been with Elimelech from the time he'd inherited his field.

"Did you clean the cucumbers?" I asked Abi. Only fourteen, she sometimes neglected doing all the steps.

"I scrubbed them good with sand."

"I'm going up to the roof," I said to Damaris.

"To decide if we put out the honey?" Damaris arched one eyebrow.

"Exactly. I'll be back shortly."

From the roof, I could judge Elimelech's mood as he returned from his day's work. We usually served honey in the mornings, but when my husband needed *sweetening* due to a hard day, we also served his favorite food at the evening meal.

Instead of the fragrance of ripe grain greeting me as I climbed from the ladder well and went to stand at the parapet, the smell of ruin filled the air. Our dwelling stood one row of houses from the town wall, and the roof rose higher than the surrounding ones so I had a good view of the destroyed crops. Both the lesser and the greater rains had failed as had the cool winds that normally blew in from the Great Sea during the month of Ziv. In their place, siroccos blasted up from the Gulf of Aqaba. The hellish winds whistled and howled, scorching the Judean hills, killing our crops, thus robbing both humans and animals of food.

I searched for Elimelech among those heading home. Though the gathering dusk blurred their faces, and the wind whipped their clothes into a frenzied dance, I recognized most by walk and posture – Eli from next door by his waddle; old Enoch by his short, clipped steps even though he had long legs; Boaz, who wasn't as tall as Elimelech, but who walked with as much purpose, head high, arms swinging; Skinny, so named because he was shaped like a stripling pine. And many others I recognized, for I'd known them all my life.

A few men gathered around the town wall. Elimelech wouldn't be among them for they'd be grumbling, and my husband seldom bothered with grumblers. "Not only will there be no barley this year," they'd say for the thousandth time, ". . . but no wheat. Sowing wheat seeds on the stone-hard ground will be as productive as arguing with the wind." Then they'd complain about the hard cracks that rutted the ground, making it impossible to plow. I'd heard them often enough to know how their conversations went.

When a gust of wind buffeted me, I gathered my hair in my hands and held it to my neck as I observed the beggars. With no harvest, there was no work to be had, so their numbers multiplied as fast as weeds in my garden. The beggars beseeched everyone they met for a bit of cheese, a crust of bread, a few olives. I gave a little huff. They shouldn't have to beg. Our laws required that we put aside a seventh part of our crops each year for times such as this. Of the portion we put aside, a tenth was supposed to go to these poor souls who had no food but, instead of acting, the elders bickered over how to dole out rations. Distributing food didn't seem difficult. Damaris and I could probably have come up with a plan in the amount of time it took to draw a bucket of water.

At last, I saw Elimelech coming from the vineyard. Instead of with the sagging shoulders of a man having just lost his prized ram, he strode with the purpose and energy of a man intent on something. He stopped near the town gate and looked about as though searching for someone. Then, raising his hand in greeting, he went toward a stranger with a humped shoulder who stood apart. Earlier, I'd seen the man loitering about the gates. Other than his unfortunate posture, he looked well off, his clothes sturdy and a bright yellow instead of the undyed wool worn by most.

When Elimelech reached the man, who was a head shorter, Elimelech glanced up to where I stood. I raised my arm to wave but dropped it when he turned abruptly away, put his hand on the stranger's shoulder, and steered him close to the wall where I couldn't see. My husband had pointedly ignored me. What business did he have with this stranger that he didn't want me to know about?

I hurried down to help finish the meal. As I passed through the back door and into the yard where most of the cooking was done, the aroma of bread baking, along with that of roast mutton made my mouth water. I preferred simple meals rather than stuffing ourselves with mutton, but because we wasted nothing, Mighty Samson's flesh roasted in the firepit. The meat wouldn't be done until the following evening, but we had carved away a small amount to make a stew. The ram's fleece, still smelling of dung and dirt for we had to conserve our water, hung on the limb of the nearby fig tree.

"It smells like the bread is almost ready," I said.

Damaris nodded. Sweat ran down her wrinkled cheeks as she peeled flat bread from the walls of the mud-brick oven with a wooden paddle. "Do we need to bring out the honey?"

"Not tonight."

Abi, her eyes vacant as though she occupied a different world chopped herbs, adding them to a cruet of oil to be poured over the cucumbers. I guessed her thoughts were probably on one of the young men I'd seen her gawking at when we were at the village well.

I went to stir the stew bubbling over the fire. "I'm sorry I left you two busy with all the work."

"At least we have food to be busy with." A piece of bread slipped from Damaris's paddle and fell to the ground. She picked it up, stared at it as though she hated to part with it, and then put it aside. "A waste," she said. "Those starving people out there in the streets would be happy to eat it covered with dust."

"Some would eat that bread even if it was covered with dung," Abi said.

I gave the stew a quick stir then tasted it. It needed more coriander. "You took bread to your grandmother?" I asked Abi as I added more spice. We had begun to bake extra bread for a few who had none.

Abi nodded. "She's grateful." She brushed her forearm across her brow.. "They say those priests of Baal climb up on the temple roofs and pour water through the lattices. If they douse the altar gods, they think it'll make the rains come."

"Well it doesn't do no good, does it?" Damaris said. "A waste of water if you ask me. The barley's already ruined." She peeled the last piece of bread from the oven wall. "Seems everybody's gods are silent right now. Not one of them up there listening to us down here." She grabbed an empty bowl. "I'll get raisins."

"And they're sacrificing babies at that altar up in the hills," Abi continued. I saw the shudder that ran through Damaris.

"I don't want to hear about babies being sacrificed," she said.

"Well, they are." Abi had raised her voice.

"That's enough, Abi." I glared at her.

Damaris shot the girl a look of contempt, then spit, the spittle landing at Abi's side, and went off grumbling.

"Don't talk about sacrificing babies around Damaris. Or around me either. I'm going to see to the wine." Abi was a good worker and never seemed to tire, but she riled Damaris a little too often.

"Don't want to hear about them babies," Damaris mumbled when I joined her in the storeroom. There was barely enough light to see, but I could have found things even during darkest night so well did I know the room.

"I'll warn her again." I removed the straining pitcher from a peg.

"That girl don't understand nothing about warnings." Damaris blew out a huff as she removed a handful of raisins from the jar. She dropped several on the ground. In the gloom I knew she dropped them only because she bent to pick them up. "More waste," she groused. "And all them people about to starve."

"No one is going to starve. There's enough food." I removed the covering from a wine container and poured wine into the pitcher.

"Yes, there's enough food. And when are they going to share it? Tell me that. Can you not talk to your husband? He has as much say as any other elder."

I had already talked to him, but to avail. Elimelech was only *one* of the elders. He couldn't decide by himself.

A familiar bray sounded from the front gate followed by Killion's coaxing as he tied the donkey beside the gate. We'd begun to leave a donkey there, knowing he'd bray if anyone tried to break into our stores during the night. The men also took turns sleeping in front of the door. About to strain the wine, I stopped to listen as Machlon taunted Killion about his handling of the animal, to which Killion retorted in kind. I smiled. *Brothers.* They loved to torment each other yet remained the best of friends.

Then I heard the booming voice of Arioch and the croak of Zacharias as they drove the oxen and remaining donkeys into the stalls. *Whoa. Not so fast.. Hold up. Move, you bloody ass.* The voices of Elimelech and Kir were missing.

Kir. I'd have been happy to *never* hear his voice for I didn't trust Elimelech's other bondsman. With his malformed face and beady eyes, he looked more like a thief than a bondsman. I didn't understand how Elimelech could rely on him.

"We need to hurry," I said as I left to get an ember from the oven to light the lamps. It wouldn't take long for the men to throw down fresh hay and feed the animals, and we hadn't yet brought the food up to the floor where we ate and slept. I hoped my husband wouldn't bring the hump-shouldered stranger to join our evening meal or offer him a place to sleep. The secrecy of their meeting hadn't sat well with me.

Chapter 3

The men ate then went into the night to relieve themselves, while we women devoured what we'd set aside for our own meal. We finished, took the dishes below, and scoured them with sand. Except for Elimelech, the men returned and, seeking a haven from the heat, climbed to the roof to sleep in temporary shelters made of branches and reeds.

After checking to make sure the fire in the oven was out, I fumbled my way along the corridor toward the front entrance for I, too, had to relieve myself. The lamp at the foot of the ladder still burned, but it's light didn't reach much further than the length of a man. I had passed the ladder well and was going past the pen where we kept lambs for fattening when I heard Elimelech's voice outside the gate. Our bondsmen were already on the roof, so puzzled as to whom my husband spoke, I stopped to listen.

"Why this decision?" I recognized the voice of Boaz, Elimelech's cousin. "You know it's wrong."

Elimelech mumbled something.

"I beg you to reconsider," Boaz said.

"I've decided." Elimelech's voice had hardened. "You, especially you, will see that it's for the best. Goodnight."

The gate closed with a click and Elimelech's sandals crunched on the straw of the corridor as he came toward the ladder. When he saw me, he stopped and narrowed an eye as though wanting to ask if I'd overheard.

"I was going out to relieve myself," I explained.

He nodded. When he didn't move, I waited, wondering if he meant to tell me about the conversation with Boaz or the one with the humped stranger. But he explained neither. Instead, he kissed me lightly on the cheek, walked away, and, at the ladder, took off his sandals. Still hoping for an explanation, I watched him immerse his feet in the foot bath, slosh his feet in the water, and then climb the ladder to the roof without a single word.

Chapter 4

The following morning after breaking fast, Elimelech took me by the hand and led me to the wool storage room where we could be alone. "We have to go," he said.

"Go?" I was puzzled. "Go where?"

"We have to leave."

I raised my hands in a question. "What are you talking about?"

"We have to leave Bethlehem. The pasturage is nearly gone. There's barely a green blade left."

Leave Bethlehem? Surely, he meant he'd have Uri take the flock to the place he'd spoken of as having plenty of grass.

"The goats manage to find weeds and a few blades of grass in rock crevices, but the sheep are trying to graze the entire day without resting. You know what that means."

I knew. When the sheep got the nourishment they needed, they'd graze for a while then rest. When the grass lacked nourishment, they'd spend every moment of the day eating. They also got their water from dew-covered plants. Since the sciroccos had robbed the grass of dew, the sheep needed another source, but the stones in the wadis hadn't been dampened by a drop of water in weeks.

"The sheep will die if we don't do something." Elimelech, usually straight and tall, slumped.

A chill ran through me as I pictured sheep falling over dead. Each year, every flock owner lost two or three out of ten to disease, predators, thieves. But *all* the sheep? Surely, he exaggerated.

"There will be no milk, no cheese, no labneh, no . . .." He squeezed his forehead between his thumb and fingers. "Without sheep, half our food will be gone. The land can no longer support two flocks the sizes of mine and Boaz's. Soon, it won't be able to support even one. And there are the smaller flocks to consider. This will be hard, Naomi, but we won't be there long."

"There?"

"I've questioned every traveler and trader who's appeared at the town gates. Good pasturage is nowhere to be found in Judea." He studied my face for a few moments. "I don't think you understand what I'm saying."

"Then tell me."

"We're leaving Bethlehem. We'll return when the rains come."

I didn't believe him.

"We'll be gone only a few seasons."

A few seasons? Gone! He hadn't told me where we were to go. Nor did I care, for I knew he wouldn't take us away from our home. Leaving was a wild idea he'd forget by tomorrow, or even by afternoon. Where did he think we'd live? In tents? I crossed my arms. "Where do you plan to take us?"

"Moab."

"Moab?" No Israelite would take his family to the country of our most despised enemy, the country through which the Moabite king refused passage to Moishe and the Israelites, the land against which we'd waged war and whose people we were prohibited to marry.

"The grass is plentiful in Moab," Elimelech said.

I was struck speechless. This couldn't be. Was it even allowed? There were laws about sacrifices and food, about inheritance and tilling the land. There was even one forbidding us to weave two different kinds of thread into one cloth. With so many laws how could there not be one forbidding us to live among our enemies?

"You'd really do this?" I asked bitterly when I found my voice.

"We must. You'll come back with stories to tell." He gave a wan smile and reached out to touch my hand. Tucking my hand inside my garment, I stepped back. He pressed his fingers to his forehead. "Today, Uri is bringing the flock to the shearing pens. In two days, in time for the Sabbath, we'll be finished shearing my flock. Then we need two days for Boaz's. His men and mine will work together as they always have." He sat down on a pile of fleeces and, head down, leaned his arms on his thighs. "I'm sorry, Naomi, but this is the way it has to be. When we've taken the wool from the last sheep, we need three days to get ready for the move. Zacharias will do what he can while the rest of us are at the pens. You'll see to the packing of household things. You need to begin now. The longer we linger here, the more sheep we'll lose."

One of my knees jerked uncontrollably.

"Damaris and Zacharias will take care of the house while we're away, along with Damaris' nephew." Without meeting my eyes, he rose and stood facing the door. "A guide will take us to the place we're going."

The man with the humped shoulder! Now I understood. "And Kir? Did he talk you into this?"

Elimelech held up a palm in question. "Why, would you . . .?

"You know nothing of Kir. Yet this . . ., this bondsman who's been with you only a little over three years advises you, and you listen."

"Yes, I listen to Kir. I'd be a fool not to consider sage advice when it's offered. But I make my own decisions. As for Kir having a hand in this, I neither asked him for advice, nor did he give any." He turned and strode away.

Chapter 5

Before I continue my own story, there is another I must tell so that you may better understand mine. This other is a story within a story, the longer one containing enough smaller ones to entertain us for many seasons. The longer story begins with Joseph being sold into slavery in Egypt. I will skip over how all of his brothers eventually wound up there, and how they had children and grandchildren and great-grandchildren, and so on, until there were thousands of Israelites in Egypt. And I will skip over how, led by Moishe, the Israelites escaped Egypt.

Let me take you to the part where the Israelites have come to a place called Kadesh, east of the Salt Sea. To continue on to the land flowing with milk and honey which Yahweh has promised them they must travel north, cross the Arnom River, and then turn west to cross the Jordan for the Promised Land lies west of the Jordan. This path will take them through the countries of Moab and Edom. Respectfully, Moishe asks the kings of Moab and Edom for permission to lead his charges through their countries, promising they will not trample their fields and vineyards, nor will they drink water from their wells. Not so respectfully, both kings decline. The King of Edom even sends out a heavy force to insure the Israelites do not enter his territory.

The only other way to get to the Promised Land is to travel through the great desert to the east where there is neither food nor water. The Israelites set out on this formidable route, suffering greatly and prolonging their journey by nearly forty years, their resentment against the Moabites and Edomites building. Finally, after many years and struggles, they reach wadi Zered near the Arnom River and pitch their tents beside the border of Moab. Frightened at their numbers, King Balak hires a man named Balaam to destroy the Israelites with a curse. The curse doesn't work, so Balaam instructs the Moabite women to seduce the men of Israel then persuade them to worship their idols. Balaam knows this will evoke Yahweh's fury at the people of Israel. The Moabite sluts seek out the Israelite youths, entice them to fornicate, then persuade the young men to worship Chemosh. As Balaam predicted, an angry Yahweh orders Moishe to impale the idolaters then sends a plague that kills twenty-four thousand Israelites.

Bitter, the Israelites have ever since despised the Moabites, writing into their laws, prohibitions against certain intermarriages. And it is to this country that my husband has decided that we must go. Even with two sons of an age to be seduced by Moabite sluts.

After receiving the abominable news from my husband, I leaned against the door frame watching Damaris and Abi while blood churned through my veins, turbulent and chaotic, like water rushing through wadis after the greater rains. Yet my serving women didn't notice how I shook, or hear my heart beating like a drum. How could they not?

Kneeling near the oven, Damaris periodically stopped the whop, whop of pestle against mortar to pick flecks from the flour – a bit of stalk, a fly's wing, a fluff of dandelion dropped by the wind. Abi stood in the shade of the fig tree setting up a tripod from which a goatskin bag dangled. When she had the tripod standing securely, she picked up the jug of milk next to it and looked toward Damaris. "Can you help?"

Leaving a white streak across her forehead, Damaris pushed back a strand of hair, rose from her crouch, and went to hold open the neck of the goatskin while Abi poured milk in. Without a word, Damaris went back to her mortar and pestle. Abi tied the neck opening tight to keep milk from splashing out, sank to her knees and, humming, began to push the skin back and forth like a pendulum, separating fat from milk.

When Damaris finally noticed me, she stopped pounding grain and tilted her face to see me better. "Did you want something?"

I shook my head. "Imla is coming to help with the weaving. I was just . . .. I need to finish setting up." I fled to the wool room and sank onto the stool I used for weaving, a thousand questions batting at me like wasps attacking a beehive. What would happen to my home while we were away? Zacharias was getting old, and I didn't trust Damaris' nephew, Matthias. He was only sixteen; what did he know? An old man and a youth were going to keep thieves from taking everything we owned? And Damaris had started to slow. It took her twice as long to grind the flour as it had a year ago and, often enough, she failed to add a needed ingredient to whatever she was making. Last week she'd neglected to put coriander in the stew. The week before, she forgot to strain the wine. Would she be careless with lamps and burn down our home?

The room lay in semi-darkness. Below the eaves, one tiny window let in barely enough light to make out items. Along with my loom, there were bundles of wool, a pile of fleeces smelling of sheep fat, containers filled with dye materials – cochineal insects, turmeric, dried red madder and safflower. Spindle whorls and extra weights for the warp were stashed in baskets.

The day before, I'd strung the warp and attached weights so Imla and I could begin straightaway. We often worked together, Imla standing behind the loom to hand the weft through the warp threads while I sat or stood in front and grabbed the weft as she passed it through. Then, after crossing it over the warp, I handed it back to her. While a piece of cloth formed on the loom between us, we'd spend the morning laughing, gossiping, bragging about children, or complaining about them when they merited complaints. When my father died, we mourned together as a length of yellow cloth formed between us. My father had been Imla's uncle, but he raised her as one of his own.

I heard the crunch of straw and moments later Imla appeared in the door – Imla, my cousin by birth, but sister by choice, fine-boned and graceful.

"You look like the moon just fell out of the sky," she said.

"We're taking the flocks to Moab," I blurted.

"Funny." She sat down on the pile of fleeces.

"No, it isn't funny. There's grass for the sheep over there." I motioned in the general direction of Moab even though I wasn't sure of its exact location, just that the land lay somewhere on the other side of the Salt Sea.

"You sound like you really mean it." Imla frowned, her normally straight eyebrows arching. "You can't go; our children are to be married in two years."

"Machlon and Galatia *will* marry. We'll return when the rains come."

"You can't live with the Moabites. They won't let you."

"I hope not. I hope they send us back straightaway." I dissolved into tears.

Imla knelt in front of me, her hand on my knee. "You aren't going anywhere, Naomi. The priest has summoned us for a public weeping. If we weep long enough and hard enough, Yahweh will take pity and make it rain."

I wiped my eyes with the sleeve of my tunic. "Nothing else has worked. Not the sacrifices. Not all the other praying and weeping."

"This time it will work." Imla's voice was firm.

All of Bethlehem wept – men, women, boys and girls; the rich, the poor; the pious and even those that weren't. Led by the priest, we wound through the streets, our cries loud enough to reach Yahweh's ears. At the altar, lambs were sacrificed, and the crowd wept louder. Surely, Yahweh heard and would withdraw his punishment.

That night, I was awakened by rain pattering below the roof opening. Overjoyed, I rushed from my bed, anticipating the feel of heavenly drops falling on my face only to discover the rain had been a dream. I lay awake for the remainder of the night, listening, hoping that my dream was an omen, that rain would come. But as black night turned to gray morning, the air was as dry as a dead leaf. Yahweh had closed his ears to our pleas.

Chapter 6

"Prepare refreshments for twelve or so," Elimelech said as he headed out the next morning. "They'll come before they begin their day's work."

"Wait," I called after him.

He turned and explained. "I'm gathering ten elders to deal with my share of the grain tithe."

I didn't have enough to do already? Now I had to stop and prepare food for a group of men who had just eaten their breakfasts?

Boaz arrived soon after. I was readying a bowl of nuts and dried fruits, when I heard him coming along the corridor, humming. After instructing Abi to bring water, I went to meet him.

"Shalom, Naomi," he said. He had brought two donkeys and was looping their halters around the top rail of the stall fence. "I'm glad to see you and sorry that soon I'll no longer have the pleasure. At least not for a while."

"I'm sorry, too. But it will be doubly pleasurable to see you when we return. How is your wife?"

He shook his head sadly. "She's slow recovering from the latest still birth."

"Tell her I hope she'll be better soon, and if there's anything she needs . . . .." What she needed most, no one could give. Sarai had had four babes die in the womb and no live births. This man, as rich, as industrious, and as honorable as Elimelech, had the misfortune to have no heirs.

"*Toda.* Thank you. I'll tell her," he said.

Abi brought a jug of water and cups. Behind her, Damaris came with nuts and figs.

"Shalom Aleichem," Boaz said and smiled at my serving women.

I stood aside while he asked Damaris' about her nephew and Abi about her grandmother. Boaz was as charming as my Killion, and almost as handsome as Elimelech. Three years younger and a whit shorter than my husband, Boaz had the same dark, curly hair, the same gray-speckled beard. Smile lines webbed from the corners of his eyes.

The elders began to arrive, one by one or in twos, until the last came accompanied by Elimelech. After wiping their hands on their tunics, they took refreshments with barely a thank you and no more than a nod to acknowledge my presence. Looks of weary impatience on their faces, they were in a hurry to get back to what they'd been doing: clearing dead crops from their fields, shearing sheep, despairing of the dried-up beads of grapes in their arbors.

Elimelech waved his hand to get their attention. "I want you to witness me turning over my grain-tithe to Boaz for safe-keeping. People need to know I did what is required. When you decide how to share the grain with the hungry, Boaz will do it for me."

"Fine, fine. Let's get on with it," one of the elders said. The others muttered in agreement.

Elimelech took them to the storeroom where we kept part of the grain in large amphorae and where the floor had been dug deep to keep out moisture. After taking note of the amount stored there, my husband led them to the structure built against the outside of the house where we stored a majority of the grain. Curious, I followed. The structure had double thick walls and there, too, the foundation had been dug nearly as deep as a man.

The elders noted the amount, determined what our tithe should be, and helped Elimelech and Boaz shovel it into baskets. As soon as the baskets were loaded on Boaz's donkeys and Elimelech's oxen, everyone left except for Elimelech and Boaz. I stood just inside the entry to the storeroom, listening, hoping for what I knew was impossible: that Boaz would persuade Elimelech to change his mind.

"There's nothing that will convince you to stay?" Boaz asked.

"Nothing," my husband replied.

"I fear for your safety. Your lives are more important than your sheep."

"With that, I agree. But nothing will happen. In Moab we have the protection of a village chief, and we'll manage the difficulties of travel." He paused before adding, "I see that look on your face, Boaz."

"What look?"

"The one you have when you're plotting or planning."

"I wasn't plotting or planning." I heard the smile in Boaz's voice. "I was just wondering if there wasn't some law among all those given us by Moishe that forbids us to set foot in Moab. After Moishe's troubles, you'd think there would be."

"No law that I know of," Elimelech replied. I heard the smile in his voice, too. "You know me. If there were such a commandment, I'd abide by it."

"Yes, you would. You don't want your sheep struck down because you faulted on a law. I'm going to miss you, cousin."

"And I you."

Though busy shearing, Elimelech found time to hire two extra men to accompany us on our journey. The first, Skinny, did itinerate work in the fields as well as odd jobs. He had a long, narrow face with a scar stretching from one ear to the corner of his mouth.

It was the hiring of the second man that shocked me.

"The bully!" I said to Elimelech when he told me. "You hired the bully?"

"Yes. I hired him." He rose from where he'd been sharpening shearing knives. "I wanted someone big, and he's learned his lesson about bullying the animals."

"The animals! What about us?"

Elimelech gave me a lopsided smile. "If you find him threatening because of his size and demeanor, that's the point. Anyone who takes it into his head to accost us will also find him threatening. I've set him straight about bullying. He'll harm neither us nor our animals. And he does have a name."

"Festus," I said. "Festus, the Bully."

"*Festus* will do."

Elimelech sent Hada and Mesha, two sisters who did our milking, to help pack. They would also accompany us on our journey. Hada, tall and square-faced, was a disciplined, hard worker who spoke little, but her short, round-faced sister Mesha did enough talking for both.

As we set ourselves to the task of packing, the days flew past. Three, then two, then one. I was barely aware of what Elimelech did, only that he sold what wool he could, sent Kir to purchase goat hair tents, and buried our valuables in a place he hoped no one would find. What Elimelech's other tasks were, I couldn't say because I was too busy with my own.

The news of our exodus spread like chaff in the wind. Sad or curious, friends and neighbors came offering help but mostly getting in the way. Nights, I crept into bed glad for quiet, solitude, and rest.

My brothers and sisters warned of lions, wolves, thieves, and whatever else they could think of to make me afraid. During the early afternoon of the last day, even though she'd interrupted my packing every day, my sister Dorcus came, bringing her four-year-old granddaughter, Esther. Hada and Mesha were in the outside storage area, shoveling the last of the barley and wheat into baskets. I had been doing the same in the inside storage room. Esther sat down beside me and began running her hands through the grain.

"Will you be taking all your grain with you?" Dorcus asked.

I flinched. What Dorcus really wanted to know was, *Will you be sharing a tenth with the poor? Will you be leaving us a portion?* With Elimelech's blessing, I had already sent Dorcus a gift of grain since her husband hadn't done as well as Elimelech. He blamed his lack of riches on misfortune – the weather, the land's lack of fertility, his bad back. The truth was he didn't work as hard as Elimelech. None of my family had done as well as my husband for the same reason. Yet, Elimelech had sent each of them a departing gift of grain.

"Elimelech gave his grain-tithe to Boaz for safe-keeping until the elders decide how to distribute it," I told her. "The elders witnessed the transfer."

"Hmmmph." She frowned. "Don't forget to enter Moab with one shoe on and one off." She gave me her big sister look, the same one she used when she ordered me around as a child.

"Why does she have to take off a shoe?" Esther asked. The child was grabbing fistfuls of grain, holding her hands above the basket, then opening them to let the grain fall through her fingers.

"To free her from Balak's curse," Dorcus explained.

"Don't frighten the child with talk of curses," I said in a low voice.

Dorcus shrugged. "She might as well know."

It wasn't only the child sitting beside me, dirtying my grain, that I didn't want Dorcus to frighten. All week, there had been references to wolves, lions, thieves. Now we had to talk about curses.

"It's a silly story," I said, hoping it *was* a silly story.

"But I want to know," Esther said.

I grabbed Esther's hands, brushed away the grain, and then held her hands between mine.

"Long ago, in the time of Moishe, Balak, the king of Moab hired a man called Balaam to put a curse on the Israelites. But it's nothing you have to worry about."

"The curse is laid back on the Moabites if an Israelite enters Moab with one shoe off and one on," Dorcus said to her granddaughter. "Naomi is right. It's nothing you have to worry about. Come . . . .." she held out her hand to Esther, ". . . it's time to go."

Shortly after Dorcus left, Zacharias helped me carry my stash of white wool to the upper floor where Damaris and Zacharias slept. If thieves broke in while we were gone, they'd probably concentrate on pillaging the storage room. I saved whatever pure white wool our sheep produced, planning to weave garments from it as a gift to my bride-daughters.

When we finished moving the wool, we returned to the wool room for Zacharias to take my loom apart.

"You'll need something to fill your time when you're there," he said as he moved the precious loom away from where it leaned against the wall and laid it on the ground.

"Yes, I imagine I will." I had no doubt that my time would be filled in Moab just as it was here. Did no man realize how much effort went into preparing his food? Or how much harder cooking was going to be without Damaris? I supposed I wouldn't have a garden to care for in Moab, and there'd be no house to tend, just tents. But other tasks would present themselves. I'd know what they were soon enough.

I watched Zacharias as he struggled to untie a cord that bound the top of the loom to one of the sides. Every day he looked a little older. His speckled beard had changed to white, another of his teeth had gone missing, and the hairs that once populated the top of his head had migrated down to sprout in the wild garden of his eyebrows.

Finally, he sat back on his haunches. "Too tight," he said. "May have to cut it." He inserted a knife in the knot, wiggled the blade back and forth until the knot loosened, and then set the knife aside.

"Zacharias . . .."

He looked up, waiting for me to go on.

"The curse of Balaam," I said finally. "You know the story?"

"I've heard it."

"Is it true?"

"Who's to say? There are so many stories, and every person tells them differently. Some tell how Yahweh created man and woman on the sixth day after he created everything else. Others say Yahweh formed man before he created the plants and animals. Only when he was done with those, did he make a woman." He moved to the other end of the loom. "Which are we to believe?" He shrugged. "I wouldn't worry about curses."

What he said was true. There were so many stories, and no two people told them the same way. Such is the nature of tales. And though some were as old as the earth itself while others were as new as yesterday, these stories bind my people together. Blown across the rock-scarred Judean hills, tales of love and hate, defeat and victory, creation and destruction land on our doorsteps, beside the village well, or in the fields where we work. We retell them, adding a little here and a little there.

"I'll build you a new loom while you're gone," Zacharias said, as he untied the chords. "This one's nearly as old as I am."

"Oh, Zacharias." I caught myself before I reached out and touched his arm. What I really wanted was to cast away convention and hug Zacharias who was more like a kind uncle than a servant.

He shrugged. "There won't be much else for me to do. Just the vineyard to keep an eye on, and the house to watch."

He removed the top of the loom, unstrung the kettle boards, and wrapped the pieces in a woven floor covering. "Better to load this on top of a bundle of wool so it won't break. The wood is brittle."

I followed him as he took the loom pieces into the corridor where our possessions were arranged in piles, each pile to be borne by a single animal.

"There." He placed the loom on top of two bundles. And then, as though I didn't remember, he said, "You made me new clothes two months ago. And Damaris, too. Your weaving is so fine those clothes will last us a long, long while." He swallowed and looked away. "But come back soon even if we don't need new clothes."

"I don't know how we can do without you and Damaris." My voice broke.

He tilted his head, a wistful look on his face. "We've been with the family since Elimelech was a boy. He's never treated us like servants, and I love him like . . .. Well, . . . like a son." He shuffled his feet and looked down, but not before I saw a tear trickle from his eye. "You'll be back before you know it, and it will seem as though you never left."

Time is its own master. While we struggled to keep pace, it moved forward, bringing us to our last supper in Bethlehem. While we waited for the men, Damaris sank down on her haunches to rest and pick at the flour stuck beneath her fingernails. Abi flapped a cloth half-heartedly at flies swarming around the figs. Hada and Mesha had come to join us for the meal and to spend the night, for we were to rise early and be the first out the city gates in the morning. Except for Uri and the mute who were with the sheep, and Damaris and Zacharias who would be remaining behind, the people at our table this evening would be my only company for as long as we remained in Moab. There'd be no friends, no kin, no neighbors.

When the men's voices billowed up from below, I picked up the lamp and moved quickly to light the incense burner to counter the inescapable odors of working men.

The ladder groaned under the bulk of Arioch. I knew it was him. Starving, thirsty, and full of good humor, he was the first to appear for every meal. Arioch, the lion. With his size and strength, I wondered if he shouldn't have been named for an ox instead. But in a way, he *did* remind me of a lion with his broad nose, large teeth, and wild mane of reddish hair. When Elimelech claimed that a ram the size of Mighty Samson would have skull bones as thick as the wrist of a large man, he was probably thinking of Arioch, for both his wrists and his hands were of extraordinary size. I was glad he was coming with us, and not only for his pleasant company. With his size and bulky muscles, who would bother us?

"Greetings," he said, his head appearing in the opening, his mane burnished by the glow from the lamp. "Greetings to the three best, wisest, and most beautiful women in all Bethlehem." He heaved his body up, stalked over, and sat down, his thick lips stretched in a grin as he eyed the food.

Damaris gave him a dismissive wave as though she cared nothing for his compliments, but there was a glint in her eyes that didn't come from the flickering flame of the lamp.

Killion scrambled up next, his cheeks bright from a day in the sun. He planted a peck on my cheek, and then threw himself onto a cushion next to Arioch. With his constant smile, Killion was certainly the best-liked young man in Bethlehem. Especially, among women. Since he'd been old enough to coo, he'd cultivated the admiration of females from newborns to grandmothers. When it came time to find him a wife, there'd be a line at our door. He was also the most handsome young man in Bethlehem. His hair fell in soft brown waves, and his eyes, of the same brown, danced with delight, curiosity, and, I'm sorry to say, mischief.

Machlon followed, hair plastered down by sweat, face drawn with exhaustion. While Killion might stir the hearts of a thousand women, I knew my older son would be the sweetest, kindest, and most faithful husband in all of Judea. In two years he'd marry Galatia, daughter of my cousin Imla. My oldest son was also handsome, but in a different way. Like me, he had straight black hair and eyes the color of filberts. Like his father, he was tall. I, too, was tall, but on a woman height isn't becoming.

Next, Zacharias, looking exhausted, poked his head through the opening.

Even his protruding ears seemed to sag. Damaris nodded to her husband who gave her a two-finger greeting before dropping onto a cushion. He crossed his legs, rested his arms on his thighs, and then closed his eyes and let his chin drop.

I felt a pang. The time probably wasn't so far away when Zacharias would no longer be with us, and I'd grieve for him almost as much as I had for my own father. Elimelech had done what he could to ease his work.

Skinny and Festus, our two new workers, joined us. Festus was almost as big as Arioch. Elimelech had been right: with two bondsmen the size of Festus and Arioch, thieves would think twice about accosting us. Unaccustomed to our company, Festus and Skinny sat down quietly, their eyes focused on the food. They were to spend the night on the roof with the other men.

I looked down through the ladder well, expecting to see Elimelech climbing up next, followed by Kir. Kir usually trailed behind my husband like a hungry lamb after its mother. But it was Kir's malformed face and black eyes that appeared in the ring of lamp light. He climbed from the opening, nodded, and, eyes averted, sat down.

"Where's Elimelech?"

"He's short on my heels." Kir rubbed at a spot on his tunic. His old, old tunic. He never wore the new ones I made for him each year. I dreaded the thought of his being often in my company when we settled in a new place. Usually, the men left the house to do their work, only returning when the sun set. In Moab, there'd be no field to go to, no vineyard, no orchard, so I'd be forced to see Kir constantly.

Finally, my husband climbed up. Behind him, came the hump-shouldered man who would eat with us, sleep on our roof this last night in Bethlehem, and then guide us to the place I dreaded going.

"Cyrus, our guide," Elimelech said, introducing us.

"Shalom," Cyrus said, dipping his head.

I muttered a welcome and invited him to sit at our table.

I had expected to be repulsed by this malformed Moabite, but as I poured wine into his cup, I softened. He had a gentle manner, warm eyes, and a melodious voice that pleased me. Earlier, Elimelech had explained that Cyrus was an agent of the chief who offered us protection in Moab, and that he traded for the Moabite chief, selling wool, grain, oil, and wine to Egyptians and others on the chief's behalf.

Though satisfied with our guide's manner, his presence disturbed me for it meant this wasn't a bad dream. We really were going to Moab.

◆ ◆ ◆

Dorcus came that evening – our last evening. I was about to go out to relieve myself; Elimelech and my sons had just returned from doing the same. Seeing Dorcus, they stopped.

"What is it?" I was alarmed that Dorcus would come so late.

She threw her arms around me and drew me into a tight embrace, her cheek pressed to mine so that her tears flowed down both of our faces. When she finally let go, she hugged my boys, even though they were past the age where they liked aunt-hugging. Then she grabbed Elimelech's hands between hers and pressed them to her heart, "Don't go; don't go," she begged.

"We must," my husband said gently.

I put my hand on her arm. "It won't be for long."

Still holding Elimelech's hands against her heart, she shook her head. "No," she said. "You won't all come back."

"We'll *all* be back," Elimelech said firmly.

"Some of you will die," she whispered.

Chapter 7

"Mother, Mother, wake up." It was Killion's voice. "They're loading the animals."

My heavy lids refused to respond.

"Mother, are you sick?" He touched my cheek.

I forced my eyes open. The glow from an oil lamp lit his face.

"No, Killion. I'm not sick." I sat up. My body was stiff, and there was a faint pounding behind my temples. I *was* sick, not of body, but of soul. I wanted time to stop, leaving me in my bedchamber so I wouldn't have to set foot outside Bethlehem.

"Damaris is up. And Abi."

My servants had risen before me? A feeling of disgust flooded my belly. They'd have been preparing food while I laid around like a dead fish. Reluctance to begin our journey was no excuse for shirking my duties.

"We're loading the donkeys." Killion's voice was thick with excitement. "The oxen are next. I have to go and help."

"Go." I waved him away.

At the door, he looked back. "Will you hurry?"

"Yes, Killion. I'll hurry. Even now I'm getting up." I stood. "See?"

I became aware of the noise below – the repeated bray of an unhappy donkey; a bullock's snort; the men's clipped orders to the animals: *Stay. Be still. Move up;* the mingling of Hada's and Mesha's voices with those of the men. Everyone was there except me. My cheeks burned with shame as I rolled up my bedding and secured it with a leather cord. Quickly, I threw an outer garment over my tunic, covered my head with a shawl, and, after tying a girdle about my waist, tucked a package containing trinkets and another of kohl inside. Cloak draped over one arm, bedding tucked under the other, I went to join the others.

The basket at the bottom of the ladder where we left our sandals contained only one pair: mine. Mortified, I slipped my feet in and tied the thongs. Knives and slings tucked into their hagoras, the men paid no attention to me as they secured baskets, jugs, and packets to the backs of skittish animals. Zacharias was draping blue beads and plaits of red woolen thread around the necks of donkeys.

Elimelech gave me a questioning look as he came and took my bedding to load. "Are you all right?" he whispered.

Biting my lips, for I didn't trust my voice, I nodded.

"I'm sorry, Naomi." He touched my hand. "I don't want to do this either, but we must."

"I understand. I'll be fine, Elimelech. I'll be fine."

He returned to the business of loading, and I hurried toward the back to help bring food.

"There's a basket of raisins and apricots ready," Damaris said as we passed in the corridor. She carried a bowl filled with dried cheese.

In the storage room, I grabbed the basket, and brought it out. Each man grabbed a handful, stuffed the food in his mouth, and then continued what he was doing. There was no time to sit and eat. The oil lamps lining the corridor, threw dancing shadows of the busy men against a wall as they strived to finish before daybreak.

When the basket was empty, I returned to the cooking area. Abi had brought out more bread and was still in the corridor, but Damaris stood aimlessly beside the oven, holding an empty bowl.

"I saved bread for you." She pointed to two pieces on the bench.

The pounding in my head had worsened and though I'd done no work, my limbs hung heavy with exhaustion. "Thank you," I managed to say. "But I can't eat anything."

"I thought you'd say that." She wrapped the bread in a rag and tucked it beneath my girdle. "There. For when you're hungry."

"Damaris, I can't manage without you."

"Of course, you can." Her voice broke. She swallowed, steadying herself. "You'll watch over Abi? She's looking at the young men, and who knows what that girl might get up to."

"Yes, I promise."

Soon afterwards, Elimelech announced that we were ready. "You and Abi will herd the sweeper ram and our three young rams," he said. "I had a goat brought from the flock to lead them."

That sheep chose to follow goats had always been a puzzle to me, yet I was glad for that. "You're putting the future of your flock in the hands of weak females?"

His eyes crinkled. "Weak? Not in a million years. But yes, you're in charge of the sweeper, and of Little Samson, Blackfoot, and the third lamb. Did we give him a name?"

"I'll call him *Springer* since he sprang higher than the others when the young lambs were jumping about."

"Well, then, *Springer* it is. Guard them well. They're our future. Nothing must happen to them."

Chapter 8

All of Bethlehem, it seemed, woke early and came to see us leave. Women and girls with their water jugs. Boys with sheep and goats. Men with tools propped over their shoulders. My household had become a show. An entertainment. We paraded through the town gates, a spectacle for the bored, a shameful exhibition for the poor, a curiosity for the misinformed.

Thus we began our exodus. Once outside the gates, I herded my charges past threshing floors, columns of white-washed stones stacked to keep jackals away, terraces built with the sweat and blood of generations. As fields, vineyards, and orchards receded, I dreaded coming to the place where I'd no longer be able to see Bethlehem.

When the sun rose, Elimelech left the front of our caravan and came to where Abi and I herded the lambs at the end. Taking my arm, he gently turned me around, and we looked back at the town of our birth. Perched on the edge of a hill, Bethlehem had shrunk to nothing more than a nest of sand-colored toy houses.

"*Bet-Lehem, the house of bread*, where there's little grain left to make bread," he said. "Next year, when the rains come there'll be plenty again, and we'll be back."

◆ ◆ ◆

Wind grated across the dry land, rustling the yellow leaves that should have been fresh and green. As early morning gave way to midday, the sun beat down on us with relentless fury; sweat dripped from beneath my arms to trickle past my ribs and down my thighs. Every step became painful as sandal straps rubbed my feet raw. I was glad for the times when No Name, as we'd begun to call the sweeper, refused to move, forcing us to stop.

Though miserable from heat and blisters, it was fear that plagued me most. My brothers had warned of thieves, lions, and wolves. My eyes darted about, watching every moving shadow; my ears pricked at every sound that didn't come from the snorting or braying of our pack animals or from their feet plodding against the brittle ground. Once, when a raucous call startled me, I dropped my shepherd's crook in alarm only to realize the caw came from a crow sweeping past.

When the donkeys became accustomed to marching in line, thus needing less supervision, I begged Hada and Mesha to keep Abi and me company. Clearly, they didn't have the same fears as I, for their faces were relaxed, and they walked with an easy gait. Hada's long legs outpaced ours so that every few steps, she had to stop and wait for us to catch up. Mesha's constant chatter soothed my fears, leaving my mind free to wander and wonder.

Our journey through the Judean Hills, the desert, and the roads on the other side of the Jordan was to last for only two weeks, yet I must dwell on it. While leaving my home was like having a limb torn from my body, in the midst of that pain came the feeling of walking from a cave into the light. Even on that first day, I marveled at how much larger the world had become in the space of a morning. The Great Sea, invisible to us, lay beyond the hills to our left. Seeing the hills stretch endlessly around me, I decided the sea must be even greater than I had imagined. How was it that the water didn't fall off the earth at the place where the sea ended? What would we see if we stood at the edge of the earth and peered over? And was there really a cold wasteland north of the land of two rivers? I'd heard tales of a barren, cold land that lay beyond where Abraham came from, but with the sun burning our skin, I wasn't sure I believed in cold wastelands though I could easily imagine the great desert to the east.

My mind diverted, I didn't see Springer wander away. Nor did Abi who talked gaily with Mesha and Hada, although it was mainly Mesha doing the talking. It took a rock nearly tripping me to notice that we only had three rams instead of four. I gasped. My three companions stopped and realized what was wrong when they saw me looking frantically about. Ahead of us, Kir kept going. Leaving Abi with the goat and the other rams, Hada, Mesha, and I hurried back in the direction from where we'd come.

The rascal had slipped behind a boulder and was chewing something. Fearing that it might be the same poison parsley that killed Mighty Samson, I pried Springer's mouth open, raked out what was inside, but found only vetch. I nearly cried with relief.

Kir, a question in his eyes, looked back when we rejoined the caravan.

"Woman business," Hada said to him. "We need to go behind the rocks more often than you men."

Abi and Mesha giggled as Kir, red-faced, turned his back to us and walked on.

Relieved that we found our errant lamb so quickly, I vowed to never again have such a lapse of attention. Lack of sleep was no excuse, nor were the headache and lightheadedness from hunger. From now on, I would compel myself to eat even when not hungry. I pulled the bread from beneath my girdle, crammed it in my mouth, and forced myself to chew and swallow it.

Late in the morning, we climbed a hill thick with acacia trees, their thirsty leaves like the flaccid hands of an old woman. As we descended the other side, a cheer went up. Our flock, which had started moving two days earlier, waited for us below. Handing the shepherd's crook to Hada, I ran to join Elimelech, for I'd seen vultures circling overhead.

Uri waved. Barefooted, as always, he ran to meet us.

"How many?" Elimelech asked, eyeing the vultures.

"Three." Uri looked miserable. "There isn't enough forage."

"The lack of food isn't your fault," Elimelech said, a catch in his voice. "The fleeces?"

"We cut them away already."

"Show Festus where they are, then drive the sheep forward." Grim-faced, Elimelech pointed in the direction we were to go.

Festus and Skinny loaded the fleeces on top of an ox and, with long faces, we set out again.

That night we camped in a grove of acacia trees near a small village. We pitched one tent, unloaded our precious grain into it, and then ate dried cheese and yesterday's bread. After the men tied the donkeys, who could crush a jackal beneath their feet, at intervals around the flock, they lay down to sleep near the donkeys. Tired to the bone, we women crept into the tent to sleep with the grain.

I expected to fall into a deep slumber the instant I lay down, but as I closed my eyes, an unearthly howling began. Wolves! I'd heard stories about wolves following people, the pack growing and growing until the moment of attack. That night, my last waking moments were filled with images of my husband and sons trying to protect our sheep from the lethal teeth of wolves with nothing more than knives.

On the second day, we fell into what became a routine. Each morning, using embers we carried in a small jug, I lit a pile of twigs and dried acacia pods gathered the evening before. As flames flickered to life, Abi squatted beside them to mix flour and water for flat cakes while I selected food from our stores to be eaten in the middle of the day. I packed the food in containers easily gotten at. Then I took a few sizzling cakes from the rock and, along with cheese and olives, carried them to Uri and the mute for they began moving the flock while the rest of us ate and broke camp. After hastily mumbled prayers, we ate.

The men reloaded the grain on the donkeys and oxen and took down the tent while Hada and Mesha milked goats. The milking season for sheep was over. When they finished, the sisters attached milk-filled goatskins to the donkeys so the skins would swing back and forth, churning the milk while we traveled

That first morning, as Abi waited for the fire to become hot enough to lay the cooking stone, I took a small basket, scooped two fistfuls of grain into it, and went to check the rams tethered beside our tent. I doubted such a small amount of grain would be missed.

"Shalom," I said to the rams as though they were people.

No Name stood still, his eyes hooded, but one ear cocked toward the sounds coming from the milking. I was apparently unworthy of his attention, but the three lambs gathered around, nuzzling at my empty hand. I held the basket out of their reach, for I wanted to first contain No Name. But Springer jumped, trying to reach the basket, while Little Samson and Black Foot reared up, landing their front feet on my thighs, trying to get at the food.

No Name took a step toward me. "This is only for the little ones," I said, brushing away the lambs and grabbing the tethering rope around his neck. "You have to find your own food."

Holding firmly to No Name's rope so he couldn't lower his head, I set the basket down. When they'd eaten it all, the lambs rattled the basket around, seeking one last kernel.

I let go of No Name and retrieved the empty basket. "Springer, you need to mind your manners," I admonished as though he were one of my sons. "Today, you'll stay with the others instead of hiding behind rocks. And if you're all good, I'll bring you a little grain every day. But don't tell."

Each day, we caught up with the flock before the sun traveled more than the span of a hand across the sky. Sweat streaking our faces and feet pained by blisters, we trudged on, breathing the dust stirred up by the sheep and treading carefully to avoid their dung.

The sheep had wilted like un-watered flowers, heads dipping, tongues hanging out. Halfway through the second morning, one of the ewes stopped moving. Ignoring the dogs nipping at her fetlocks, she let the flock pass her by then toppled over.

Uri was the first one there, although I arrived soon after. I'd thrust the shepherd's crook into Hada's hands when I saw the ewe fall.

Uri pressed two fingers to her neck. "Dead," he said looking up at Elimelech who had come running back. My husband had eyes all around his head when it came to the sheep. When a ewe dropped dead at the back of the flock, he saw it.

"She was old," he said, his voice brusque as he tried to hide his dismay. "Old," he repeated.

I caught Uri's eye. We both knew had the ewe been too old to produce lambs, she would already have been roasted and eaten. Her malady was neither age nor one of the diseases sheep die of, but lack of food and water. How many more would perish before we reached Moab? Like the morning milking and bread making, their dying would become part of our routine.

The howling of wolves also became part of our routine.

On the third day, we stopped late in the afternoon for the Sabbath was about to begin. The men positioned the flock between two escarpments, piled thorn bushes at one end, and erected the storage tent at the other. Next to the storage tent, Elimelech put up a smaller tent.

"Will the donkeys keep the wolves as well as the jackals away?" I asked Elimelech as I gathered kindling. He was unloading grain into the large tent.

"Wolves won't dare attack," he said, straining under a large basket.

"Why not?" I threw my armful of twigs on the wood stack.

"Because of a dozen donkeys and nine men." He gave me an exasperated look.

"Why do you look at me like that?"

"Like everyone else, I'm tired. I don't want to worry about wolves."

"Then *don't* worry," I snapped.

His face hardened as he shouldered his load toward the tent.

I spent that night in the small tent without my husband, wondering why he'd bothered to put it up if I was to sleep without him. Rather than being alone, I would have preferred the company of the other women whose chatter and giggles would have helped keep my mind off wolves.

When the Sabbath ended, I went to bed in the small tent, sure that our exodus had been a miserable mistake. Another ewe had died. Tomorrow, one or two others would die, and in the days that followed even more. How high would the pile of unwashed fleeces become?

And water had become a problem, not just for the sheep, but for us. Villagers didn't refuse to let us fill our skins at their wells but, faces etched with resentment, they watched our every move as we took their precious water. I feared that soon we might run out altogether.

The door flap snapped shut as Elimelech entered the tent. Keeping my eyes closed, I listened to the crackle of dry leaves and twigs as he moved toward me and the thud of his clothes landing on the ground. Smelling of dust and sweat, and of the garlic and cheese he'd eaten, he lay down beside me. I rolled away.

"Naomi?" He touched my arm.

"Not now." I brushed his hand away.

Abruptly, he rose, drew on his clothes, and left.

I lay sweating in fear as I listened to the coming and going of silent travelers, the complaints of tethered goats, the howling of wolves. I even thought I heard the panting of dogs as they guarded the sheep. I longed for my husband to lie beside me, yet I'd driven him away. What had happened to the Naomi who laughed? The happy Naomi? Until now, things had gone easily for me. I had the best of husbands. Due to his diligence and hard work we were rich with many sheep, a well-tended field, a productive vineyard. While many families had none, we had six servants and bondsmen. Every member of our household had his own drinking cup so there was no need to share cups at meals. My husband and sons had threads of tekhelet blue in their prayer shawls; most couldn't afford the rare blue dye. I even possessed a few bracelets and necklaces from Egypt. With all this, being happy had been easy. But it seemed that now I was being put to some sort of test, and I was failing. I'd become angry, resentful, and full of bitterness, *mara*. We were going to Moab, and there was nothing I could do to stop us, so I needed to accept that. I only hoped we still had sheep when we got there.

Chapter 9

"You abandoned your three new sons? The young rams?" Killion asked when I went to walk with him and Machlon the next day. Hada and Mesha were herding my charges, giving Abi and me a break.

"Why do you call them my sons?"

"Everybody sees how attached you've become." Killion picked up a stone. While they walked, he and Machlon had been engaged in a contest with their slings. "Samson wasn't a good choice of names for our departed ram nor for Little Samson."

"Why not?"

"You know the story." He fitted a stone into the pocket of his sling.

"Over there," Machlon said, pointing to where a sandgrouse perched on a fallen limb. "You first."

Still moving with the caravan, Killion swung his sling several times around and then let the rock fly, missing the grouse by the length of an arm. The grouse flew to a different tree.

"Ha," Machlon said. "You have the aim of a five-year-old."

Killion made a sound of exasperation.

Machlon stopped walking, placed a rock in his sling, and swung it until the sling whistled, then let go.

"Donkey shit," Killion said as Machlon's rock found its mark.

"Killion!" I protested.

"Sorry."

"Your second son is a lame ass with his sling," Machlon said.

I stopped and held up my hands, bringing my sons to a halt. "Control your language. I didn't join you to hear such."

They raised their eyebrows at each other and, mouths twitching, fought to contain grins. I failed to see the humor in coarse language and, even less, humor at my reprimanding them for using it.

"You said we shouldn't have named our ram Samson," I reminded Killion as we resumed our wretched march. "Tell me why."

"Because Samson was as dumb as a log."

Machlon laughed.

"Why do you say that?" I asked Killion.

"You think he was brave, innocent, and holy, don't you?"

"Wasn't he?"

"Ha. First, he marries a Philistine girl. Which he shouldn't have done. He tells a riddle at their wedding feast and taunts the guests by claiming they'll never be able to solve it. The guests tell his bride they'll kill both her and her father unless she can find out the answer so she nags Samson until he tells her. He's as mad as a hornet when he finds out she's passed along the answer to the guests. You remember what happened then?"

Machlon burst out with the answer before I could reply. "In his rage, Samson killed thirty Philistines."

"And rage means *dumb*?" I thought *dumb* the better trait if *rage* led to killing.

"Then the bride's father gives the bride to Samson's best man and offers Samson his wife's sister to replace her," Killion continued. "Now Samson is really mad."

"I don't blame him," Machlon muttered. "I'd have done the same thing he did next."

"No, you wouldn't," I said. "You're much too kind and sensible." I could understand Samson's anger, but his next actions resulted in full-scale war. One atrocity followed another until Samson finally gave himself over to the Philistines only to escape later.

Killion seemed to have forgotten the story momentarily while he collected rocks for his sling.

"I've heard the cruel and angry part of the story," I said, impatiently. "I'm waiting for the *Samson was as dumb as a log* part."

Killion tucked the rocks in his agora. "He wasn't just dumb; he was sex-crazed."

My seventeen-year-old son was speaking of *sex-crazed*?

Not recognizing my distaste, he continued. "One Philistine temptress wasn't enough, so Samson falls for Delilah. And guess what? Like the first wife, Delilah nags him. Only this time it isn't the answer to a riddle she wants; she nags him until he reveals that the source of his strength is his hair, and then . . ." He grabbed his hair and pantomimed cutting it off.

Machlon laughed. "A bad hair-cut, I'd say."

"And that's how the Philistines put an end to Mighty Samson's strength," Killion said. "Now tell me that revealing your secrets to two Philistine women isn't dumb."

"Lesson learned," Machlon said in a mocking voice. "Stay away from Philistine women."

"Stay away from Moabite women," I said.

Machlon grimaced. "Wouldn't think of it. I'm going to marry Galatia."

Killion shrugged and rolled his eyes as though to say my worrying about Moabite women was a silly idea.

Each day, Elimelech worked through the flock, pinching the skin on the sheep's backs into a tent and then letting it go to see how long it took for the skin to return to normal. Each day, it took longer. But we didn't need Elimelech's pinch-test to know the sheep suffered from lack of water; we knew from the stink of their dung. The more dehydrated they became, the more the dung stunk. The suffocating smell enveloped us day and night. Circling above us, buzzards became a constant presence as they waited to feast on a lamb, a ewe, one of the wethers.

The grass covering the Judean hills normally looked like the head of an old man whose hair has grown sparse – blades poking at intervals out of white, rocky ground – but the growth had become so meager the pate was nearly bald. Cyrus promised that in Moab the blades of grass grew so close together you couldn't see the ground in between. Though I knew that couldn't possibly be true, the idea improved my mood by a hair's breadth.

Elimelech was kneeling in front of No Name when I brought grain for the young rams on the fourth morning of our journey. Quickly, I hid the basket behind my back. He glanced at me, then went back to examining our sweeper.

"No Name is dehydrated," he said. "We'll have to set aside a portion of water for him. We'll tie a skin to one of the donkeys walking with Kir and he, or you, can see that No Name drinks." He stood up and watched the three young rams who had crowded around me, expecting their morning treat. "At least our three young rams appear to be weathering the trip well."

I felt guilty about sneaking food to them, and at the same time, not guilty. We had to keep these three alive, even if that meant giving them a portion of food meant for us. Springer and Little Samson reared up onto my thighs, but Blackfoot, the smarter of the three, pushed behind and attacked the basket of grain, causing it to spill.

"Now, look what you've done." I was peeved at Blackfoot for revealing my secret.

The other two quickly joined Blackfoot, devouring the grain from the ground, while No Name pushed his way in for his share. I grabbed his rope and pulled him away.

"No," I said. "This isn't for you."

I dared a look at Elimelech.

"Is this the reason these three appear so energetic?" he asked. "You're feeding them our food?" His eyes were unblinking.

"Only a couple handfuls."

"No wonder they were so glad to see you." There was a smile in his voice. "Bring some for No Name each day, too." He touched my cheek lightly with his fingertips. "We won't mention this to the others. We have enough grain, but they might worry that we'll start feeding the entire flock." Then the dark cloud that had been so much on his face lately, settled there again. "The drought is destroying the forage even faster than I expected. In Bethlehem there'll soon be none."

◆ ◆ ◆

That morning, we turned east, heading toward the descent from the hills into the desert. As bad as the desert might be, at least the wolves wouldn't follow us there. Then I wondered if I really knew what wolves would or wouldn't do.

Kir surprised me by falling back to walk beside me. "We'll be coming to the bad part soon," he said. It was the first time Kir had spoken to me without my speaking to him first.

"The bad part?"

"Where we drive the flock down from the hills. Then there's the desert between the hills and the Salt Sea."

"How soon?" I hated asking Kir for information, but Elimelech was too busy helping Uri prod the sheep onward.

"By the end of the day." He pointed eastward. "The land is hot and dry down there."

What was it now, if not hot and dry? I let out such a sound of displeasure that Kir looked alarmed.

"There's an oasis beside the Jordan River," he said quickly. "Near where Jericho once stood. The springs there have clear, sweet water."

"And after the oasis?"

"We cross the river into the land of Gad, travel east for a day, then turn south into the land of Reuben, and after that . . .."

"Moab," I filled in.

"If you like, I can teach you some of their words."

"And how is it that you know all this, Kir? The Moabite's language. The lay of the land."

He didn't answer for several moments. "I've been to those places," he said finally, and as though he didn't want to talk about it further, moved back up to walk beside a donkey.

It wasn't Kir that I began learning the Moabite language from, but Cyrus. I went to walk with him for a short while, and he began teaching me. He'd already been teaching Elimelech and my sons. I no longer took notice of his humped shoulder, focusing instead on his warm brown eyes and the honeyed voice that could have persuaded birds to fly backwards had birds understood his speech. As we made our way through the rough landscape – the ridges, chasms, rocks – I learned the words for things we saw around us, the food we ate, the clothes we wore. Many words were similar to ours.

"The Moabite language is a cousin of your language," Cyrus explained. "You'll learn it easily."

I mused on the strange idea that if our languages were akin, maybe there had been a time in the far, far past when we and the Moabites had been cousins. Now, two different gods had claimed us. Or was it we ourselves who had claimed two different gods? It was all very confusing.

That evening, I sat leaning against a bag of wool and stared at the heavens. With the dust from our caravan settled, the sky had become a stark black fabric filled with glittering stars. Cyrus and Elimelech sat nearby discussing the following day's journey. The others had gone to bed.

"The descent is short but difficult for both man and animal," Cyrus said.

Elimelech frowned at a twig he'd been rolling back and forth between his fingers, then threw it aside,. "Seventy-eight sheep left," he mumbled. "Seventy-eight out of a hundred and eleven, and the hardest part of our journey yet to come."

He stood suddenly and strode into the dark.

"Elimelech," I called, chasing after him. I caught up and laid my hand on his arm.

"Am I a fool, Naomi?"

"Had we remained in Bethlehem, we'd have lost most of the flock. Those were your words."

"We'll be lucky to arrive in Moab with half our flock."

"Then we'll have half instead of none. Think of how Cyrus described the grass there: the blades growing so close together you can't see the ground in between."

"The grass won't benefit us if there are no sheep." A look of intense sadness withered his face. He hugged me to him and ran his fingers through my hair, combing it distractedly. "If we went back now, we'd lose even more sheep than on the way here. There's no choice; we have to go forward."

That night the wolves struck.

Chapter 10

We pitched our camp near a grove of pines. The dried needles provided kindling and, when raked into a pile, softened the ground beneath our sleeping mats and filled the tent with an earthy smell. The grove also served an evil purpose. Unknown to us, a pack of wolves hid among the trees, keeping quiet as our fire burned low, waiting for us to lie down to sleep.

Something jolted me awake. A nightmare. But no, something was happening. My heart stopped. It wasn't a dream, not this tempest of sound — brays, barking, bleating, growling, men shouting. I rushed from the tent, the other women behind me. Streaks of reflected moonlight flashed and darted in confusion making it impossible to tell man from beast. Something raced past me, and half a breath later I heard the surprised bleat of a lamb.

"No!" I cried and grabbed the only weapon available: the empty water jug standing beside the tent opening. I rushed to save the rams tethered beside the tent, but the donkey tied there was already rearing and braying. Breathless, I watched the dark form rear again and again, and I heard the crack of bones as the donkey crushed the ribs and skull of the wolf. Finally, the wolf's whimpering ceased, and the donkey, after a snort and a toss of his head, moved away and became still.

Two small forms and a bigger one cowered nearby, but a lump of dark lay on the ground beside the larger mound of the wolf. I couldn't breathe. "Please, don't let it be one of the rams," I pleaded. But I knew. One of them was gone. First, Mighty Samson had been taken from us and now one of the young rams meant to take his place.

The snarling of wolves had ceased, and bleats from the fold sounded more like the aftermath of fright rather than fear itself. Still barking, Uri's dogs chased the demons away while the men called to each other, checking to see that the humans in our party were alive and well.

"Mother?" Machlon ran up to me. "You're all right?"

"One of the rams," I managed, my voice hoarse.

I stared at the two dark mounds lying side by side. One large, one small. One a wolf, the other . . ..

"Which one?" Machlon asked.

Which one indeed? It was too dark to tell.

"There are other sheep gone, too," he said. "We can't count in the dark. Tomorrow we'll know."

At dawn, I sat with Abi, Mesha, and Hada in front of our tent, trying to ignore the buzzards that circled and swooped to land beyond the trees where the men had thrown the carcasses. One of the carcasses was Springer's. The men had cut away the fleeces, adding them to the growing pile atop the oxen. Swarms of flies buzzed nearby, the females gorging on the blood.

Had my husband not done everything he was supposed to do? Had he not kept the laws of Moishe with rigor? Had not every action of his been done in good conscience? He was a good and kind man, fair to everyone. He worked hard. So how was it that a pack of wolves could attack what he had worked for, and one of the vile creatures be allowed to murder my favorite ram? Where was the fairness?

We moved on. Was there any choice? Soon, we discovered that what Cyrus had described as a *descent* into the desert was more like a plunge.

"Our animals can't do this," I said to Elimelech as we looked at the steep path leading around boulders and chasms, cliffs and ridges.

My husband's face had turned white.

"Others do," Cyrus said.

"I didn't understand that it would be this . . .." Elimelech held his palm toward the path. ". . . this steep," he said finally.

"Ahead of us are two difficult days of travel," Cyrus said. "First, going down." Like Elimelech, he held out his palm indicating the descent. "A short distance but a long day. Then we cross a stretch of desert."

"We have little water for the humans in our party," Elimelech said. "As for the sheep, in the desert they'll have neither food nor water."

My husband grimaced at the ragged terrain, but I knew that whatever troubled thoughts he had, whatever reservations, we'd continue this journey. He was a stubborn man.

"The flock will revive once we're at the oasis," he said finally. Then he looked at Cyrus. "In Moab, the sheep will flourish if the grass is as plentiful as you say."

"It is as I say." Cyrus pointed toward the hazy gray mountains in the distance. "Those are the hills of Moab where grass grows like a green carpet."

"Then let's not waste any more time."

The goats led the way, hopping from boulder to boulder, leaping over crevasses, stopping to nibble at weeds between the rocks. Sometimes they seemed to sneer as they looked back at the sheep who, not nearly so nimble-footed, laboriously picked their way down. Uri's dogs earned their keep that day, running back and forth, barking, nipping at hocks. Exhausted, the sheep could barely hold up their heads; they stumbled; sometimes one would stop and let her legs fold beneath her. Then one of the men would rush over and raise her from the ground. Two ewes fell to never rise again.

The worst were the oxen. They balked at treading the steep slopes. Elimelech charged the women, except for me, with cajoling the donkeys down, while he, Arioch, and Festus prodded, pushed, and cursed at the oxen to follow.

As I urged my rams around chasms and boulders, No Name became belligerent. He'd walk a few steps then stop to stare at something on the ground while his nostrils quivered. He'd remain like that until I gave him a good, hard push from behind.

Half-way through the morning, Little Sampson began to hesitate each time he had to set a rear foot down.

"Is everything all right?" Elimelech asked, coming up beside me.

"No Name isn't being cooperative, and Little Sampson seems to have a problem with his back hooves."

Elimelech put his hand on Little Sampson's head to keep him still, then lifted first one back hoof and then the other. "Pebbles," he said and pushed on the ram's rear. "Lie down, little fella."

Little Sampson sank down and, at Elimelech's urging, lay on one side. Using his fingernails, Elimelech probed, working to dislodge a pebble. The young ram flinched as the first pebble came out. Elimelech let go of the hoof, picked up the other, and tried to remove the pebble from the second hoof. Little Sampson kicked and bleated.

"Hold his leg still," Elimelech said.

I grabbed Little Samson's hock and held tight.

When the second pebble finally came out, Elimelech watched the ram struggle to his feet, only to sink back down.

"It hurts when he walks," I said. There was the possibility of his hooves becoming infected, especially considering what we were putting him through.

Elimelech gathered the ram in his arms. "The oxen can bear a little more weight."

We struggled on, the heat from the desert below rising to make us swelter like wet fish on a hot stone. Late in the afternoon, we reached the bottom, stepped into the furnace that was the desert, and erected our tent on the scorching sand. We wouldn't need a fire to heat our cooking stone that evening. The sand would do.

Night, and the relief it brought, passed too soon. The steep descent was behind us but the desert stretched before us, hazy with moisture from the Salt Sea and burning with the heat of Hell. The cliffs beyond the Salt Sea where Moab looked down on the pallid waters were a blur, like something imagined instead of real. Around us, the air stunk from the slimy excrement of sheep who were near thirsting to death.

"We have to travel at night," Elimelech said, his voice grim.

Cyrus nodded. "If you know the way, and I do, it's possible."

"Some of the sheep might slip away," Kir said. "Or lie down to die without us knowing it."

"Are you saying we shouldn't travel at night?" Elimelech furrowed his brow at his bondsman.

"I think it wise to travel at night. I'm only pointing out what you already know. We'll be missing members of our flock when we arrive. If we travel during the day, we'll lose even more."

Elimelech called to Arioch who had just come from feeding the oxen the last of the hay, "Go and take Uri's place with the sheep and send him to me."

Uri came quickly.

"The sheep won't survive a daytime march across the desert," Elimelech said.

"Nor will we," Uri replied. "Our water is almost gone."

"We'll go at night. Be prepared."

Uri nodded and went back to the flock.

The sheep had given up trying to find food. They lay on the rough, hot ground, dazed, eyes sunken, mouths and nostrils dry.

We spent the day in the tent, at first with the sides rolled up in hopes of catching a breeze. But there was none, only a scorching inferno. We let down the sides, but then the tent was filled with the oppressive heat of our bodies. My mouth was parched. Even my skin cried for water. Never had I wished so desperately for a bath. Finally, the men abandoned the tent to loll in its shade, changing their location as the sun rolled from one side of the sky to the other. Neither man nor beast cared to eat.

"How much longer?" Abi whined at one point. Unwilling to leave the shelter of the tent, I had no idea where the sun sat in the sky. It could have been morning or afternoon. Nor did I care. I only wanted to fall into a deep sleep and not feel anything.

"Are you asking how much longer until the sun sets, or do you mean how much longer we have to journey?" Mesha asked. Like everyone else, her garment was soaked, her nose and cheeks red from sunburn, her face streaked with black from the kohl we used around our eyes to cut the sun's glare.

"When the sun goes down, it will be cooler," I said, as if they didn't know. "We should try to sleep since we'll be walking all night."

The three women looked at me as though I'd asked them to jump over the moon. I knew what they thought, for I felt it, too. *Sleep in this misery?*

"Tomorrow, we'll arrive at the oasis, and then . . . .." I tried to smile, ". . . there'll be more water than we've seen for a long, long time. Streams. A river nearby."

"Water," Hada repeated dumbly. "Water." In an attempt to cool herself, she poked out her bottom lip and blew, directing a stream of air to her upper face.

". . . and fruit. The limbs of the trees will be heavy with dates, bananas, lemons."

They looked at me, half in disbelief, but also with a glimmer of hope in their eyes.

My fingers inched toward my water skin. I needed to set an example by conserving water, but my tongue was swollen, my lips cracked and peeling. Three drops, I thought.

A bleat came from where the men had piled the grain containers. Quietly, I took the water skin, went to where the rams huddled in the shade of baskets, and found Elimelech doing what I had intended to do. Squatting in front of Little Samson, he poured a few drops of water onto his palm. As he held his hand out to the young ram, Elimelech looked up at me and then at the water skin in my hand.

I knelt beside him and did as he had, offering my palm to Blackfoot who had been trying to nudge Little Sampson aside. No Name looked too miserable to fight for a swallow.

"No more," Elimelech said when Blackfoot had licked my palm dry. He put his hand on mine as though to stop me should I decide not to heed his request.

Still squatting, he said, "We'll rest at the oasis and let the sheep graze for a few days. I'll have to pay someone for grazing rights, but it will be well worth it." He looked at me for confirmation.

"You're right."

He stood and bent over Little Samson, picking up first one back hoof and then the other, examining them. "Tonight, he'll continue to ride atop one of the oxen. And you'll hold tight to Blackfoot's rope so we won't lose him in the dark?"

"As though he were my son."

"Good." He started to walk away.

"Elimelech," I said, stopping him. "I don't like for you to . . ." I drew in a breath, not sure that I should say what I was about to.

"You don't like for me to *what?*" He spoke softly, as I had. We didn't want the others to hear.

"I don't like for you to doubt yourself."

"But you doubted me."

"No, I didn't doubt you. I just didn't want to leave my home."

"I didn't know how bad it was going to be. I knew a few sheep would die, but I thought there'd be scraps of grass here and there. Instead, there's been next to none. I also knew we'd be tired and cranky sometimes. And worried. I've awakened more than once in the middle of the night wondering if the drought will kill us all."

"The drought won't kill us. Next year after the rains, we'll return to Bethlehem happy and healthy, and with a large flock. Don't doubt that."

Chapter 11

We set out before the last dregs of daylight disappeared. Uri, Festus, Skinny, and the Mute, along with Uri's dogs, drove the flock from behind. The donkeys were split into two groups. To form a kind of fence, they were roped together head to tail with a long stretch of rope between the tail of one donkey and the head of the one behind. The sheep were positioned between the two lines of donkeys. Kir led one line and Hada the other. Mesha and Abi moved back and forth along the lines, prodding the donkeys when necessary and checking that ropes hadn't come undone. Holding tightly to the ropes of my goat and two rams, I walked at the front with Cyrus along with Arioch and the oxen. As for Elimelech, he was everywhere, checking our progress or lack of progress, helping where help was needed, offering encouragement when we lagged.

Our goal was to cross the desert and reach the oasis before the sun rose to broil both humans and animals to a crisp. As we entered the desert, we left the land assigned to the tribe of Judah. At the oasis, we'd enter the territory belonging to Manasseh's tribe.

The stars blazed, and the moon shone full and bright as we stumbled along, crashing into thorn bushes, falling over rocks, but throughout I held tightly to the ropes of my charges. Terrified of stepping on a snake, my fear was magnified by the feeling of being alone. The others – the people, the pack animals, the sheep – were mysterious forms touched by moonbeams or not seen at all. I had never wished so mightily for a night to end.

Our rests were short. Once, Elimelech came to sit on the sand with me.

He spoke in awe about the blackness of the sky and the quiet of the desert as though these were something wonderful. "If you stand on my shoulders it's almost like you could pluck a star from the sky," he said. "They seem that close."

"And what would I do with a star?"

We sat shoulder to shoulder, so I felt his shrug. "Who knows what's to be done with a star. Something good, I think."

The things that left him in awe disturbed me. I wondered if those ill-conceived thoughts that sometimes appeared in my mind were more visible to the gods without the distractions of things seen and heard during the day. I wondered, too, if the gods fought over territory in the sky as we humans did on earth. If so, would it mean that beneath the sky of Moab, we'd be under the dominion of Chemosh? Or did people belong to certain gods because of having been created by that god? Israelites to Yahweh, Moabites to Chemosh, Canaanites to Baal? It was confusing. And to which god did the desert belong? Not knowing, I felt unprotected and naked. I trembled.

Thinking I shivered from the cold, Elimelech put his arm around me. "We'll be moving again shortly." He rubbed my arm trying to warm it. A few heartbeats later, he stood, held out his hand to drag me to my feet, and said, "It's time to go."

We stumbled on through the dark, thirsty and exhausted. When I thought the night would never end, black turned to gray, and then to a lighter gray. My spirits lifted. At least I could see where I was going. Just as quickly, my spirits sank for the same reason, and a shudder ran through me. We could have fallen at any time into one of the chasms or from one of the escarpments that rose around us.

When the rim of the sun finally peeked at us, a murmuring arose. A strip of blue-black that looked to be a half-day's walk away had appeared.

"The Salt Sea!" someone called out.

"Moab is on the other side," someone else shouted.

The cliffs of Moab rose from the sea's eastern side, steep, gray, menacing. Dragging my tired rams with me, I hurried to join Elimelech and Cyrus.

Our guide pointed out a haze of gray-green hovering at the north end of the sea. "That's where the River Jordan flows into the Salt Sea. And there . . .." He pointed farther to the left. ". . . is the spot where Jericho once stood, and where lies the oasis of Ain-es-Sultan."

The oasis was a thin cloud of gray-green.

"You Israelites call it the Spring of Elisha," Cyrus added.

I didn't care what it was called, just that it *was*. My feet felt lighter, and a spark of excitement led me to glance around to see the others walking faster, heads turned toward the good news, fingers pointing. The animals must have smelled green growth, for the sheep raised their heads and, sniffing at the air, moved more willingly. The donkeys sped up despite having walked throughout the night.

The tension present on Elimelech's face during the past week eased, and he allowed himself a fleeting smile before busying himself organizing our arrival. He strode along one side of the flock, around the back, and then up the other side, giving instructions. He, Uri, and the mute, along with Festus and Skinny, would accompany the flock to the western edge of the oasis where there'd be grass. Kir and Arioch, with the help of Killion and Machlon, would lead the pack animals into the oasis. They'd water the animals and then find a camp site near the sheep. We women were to drink to our heart's content, then fill skins and bring them to the men who accompanied the sheep.

The haze became more distinct, drawing us forward until, at last, a vivid green jumped out of the arid wasteland of tans and browns. A faint aroma — a combination of cucumber, citrus, mint, and ripe dates – grew stronger with each step, pulling us like bees to nectar. When we came close enough to make out individual trees, the flock split away to the west.

When I didn't think I could go another step, that I might fall over and blow away like a dead leaf, we arrived at a sparse growth of date palms which, along with a breeze, marked the beginning of the oasis. A few steps later, the growth thickened. I was too desperate for water to note which plants and trees grew there, nor did I heed the few strangers who wandered about. My only thought was to find the trickling stream I'd heard as soon as we entered the oasis. With my women at my heels, I forged through the trees, ignoring branches slapping at my face, thistles clinging to my clothes, over-ripe fruit beneath my feet.

A dense growth of weeds and grass where snakes could have been concealed surrounded the stream, but our thirst was stronger than our fear. We dropped our shawls on the bank and, wearing only our tunics, plunged in, laughing. Cupping our hands, we drank. We splashed our faces and drank more. When Abi sat down in the stream, Hada, Mesha, and I did the same, soaking our clothes. Leaning back on my elbows, I let the ends of my hair float in the stream. My head sank back further, wetting my ears. Finally, I doused my head in the water then came up sputtering and laughing. The others laughed and dunked their heads, too. In a few short moments we'd changed from haggard, dried-up crones to happy, young women.

My thirst quenched, I climbed from the stream, dripping water, and noticed, for the first time, the orange and lemon trees loaded with fat, ripe fruit, palms lush with clumps of dates, bananas growing everywhere. There were acacias, thorny canopies of jujubes, and giant phragmites reeds.

The men leading the pack animals found us. Laughing, they, too, splashed into the water. The animals needed no urging to follow.

We filled water skins, loaded them on a donkey, and set off to find the flock. For the first time since Elimelech announced we were leaving Bethlehem, I felt a tiny ray of hope.

Chapter 12

Elimelech decided we'd remain at the Spring of Elisha five days, giving us and the sheep time to recover. We gave in to lethargy when we weren't doing what had to be done – cooking, tending the animals, repairing harnesses and ropes. Only Kir didn't seem content to relax but kept looking around as though expecting someone. Sometimes, he left us to wander around the oasis, only to come back frowning.

The day after our arrival, I left our encampment to gather fruit, but mostly I just strolled, enjoying the shade and the greenery. When I stopped to admire a patch of carmelite with their deep lavender blooms, I looked up to see Kir passing nearby. Curious, I trailed behind. Half-hidden in the shadows of trees, I stopped occasionally to pick dates or figs. If he saw me, he'd think nothing of my gathering food.

He slithered about like a serpent, stopping and coiling when he encountered someone. Sometimes he questioned the person. Other times, his dark, beady eyes narrowed, he studied the stranger's face as though trying to place the person. Finally, he'd shake his head slowly and wander to some other part of the oasis. Clearly, he was looking for someone.

When I returned to our campsite, Elimelech was busy examining Little Samson's feet for probably the third time that day, and I had to help prepare the evening meal, so talk about Kir would have to wait. While Abi mixed dough and Hada fanned embers, Mesha rolled balls of cheese in a mixture of herbs, but she paid more attention to Arioch than to making cheese balls. She could have been rolling them in sand for all the care she took. Seated on the ground nearby, Arioch appeared to struggle with a frayed rope, trying to repair it. I wondered if he actually struggled or just pretended to in order to stay near Mesha. We'd have to marry the two. *That* should bring their attention back to their duties instead of to each other.

"A story, a story." Killion nudged Uri's foot with his own, urging him to entertain us that evening. Festus and Skinny watched the flock, allowing Uri to join us for our evening meal. We'd finished and were lingering around the fire.

Uri stretched, rolled his shoulders, and closed one eye as though considering. "A story..... Hmmmm....... What story?"

"The one about Joshua and Jericho," Machlon said.

"You've heard about the Battle of Jericho so many times you could repeat it in your sleep."

"But it's a good story," Killion protested. "And the ruins of Jericho are over there." He pointed in the direction we'd been told the ruins lay. "They say the ground is still full of rubble and charred wood."

Uri picked up a twig and twisted it back and forth between his fingers. "It *is* an excellent story – the Israelites silently circling the town once each day for six days; then marching around seven times on the seventh day with seven priests blowing ram's horn trumpets; Joshua yelling 'shout,' and the people shouting at the tops of their lungs."

"Then the walls falling in." Machlon gave a loud clap. "Crash."

"Don't forget about the harlot, Rehab," Killion said.

"*Do* forget about Rehab." Elimelech lay on his back gazing at the stars. "You're quite right, Uri. We've heard about the Battle of Jericho enough. Let's hear a different story,"

Before Uri could reply, Arioch began to chant.

JOSHua, JOSHua, *clap, clap, clap.*

JOSHua, JOSHua, *shout, shout, shout.*

BLOW the horn, BLOW the horn, *snap, snap, snap.*

CRASH bang, CRASH bang . . ..

Whoooooops . . ..
The walls
came
tumbling
dowwnnnn.

My sons joined in, leaving Arioch to sing the *dowwnnnn* in his deep voice, but after two repetitions, Elimelech held up both hands. "Enough."

"Can we see the ruins of Jericho?" Killion asked.

"The place is cursed." Arioch said, contorting his face as though he'd eaten something sour.

"*Cursed before God is the man who sets out to rebuild this city of Jericho. He'll pay for the foundation with his first born son and for the gates with his youngest,*" Elimelech quoted.

"I was asking to *see* it, not rebuild it," Killion said.

Machlon, who had taken on a thoughtful look, said, "I wish I could write."

"Write?" Abi pulled a face at him. "Whatever for? That's a servant's job."

"It's a scribe's job."

"You're the son of a rich man. You'd want to earn a pittance by writing?" Abi looked at him with disbelief.

I, too, wondered what had put such a thought in Machlon's head.

"I could write down stories," Machlon said. "Like the one about the Battle of Jericho."

Abi made a little sound and raised her palms as though questioning my son's sanity. "That's silly. Stories aren't for writing; they're for telling." She looked at the others for confirmation.

Our servants looked away or downward, not wanting to go against their master's son. The master, however, gave Machlon a look of disbelief.

"For once, I agree with Abi," Killion said, a smirk on his face. "Why write stories when no one can read them? A story written down would be a dead thing. Like a rotting carcass."

"Enough," Elimelech said. "It's time we retire for the night." He rose. "I bid you all a good night."

Chapter 13

We cut hair the following day. The cutting of hair happened once a year and was like a celebration, Damaris making special treats and everyone laughing at each other as both head hair and beards were much diminished. When the job was finished, there was always a great pile of hair and jokes about how to dispose of it. Only Uri didn't submit for he wore his hair long like the other shepherds.

Since Damaris wasn't with us, Hada and Mesha molded goat cheese around dates and then rolled the balls in crushed pistachios. Abi strained and served wine. Elimelech did the cutting while I stood by with a basket to collect the shorn hair. We finished in a merry mood, and then lay down to rest though the energy we'd expended amounted to no more than walking from one end of a field to the other.

That same afternoon, when a caravan from the east crossed the Jordan, I ran with my three women to watch the procession wade through the water. Adorned with red, yellow, and blue ornaments and heavily laden, camels, donkeys, and mules sloshed across. The camels I'd seen in the past could be counted on one hand, thus I had no idea the hump-backed animals were so plentiful there could be almost a hundred in a single caravan.

The procession stopped at the edge of the oasis, and the animal drivers began shouting back and forth to each other in strange languages. Some led their animals into the oasis to drink, while those awaiting their turns adjusted the straps holding their loads or flopped down to rest on the ground.

"What could be in all those packs?" Mesha asked.

Abi's eyes were round with excitement. "Can we go closer?" She took a step forward.

"Not too close." I pointed to a camel aiming his feet at his driver.

Curious, my three women edged toward the caravan.

I, too, wondered what could be in all the packs but knew it would remain a mystery for surely the caravaners wouldn't uncover their goods until they unloaded them at a market somewhere. The camels spit, bellowed, and made sounds like *nuzzing*. Mesmerized, I watched them kneel for their drivers to adjust a strap or remove something from their load. When the beasts rose from their kneeling positions, they'd unfold their legs and jerk their bodies to stand. They were like clumsy adolescents: all arms and legs.

I caught a glimpse of a familiar tunic. Kir was hurrying to catch up with one of the caravaners who led his donkey into the trees. I slipped away to follow. When Kir caught up with the man, I stopped beneath the branches of a lemon tree, my upper body concealed by its foliage, but with my basket ready to pick lemons should our bondsman glimpse my way. Kir said something to the man in a strange language, and the man responded. Kir seemed to be asking questions, leaning his head slightly toward the man, right palm raised, fingers spread, eyes narrowed. Finally, the man shook his head. Frowning, Kir went away.

I told Elimelech when I returned to our camp.

"You're spying on our bondsman?" My husband looked at me in disbelief. "I know you don't like Kir, but spying on him?"

My face flamed. I had done exactly that. But was it wrong to worry about our bondsman's intentions?

"Kir had a life before he came to us," Elimelech said. "He was probably asking after old acquaintances. I trust him. Why can't you?"

I dreamed that night. A dark figure lured Elimelech to Moab under the pretense of providing grazing. Magically, as can only happen in dreams, we were suddenly in Moab, and the unidentifiable figure set about stealing everything we had – our flocks, our grain, and our lives.

Chapter 14

We stood on the banks of the Jordan, watching the rising sun turn its waters from black to gray. Until now, I'd harbored a tiny hope that Elimelech would change his mind. Once we crossed the river there would be no turning back. That certainty lodged in my heart like a thorn.

"It's time," Cyrus said and, without another word, waded in.

The men with the pack animals plunged in after Cyrus. We women were supposed to follow and then tend the pack animals, while the men crossed back over to herd the sheep and goats through the water. But we hesitated. The streams that meandered through the Judean hills were narrow enough to leap over, but the Jordan looked to be the width of eight or ten men laid head to toe.

"Naomi?" Elimelech touched my arm. "You have to go. It isn't deep."

I took a deep breath and waded in, repeating, "*It isn't deep. It isn't deep.*"

The muddy, yellow water came almost to the tops of my thighs before I'd gone more than a dozen steps. Behind me Abi squealed at every limb and rock on the riverbed. I looked back to see Mesha's eyes widened in fear and her fingernails in her mouth, though I held the opinion that her fear was mainly a show to attract Arioch's attention. She succeeded. Leaving the oxen, he waded out to take her hand and utter consoling words. *You'll make it. Just a little further. It's nothing, this river.* Hada waded in as bravely as the men, grasping two lambs by their napes to bring with her.

Before the main flock was driven over, the lambs, too small to cross on their own, had to be helped to the other side. The men grabbed two at the

64

time, dragged them across, and then returned for two more. Taking no chances with the future breeder of his flock, Elimelech hoisted Little Sampson to his shoulders, carried him over, and deposited him at my feet. Then he returned for Blackfoot. Only then did he turn his attention to the remainder of the sheep. Eventually, both humans and animals stood on dry ground.

We were now in the territory given to the tribe of Gad, Jacob's seventh son. While the men reorganized the pack animals and the herd, I surveyed the surrounding mountains, wondering which was Mount Nebo. Moishe had climbed the mountain to view the land which Yahweh forbade him enter and, after the one look Yahweh allowed him, Moishe died.

We traversed only a corner of Gad, the following day entering the land Reuben's tribe settled. Reuben, Jacob's first-born and the son of Leah, had requested this area because it afforded good grazing. Mid-morning, still in the land of Reuben, we turned south to travel along a dirt-packed road that stretched into the distance. We were no longer lone travelers but encountered other groups, including a large caravan.

"They call this the King's Highway," Machlon said when he came to walk with me. "We'll cross the Arnon River and keep following the highway until we come to a path that leads into the mountains."

The mountains rose steeply on our right. To our left ran a strip of habitable land separating the King's Highway from the great desert. Cyrus had explained all this to me, but I let Machlon babble on.

"Why do they call this the King's Highway?" I asked.

"Maybe because the king moves his army along here? Or because he can collect tolls?" Without breaking stride, he picked up a rock and threw it.

"How do you know this?" We had no such thing as tolls in the Judean Hills.

"I listen, and I ask questions. Out there, a day's walk away . . .," he pointed east, ". . . lies the great desert which takes weeks to cross. It's so large and barren that people get lost and die of thirst out there. But the caravans know the way. They bring frankincense and myrrh from a country on the other side."

"What lies beyond the country with the frankincense and myrrh?"

He shrugged. "Maybe that's where the world ends."

"I like it when you tell me these things, so I'm glad you ask questions."

I ruffled my son's hair. He drew away with an annoyed look and went back to his place in the caravan. Or perhaps he went to ask more questions of Cyrus.

A little later, Killion came and related the same things, only he had a different answer for why the highway was called what it was.

"Moishe wanted to lead the Israelites along the King's Highway," he explained. "But there were so many Israelites the King of Moab was afraid and refused to let them pass. They had to travel through the desert instead."

"But we're not in Moab yet."

"The King's Highway runs all . . ." he stretched out the *all* ". . . the way from down in Egypt . . .," he turned around and walked backwards as he pointed north, ". . . to somewhere up there. If you go far enough north, there are two big rivers. It's where Abraham came from, and where Jacob went to find wives."

"Rachel and Leah."

Killion's lively eyes had a puzzled look in them. "I wonder why Moishe didn't travel through Moab anyway. The Israelites could have beaten the king's army."

I shrugged. "Ask your father. Or Cyrus."

I reached out to ruffle his hair as I had done with Machlon, but Killion was quicker than his brother. He drew back, scowled at my attempt at intimacy, and left.

◆ ◆ ◆

That evening, we raised camp beside the Arnon River. Moab lay on the other side. We ate our meal in silence, avoiding each other's eyes as we cast nervous glances at the opposite bank.

Kir and Festus were watching the sheep, so Uri was with us. "Somewhere up there . . .," he said, pointing to the mountains, ". . . Lot settled in a cave after his escape from Gomorrah."

Arioch gave a sniff. "Him and his two daughters."

"It's a shameful story," Abi said. "His daughters getting Lot drunk, and then . . .." She stopped.

"And then?" Killion had a wicked glint in his eyes.

Abi scowled at Killion. "You know what happened."

"Of course I know what happened."

"Let's leave this story alone," I said.

I didn't want to see Killion smirking during the retelling of how Lot's daughters got their father drunk, lay with him, and then produced sons, one of whom was named Moab. It was this offspring, conceived in sin, for whom the country had been named.

We sat around the embers of our campfire, listening to crickets, the crackle of logs, and the occasional yelp of Uri's dogs. In the gathering darkness, the Arnon soon became invisible but Abi kept her eyes glued to where it flowed as though on guard for evil spirits that might rise from its waters. Hada leaned against the trunk of a date palm, her eyes closed while Mesha, sitting behind Arioch, had drawn her legs up and wrapped her arms around them. Uri and Elimelech were adrift in their own thoughts, which probably had to do with counting our surviving sheep or wondering how many new lambs we'd have in the spring.

Machlon and Killion, their youthful energy unexpended, drew circles on the ground with twigs, then stood up to walk around, then, becoming bored with that, sat down again to throw yet another stick on the fire even though Elimelech had asked them not to.

Finally, Arioch stirred, rearranged his legs, and leaned back on one elbow. "We have to enter Moab with one shoe off and one on," he said. "Throw Balaam's curse back on the Moabites."

"Tell us that story," Killion said to Uri.

Machlon, who had been making yet another circuit of the campfire, sat down beside his brother. "Yes, tell it before we cross the Arnon."

"It's the story of a curse that went wrong." Uri threw aside the twig, crossed his legs, and interlaced his fingers. "Once, many years ago," he began, ". . . when our ancestors had been traveling for ages and ages to escape slavery and the Pharaoh, they came to the plains of Moab and set up their tents. King Balak of Moab was afraid. The Israelites had already defeated the King of the Amorites and the King of Bashan so King Balak sent some of his elders to Ammon to a man called Balaam. 'You must come with us to the king'," they said to Balaam.

"I can only do what Yahweh commands," Arioch said in his deep voice, acting the part of Balaam, ". . . and Yahweh told me not to go."

"So, King Balak sends higher-ranking priests and offers Balaam honors," Uri continued.

"I can only do what Yahweh commands," Arioch rumbled, ". . . and Yahweh told me not to go."

Uri's eyes rounded. "King Balak keeps begging and offering rewards. Finally, Yahweh gives Balaam permission to go. Balaam sets off on his donkey. But then . . ." Uri flitted his eyes from person to person and said in a whispery voice, ". . . Yahweh changed his mind."

"Chaaaaanged his mind," Arioch repeated.

Everyone leaned toward Uri, while I sat back, questioning why Yahweh changed his mind. Wasn't Yahweh supposed to be all-knowing, and not make mistakes?

"And so old Balaam is going along, and going along, and suddenly the donkey stops. The donkey won't move another foot. 'Get going, you stinking, lousy ass,' Balaam says and jerks at the reins. But the donkey won't budge. 'You cursed beast, move your butt!' Still the donkey won't move. Balaam gets off the donkey and looks the animal in the eye. 'What's wrong with you, you miserable sack of bones?' Balaam grabs his whip and is about to flog the donkey, when the donkey speaks." Uri motioned to Arioch.

"Balaam, you're the ass," Arioch roared, pretending to be Balaam's donkey. "Can you not see the angel in front of me blocking the way?"

Everyone laughed.

"Finally, Balaam is allowed to see the angel," Uri continued. "The angel says, 'Yahweh is angry at you for going to the king.' Balaam falls to his knees. 'Forgive me, forgive me,' he says. 'I am truly repentant. I will turn around and go back.' But then the angel tells him he will be allowed to go ahead."

"Yahweh has a hard time making up his mind, doesn't he?" Killion asked.

Elimelech gave our younger son a sharp look but said nothing.

"And so . . . .." Uri said, "Balaam is brought to King Balak. The king takes him to the high place of Baal, and they offer sacrifices on seven altars, but when Balaam speaks the prophecy Yahweh put in his mouth, he blesses the Israelites instead of putting a curse on them. So King Balak takes Balaam to another high place at Pisgah to try again. They build another seven altars and offer sacrifices, yet again, the prophecy that's put into Balaam's mouth blesses the Israelites instead of cursing them. Now King Balak is really frustrated."

"Reaaallly frustrated," Arioch repeated.

"King Balak takes Balaam to a third high place, Peor, and after the seven sacrifices, Balaam looks down at the Israelites' camp from the peak and delivers a third prophecy that favors the Israelites."

"And then . . . .." Killion interjected, "the young Israelites give in to temptation and fornicate with Moabite women."

"As punishment for what the young Israelite men do . . .," Uri said, regaining control of the story, ". . . a deadly plague besets the tribes. The Israelites seek revenge by going to war with the Moabites. They kill many, including Balaam. But not before Balaam has taught King Balak how to curse the Israelites."

"Which we can overcome by entering the land with one shoe off?" Killion asked.

From his tone, I knew Killion jeered at the notion.

Uri smiled. "It couldn't have been a very strong curse if that's all we have to do. But tomorrow we'll put that to the test."

Chapter 15

I waded out of the Arnon with one shoe off for there was no point in putting a curse to the test. While I retied the thongs of my sandals, I heard behind me the protests of our animals being forced across the river and the men prodding them to move. As I waited for the last sheep to climb from the river, I examined the town we'd seen the previous day from the opposite shore. Homes, much like the ones we left behind in Bethlehem, rose above a surrounding stone wall. The lively market outside the gates was much larger than ours but gave off familiar smells – tanned leather, roasting meat, spices, the stink of dung. There were other odors I couldn't identify, leading me to wonder what strange goods were sold here. Even had time allowed, I was reluctant to enter the throng of pushing, shoving foreigners to find out. Then I remembered: it was I who was the foreigner.

Holding a shoe, Hada came to stand beside me, her clothes still dripping. "Look," she said pointing to an oncoming caravan.

The jingle and clack of beads around the necks of their animals grew louder as the caravan approached. The men walking alongside the animals wore knee-length, wrap-around skirts tied with belts.

"Those are the clothes of Egypt," Cyrus said, joining us.

"But look." Hada pointed again.

Lifting my hand to shield my eyes against the sun's glare, I recognized what had caught Hada's attention. Among the caravaners were two men with skin as black and shiny as onyx. I stared. I'd been told there were such people. I'd also been told there were people with slanted eyes, and that in the land of two rivers, they'd built a tower that touched the clouds. Some said that in the higher mountain regions, snow piled up on the ground and, instead of melting, lay there for days. Many such tales I'd heard, believing them to be either exaggerations or inventions of fantasy. Yet the two black-skinned men coming toward us were as real as the ground I walked on.

We had little time for staring. As soon as the last ewe set her hooves on the soil of Moab, Elimelech pressed us onward. The men herded the sheep along the side of the road for there were others traveling the King's Highway in both directions. Mid-morning, I went to walk a while with Elimelech and Cyrus.

"Our destination is up there, only a little further south." Cyrus pointed to the mountains that rose steeply on our right.

"Then why aren't we climbing into the mountains now?"

"Up there, the rivers' currents have carved crevasses as deep as ten or more houses stacked on top of each other. There's no way to bridge the rivers, so we have to travel along the highway until we're past them."

"If the rivers are in such deep chasms how will we get water?"

"A shallow well produces water. Sometimes just a ditch will do."

I returned to the rams, watching over them from the corners of my eyes for my main attention dwelled on the new things I saw and heard – the garble of languages, the strange dress of people from foreign lands, the color of their skin, their eyes. People came from the south – from Egypt and countries whose names I'd never heard. They came from the north where the two rivers flowed and from places far to the east of the two rivers. Some came from the desert where the men twisted one end of their long, narrow scarves into turbans and then wrapped the other end around their faces so that only their eyes showed. Both night and day, Cyrus explained, the desert men wore their scarves wrapped in such a way so as not to breathe in the sand.

Before the morning ended, I realized why Moishe took the Israelites through the edge of the desert instead of defying the King of Moab by bringing them through his country. Overlooking the highway was a large fortress built above the bedrock. We passed beneath with heads tilted back and eyes focused on the foreboding structure looming above us.

Excited, Killion came running to me. "See the parapets?" He pointed. "Archers shoot at enemies from up there. When the archers have done all the damage they can, soldiers *sweeeeep* down with swords and slings and bows." He swept his hand through the air, showing how the soldiers came rushing down.

"And they kill people."

"Well . . .. Yes." Killion eyed me as though I had turned simple-minded. "That's what they're supposed to do."

"Why?"

"Why what?"

"Why are they supposed to kill people?"

"Because . . .." He raised his palms as though the answer was self-evident. "They kill their enemies."

"Wouldn't it be marvelous if we didn't kill each other?"

He shrugged again and said, "That's the way things are. Cyrus said there are other fortresses along the highway: Ara'ir, Balu'a, Khirbet el-Medeiniveh. Some say . . ..," Killion's voice grew low, ". . . that a race of giants, the Emion, occupied this land before the Moabites. Maybe they're the ones who built the fortresses." He shrugged. "But that's probably just a tale."

I hoped so. Up until that morning, I'd thought black-skinned people were just a tale.

The sound of dogs barking and our sentries yelling woke me that night. My first thought: *wolves*. I rushed out to see Arioch straddling a man, pounding him with his large, beefy hands. The moon cast a ghastly glow on the blood spurting from the man's face.

Three figures, streaks of moonlight on their backs, dashed away, our men close on their heels. Kir's knife caught a moonbeam and flashed in the dark as he chased after them, screaming. Heart racing, I searched through the confusion until I saw that husband, sons, and rams were safe.

Elimelech pulled Arioch off the thief. Still panting, Arioch grabbed the man by his neck, jerked him to his feet, and gave him a punch in the stomach, sending him sprawling. Kir, who had run over, kicked the thief in the ribs and let out a stream of curses in another language. I didn't have to understand the language to grasp that he'd used vile and menacing words. Kir's anger made him seem more human.

"Enough," Elimelech said. His heavy breathing sounded as though he'd run all the way from the Arnon. "Pitch the swine out."

Kir and Arioch picked up the writhing man by his arms and legs, dragged him away from the camp, and swung him into the night. I and my women watched, shivering.

"Go back to bed," Elimelech said. "All of you." He was about to walk away, but when none of us moved, he repeated, "Go to bed."

Trembling, I remained where I was while the other women went cowering into the tent. "We could have been killed." I kept my voice low. I didn't want to disturb my women any more than they'd already been disturbed.

"But we weren't." Elimelech came and drew me to him for a few moments before holding me at arm's length. "Go back to bed and let me do the worrying."

"*You*. Has it never entered your head that I'm also capable of worry? That I have a mind that works just as you have?"

A tired look crossed his face. "I know quite well you're capable of worry, Naomi, and that your mind works equally well as mine. But what *you* don't understand is that it's my place to take care of you. And that means, among other things, protecting you from fear."

"Ordering me back to bed when I'm scared half to death is protecting me from fear?"

"What is it that you want?"

What I wanted was for him to come to bed with me and hold me in his arms. My anger was a cover for fear, loneliness, and doubt. I rested my head on his shoulder. As he ran his hand over my hair, smoothing it, I was calmed by his warm hand, the sound of his heart beating, the scratch of his beard on my forehead.

"I'm sorry," I said. "I'll go to bed now and leave the worrying to you."

We set out at daybreak, wary of encountering more thieves, but also alive with anticipation, for on the morrow we'd turn east and climb into the hills of Moab.

Late in the afternoon, we encamped on the outskirts of Kir-Harseth. Elimelech announced that while he went to replenish supplies, including four new pairs of sandals for those whose shoes had fallen apart, the women, accompanied by Kir, could explore the market. He'd take our two sons and Cyrus with him.

"Will our flock and supplies be safe?" I asked, still haunted by the previous evening.

"Uri and the mute are guarding the herd, Arioch the supplies, and Festus and Skinny will roam back and forth between tents and sheep. Besides, thieves tend to lose their confidence when the sun sheds light on their activities." He tweaked me on the cheek. "Go and enjoy yourself. You deserve a little pleasure."

We set out, Kir and four women who, before this journey, had never left the hill we were born on. Soon, we discovered that the market was enormous enough to hold in only one of its corners several bazaars the size of ours in Bethlehem.

"We'll get lost," Abi said.

"Not with Kir along," I replied though I wasn't so sure.

We entered the maze of alleyways ill at ease for we were outsiders. Foreigners. But even though my heart beat loud and fast with nervousness, I could hardly wait to see what new and strange things we'd discover.

Never had I seen so many people packed together, heard such noise, or imagined such a babble of languages. How did the gods keep track of their people when they were jumbled together? And the odors! We covered our noses with our scarves for the smells were overwhelming – urine, sweat, feces, rotten fruit. And incense – the clothes of the women all but shouted with the aroma.

We wound our way through the corridors of the butchers and then through those of the carpenters, tanners, and basket-makers. In the potters' row, we caught glimpses of earthen- and stoneware decorated with spirals, bird designs, and preening swans. In the alley where ornaments were sold, we examined scarabs of quartz from Egypt along with brooches of bone and ivory. Kir waited patiently, arms crossed, an unreadable expression on his face, as we admired silver bracelets and necklaces embedded with lapis lazuli and obsidian. A few contained a yellowish stone. When I bent to get a better look, the merchant picked up a bracelet, stuck it in my face, and jabbered. I drew back. He came from behind his display and held the piece in front of my nose. I put up my hands to keep the man away and took a step backwards. Only when Kir interceded, barking at him in his own language, did the man back off.

"The yellowish stone is called amber, but it isn't really a stone," Kir explained as we moved on. "It's the hardened sap of a tree that grows far to the north of the land of two rivers."

Just as I had during our trek through the Judean Hills, I reconsidered the size of the earth. In a few days' time it seemed to have grown even bigger. With so many goods for sale, certainly the earth's boundaries stretched much further than I'd ever imagined.

Abi wanted to dawdle at the perfumers' booths, stocked not only with perfume and incense, but with balm, incense burners, alabaster boxes to hold the containers, and I hardly knew what else. I urged her to keep going for we didn't have time to dawdle at every display.

We elbowed our way through an alleyway filled with booths selling cult shrines, carved human figures wearing masks, serpent amulets, figurines of wild animals. Finally, we came to a corridor where a man seated on the ground used a wooden mallet to beat flax placed on a stone, and I knew we were in the place where woven goods were traded.

As we pushed through the crowd, Mesha grabbed my sleeve and brought her face close to mine so as to be heard above the throng. "The pieces here aren't any better than the ones you weave."

"You're being kind," I said although I knew of no one who wove a smoother fabric than I.

"No, it's true."

"She's right," Hada said. "Your weaving is the best in Bethlehem."

The first few booths sold wool or linen, but when we pushed our way through a cluster of people surrounding one booth, I stopped in awe. Piled on the table were fabrics with shimmering colors and a weave so tight I couldn't tell warp from weft. The thinness of the fabric puzzled me. What kind of thread could it possibly be?

"Silk," Kir said.

I stepped closer. The merchant, engaged with a customer, paid no attention when I touched the silk. I caught my breath as my hand slid over the glossy material. Never had I imagined such softness, such gleeful colors, such joy in a piece of cloth, and, for the first time, I felt the desire to have something I didn't have.

But the afternoon was passing. Reluctantly, I moved on until, once again, we saw something that left me in wonderment. We'd passed several booths piled with mats and rugs when we came upon a merchant selling rugs with patterns I'd never dreamed possible – swirls, animals, tree-shapes, medallions. How did someone weave these designs? And I was puzzled at the thickness. What made the rugs so thick?

The merchant, seeing my interest, babbled at me while running his hand over a rug with a red background and yellow, blue, and white designs. Still babbling, he pointed to various figures and symbols, not grasping that I understood no word of what he said. Nodding, I pretended to listen for I wanted to examine the piece, and the more time he spent talking, the more I could examine. Finally, the merchant, realizing I understood nothing, turned to someone else.

Some rugs were stacked flat while others were rolled. I ran my hands over several, admiring their rich colors and intricate designs. But I was puzzled. Instead of a weave, threads poked up like stubble on a man's face only much closer together and softer.

Kir whispered in my ear, "The rug isn't made by weaving. Instead, threads are knotted in the back." He lifted the corner and showed me the knots.

I was stunned. It must have taken months to make a rug such as this.

"It's time to go," Kir said. "Soon, we won't be able to see."

Reluctantly, we hurried out of the labyrinth. For the space of an afternoon,

I'd forgotten about dying sheep, about living among strangers. I'd been mesmerized by all the strange new things. Especially, the brightly-colored silk. Smooth, glossy, and fit for a king. And the knotted rugs. The patterns, the rich colors. What kind of skill, what kind of witchery did the weaver possess that enabled her to weave birds and trees into a rug?

Elimelech was with the sheep when we returned. He knelt beside one of the ewes while Uri held the ewe's head and the mute watched. Festus and Skinny stood on opposite sides of the flock, keeping watch. Stretched out in front of the tent, Cyrus' hand rested on his stomach which rose and fell as he slept. Arioch, who was supposed to be guarding the campsite, was nowhere to be seen. Nor did I see my sons.

Kir went to join Elimelech, leaving us to walk the few remaining paces alone. My sons appeared from behind the tent and hurried to meet us, greeting me with more enthusiasm than I thought the occasion merited.

"You saw lots of wonderful things," I said without stopping. It was past time to begin preparing the meal.

"Yes, yes. Lots of strange and wonderful things." Giving Machlon a look of which I couldn't guess the meaning, Killion turned to walk beside me.

"Lots of things we've never seen before." Machlon walked on my other side so that I was hemmed in between them.

I stopped. Something about the way they looked at each other alerted me that there was a story they wanted to tell. Or more likely, one they *didn't* want to tell.

"What did you see?" I looked from one to the other. Killion was trying to keep an expressionless face, his gaze roaming, never looking directly at me. Machlon crossed his arms and stared at his feet.

"What did you see?" I asked again.

"We saw lots of strange food," Killion said. He shot a glance at Machlon.

Machlon finally looked me in the eyes. "There were so many things we've never seen before, I can't even name them all."

While I talked with my sons, Hada filled a bowl with lentils and began picking out hulls while Abi laid out bread and honey. Mesha took the fire cylinder from its basket, plugged a bit of dry straw into the hole of the fireboard, and began rotating the cylinder in an effort to create a spark. The live embers we carried with us in a clay pot had died when water from the Arnon splashed into the pot.

"You saw lots of new things, too, didn't you Mother?" Turning on his charm, Killion smiled at me, his eyes bright, the dimple in his left cheek deepening.

I decided to let it go. They'd probably seen something indecent. While not wanting to tell me about it, at the same time they wanted me to know they were almost men and had observed something that only men appreciated. Eventually it would come out.

"We can talk about it later," I said, starting toward the back of the tent. "I need to get fuel for the fire."

"Wait, wait," Machlon cried out, putting his hand on my arm.

Killion grabbed me by the sleeve of the opposite arm. "We'll get it for you. Stay here and rest a bit."

The two hurried toward the back of the tent for the dried palm fronds we'd gathered the previous evening.

Stay here and rest a bit? I followed them.

Elimelech was too far away to hear my exclamation, but the three women heard. They ran to where I stood over Arioch sprawled on the ground, a smirk on his face, and an empty flagon beside him. I picked it up and sniffed a sickeningly sweet smell.

"Date wine!"

Mesha gasped.

I glared at my sons. "You were trying to cover for him? Go get your father."

"Oh, please Ma'am, don't." Mesha threw herself at my feet. "Please, please let it go this time. He won't do it again." She sent Arioch a pleading look and received a stupid grin in reply. "This is the first time . . .," she flitted her eyes at me and then looked away because we both knew there'd been other times when Arioch had drunk to excess. "Those other times," she said, ". . . they were a long time ago, and it was during celebrations, and . . .." Her eyes filled with tears. "I promise I'll watch him. I'll give him a good talking to, and . . .. Please."

She gave me such a beseeching look that I relented. A little. It would be nearly impossible to find someone to fill Arioch's place and, until now, he'd been a good and faithful servant. The vision of him straddling the thief was vivid in my memory, and it was true that his other episodes of drunkenness had been during celebrations. The journey had been hard for all of us. Our bondsmen must also feel some of the pressure that Elimelech and I felt.

Everyone looked at me, waiting. I glanced out to where the men were. Occupied with their tasks, they hadn't noticed us gathered at the rear of the tent. "Alright," I said. "Ply him with water and get him on his feet before Elimelech returns." I handed the empty flagon to Machlon. "Get rid of this. Away from the camp. And you . . .," I said to Killion, ". . . if you and your brother ever cover for him again, you'll be in deep trouble with your father. If there *is* a next time, I'll tell him everything."

Killion sucked in his cheeks and nodded.

"And get busy doing something useful," I snapped. "Bring fuel for the fire."

It was past time to prepare the meal. I'd worry about Arioch later. For now, uppermost in my mind was what tomorrow would bring. I both wanted to get where we were going and *not* get there. I was more than ready to end our journey, yet the thought of living among our enemies troubled me greatly. What I didn't know and was afraid to ask Cyrus was, *Do the Moabites despise the Israelites as much we despise them?*

Part II
MOAB

Chapter 16

On the third day after leaving the King's Highway, we reached our journey's end in mid-afternoon.

"This is it," Cyrus said, lifting his arm to indicate a valley so narrow it looked more like a giant's plough-row.

The valley was perfect for us. One end pointed west toward the Salt Sea, the other east toward the great desert. Hemmed in by hills, our flock could graze within sight. Grass sprouted as thick as threads in the knotted carpets I'd seen in the market. Trees for shade and firewood grew in abundance. Behind the spot chosen for our tents stood a copse of pines intermingled with cinnabars, junipers, fledgling oaks, and saltbushes. A large oak, uprooted by some disaster, had fallen over, its roots displayed like a giant spiderweb. The oak provided a bench for when we wanted to relax amid the trees. Forests covered the south hill. The north hill contained patches of trees, and a few grew here and there in the pasture. The fresh air was heavy with the smell of green leaves and grass. If trees could be counted as riches, then we were to be very rich while we remained in Moab.

I helped unload food while the men erected tents. For the first time since leaving Bethlehem, they all went up. Elimelech's and mine stood closest to the north hill, with the fallen oak lying a few paces behind. Next to ours was the cooking tent where the women would sleep as well as cook. Then came the one for storage and, closest to the south hill, the men's tent.

As soon as our goat hair homes were up, the men hastily constructed an enclosure of thorn bushes between the men's tent and the south hill. They penned the rams in the enclosure, tethered the oxen behind, and put the donkeys, except for one, to pasture with the sheep. One donkey remained with the rams as protection against wild animals.

Exhausted, we looked forward to finishing our few remaining chores so we could eat and then fall onto our mats for a well-deserved night's sleep. Hada was attempting to bring order to the cooking tent while Mesha and Abi gathered firewood. The men were finishing a few loose ends – sharpening an extra stake for one of the tents; seeing to an unhappy ox; adding another thorn bush to the rams' enclosure.

I had just filled a clay pot with water from a skin, preparing to make a stew, when I realized there were no streams nearby. Cyrus had said we'd find plenty of water in Moab, yet I saw none. We had enough for the evening and morning, but then we'd need more. As I looked around trying to locate a source, a movement drew my eyes to the north hill. My heart dropped. A group of six men strode down the hill toward us. Were they coming to drive us off? Or worse?

The leader, a stalwart man of medium-height, walked with head held high and shoulders drawn back. He carried a staff with which he punched the ground at every step as though making holes for seeds. Before I could alert my husband, Cyrus called out a welcome and went to meet them at the bottom of the hill, greeting each with a kiss on the cheek. A younger man resembling the one I took to be a chief wore a brightly striped cloak. A third companion had a thick, black beard, while an older man with a pregnant pouch of a stomach and a stiff neck, rotated his head back and forth, studying our camp. Two young men in the group looked to be about the same age as my sons.

Elimelech had followed Cyrus but stopped a short distance away until Cyrus beckoned him closer. My husband greeted the strangers and then motioned toward our tent. As they made their way slowly, exchanging pleasantries, I wondered what I should do. I had never entertained in a tent. Should I roll up the sides? Or bring out cushions and arrange them beneath the gnarled cedar in front of our tent?

"Shall I help bring out cushions?" Kir asked in a low voice. He'd slipped up behind me.

Grateful, I met his gaze and said, "Thank you, I'll bring the cushions. I'm sure Elimelech wants you with him."

My women were waiting for instructions. "Abi, strain the wine. Mesha, help Hada see to food and then serve the wine."

After I brought out cushions and arranged them beneath the cedar, I went to the cooking tent where Hada coated balls of goat cheese in honey.

"The serving platters . . . . I can't find them." Mesha searched frantically through the utensils and containers we'd piled inside.

"And I need cups and the large ewer," Abi said. She was pouring wine from our last jug into the straining pitcher.

I shuffled through the stacks of utensils, found cups and a platter. Our large wine ewer, probably hidden at the bottom of a pile, wasn't to be seen, so I gave Abi two smaller ones. On a second platter I arranged nuts and olives, took them to the men who had been joined by Machlon and Killion. While I held out the platter to each man, Mesha handed out cups and poured wine.

Elimelech's face was tense. He'd been forced to meet our Moabite neighbors though exhausted and with much still to do before we retired for the night. When I held out the platter to him, instead of taking food, he rose and put his hand on my arm.

"My wife, Naomi," he said. Then to me, "These are our neighbors." First, he introduced Achilla, the leader of the group whose salt and pepper hair and beard were closely clipped. Then, indicating each of the others with a nod of his head, he told me their names. Lechben, the older man with a big belly and who smelled strongly of garlic, was Achilla's cousin. Aaron, Achilla's younger, better-looking brother in the striped cloak, also had closely clipped hair and beard. The bushy, black-bearded man was Achilla's steward Jerel.

The two young men were Aaron's sons, Gideon and Habish. With their dark, oily hair, bony wrists, and almond-shaped eyes they weren't as comely as my handsome sons. Gideon had pushed up the sleeves of his tunic to reveal thin arms but with muscles that appeared to be as hard as the iron tools made by the Philistines. Habish, not so tall as Gideon, was better-looking but only by an amount the size of a pea. Both had hooked noses and wore clothes of a yellowish hue that made their skin appear sallow.

I took all this in in a matter of moments as I muttered, "Shalom" to each man. They went back to their conversation, and I circled the group a second time, holding out the platter. I didn't expect to remember every name. Achilla's, I would. His commanding presence was such that I imagined everyone must remember his name.

As I watched Aaron's sons eyeing my sons, and my sons eyeing them back, I knew I'd also remember their names. Gideon and Habish. Habish and Gideon.

I hurried back for more food, meeting Mesha on her way out with a second ewer of wine. Inside the tent, Hada, her back to me, still rolled cheese balls. Her back was also to Abi. I hadn't entered quietly on purpose for it wasn't my habit to spy on my serving women. Yet neither heard me. Unaware of my presence, Abi picked up the refilled ewer from which Mesha had poured the men their first cups of wine, brought it close to her mouth, and spit.

"Abi!"

She jumped and then hid the ewer behind her as though that would prevent my seeing what I'd already seen.

"You spit in the wine!"

She gave me a defiant look. "They're Moabites."

My face flamed. "Did you spit in both ewers?" I could barely contain my fury.

She dipped her head and looked at me from beneath lowered eye-lids. "Just this one."

I narrowed my eyes, daring her to lie.

"Just this one," she repeated.

Hada stared at us.

"Hada?" I asked.

"I was facing away and didn't see." Hada's voice shook.

"Enemies, or no," I said, glaring at Abi, "Our hospitality will be honorable. Pour out the wine, scrub the ewer, then strain more. Somehow, you'll make up for what you've wasted."

◆ ◆ ◆

The men went to look at the sheep. Curious, I followed, using as my excuse that I wanted to deliver treats to Uri and the mute.

Usually, Uri greeted me with a cheerful comment, especially when I brought food, so I was surprised when he reached out absently and took the food without thanking me. His gaze followed Achilla and Aaron who wandered among the sheep, examining the lambs.

While Elimelech stood by stone-faced, Machlon and Killion scowling at his side, Achilla pointed to a lamb and then to another. Aaron grabbed the two by their napes and dragged them to Achilla's steward, Jerel, who looped a rope around their necks. Jerel then passed the rope to Gideon to hold. Puzzled, but with a growing darkness inside, I watched three more lambs pulled aside. Then Achilla and Aaron walked from one end of the flock to the other, choosing five more.

Ten lambs now stood roped at the edge of our flock. A look of misery on his face, Elimelech avoided my eyes.

I followed the men back to our tents, Achilla's steward and nephews pulling the ten lambs behind. Fury welled inside me for I guessed that Elimelech had promised lambs as payment for the village chief's protection. I was angry both with Achilla for taking our lambs and at my husband for the promise he'd made and hidden from me.

As the group neared the tents, Aaron looked to where the three rams nosed about their enclosure. "There are more sheep," he said to Achilla, pointing.

"Those are our rams," Elimelech said quickly. A bead of sweat ran down his forehead.

With the others at his heels, Achilla headed toward the enclosure. Elimelech threw me a miserable look as I trailed behind, heavy with foreboding.

No Name backed away as the men approached, but Little Samson and Blackfoot ran over to nuzzle at Elimelech's hand when he let it dangle over the fence of thorn bushes. "These are my rams," my husband said in the Moabite tongue.

Achilla studied the two young rams.

Kir said something in Moabite and, as though trying to draw Achilla's attention away, pointed toward the cushions where the men had sat a short while ago.

Ignoring Kir, Achilla pulled aside a thorn bush, entered the enclosure, and bent to examine Little Samson and Blackfoot. He ran his hand along their backs, looked in their eyes, examined their hind quarters.

Again, Kir spoke and pointed toward the cushions. Elimelech threw me a desperate look.

"There's more wine," I said, stepping forward. "And more food." I looked at Cyrus for help.

Cyrus repeated my words in Moabite and, like Kir, pointed to the cushions.

Finally, Achilla spoke.

"The agreement," Cyrus said, translating, ". . . was that I be allowed to choose any ten lambs."

"I assumed you meant ewe lambs." Darkness consumed Elimelech's face.

"Sheep are sheep." Achilla had pried open the mouth of Little Samson and was looking inside. "I think this one will do nicely." Achilla straightened, his eyes still on Little Samson. "What do you think Lechben? Aaron?"

"Take it," Lechben said. "It's a fine ram."

Aaron entered the enclosure and pulled back each of Little Sampson's ears. "Yes, a fine ram. Which of the ewe lambs should I let go?"

"Whichever you choose." Achilla patted Little Samson on the head and then, taking a rope handed him by Jerel, looped it around the neck of our most precious ram and walked him out of the enclosure.

Fighting nausea, I clenched my hands.

Gideon, the older of Aaron's sons, grinned at Machlon and Killion, who were too stricken to notice. Arioch's nostrils flared, and Kir wore an expression of stone, while Festus and Skinny watched with troubled faces. Even Cyrus's face tightened.

Elimelech, however, looked as though he'd lost his soul. Never, had my husband appeared so defeated.

Achilla's party departed, herding away Little Samson and the best of our ewe lambs. Cyrus left with Achilla, his employ with us at an end. As they began the ascent over the hill to their village, Cyrus stopped, looked back, and gave us a long, sad look. He'd been as surprised as Elimelech over Achilla's interpretation of the agreement. Having grown to like Cyrus despite his being a Moabite and despite his humped shoulder, I regretted I hadn't given him a proper goodbye.

Our bondsmen and serving women drifted quietly back to their tasks, none daring to look at Elimelech. I took my husband by the hand and, as docile as a lamb, he let me lead him into our tent.

"I was wrong," he whispered.

I embraced him. He lay his head on my shoulder, his sunburnt cheek against mine, his beard tickling my chin.

"Half the flock is gone," he said and shuddered.

"Half would have died had we remained in Bethlehem."

"But we had our home, our kin, our friends."

While I had the happiness of counting off the days until we returned to our home, kin, and friends, Elimelech had the task of ensuring that the reason we came to Moab would be fulfilled. He couldn't return a failure, nor did I want him to. I drew back, took his hand, and squeezed it, fighting back my tears. I'd cry when I was alone. "We've never seen such rich grass," I said. "And so much of it. With these wonderful pastures and your talent for husbandry, the flock will double in no time. Next lambing season, I wager we'll have more lambs than you ever imagined." I tried to smile.

"It was agreed on. In exchange for Achilla's protection, ten lambs of his choice. I just didn't think . . .. Achilla wanted to bolster his animals with new blood. During his travels, Cyrus had been watching for a good flock."

"And yours was the best." I let go of his hand and reached beneath the sleeve of his tunic to massage his arm.

A sad attempt at a smile tugged at his lips. "Had he seen Boaz's flock, Cyrus might have had a problem deciding whose sheep were the best." He shook his head slowly. "We couldn't have come here without the protection of someone."

"Yes, I know." I ran my finger around his lips. "And who's to say that Blackfoot won't be the best ram, after all?"

"Blackfoot is a fine ram."

The smell of wood smoke drifted into the tent, and I heard the voices of my women as they prepared to bake bread. In the distance, one of Uri's dogs barked and then became quiet. The notes of a sprightly tune came from our shepherd's pipe, soft and distant like a whisper of wind.

"Our family is safe and happy," I said. "And the flock will recover." At least, I hoped it would be so.

Chapter 17

A chorus of birds woke me. I draped my arm over my husband and molded my body around his back, hoping the birds wouldn't waken him yet. I wanted to enjoy the warmth of his flesh and feel his ribs rising and falling beneath my arm for a few moments, but the creatures chirped and tweeted so loudly, I doubted he'd sleep much longer.

Two thoughts filled my mind, one of which I was thoroughly ashamed, yet the thought refused to go away. Had I known that Achilla was about to take ten of our best lambs, including Little Samson, I might have added my spit to Abi's. Thankfully, the other thought, that we were one day closer to our return, sang joyfully in my head and would eventually drown out the evil image of tainting Achilla's drink. Every sunrise would bring our return one day closer. Every moonrise meant one less night in this land. Weeks would fly by. One day we'd take down the tents, round up the sheep, and say goodbye to the valley.

Meanwhile, there was much to do – for the men, animals seen to, a cistern to be carved in the rock, stones collected for stall fences and a bread oven. As for the women, our tasks were the same no matter where we were, house, tent, or on-the-road: feed the men, take care of their clothes and tempers, keep them happy.

Elimelech's breathing stilled. Then he drew in a deep breath and expelled it in a long whoosh. He stretched, rolled over to lay his hand on my hip, and stroked it lightly.

"You and Abi have to go to the village for water," he said.

I sat up abruptly. On the previous evening, I'd been so upset I'd forgotten to ask Cyrus where we'd find water. "I don't know where the village is."

"Just over the north hill."

"Abi and I can't go alone to a strange village. And we need more water than the two of us can carry."

"Hada and Mesha have to milk the goats." The blanket fell away from his broad chest as he sat up. "Cyrus promised to tell the village women you're coming and that we're guests of Achilla."

"Abi and I can't go alone," I repeated, running my hand over his chest hair.

"Keep doing that, and neither of us will be going anywhere for a while." He put his hand on mine, stopping its further progress. "What would our servants say if we didn't appear promptly for our morning chores?" He brought my fingers to his lips and kissed them.

Too dark to see, I heard the smile in his voice.

"I'll send Machlon and Killion with you," he said. "*That* will serve a dual purpose. They won't be fully engaged in their chores until they've satisfied their curiosity about what lies over the hill. Take two donkeys to carry the water."

Muffled voices came from outside.

Elimelech tossed aside the blanket and stood up. "Our disappointment of yesterday is no excuse for lingering in bed and neglecting our duties." Holding out his hand, he pulled me to my feet.

While I wrapped my outer garment around my tunic, which I'd worn to bed, he slipped into his. About to push open the flap to the tent, he stopped and let it fall back.

"Last night, I was distraught," he said softly.

"So was I."

"We've lost sheep before. Every year we lose sheep. Just not this many. But we won't dwell on it; we're going forward."

"Yes. We're going forward."

◆ ◆ ◆

After breaking fast, Abi and I loaded two donkeys with water skins and set out for the village accompanied by my sons. The world lay gray and silver in the dawn, and, except for the birds, quiet. The air smelled fresh, untainted by dust and foul smells.

"We'll be safe," Machlon said.

He'd sensed my discomfort in going to a Moabite village whose chief had taken ten of our best lambs.

"Yes, we'll be safe," Killion repeated, his eyes eager with the anticipation of adventure. "We have our slings," he patted his agora. Then, winking at Machlon, he said, "If wild animals attack, we're ready."

And if Moabites attack, I wondered? Or if Achilla captures us and demands the rest of our flock in ransom? In my mind, I knew these things wouldn't happen, yet my heart didn't always listen to my mind.

The gentle slope of the hill made it easy to climb, and the thick growth of grass and plants cushioned our steps although the dew soaked our feet. Trees dotting the hill were nothing more than gray blurs.

Half-way to the top, I realized Abi was missing and looked back to see her returning to our encampment.

"Abi, what are you doing?" I called.

She stopped. Her back still to me, she shouted, "I can't go."

"Why not?"

"It's a Moabite village."

"There's nothing to be afraid of." Yet, *I* was nervous. Along the King's Highway, no one noticed us. We were a few strangers among many, and people were interested only in what they bought and sold. Here, we were invading someone's home.

She turned around. "What if they take our donkeys?"

"Then we'll have two less donkeys."

"They might want to sacrifice us to Chemosh."

"Abi, that's enough. You're coming with us."

I glared at her until she rejoined us, albeit slowly. Machlon and Killion exchanged looks, no doubt at the silliness of women afraid to walk into an enemy village accompanied by two fierce fighters such as them, each armed with a sling tucked into his agora.

When we reached the summit, we looked down into a valley several times bigger than ours and saw a cluster of houses surrounding a commons where the well would be. A tall column rose at the center of the commons, a figure perched on top. The sun not yet risen, I tried in vain to make out the figure.

On the western side of the village, one house appeared to be twice the size of the others. Achilla's, no doubt. Did he also make demands on the villagers for *his protection*? Perhaps he had a band of strongmen led by his brother, Aaron, whose job it was to extract a tax from his neighbors, a *protection tax*. I swallowed. No, I wouldn't be bitter today. Nor would I be bitter tomorrow. *Mara* profited nothing.

Machlon and Killion started down the hill, engaged in a lively conversation as they looked about, pointing. I walked slowly, examining the village. Abi, consumed with a look of righteous indignation, was content to dawdle.

East of the village, the dark forms of men moved toward fields. I didn't need the risen sun to know what grew there. The nutty smell of ripe barley had reached me the moment we topped the crest. Had Yahweh not been angry and withheld the rains, we'd have been doing this very thing today in our own field.

A large flock grazed on the southwest side of the village. Seeing no other sheep in the area, I guessed flocks belonging to the villagers had been mixed with Achilla's, each owner marking his animals with his own colors and marks. Our ten lambs would be among them, each with two round splashes of indigo on the forehead.

"If we found Little Samson, we could steal him back," Killion said when Abi and I caught up with him and Machlon half-way down the hill.

"Killion!" I snapped. "Don't ever speak of stealing. Even to speak of it is . . . .."

"They'd kill you for sure," Abi said.

Killion shrugged. "They wouldn't know who stole him."

"You're right," Machlon said. "They wouldn't know, so they'd kill us all. And you'd better not spit in their well, Abi. Else, they'll kill us for that, too."

"I'm not that stupid." Abi raised her chin and walked straighter as though to prove her intelligence. "Who told you that?"

"Aaahh, word gets out."

"Enough," I said, putting an end to the conversation. We were almost at the bottom of the hill and moving rapidly toward the first houses.

The dwellings had the same stone foundations, mud brick walls, and wooden troughs as ours. Fuel for ovens was piled beside the houses – kindling, stacks of dung, olive pits, straw. I imagined the interiors must also look the same – stalls, storage rooms, ladders for climbing to the next floor, herbs hanging from rafters emitting fragrances of rue, myrtle, yellow apples of mandrake.

"Everything looks the same." Machlon sounded disappointed. "I thought things would be different in Moab."

"Things *are* different," Killion said. "It's greener. Why didn't Yahweh give *this* land to the Israelites? It's a lot better."

"Killion!" My sons were trying my patience. "Don't question Yahweh's wisdom."

Following a dirt-beaten path, we wound through the village until the column we'd seen from the hill brought us to a stop. On top, staring in the direction of our encampment, stood the naked figure of Astarte, Chemosh's consort. I shuddered. Neither the caravans, the strange towns, the fortresses, the markets – none of these – had announced to me so clearly that we were in the land of Chemosh.

"It's Astarte," Abi whispered.

"It's a statue," Killion said. Too loud. "Nothing but a statue. It has no power."

"Shhhh." I looked around, hoping no one had heard my younger son.

"Don't talk so loud, you idiot," Machlon said to his brother, a tease in his voice. "Chemosh might turn you into a donkey."

"Shhhh," I said again, shushing them both. "Come. We have to get water and be on our way. Go, go, go." I put my hand on Killion's back and pushed him forward.

Women were gathered at the well, some waiting in line, others grouped together talking – a scene I was well familiar with. They'd be filling each other in on their aunt's bad back, the death of an ox, the failure of someone's bread to rise, a new baby. Today, they'd also be wondering about the Israelite family settled just over the hill.

We'd gone only a few steps when someone saw us and alerted the others. Everyone turned to look. Even the person drawing water stopped mid-pull and stared.

Keeping my eyes on the bucket beam, I kept going. Shawl drawn close around my face and head down, I joined the line. Abi fell in behind me while Killion and Machlon held the donkeys aside, waiting for the women to finish. There were no men, for they would have finished watering their animals and left before the women began to draw water.

A few began to whisper. Then the whispers became words spoken aloud. The line moved forward, woman by woman. Avoiding eyes fixed on us, I looked at my feet, and at theirs, observing tattered sandals, torn toenails, raveled hems of garments. Like the women in the bazaar, their dress smelled of incense.

Our turn came, yet no woman left even though she'd already drawn water. Face flaming, I lowered the bucket into the well. Who did they think we were to stare so? Israelites drew water the same way as Moabites. We let the rope slip through our hands as the bucket plunged into the well and then tugged the filled container back up, arms straining. Red welts from the rope showed on our hands, the same red, the same pattern across our palms as on theirs. Yet they stared.

"Shalom," a raspy voice said to my back when we finished. I turned to look down at the wrinkled forehead and white hair of an old woman whose head came only to my shoulders.

"Shalom," she said again and then rattled off a string of words.

Dumbly, I stood there, not understanding. Another torrent of words issued from her while she pointed to her left. This time, I understood the word "house." I held out my palms in a question. The third time, she spoke more slowly. Still, other than the word "house," I understood nothing.

She shrugged, pinched a fold of my shawl between her thumb and forefinger, and brought it close to her clouded eyes, examining it. Whoever had dyed her own shawl had not spared the indigo. Narrow stripes of yellow ran through the vibrant blue background, and a broad band of the same yellow edged the shawl. The bright colors bespoke a person of means, yet the weaving was course.

As she continued to examine my shawl, the woman said a word I did understand. "Good." Cyrus said that often. *Good* when there was food he liked. *Good* when the trail was clear or the weather fine. The woman smiled, revealing a mouth nearly bereft of teeth. "Good," she repeated. She let go of my shawl, muttered something, and left.

"She was a witch." Killion's eyes sparkled with amusement as we re-climbed the hill.

"Don't be absurd," I said.

"Do you not think the old woman a witch, Machlon?" Killion raised his brows at his brother.

"You're bedeviling our mother. Don't worry her."

"I'm not worried," I protested. "I put no importance in Killion's silly words."

"But you saw her sandals, did you not?" A light danced in Killion's eyes.

"I saw that her sandals were good, not worn like the others."

Killion propped his arm on the neck of the donkey he walked beside. "Good sandals, bright shawl, and no teeth. Signs of a witch, I'd say."

"And *I'd* say your father needs to increase your chores, so you'll be too tired to tease your mother." I tweaked his cheek.

Killion tried to pretend seriousness, something that was becoming more and more difficult for him. "There *are* witches in Moab, I've been told, and maybe the old woman really is one."

Chapter 18

When we came to the top of the hill, I sent Machlon and Killion ahead with the donkeys while Abi and I stayed to pick wild greens. Onions and dandelions grew in abundance, and, once we started looking, I knew we'd find much more.

"It's like a feast growing here," Abi said as she began breaking off dandelions and stuffing them in the lap of her gathered up garment.

I lifted the lap of my garment, too, but then let it drop. The sun had risen to reveal the hill bursting with the reds, blues, and yellows of anemones, poppies, buttercups, and henbane. The aroma of acacias wafted as strong as that of the barley being harvested in the fields behind us. Dragonflies fluttered back and forth. A large bird, flying too fast to identify, swooped past, its wings flapping noisily, and I heard the squawk of a grackle. To my delight, I also heard the drone of bees. There would be honey nearby! When I saw two wild fig trees, my delight in our surroundings doubled.

"Look at what all I've found," Abi said, holding out her gathered tunic to show me the pile of greens.

"Abi, you did all that while I stood here gawking. How good you are."

She drew back her shoulders and smiled.

"Go on ahead," I said. "I'll stay and pick my share."

She pointed to a patch of plants with feathery leaves and white blossoms. "Be careful. There's poison parsley over there. Poor Mighty Samson."

"Some call it hemlock." I sighed. "If only our ram hadn't been so hungry."

"I'll be going now." She set off down the hill.

I returned to our camp with a lapful of prickly lettuce. Abi had filled a vessel with water and was washing the greens she'd picked while Uri sat nearby watching Hada tie the neck of a skin filled with goat milk.

"You could make yourself useful and find a limb to hang this on and then churn the milk," I heard Hada say to our shepherd.

Uri stretched lazily. "Useful? I'm taking a respite from work for the remainder of the day."

"Why should you be idle when the rest of us aren't?" Hada's jibe was good-natured. Such was the sweetness of Uri's disposition that no one ever became angry with him.

"I'll answer that when you tell me why the rest of you get to sleep through the night while I watch the sheep from sunrise to sunrise or, if you prefer, moonrise to moonrise."

"Surely, you sleep out there." Hada gave the string another tug to ensure the milk wouldn't splash out.

"I sleep when the dogs let me. They yip and yap at every little thing. Today is a holiday, which I've rightly earned." He lay down and closed his eyes. "Wake me for the next meal."

"Who's with the sheep?" I asked, dumping my load of greens into an empty basket.

"Killion," Hada said. "Elimelech sent him as soon as he returned." Searching for a suitable limb, she eyed the large oak in front of the cooking tent and the fledgling oak a little further away. She went to the fledgling and held up her hand to one of the limbs, measuring its height. "This should do." Standing on her toes, she attached the skin. "If the mute had come with Uri, he could have done the churning, but he wanted to stay out there." She nodded toward the flock.

"Abi can do the churning. Unless you prefer to do it yourself."

Abi glanced up from where she washed the greens, laying the clean sprigs to dry on a bit of wool.

"I'll let Abi do it," Hada said. "I'm going to help Machlon collect last night's dung and lay it in the sun to dry. I doubt Abi would be much help doing that." She raised an eyebrow at Abi. "Is that not right?"

Abi frowned. "Dung stinks."

"It stinks for all of us," Hada turned to me. "Mesha is attempting to bring order to the chaos in the cooking tent."

Which is what I'd do after I'd gone to see how the men were progressing.

At intervals along the south hill, rock face rose part way up. Elimelech had chosen one of these spots located near the rams' stall to carve a cistern. Expecting to find either the beginning of a cistern being chipped into the rock or else the beginning of a basin made with limestone, I found neither. Instead, the men were digging a ditch along the bottom of the rockface. They paid no attention to me, so I watched, trying to understand what they intended.

Thus far, the ditch ran the length of two men and extended into the rams' enclosure from which a few thorn bushes had been removed to make room for the channel. At its beginning, the ditch was as deep as a man's knee, but it became deeper and deeper until where the men now dug, it came to the midpoint of their thighs. Since the ditch abutted the rockface, the men had to pile the dirt they removed from the ditch along its front. Arioch and Festus had shovels. Elimelech loosened soil with a hoe, leaving it for Skinny and Kir to scoop out with clay pots. Water seeped down the rockface, wetting the dirt so that both the ditch itself and the wall forming in front of the ditch oozed with mud.

The men, stinking with sweat, had tucked the ends of their tunics into their agoras, exposing their legs. I stifled a laugh at the sight of five pairs of hairy legs covered with mud. Hands were thick with muck; tunics hung heavy with ooze; mud ran in streaks down faces. What a mess it was going to be to clean the clothes. At least they'd piled their sandals a safe distance away.

Finally, I burst out laughing. The men stopped and stared then looked at each other, searching for the source of my amusement. Arioch ran his fingers through his hair, brushing it into a mud-brown haystack. I laughed louder.

Finally, Elimelech, seeming to understand, smiled and said, "We're quite a sight."

The men began to laugh, too, and the women, along with Uri and Machlon, rushed over to see what they were missing. Elimelech crawled from the ditch.

"What about the cistern?" I finally managed to ask.

"With a watering ditch for the animals, you won't have to bring so much from the well. A cistern will take longer to build, so I thought it better to begin with the ditch." He squatted down to rest. "See how the water runs down the rock?" He pointed to the wet, black marks where the water trickled. "It gets to the bottom and turns the ground to mud. We're going to line the ditch with flat stones to collect the run-off, shingling the stones so the water runs toward the end of the ditch. The channel will extend through the ram's enclosure and into that of the oxen. They'll have drink without us fetching it." He looked around at the men who looked as satisfied as if they'd invented the Tower of Babel.

"We still have to go to the village to get water for us." No sooner were the words out, than I knew they sounded like a complaint. I suppose they were. The idea of facing the villagers every morning dissolved my humor.

"We'll carve a cistern." Elimelech's smile vanished. "If going to the village is so repulsive to you, we can also dig a well. Water is close to the surface, so we won't have to dig deep. Though there are better things to do with our time."

The others were watching and listening, so I bit back the rebuke that danced on the tip of my tongue, forcing a smile instead. "I have no objection to going to the village," I said.

After years of marriage, Elimelech knew when I told the truth and when I didn't. Our eyes held and, in the silent communication between husband and wife, he acknowledged that he understood what I really thought.

"Back to work, men," he said finally and crawled into the ditch.

In Bethlehem, I knew what to do every moment of the day. When the sun sat in a certain place in the sky, I did this, and when it rose higher, I did that. When it stood just above us, I did something else. And so on. Now, I couldn't see the sun during the morning because of the trees behind our tents. Only when the sun moved past midday would I be able to see its exact location in the sky.

I set about bringing order to the piles of things we'd thrown into tents, first, the tent with the cooking implements and then the supply tent. With Mesha's help, it went quickly.

At midday, Abi and I took food to the men. They climbed from the ditch, wiped muddy hands on muddy tunics before dipping them into the bowl of water I brought. After the first pair of hands went in the water it became so muddy there was little point in washing, but I said nothing.

I took food to Killion and the mute, handing the mute his as he wandered among the sheep. Killion sulked on the far side of the flock. Alone. Bored. Impatient. My younger son, fond of the sheep as pets, hated being alone with them. He hated being alone for any reason. To spend a day, or even part of a day with no company, was torture.

"Father could have sent Machlon to watch the sheep," Killion groused as he took the bowl of greens, cheese, and cold lentils. "I'd rather shovel shit with people to keep me company than be out here with no one to talk to."

"Talk to the sheep." I felt no sympathy. Everyone was expected to do his or her job without complaint.

"Do you know how long it's been since I've had a fun day? A holiday to celebrate? Time to spend with friends?"

A retort that *none* of us had had such a day for a long while almost escaped my lips, but Killion had buried himself so deep in self-pity a reprimand would only have made things worse. I sat on the ground beside him while he shoved food in his mouth, chewing noisily. He finished, wiped the back of his hand across his mouth, and handed the bowl back to me.

"Thank you for the food," he said. "I'll make the rounds of the sheep now. Father will ask what I did, and I need to answer him honestly. *Yes, father, I kept good watch. Yes, father, I walked among the flock and checked the sheep for all those things you've taught me to check them for. Yes, father, I chased away two wolves, a hyena, and a red lion.*" Killion grinned. "Now *that* would make the day exciting, wouldn't it?"

And so went our first day. One day gone. That evening, after consuming our meal down to the last crumb, we watched the sparks of a dying fire float into the darkness. Uri had gone back to the flock so Killion, in a better mood, sat with us. He and Machlon described the village to the others. In particular, the column with Astarte at the top.

Finally, Elimelech rose. "It's time to say good-night. Tomorrow we collect stones to line the ditch. Men, you'll need all your strength for lifting and stacking, so I bid you a good sleep."

Accompanied by the distant sound of Uri's pipe, we drifted away to our sleeping places. The sad and lonely notes coming from where Uri kept vigil at the far side of the flock were from a tune he often sang.

Forget me not; Forget me not.
For the wicked bend their bows and set arrows on the strings.
Forget me not; Forget me not.
For the wicked sharpen knives and prepare their slings.
Remember me; remember me.
And for our enemies, fire and brimstone,
And for our enemies, a tempest on their dwellings.

I tensed, wishing his song hadn't reminded me of enemies. Here, in the midst of ours, for protection we depended on Achilla, who was likewise an enemy. The arrangement seemed neither right nor safe.

Chapter 19

The second day when we went to the village, I squared my shoulders, held my head high, and led the way into the commons, walking past the column without looking at the naked goddess on top. I headed for the well as though I'd gone to this particular well all my life. I would not display my discomfort for all to see.

Again, they stared, but this time I smiled, nodded, and to two women who smiled back, muttered *Shalom*. A young woman with a baby tied at her breast and a toddler clinging to her skirts, stepped back in alarm when I passed too near, and a buxom woman scrutinized me with the same intensity with which I'd observed the two black men. In the eyes of some, I saw the first spark of a friendly light. A wide-hipped woman wearing a shawl the color of moss and a tunic flecked with crumbs from her breakfast, raised her hand in greeting.

Instead of bringing two donkeys as we had on the previous day, we brought four. The Sabbath began at sunset so tomorrow there'd be no trip to the well. I wondered if Moabites observed a day of rest. I wondered, too, about the altar at the opposite end of the commons. What did they sacrifice there? Animals and grain as we did? Babies?

Without incident, we returned to our campsite and prepared meals for the Sabbath, tonight's and tomorrow's. Until our flock replenished its numbers, there'd be no roast lamb but we'd have fresh greens. After a day of baking, dicing, and stirring, we lit candles as the sun disappeared behind the mountains. Then we recited prayers and ate our meatless meal.

As always, we were glad for a day of rest the following morning. After breaking fast and listening to the men recite the Torah, I returned to my tent where the sides had been rolled up. Breathing in the scents of pine, cyclamen, and cedar, I lay down on my sleeping mat, happy that there were no looming crises, no causes for immediate worry.

The men milled about, searching for a place to stretch out. Until the moment the Sabbath began, they'd lifted and placed stones to line the ditch. Already, water had begun to accumulate – a sodden, muddy mess, undrinkable by any animal – but Elimelech assured us that after a few days of running over stones the water would clear.

Unaccustomed to a ground cushioned by thick grass and small plants, the men, as they stretched out in their chosen places to rest, remarked on their good fortune in having a comfortable outdoor place to sleep. Or not sleep. Sometimes they simply gazed at the sky or talked among themselves. Or they'd doze for a while, then wake to look around before dozing off again. Arioch woke at intervals to talk to Mesha who, along with Hada and Abi, sat with her back propped against the large oak in front of the cooking tent.

The smell of barley drifted over the hill. When Elimelech, lying just outside our tent, widened his nostrils and took a deep breath, I knew that along with the nutty smell came the painful memory of our ruined fields.

He rolled over, propped himself on his elbow, and looked at me. "Did you ever imagine there were so many birds in the world?"

"Never." I understood he was trying not to think of our scorched crop.

"Or that they could be so noisy?"

"There should be a bird god who declares a day of rest for the birds. No chirping, no tweeting, no keeping tired Israelites awake when they want to spend the Sabbath napping."

"What are our sons up to?" He nodded to where Machlon and Killion sat off to themselves engaged in a whispered conversation that brought their eyes repeatedly our way, a sure sign that something hatched in their heads. A plan. An adventure. The sun hadn't reached the mid-point of the sky, yet they were already bored with resting.

◆ ◆ ◆

"We're going for a walk," Killion said, rising after our mid-day meal.

Machlon rose, too. A little *too* casually. It was usually Machlon's demeanor that aroused my suspicions that something was afoot. Killion was a better actor.

Elimelech raised his brows. "A walk? Where to?"

Killion swept his arm in a vague half-arc. "Wherever the path leads."

Elimelech studied Machlon. "Wherever the path leads?" My husband was as aware as I that Killion had the gift of deceiving with charm while our older son did not.

"Just . . . .. Wherever our feet take us." Machlon studied his fingernails for a few moments before looking Elimelech in the eyes. "It's hard to sit and do nothing."

"Very well," Elimelech said. "You know what's acceptable on the Sabbath and what isn't. Go."

By late afternoon, my sons hadn't returned. Elimelech paced, looking for them first in one direction and then another. Finally, he wrapped his agora around his waist and motioned to Kir to do the same. They tucked their knives in and were about to set off when Hada called out.

"There." She pointed to the hill that separated us from the village.

Machlon was stumbling down the hill. Alone. My heart stopped. We – all of us; every person in the camp – ran to meet him.

Breathless, Machlon muddled his words. "Killion . . . .. In sheaves . . . .. Reapers seized him . . . .. The corn spirit."

Elimelech grabbed him by the shoulders. "Take a breath. What happened? Where is he?"

Machlon took two quick breaths. "We went to watch them harvesting barley. They saw us. They seized Killion, wrapped him in sheaves, and tied him up. They're going to sacrifice him. Behead him. And throw his body in the river."

As one, we dashed up the hill. At the summit, Machlon pointed to a field and then

collapsed. We sped down the hill, bolted through the stubble of a field already harvested, then through another, and another, my heart nearly bursting, my lungs burning. Running. Running. Running to where reapers, still holding their sickles, huddled, laughing.

Elimelech shoved his way through, Kir short on his heels, the rest of us behind Kir.

Killion, bound tightly inside sheaves of barley, lay on the ground, his face contorted with rage and fear. I threw myself down beside him, and held his head between my hands, ensuring it was still attached to his body.

Elimelech, knife drawn, shouted at the reapers who had fallen quiet, "What are you doing?" Rage billowed from his eyes.

Gideon and Habish were among the reapers who shrank back and lowered their eyes. It was *them*, Achilla's evil nephews, who had goaded the workers to do this.

Elimelech knelt and began cutting the ropes. Kir, his knife drawn, faced the reapers, eyeing each, daring anyone to stop Elimelech from freeing our son. Arioch, Festus, and Skinny stood with Kir, their knives also drawn.

"What's going on?" a voice roared from outside the group.

Cyrus! He spoke in the language of the Moabites, but I understood his words. He shoved his way through, arriving just as Killion brushed aside the last barley sheaf, sprang to his feet, and lunged at Gideon.

Together, Cyrus and Elimelech held Killion back.

"Restrain your son," Cyrus said to Elimelech, but his eyes, full of fire, were on Gideon. "What were you up to?"

Gideon looked at Cyrus from beneath half-lowered lids and muttered something.

Still glaring at Gideon, Cyrus held his hand toward Elimelech and me and said, "Speak so they can understand."

"It was a joke," Gideon repeated in our language. His lips twitched.

"A joke?" Cyrus shouted. Then he narrowed his eyes at Habish. "And *you*. Did you think this was a joke, too?"

Habish nodded. "A joke," he said weakly.

"Go," Cyrus said, jabbing his forefinger at Gideon and Habish. "Go to Achilla and wait there." Then he said something to the reapers in Moabite, and they backed away.

He turned to Elimelech. "Bring Killion to my house. It's the small one at the end of the commons. The end opposite the well."

Instead of telling us *the end opposite the well,* Cyrus could have said *the end near the altar.* I shivered as we went past the blood-stained, stone structure. Though the smell of incense was strong, it didn't mask the stink of recent sacrifices.

Kir and Arioch stationed themselves outside Cyrus' house, fingering their knife hilts, while Elimelech, my sons, and I went inside. Elimelech had sent the others back to our encampment.

Cyrus led us to the roof of his two-room house which had neither animal stalls, tools, nor storage rooms. A cooking room filled the ground floor and a sleeping chamber the one above. He invited us to sit on cushions made from sheepskins, then motioned to his serving woman to pour wine. "A generous amount for everyone, especially the young man." Then he said to us, "Achilla will see there are no further such *jokes.*"

I took the wine offered me, but set it aside while Elimelech, a thunderstorm still brewing on his face, waved away the cup and said, "You promised that Achilla was a man of his word."

"He is. Whatever other faults Achilla has, when he makes a promise, he keeps it." Cyrus took a cup from his serving woman and drank. "He won't abide his nephews scaring your sons witless when he's offered you his protection." He looked at Killion who had shaken his head when offered a drink. "Other than your pride, you're unharmed."

Killion swallowed, fighting back tears. I willed him the power to do so, for shedding tears would embarrass him more than the events of the afternoon.

"How is it that Achilla's nephews know our language?" I asked.

"I taught them. Sometimes they accompany me on trips. Eventually, one of them will replace me." He interlaced his fingers. "Gideon and Habish have listened to too many stories along the way. Like the ones they tell in some places of how a stranger passing a field being harvested is regarded as the embodiment of the corn-spirit. The reapers seize the stranger, wrap him in sheaves, and behead him. They throw the body into water as a rain charm."

I gasped.

He fixed his warm, brown eyes on me. "It wouldn't have happened, Naomi. Gideon and Habish spoke truth when they said it was a joke. A nasty joke, but a joke. They know Achilla would blast them with the rage of every god in the universe had they done what they threatened."

I myself would do the same to those two merciless boys if they ever again threatened my sons, joke or not.

"The worse that ever happens in this village," Cyrus continued, "is that the person who cuts the last sheaf is bound in it, carried to the well, and drenched with water."

Elimelech, his face as hard as the stones he'd been lifting, leaned toward our former guide. "Tell your chief that no harm will come to my family, nor to my bondsmen, nor to my serving women. If anyone so much as touches one hair . . .."

Cyrus held up his hand, stopping Elimelech. "I'm going to Achilla now. Gideon and Habish are there, quaking in fear. As they should be." He allowed himself a smirk. "When they recover from Achilla's rage, I expect they'll head down your side of the hill offering eternal peace and everlasting friendship."

I acknowledged Cyrus's attempt at peace-making with a flicker of my eyelids, but while Gideon and Habish might recover from Achilla's wrath, I'd neither forget nor forgive what they'd done. Nor, I expected, would Killion.

Chapter 20

The old woman approached me almost every day at the well until, finally, I understood her to be saying, "Come house, Achilla's wife." I shrugged, pretending not to comprehend, but as she became more persistent I learned from Kir how to say, "Sorry, busy." I couldn't guess why she wanted to lure us to Achilla's house, nor could I imagine how surprised Achilla's wife would be if we showed up.

One day, two girls I judged to be two or three years younger than my sons strolled up to the well, bringing no water jugs. Their diffident air made it look as though they had no purpose in life other than to stroll about the village, visiting friends and gossiping. The younger had copper-colored hair that fell in soft waves down to her waist and pleasing curves for one of such a young age. From the way she bestowed her practiced smile on the villagers, I knew she was aware of her beauty and accustomed to being the center of attention.

The second had soft, brown hair, large eyes of the same color, and would have been considered pretty in any company other than her sister's, for I took them to be sisters from the identical shape of their perfect noses, high cheekbones, and arched eyebrows.

They mingled with the women and girls, exchanging greetings, while flicking their gazes sideways at Abi and me. When they tired of looking at us, they focused on my sons. Killion made no attempt to mask his admiration, especially of the younger one, gawking as though she were the last bit of honey in the jar.

"It was unbecoming of you to look at her that way," I said to him on the way home.

"Is that one of Father's rules: *Don't look at girls?*"

"Your father didn't make the rules." I was displeased with Killion's impudence.

"One of Moishe' rules then?"

"You know very well Moishe didn't make the rules either. You're not listening to your father's teachings, or else you're just being insolent. Don't compound your lustful gaze with other sins."

"My lustful gaze? Must I turn my eyes away from every beautiful girl?" He looked at me in disbelief, but then, trying to hide a smirk, asked, "Is it all right to look at the ugly ones?"

We had come to the top of the hill. I held up my hand for him to stop while Abi and Machlon, casting backward glances at us, went ahead.

"Killion, don't make our stay in this place any more difficult than it already is. You will marry a girl from Bethlehem, not a Moabite girl."

"Mother! . . . I'm seventeen. I have no thought of marrying anyone. A pretty girl came to the well; I looked at her like I would have looked at a beautiful falcon, or . . . .." He shrugged, unable to think what else he might have enjoyed looking at.

I closed my eyes and took a deep breath. Killion was right; I was being unreasonable.

When I'd been going to the well for almost three weeks, the old woman came, dragging Achilla's nephew, Habish, with her. Pointing to me, she said to Habish, "Tell her."

"My aunt, the wife of Achilla, wishes you to visit her home," Habish said.

By now, I knew the villagers weren't going to harm us. Isolated in the hills as they were, maybe they didn't even know we were enemies. Yet, I was wary.

The old woman tilted her head, waiting for an answer while Habish made a show of not caring whether I visited Achilla's wife or not. Crossing his arms and shuffling from foot to foot, he let his gaze roam over the women at the well.

"Come, come," the old woman said and beckoned to me.

"I'll stay and draw water," Abi offered.

Still, I hesitated. The idea of going alone to a stranger's home worried me. Yet, I was lonely. Serving women didn't offer the same companionship as friends or kin so a spark of excitement had ignited over the prospect of visiting another woman's home. But how would I converse when my ability to do so lay in only a few words and broken sentences?

"Come," the old woman said again. It was a command.

Habish let out a huff. The old woman slapped his chest and rattled off a string of words that sounded as though they were a threat.

"Please, will you come," Habish said. "My aunt wants to meet you. And she asks about your fine weaving."

Killion, leaving the animals in Machlon's care, had slipped up to listen. "We'll wait with the animals," he said.

"*I not speak language good*," I said in Moabite to the old woman.

"Habish will come too."

Habish shot her a sour look but followed as she led the way.

Achilla's dwelling was bigger than ours in Bethlehem and twice as big as the others in the village. Workers were unloading baskets of barley into his underground storage pit. From the smell, I knew the barley had already been heated to prevent it sprouting in storage. Storage rooms and animal pens occupied the bottom level of his house just as they did ours. The same smell of straw and dung filled the air. The same herbs hung in bunches from the rafters.

We'd removed our sandals and the old woman was halfway up the ladder when I heard the bleat of a lamb. Little Samson? Had he detected my scent?

"Come," the old woman said, beckoning.

Swallowing the bile that filled my mouth as I thought of our lost ram, I climbed to the first floor, where the aroma of incense hung heavy in the air. A shaft of sunlight from the roof opening lit a stack of cushions and a small alcove containing figures of Astarte.

The old woman made her way up the next ladder as sprightly as someone half her age. I followed and climbed out onto the roof to glimpse two women, one with the same mass of curly, copper-colored hair as the girl at the well. She remained seated as she dipped her head in welcome. The second woman, a few years my senior, rose with difficulty, using her arms to push herself up. Neither beautiful nor unattractive, she had a long face, narrow nose, and a widow's peak.

The older woman pointed to herself. "Hoglah," she said in a deep, melodious voice. "You are Naomi."

"Shalom," I murmured wondering why Achilla's wife would be on the roof so early in the day? Did she not have chores? Or was the younger woman his wife?

Hoglah pointed to the copper-haired woman. "That's Noa."

"Shalom," I murmured again.

Noa rose, smiled prettily as she dipped her head, and then sat down again.

Hoglah motioned to a cushion. "Please, sit."

I did, but nearly sprang up again to offer Hoglah my hand when I saw with what difficulty she folded her body to sit. Her face showed only faint signs of aging – thought lines between her eyes, a barely visible web from the corners of her eyes – yet she appeared to suffer from the joint sickness.

"You can sit, too," Hoglah said to Habish who had gone to lean against the parapet.

"I'm fine standing."

The old woman, whom I had almost forgotten, said something and then descended the ladder.

"The weather is good," Hoglah said, and I understood. Then she asked, and Habish translated, if we'd settled comfortably on the other side of the hill.

Through Habish, I answered her questions about our encampment. But I was puzzled. Which woman was Achilla's wife? Hoglah seemed to be the one in charge. She wasn't old enough to be Achilla's mother, yet I imagined him with a younger wife. Perhaps Hoglah was his sister. Noa, on the other hand, fit the image in my imagination of what Achilla's wife would be like: young, pretty, and empty-headed. Yes, despite being aware of my unkindness, I made that judgement — *empty headed.*. And despite having known her for as long as it takes a bird to fly from one branch to another, contributing to my rush to judgement were her soft, unblemished hands. Those fine fingers had no callouses, nor were there rope marks from the well, or dirty fingernails from working in the dirt. And I judged her because of the way she toyed with her spindle. A pile of wool rose in front of her along with a basket for yarn, but only three skeins lay in the basket. A smaller pile of wool lay in front of Hoglah. Even with hands beginning to gnarl from the joint disease, she'd spun enough wool to fill her basket to the half-way mark with skeins.

"You have two handsome sons," Hoglah said, veering from the topic of our living arrangements.

I didn't need Habish to translate that. "*Toda,*" I said. Thank you. Then, becoming bold, I asked, "Which of you is Achilla's wife?"

Hoglah raised an eyebrow, and Noa's eyes sparkled with amusement."

"They're both his wives," Habish said.

My face grew warm.

"Do men in Bethlehem not have more than one wife?" Noa asked.

"A few do."

"If a man is rich," Hoglah said. ". . . and needs heirs, then it profits him to take another wife. I had no children, so Achilla took Noa."

Noa set the spindle aside, dropping all pretense of spinning. "You have two sons," she said. "And I have two daughters."

"They must be a comfort to you." I wondered if Achilla would take a third wife if Noa didn't produce sons.

"They're beautiful girls," Hoglah said. "We have only to find them good husbands."

"Will they marry soon?"

"In a couple of years," Hoglah answered. "Tell me about Bethlehem. We wonder what it's like on the other side of the Salt Sea."

With Habish repeating everything, I described Bethlehem, our journey, the drought.

"Could your priests not make it rain?" Noa asked. Then turning to Habish, she said, "Tell her what we do here to make the rains come."

The bored look in his eyes vanished as Habish described how Chemosh's representative in the village put a burning brand on the grave of a man who had died of burns, quenched the brand with water, and then prayed for rain.

"When midsummer comes, and the star Adonus rises . . .," Habish continued, ". . . we build bonfires in the middle of the village and the men and boys leap over them to make the crops grow taller. The women cheer us on. We leap and shout until the fires burn down."

"And everyone eats and drinks, and we dance with wild abandon," Noa added.

"Down in Kir-Harseth," Habish said, "they dress a winnowing fork in women's clothes. The girls and women carry it from house to house singing."

"The Mother of the Rain." Hoglah added. "I come from Kir-Harseth."

Not wanting to hear more about their pagan customs, I felt the visit had become too long. "I thank you for your hospitality," I said and started to rise. "I must see to my duties."

"You can't go now." Hoglah held out her hand to stop me. "The Mother is bringing refreshments."

The old woman, *The Mother,* but whose mother I didn't know, appeared with a bowl of dove eggs, boiled, peeled, and coated with herbs. Behind her, a serving woman brought a pitcher of water, and a second serving woman brought a brightly colored incense burner, a palm-sized packet of something wrapped in wool, and a small bowl.

I settled back down and took what was offered. The Mother, after serving us, took an egg in each of her hands and settled nearby. We ate and drank while Habish showed increased boredom as he translated Hoglah's and Noa's chatter about their families and the people in the village.

Finally, Hoglah leaned over to touch the sleeve of my outer-garment. "Your garments are finely woven," she said. "Did you do the weaving?"

I nodded. I had just taken a bite of egg and my mouth was full. The eggs were delicious and a rarity for me.

Hoglah let her fingers slide away. "Cyrus brought us frankincense from his latest trip." She beckoned to the woman with the incense burner.

The woman brought the burner, knelt down, and sprinkled frankincense from the package into the top cavity of the burner. Then she took embers from the bowl and placed them in the bottom cavity so that curls of spiced smoke rose from the burner. The serving woman held the burner out to me.

Confused, I looked at Habish. "What am I supposed to do?"

His mouth widened into a grin. "Take it," he said.

"Why?"

"Do you not do this where you come from?"

"Do what?"

He said something to Hoglah who took the burner and, her eyes focused on me, placed the burner beneath her tunic.

"Why is she doing that?" I asked Habish.

"That's what women do here." His grin stretched from ear to ear. "They smoke their clothes with incense."

Understanding dawned as I recalled the women in the market smelling strongly of incense. After an interval, Hoglah removed the burner from beneath her clothes and handed it to Noa. Noa stuck the burner beneath her tunic, all the while looking at me as though to say, *See, see, this is what we do and how we do it.*

Finally, Noa handed the burner to me. Reluctantly, I stuck it beneath my tunic. I liked neither the heat of the embers nor the feel of rough clay against my legs. Least of all, did I want my clothes to be saturated with the smell of incense. In my mind, incense had no purpose other than to rid the house of the smell of men's sweat and the altar of the stink of sacrifices. But I endured, while Noa chattered on, oblivious to Habish's inability to translate as fast as trivia poured from her mouth. Once, I caught his eyes, and for a heartbeat, something like understanding passed between us. I supposed someday I'd have to forgive him for his part in the thoughtless joke with Killion and the sheaves. But not yet.

When a serving woman appeared with a bowl of water for us to dip our hands in and a cloth for drying, I set the burner aside and washed my hands. "Again, I thank you for your hospitality," I said, wiping my fingers on the cloth. "But I must go and attend to my duties."

Hoglah rose, the discomfort of moving her limbs showing in her face.

"You'll come again. It isn't often we get to visit with people from faraway places."

Noa jumped up. "You must come back and meet my two daughters, Ruth and Orpah."

Ruth and *Orpah.* The two girls at the well.

Habish descended the ladder and then waited for me.

"Toda," I said when I stepped from the last rung and reached for my shoes. "I can find my way back. You needn't wait for me."

"I'll wait." He crossed his arms.

I wanted to see if Little Samson was in a stall but couldn't think of a way to make Habish leave, so after tying my sandals, I ignored him. Searching along the corridor, I came to a stall with four rams – an adult, two yearlings, and Little Samson.

"Achilla wouldn't like you doing this," Habish said.

"And I didn't like Achilla taking our finest ram." I draped both arms over the stone fence, and Little Samson trotted over to sniff and lick my hand. My heart in pieces, I stroked his neck with my other hand.

"He's a fine ram." Habish propped his arms on the wall. "My uncle is proud to have a good breeder."

For the length of a heartbeat, I imagined slipping into the dwelling in the dead of night and stealing back Little Samson. I dared think this after reprimanding my son for having the same thought.

"You have to get back to your chores," I said finally and, heavy-hearted, left our young ram in his new home.

Chapter 21

Elimelech met us at the bottom of the hill. "Where have . . ..?"

"Ask Mother," Killion interrupted and, leaving me to explain, continued on with Machlon, Abi, and the donkeys.

Elimelech raised an eyebrow. "You were a long time."

"An unexpected visit." I kept walking, Elimelech beside me. Not only were the boys behind with their work, but so was I.

"You smell of incense."

"I had a good dose of it this morning. The old woman, someone's mother, I'm not sure whose, took me to meet Achilla's wives."

"Wives?"

"He has two. One young and pretty with two daughters, the other older with no children." Then I explained the custom of women burning incense beneath their clothes.

He gave a little snort. "Thus the smell of the women at the market. Now that you're safe at home, I'll go back to work."

He hadn't gone far before he stopped and turned around. "I like your natural smell better," he said. "The one you were born with."

That afternoon, I put on my second set of clothes and washed the ones I'd worn into the village, washing away the smell of Moabite women.

◆ ◆ ◆

The weeks folded one into another. So busy were we, had we not kept count of the days so as to know when the Sabbath arrived, I would have lost track of what day it was altogether. When we women weren't preparing food, milking, and churning, we began the endless task of clearing ground for a garden. I had chosen a spot near the watering ditch. The moist, loose soil made digging easy, but that same moist, loose soil enabled weeds to grow as fast as a butterfly can flap its wings. We'd clear a small section only to find purslane or wiry-stemmed knotweed popping up through the dirt the next morning. Before clearing more ground, we had to re-clear what we'd done the previous day, and the day before that. By the time we had the plot ready, it would be too late for a summer garden. We'd have to be content with winter vegetables: broad beans, lentils, chick-peas, fenugreek, cumin. If these grew as readily as the weeds, we'd have a bountiful supply.

The water in the ditch had cleared, so we no longer had to bring water for the oxen. During the rainy season, we wouldn't have to go to the village at all, for the men had carved a cistern. When Elimelech again mentioned digging a well so we'd have water during the other seasons, I objected.

"It isn't necessary," I said. "I don't mind going to the village."

"You don't mind?" He studied my face, perhaps thinking I was saying this just to please him.

"No, I'd rather you build a bread oven, and you need to replace the thorn bush stalls with real fences."

I didn't tell my husband that seeing other people and hearing their voices eased my loneliness. I missed my kin, my neighbors, even the people who ran the shops – the potter, the basket maker, the tanner. I longed for our roof where my neighbors and I called back and forth, reporting everything that went on in Bethlehem. The roof was also where my sons indulged in mischief. Many a time, I'd caught them tossing olive pits over the parapets onto the heads of friends.

Nearly every day of my life, I'd gone to the well first thing each morning, and, now that the villagers greeted us openly, it seemed natural to continue doing what women all over the world had always done. My ability to speak the language had improved, making conversation possible. I knew a few women by name and recognized which children were theirs – Sarai, with her nest of red hair and two wild little boys with the same red nests atop their heads; tall, thin Esther with twin girls; plump Leah, with her beautiful grandchildren; and several others. I was very willing for Elimelech to abandon the idea of digging of a well.

◆　◆　◆

Kir took a break from stacking stones for animal stalls to put my loom together. While he reassembled it, I accompanied Elimelech on his daily trip to examine the flock.

"We need another tent," I said as he knelt in front of a ewe to examine her mouth.

"Why?"

"Actually, we need two more."

He gave me a sharp look.

"We need one for my loom and weaving supplies and for storing wool after the spring shearing. My supplies are stacked in whatever corner I can find space; there's no room to arrange them, so I don't know what's where."

"Why do we need *two* tents? Do you think our sheep are going to grow longer wool because the grass here is longer?" He grinned at his joke.

"The second tent is for Arioch and Mesha."

I laughed at his uncomprehending look. "Have you not noticed?" From his expression I realized he hadn't. I laughed again. "How can you be so clever, Elimelech, and so successful, and not have noticed?"

Finally understanding, he smiled. "Two tents, then. A wife will be good for Arioch." He moved to a ewe with a wide black stripe across her neck and pulled up her lids. "But we have to be careful."

"Careful?"

"I'll send Kir to the market for tents. After that, we need to conserve our silver for the return trip." He ran his hand over the ewe's hocks. "With no grain to sell, our only income will be from the sale of wool and fattened lambs." He straightened and looked out across his flock. "A wise man plans for the worst. It could be . . . .."

"Surely, the rains will come." I couldn't bear to think of not returning to Bethlehem in the spring.

Chapter 22

Resentment sticks like flies in honey. Late one afternoon, I looked up to see Achilla coming down the hill, accompanied by Gideon and Habish who led donkeys laden with baskets. Not wanting to speak to Achilla or his nephews, I escaped to the cooking tent to prepare refreshments, intending to let Hada and Mesha serve them. As for Abi, I still didn't trust her to not spit in their food so I sent her to spread cushions beneath the cedar.

Elimelech, covered with grime and smelling of damp earth from digging a storage cellar for our grain went to greet our guests. He invited them to sit and rest and then called for Machlon and Killion to join them.

I strained wine, handed the ewer to Mesha, and instructed Hada to carry out olives while I filled a bowl with pistachios. That was quite enough refreshment for someone appearing unannounced late in the day. No sooner had Mesha left the tent with the wine than I regretted not having sent water instead for we only had one jug of wine left.

The sides of the cooking tent were rolled up, enabling me to listen to the conversation as the men discussed sheep, the yield of the wheat harvest, the sighting of a pack of jackals nearby. Once, I looked over to see Elimelech cast a puzzled look at the two laden donkeys tethered nearby.

At length, the men set their cups aside and rose to follow Elimelech to the watering ditch and the partially-dug storage cellar. Men liked showing off their work just as we women liked to display our weaving. Relieved that I hadn't been invited to speak with our visitors, I filled a bowl with lentils and began picking through them, discarding bits of hull and stem. I'd almost finished, when Elimelech and Achilla returned to their cushions, leaving our sons to wander about the encampment with Gideon and Habish.

"Shall I pour more wine?" Mesha asked.

"Yes, please." I sighed. Not only had Achilla taken our best sheep, but now he was drinking the last of our wine.

"Naomi," Elimelech called after Mesha had refilled their cups. "Achilla wishes to speak with you."

Swallowing my displeasure, I set aside the onions I was about to dice and went to where they sat.

"Welcome to our encampment," I said, and added a few pleasantries – something about the weather, his wives' hospitality, the approaching winter, and finally, "It was good of you to come. I'll go back to my chores now."

"Stay, Naomi, I came here to speak with you," Achilla said. He turned to Elimelech. "My wives praised Naomi's weaving. The best they've seen, they claim." He lifted his wine cup, took a drink, and then wiped a sleeve across his mouth. "I've brought wool." He motioned to the donkeys. "Noa begs for cloth from you. For herself and our two daughters."

Was the gall of this Moabite chieftain such that he assumed my compliance and brought wool without first asking? Shocked, I glanced at Elimelech whose face had hardened.

"If you can find the time." Achilla made an attempt at a smile.

If I could find the time. Indeed. Achilla was a man accustomed to being obeyed, but I had enough to do without becoming his family's weaver. Nor would I have wanted to do their weaving had I nothing at all to do.

"Hoglah's hands are too crippled, and Noa is clumsy at the loom," Achilla said. He leaned toward Elimelech and, smirking, added in an undertone, "Noa's talents lie elsewhere."

Stone-faced, Elimelech looked straight ahead, his mouth moving. I knew he was trying to compose a carefully worded response for our *protector*.

"Let me show you what I've brought," Achilla said and rose with a grunt. He went to one of the donkeys who, despite her load, chomped at grass while swatting flies with her tale. He removed the cover from a basket and pulled out a handful of wool. "Wool from the sheep's shoulders," he said. ". . . the softest of all, and it's already been beaten and combed." He handed the wool to me. "See for yourself."

Reluctantly I took the wool.

"I'll pay you in barley," he said.

"My wife doesn't do the bidding of other men," Elimelech said, finding his voice.

"My husband is right," I said to Achilla. "But as a friendly gesture of one neighbor to another, I will weave cloth for one set of clothes for each of your daughters and for Noa. But then . . . .." I forced a smile, ". . . I have weaving of my own to do, for we owe our servants their yearly set of clothes."

Achilla studied me with narrowed eyes.

I widened my smile as though he honored me by asking this favor.

"Hoglah will bring dyes and tell you which colors they want," he said finally. "My daughters are very particular, as is Noa."

"I'll welcome their visit." I said this while thinking his daughters could be as particular as they liked if they learned to weave for themselves instead of wandering aimlessly around the village practicing the art of idleness. As for Noa, she wouldn't be so clumsy at the task were she to work at it instead of sitting around smoking her undergarments with incense.

Achilla called to his nephews to come and help unload the wool. I stole a glance at Elimelech who gave a nod that only I would have recognized as a nod. The tiny glint in his eyes told me he approved of my handling of the village chief.

With the help of my sons, the baskets were soon unloaded. The last item wasn't wool.

"I brought you this," Achilla said, throwing a glance at Elimelech as he heaved the last basket from the donkey. Achilla's muscles tightened from the heavy load as he brought the gift to my husband, setting it down at his feet. Inside, were three wine skins. "You may be the best breeder of sheep, but I make the best wine in Moab."

"Thank you," Elimelech said with a guarded smile as he hoisted the basket to his shoulder. "Our wine is nearly depleted so this is very welcome. But what do you base this claim on? Have you tasted all the wine in Moab?"

"Most of it." For once, Achilla's smile wasn't that of a jackal but of a man.

"Then I look forward to sampling yours."

"Machlon is better with the sling than Gideon," Killian said when Achilla and his nephews had gone. "Gideon was annoyed."

Machlon looked pleased. I was pleased, too. What mother isn't pleased at her child's superiority even if it's flinging rocks?

"What's the wool for?" Machlon asked.

"Achilla wants me to weave cloth for his wife and daughters."

"Ruth and Orpah," Machlon said.

"How do you know their names?"

He rolled his eyes. "What do you think we do when we're standing at the well waiting for you to draw water? We know the names of all the girls in the village."

"Orpah is pretty," Killion said.

"She's the one with the copper-colored hair?"

"Yes."

"Go back to your chores." I spoke more snappishly than necessary. Orpah was pretty but she was also a Moabitess and idle. "The dung pile in back of the cooking tent needs to grow a lot higher before we have enough fuel for winter. Get busy."

"Why do we need dung when we have all these fallen branches?" Machlon protested.

"Then go and collect wood. Pile the dung somewhere else."

They gave each other *the look*, the one that asked *What did we do wrong?*

What they were doing wrong was growing up. In another month, Machlon would turn nineteen and, two months later, Killion would be eighteen. Even though I persisted in calling them boys, they were becoming men. It was time for Elimelech to have a talk with them about controlling their manly desires.

Chapter 23

The women of Achilla's household came, Hoglah and Noa on donkeys, Orpah, Ruth, and The Mother walking alongside, carrying baskets.

I met them at the bottom of the hill. "Shalom," I said. "I'm happy to see you."

Hoglah slid from the donkey. "We brought dyes."

"When you find out how particular these women are you might not be so glad to see us," The Mother croaked. "*Not this color, that color. Brighter. Not so bright. Stripes this wide, no less, no more.*"

A little too eagerly, Killion ran over to hobble the donkeys. Looking over his shoulder at the beautiful Orpah, he nearly tripped as he tethered the animals. The moment the donkeys were secured, I waved him back to his chores.

My visitors settled on cushions beneath the cedar. Abi and Mesha were on the south hill collecting onions, so Hada brought a pitcher of water flavored with dried lemons then went to prepare refreshments.

We fell into idle talk, I, still struggling with the language. As was proper in the company of older women, the two girls sat quietly, Orpah examining our encampment with curiosity and Ruth studying me.

"You brought dyes," I said finally, prompting them to get on with the business at hand.

Excitedly, Noa, Orpah, and Ruth, described what they wanted while Hoglah listened with a bemused expression. The Mother gave a little sniff, closed her eyes, and nodded. *See, see,* her nod seemed to say, for she'd spoken truth when she claimed the women of Achilla's family were particular.

Noa wanted a tunic of red and a cloak of the same red bordered by indigo. The indigo should be neither too bright nor too dull. "And the red should be the color of . . .." She looked around trying to find something to serve as an example. "The bright red of an amaryllis," she said finally.

Orpah asked for a yellow tunic and a cloak of yellow patterned with black stripes. The black stripes should be the width of a thumb.

"Will the width of mine do?" I held up my thumb.

Orpah studied it for a few moments and then nodded.

"And between the black stripes, two narrow red stripes the width of a piece of straw." Orpah looked at my thumb again. "The stripes should all be a thumb's width apart."

The Mother sniffed and rolled her eyes.

Ruth chose blue. The color of the sky.

"The sky on which day or at what time of day?" I asked, hoping no one realized I made fun of their demands "A bright, summer sky? A wintry sky? The silvery sky of early morning?"

"Late afternoon sky. Dark, but clear."

I'd have to study the late afternoon sky.

By the time we said our goodbyes, my headache inclined me to agree with The Mother: the women of Achilla's household were too particular. I vowed to think of a list of excuses so the next time Achilla asked something of me I'd have one ready.

As I watched my visitors disappear over the hill, I wondered about Ruth. Unlike her mother and sister, she wanted garments unadorned by colors or patterns that drew attention. Her modesty pleased me. If only she were industrious, I thought I might even grow to like her.

Worried that the moist grass of Moab might cause foot rot, Elimelech had taken Machlon and Killion with him to check hooves while my visitors were there. When they returned, Machlon joined me at the firepit where I was stirring a stew. The aroma of garlic and cumin set my stomach rumbling.

"Killion wasn't much help while Orpah was around," Machlon complained. He swished his hands in the bowl of water I kept near where we ate, then shook them, sending droplets flying. "He thinks she's the prettiest girl he's ever seen." He wiped his hands on his tunic and then squatted down beside the fire.

"He'll see lots of pretty girls before we settle on one," I said. "*Israelite* girls."

"Galatia is prettier than Orpah."

"Galatia has much to recommend her and, unlike Orpah, she's industrious." I had yet to see either of Achilla's daughters engaged in a meaningful task.

"When will I marry Galatia?" Reflections from the flames danced in his dark eyes.

"In two years."

I looked forward to welcoming bride-daughters into my home and to the babies they'd bear. My grandchildren! As soon as we returned I'd find a wife for Killion, even though they wouldn't marry until he was older.

"Why are you smiling, Mother?"

Why indeed? Because I was lucky to have two handsome sons and a husband with the means to provide enviable bride prices. I could already smell the roasting lamb of a wedding feast, the honeyed fruit, Damaris' bread which the rest of us couldn't equal no matter how hard we tried. I imagined the celebratory sounds of cymbals, the plucking of lyres and lutes, the steady beat of drums as we danced, we, our kin, our friends, our neighbors – the ones we'd left behind.

"What happened to your smile, Mother?" Machlon asked. "There are tears in your eyes."

Two small oaks stood near the wadi that ran along the bottom of the north hill. Arioch strung ropes between them to hold the dyed wool while it dried. I worried about the birds. Their droppings threatened not only the wool, but the food we ate, the water we drank, and, always, our sandals.

"Don't you dare," I called to a grackle flying past. Baskets of wet yarn waiting to be hung sat beneath the bird's flight path.

Arioch tied the last knot, tested the ropes to make sure they would hold, and then turned to Mesha and I with a grin. "It was my privilege to serve two beautiful, blue-handed ladies," he said, nodding to our hands, blue from indigo dye.

"Better blue hands than stinky feet." Mesha pointed to the bird droppings stuck to Arioch's shoes.

"Aaahh, *that*. Can't seem to avoid it." Tilting his feet first one way and then the other, he scraped the sides of his sandals on the grass. "Anything else I can do for you ladies?" He looked at Mesha, clearly hoping for a directive that would keep him near her.

"Thank you, Arioch," I said. "We'll call you when we need something."

Casting a backward glance and a smile at Mesha, he went back to where he'd been pounding limestone to make plaster to line the grain pit.

Until Elimelech could send Kir to the market in Kir Harseth for more tents, the loom had been placed inside mine. This left little room for our bed mats but I couldn't risk birds ruining the cloth. I decided to begin with Noa's fabric. I strung the red warp threads, weighting them with clay weights then set the basket containing the weft beside my stool.

I left my loom only to take charge of meals, gather greens, and work a little each day in my garden where cumin and broad beans had begun poking through the soil. Unhappily, weeds still poked their nasty heads through, too, no matter how hard I worked to rid my little plot of them.

These were peaceful days. I watched the cloth form beneath my fingers while the heat, the blistered feet, the uncertainties of our journey receded like water disappearing from wadis during the dry season. When I felt the need to stretch, I roamed the hills in search of dandelion greens and wild mint. Breezes, rife with the smell of pine, breathed through the rifts and hollows. Sometimes on the Sabbath, Elimelech and I climbed the south hill and, though I couldn't pick greens on the Day of Rest, I made note of where patches of wild garlic and thyme grew.

But it was while seated at my loom that I found real contentment. As each span of yellow, blue, or red formed beneath my hands, I felt as though I partnered with the Creator to produce something beautiful.

Early one morning when the trees were nothing more than blurs against a silver sky, Kir set out for the King's Highway to purchase two tents. He carried silver in a pouch hidden beneath his tunic. Attached to his donkey was a bundle of something wrapped in skins. Curious, I asked Elimelech about the contents as we watched Kir disappear into the trees.

"Nothing of significance," Elimelech said. Shrugging, he walked away.

Annoyed that my husband wouldn't tell me what was in the package but had entrusted our twisted-faced bondsman with our precious silver and a mysterious bundle, I frowned at Elimelech's back. We knew nothing of Kir's past. I half-expected him to take our silver and run.

Toward the end of the second day after Kir's departure, Elimelech climbed the north hill and looked eastward, watching for our bondsman.

"It's unlikely Kir would make the trip to and from Kir-Harseth, do his errands, and then return in only two days," Elimelech said when he joined me at the firepit. I was fanning at the embers, inviting a flame. He squatted down to watch, he on one side of the pit, I on the other.

"Yes, it's unlikely," I agreed.

The flame caught. I added twigs from the cedar tree, knowing I shouldn't grow accustomed to the delightful aroma of burning cedar since there'd be none when we returned. Cedar would be one of the good things I remembered about Moab.

"Arioch is almost done with the bread oven," Elimelech said.

"Yes, I can see." The structure stood a few arm lengths away. "Are you afraid Kir won't return?"

"Of course I'm not afraid Kir won't return." He frowned at me. "Why would I think that?"

"You were watching for him from the hill."

"Watching for him means I'm afraid he won't come back?"

"Of course, he'll return," I said. "I don't know why I even suggested that."

Trying to convince myself that my worries were unfounded, I added a few more twigs to the flames. Had Elimelech harbored any suspicion of Kir slipping away with our silver, he wouldn't have given it to him in the first place.

On the third morning after Kir's departure, the men stacked stones in the pasture, forming columns the height of a man to keep away the jackals. The jackals couldn't be very smart if they mistook a stack of stones for a person, but it seemed to work.

By mid-afternoon, they'd finished and were resting when Achilla's nephews walked proudly into our encampment, a hooded falcon resting on Gideon's leather-wrapped arm. Habish carried a basked and had a rope coiled around his shoulder.

We all gathered around to admire the bird.

"Where did you get her?" Killion asked, his voice full of envy. He and Machlon had their hands out, wanting to touch the bird's feathers but not daring.

"Go ahead," Gideon said. "Touch gently with the back of your finger. One person at the time."

Killion stroked the falcon along the back of her neck.

"Let me," Machlon said reaching out his forefinger.

"Achilla's steward, Jerel, caught her for us," Habish said. "Why don't you come to the top of the hill and watch us train her?"

Eyes brimming with excitement, my sons looked at their father,

"Go," he said and waved them away.

Forgetting the jobs that needed doing, we watched from the bottom of the hill as the falcon soared from Gideon's arm and then swooped to capture bits of meat tied to the end of the rope swung by Habish. Engrossed, we didn't hear Kir slip up behind us. When I turned, remembering it was time to begin preparing the next meal, I found him watching the falcon with the same intensity as the others.

"Shalom," I muttered and hurried away to chop onions.

The following day, I roamed a section of the south hill, searching for wild dill and whatever else I might find. I'd learned to enjoy exploring, something I'd never done around Bethlehem. Truly, why would one think of exploring a place where one has always lived, where one's parents and grandparents lived, and where one knows every cubit? New places, new things, new thoughts had previously been as far from my mind as the moon from the earth.

I stepped over a fallen log, rotten and stinking of wet moss, and was about to enter a clearing when I heard humming. Thinking it to be bees, I went toward the sound but stopped when I realized it was a human voice. My first impulse was to run, but it was a man's voice and a man could outrun me. Pulse racing, I backed away, putting each foot down carefully so as not to rattle twigs and dried leaves.

"In time, in time," I heard someone say.

Kir! I breathed a sigh of relief. But what was he doing here? Curious, I crept through a stand of evergreens, concealed myself behind a low-growing jujube, and peeked around its limbs. He stood in front of an oak, his back to me. Cautiously, I moved a few steps to my right and saw him cramming moss in a large knot hole in the oak's trunk. Then he knelt, scraped more moss from the ground, and stuffed that, too, into the hole.

As I crept away, I heard him repeat: "In time, in time." There followed a sound which, had it been anyone other than Kir, I would have thought to be a sob.

Chapter 24

The men were shearing goats when I returned. Elimelech knelt beside Killion, helping him. Machlon, more adept with his hands, had learned to shear both sheep and goats almost as well as the more experienced men.

Before telling Elimelech what I'd seen, I'd find the tree and confirm what I suspected. Only then would I tell my husband that his trusted bondsman was hiding silver. Kir had been sent on similar business on several occasions, and I suspected he siphoned off a bit of silver each time.

That afternoon, Elimelech, Arioch, and Kir erected the tent we were to use for weaving and storing wool. I teased my husband and Arioch, playfully exhorting them to hurry up, or to orient the tent where I could get the best light. I turned a cold shoulder to Kir, though ignoring his presence was like ignoring a hungry wolf in the midst of a flock of sheep.

We left the second new tent lying on the ground. While we prepared meals, churned, weeded the garden, or performed any of a hundred other tasks, Mesha would look in the direction of the collapsed tent and then at me. Feeling sly, I kept my gaze focused on whatever I was doing, but I'm sure the smile that crept across my face gave away my and Elimelech's intentions. If not, Mesha and Arioch would find out soon enough.

A few days later, Elimelech returned from the village with a jug of olive oil he'd received from the rope maker in exchange for goat hair. Still carrying the jug, he came to the watering ditch where I was scrubbing red dye from my hands.

"We've been invited to the harvest festival,"

"The harvest festival," I repeated absently. He wouldn't agree to attend a celebration in the village, so I paid him only half-attention as I lathered a bar of lye soap between my palms. The batch of yarn I dyed for Noa's garments hadn't been enough, so I'd done a second batch, hoping the color would match that of the first. Not only was my mind preoccupied with weaving and dying, but with Kir. I had found neither time nor excuse to go alone to find his hiding tree.

Elimelech set the jug of oil on the ground and leaned against a tree, waiting for me to respond with something other than just a repetition of his words.

My hands whispered and squeaked as I rubbed them across the soap. The red wouldn't come off altogether for a few days, but the color would be reduced to a pale pink. Finally, I dried my hands and faced my husband. "You told them 'no'?"

He was rotating a twig back and forth between his fingers. Now that his sheep were growing fat again, he looked relaxed and happy. "I didn't tell them 'no.'"

"They'll offer sacrifices to Chemosh for the harvest, and then beg him to bless the seed that will go in the ground come spring."

"They've already thanked Chemosh for the harvest, and they'll wait until spring to ask him to bless the seed. As for the laws of kashrut, I've been assured the food they serve will be acceptable." He dropped the twig. "The harvest festival is for getting together and enjoying each other's company. Like our celebration of the first fruits."

"That's something we do to get together and enjoy each other's company?"

"Isn't it? We've already thanked, sacrificed, and been blessed by that time." His eyes twinkled.

"The air up here is going to your head, Elimelech."

"I told them that if my beautiful wife, who is also industrious, modest, and talented, agreed, we'd come." In a more sober voice, he added, "The boys would like it. It's hard for them here. They have no friends and nothing other than work. They need a respite."

I blew out a sigh. "Yes, that's true. If you're sure we won't be expected to acknowledge Chemosh in any way, then . . .. Yes, I suppose we could go."

"You didn't really think I'd accept if we had to acknowledge Chemosh, did you?"

"No, dear-husband-who-follows-all-the-rules, I did not."

He pulled me to him and planted a kiss on my forehead. "I also told them that among your other talents, you were an incredible woman on our mat at night."

I gave him a playful slap on his check, though, judging by his wince, the slap landed harder than I intended. "Go plow your field," I said, pretending annoyance.

As the sun reached the middle of the sky on the day of the festival, we climbed the hill separating us from the village. Our servants and bondsmen stayed behind. Before we allowed them to join the villagers in a celebration we wanted to make sure everything was acceptable. Elimelech had instructed Kir to guard our wine lest Arioch decide a celebration in the village meant one for him, too. I hadn't washed my clothes as I did in Bethlehem before such occasions for I'd either have to wash them again afterwards or put up with the odor of incense clinging to me day and night.

Long tables, constructed of split pine logs, filled Achilla's courtyard. Servants milled around, fanning at insects and adding more food to the already full tables. Men and boys gathered there while women and small children made their way to the roof. As I went toward the entrance of the house so that I too could climb to the roof, I spotted Cyrus across the courtyard talking to a group of men. He looked up and waved. Though I wanted to, it wasn't appropriate that I wander through a crowd of men to speak with him. Standing next to Cyrus, Achilla's fat-bellied cousin Lechben raised his chin and gaped at me. I felt his unseemly look burning my back as I disappeared through the door of Achilla's house.

On the roof, women sat around cloths spread with food. Toddlers squeezed in beside their mothers or climbed on their laps, while older siblings dashed about ignoring admonitions to stop running lest they upset a servant carrying food. Women I recognized from the well sang out to me and raised their hands in greeting. Hesitating, I wondered where to sit.

"Here, here," called The Mother beckoning me to her side and forcing the woman next to her to slide over. Hoglah sat across from us while Noa had settled on the far side of the roof with a group of younger women. Noa's daughters were at yet another cloth.

Hoglah clapped her hands, getting everyone's attention. "Our guest of honor is here," she said in a loud voice.

Everyone looked in our direction, clapping and saying things I didn't understand. Puzzled, I looked around to see who the guest of honor was, but everyone was looking at me. Then a servant offered me meat.

"We've saved you the right thigh as our honored guest," Hoglah said.

Confused and embarrassed, I murmured my thanks, and accepted the thigh, uneasy over why they'd chosen to honor an enemy.

I ate, trying to make sense of being chosen as guest of honor while also seeking to understand the conversation around me which became more and more difficult as voices rose, laughter bubbled up, and more wine was consumed. At intervals, The Mother elbowed me and said, "Funny." Then she'd break out cackling. Though I had no idea what was funny, I laughed and tried to be merry.

A girl began clapping, then another and another. By the time the servants had removed the dishes, every woman on the roof clapped, chanted, or sang. Unfamiliar with their songs and chants, I clapped anyway. A drum appeared, then a cymbal, a lyre, two halils. The younger girls were the first to jump up to dance, but soon, most of the women joined in. Not knowing the steps, I remained beside The Mother. Eventually the music changed, and the older women sat down to watch the slow, erotic dances that unfolded.

"Beautiful, isn't she?" The Mother raised her palm to where Orpah undulated her hips while weaving her raised arms in serpent-like movements.

I nodded. Achilla's daughter was beautiful, but much too alluring for one so young.

Ruth danced too, her movements fluid and rhythmic as though she were part of the music, but in Orpah's presence she was the moon to Orpah's sun.

"We have to find husbands for them," The Mother said.

Other than Gideon and Habish, I knew no boys in the village, so had little interest in who Achilla would choose for his daughters. Naturally, they'd be boys whose fathers agreed to pay a healthy bride price in sheep. Maybe they'd even have to give up their prize ram.

The sun, no slave to merriment, began to set. Not wanting to walk home in the dark, we tore ourselves away. Annoyed because we insisted on leaving early, Machlon and Killion walked ahead of us complaining.

"As honored guest, they presented me with the lamb's right thigh," Elimelech said when we were far enough away not to be overheard, but still close enough for music and laughter to ring in our ears.

"They also served me a right thigh," I said.

Elimelech cocked his head at me. "Why were we their honored guests?"

"Because Achilla feels guilty about taking ten of our lambs when we've lost so many? Because he took Little Samson?"

"I doubt Achilla is familiar with the emotion of guilt."

We'd come to the village commons. Astarte looked out from her pedestal, the expression on her stone face unreadable. Having been walking on the side of my husband closest to the statue, I moved to his other side, putting him between me and Chemosh's consort.

Elimelech looked up at the goddess. "We've done nothing wrong," he assured me. "We've kept our own laws. No harm will come to us." A few steps later, when Astarte was behind us, he said, "Yahweh expects us to earn our keep, and that was no longer possible in Bethlehem, so we've done no wrong in coming here."

I wondered if he was trying to convince me or himself.

Machlon and Killion waited for us at the top of the hill, and we stood for a few moments looking down at the dark forms of our tents and at the fire in the pit. Someone stood up from the fire and moved toward the animal enclosure. Kir, I guessed. The shape didn't look large enough to be Arioch or Festus.

"Gideon says he's going to marry Orpah," Killion said.

"That could be," Elimelech responded.

I hoped Gideon spoke truth. A suspicion had niggled at me that the women of Achilla's family had their eyes on my boys.

"They're cousins," Elimelech said, ". . . and Gideon's father has a small flock which would be added to Achilla's in time."

"Our flock is three times bigger than Aaron's."

I wondered how Killion knew the size of Aaron's flock.

"That may be, but Aaron's flock is bigger than that of the other villagers." Elimelech studied his son. "Unless the marriage happens quickly, we'll never know if they marry or not. We're returning to Bethlehem as soon as next year's barley is harvested."

"What were we celebrating tonight?" Machlon asked.

Elimelech's mouth curled in a cynical smile. "An abundant harvest, they claimed. But I expect we were really celebrating Achilla's show of wealth and his ability to control the village. And us."

Chapter 25

The fabric for Noa, Ruth, and Orpah turned out magnificent – the colors perfect, the weaving tight and even. Perhaps I was prideful, but I imagined they'd never before had such beautifully woven cloth.

When I delivered the pieces, they *oohed* and *aahed* as they ran their hands over them. They brought each piece close to their eyes to examine the fine weave and then draped the cloth in front of their bodies, welcoming compliments on how the colors suited. Hoglah watched with a vague smile. Wondering why she had requested nothing, I decided I would weave something for her anyway. A gift. Dark, dark red would suit.

We chose a day during the month of Sivan for the wedding of Arioch and Mesha. The men erected their tent, and we filled it with new sleeping mats, fleece cushions, and rush floor coverings. I wove a white shawl as a wedding gift. With so much weaving, my fingers had become calloused, my back sore, and my arms tired, but being busy was a blessing for it helped time pass quickly.

"Mesha isn't pretty," Abi said to me a few days before the wedding. We were working together at the loom, she taking the weft when I handed it through the warp and then returning it after crossing it over. "Her face is round, and she's squat."

"Mesha is beautiful inside. We'll find a good husband for you when we return to Bethlehem."

"When I marry, can I live with you still? And my husband?"

"I think so. The drought will be over, and the barley and wheat will be so plentiful that Elimelech will need extra help."

"I miss Damaris." Forgetting that she was supposed to be handing the weft through, she let her hand dangle.

"I'm sure she misses you, too."

"Do you think she'll be glad to see me?"

"She'll be overjoyed. Of that, I'm certain. Now hand back the weft. We need to get this finished."

Seven days before the wedding, Mesha began covering her face with a veil. I thought it absurd to adhere to tradition since Arioch had seen her face daily for the past three months but I said nothing.

Hada, Mesha, and I worked for three days getting ready for the feast. There was much to prepare for we'd invited Achilla and his family, Aaron and his, and several women from the village with their families. Against my wishes, Elimelech invited Lechben and his wife. Such people wouldn't normally attend the wedding of a bondsman and a servant, but we invited them, nevertheless, and they accepted.

I set Abi to tasks having nothing to do with food. She grumbled, especially when I asked her to sweep bird droppings from beneath the cedar tree. Lips in a pout, she made a stick broom, but instead of going straight to work, she protested.

"Damaris spits, too," she whined.

"Damaris doesn't spit in food."

"She might if she were here. She hates Moabites." Her hands clenched and unclenched the broom handle.

I'd never heard Damaris say she hated anyone. I stopped pressing figs into cakes and sat back on my heels. "No, Abi. Damaris wouldn't spit in the food of Moabites. Must Israelites and Moabites remain enemies because of what happened two hundred years ago?" My question was directed more to myself than to her. If we were to harbor every grudge from now to the end of time, before we got to the end, there'd be so many grudges we'd annihilate each other. And there weren't just the Moabites who had become our enemies, but the Hittites, Girgahites, Amorites, Canaanites, Perizzites, Hivites, and Jebusites. And those were the ones I knew about. How many others were there?

"How do you know Achilla and his men won't come and slice our throats and take all your sheep?" Abi asked.

"Well, I suppose they could. Make sure you tuck a knife inside your tunic in case that's their plan."

Her mouth fell open. "You think . . ..?"

"Abi, I'm joking. Nothing other than a good time is going to happen."

The day before the wedding, Ruth and Orpah came unannounced, chaperoned by The Mother and accompanied by a servant. All four carried packets wrapped in bits of cloth.

"We've come to prepare the bride," Orpah called gaily when they walked into our encampment.

I welcomed them, hoping that *preparing the bride* had nothing to do with Astarte. "How do you plan to prepare her?"

"We brought henna." Ruth held out her hands, displaying several small packets.

"We'll make her beautiful," Orpah said. "Like this." She pushed up a sleeve for me to see the intricate designs painted on her skin. "And when we're finished with the bride, we'll decorate you and Hada and Abi."

The Mother bobbed her head, "Yes, you too."

My three women gathered around and looked with interest at Orpah's arm. The distaste on Abi's face when she was around Moabites was replaced by curiosity.

"We could work behind your tent at the fallen oak," Ruth said. "Out of the way of the men." She looked at me, a question in her eyes. "They won't come there will they?"

"I'll tell them to stay away."

"We need water and some cushions to sit on," Orpah said.

I directed Abi to fetch cushions and Hada to get water, promising them that when Achilla's daughters were finished with Mesha they could have their arms and hands decorated. Even Hada looked intrigued at the prospect.

Their servant mixed henna while Orpah and Ruth worked on Mesha throughout the morning, each decorating a separate arm. Whenever I went to check their progress, I found The Mother offering advice which both Orpah and Ruth ignored after thanking her.

I prepared the midday meal alone, unwrapping bread we'd baked earlier, tearing off hunks of cheese, filling a bowl with olives and onions. After packing a basket for the men, I took the food past the trees behind our tents to where they removed brush and stones from a section they'd laid out for barley. Though the planting season was months away, they had much to do to clear the ground by then.

"You'll stop early today, won't you?" I asked Elimelech as the men collapsed onto the ground, starving as always.

"Yes, we'll stop early." Elimelech grinned as he took the food. "In time for Arioch to get cleaned up for tomorrow."

"And so that Arioch can get a good rest," Festus said with an even bigger grin. "He'll need extra energy these next few days."

The men laughed. It galled me that Killion and Machlon laughed the longest and loudest. They were recently eighteen and nineteen, practically still boys, certainly too young to dwell on Arioch's pleasures during the coming week.

"Stay away from the log behind our tent," I said to the men.

"Why do we have to stay away?" Elimelech asked.

"Ruth and Orpah are there preparing the bride."

A light flared in Killion's eyes. "Orpah is here?"

"Stay away." I shot him a look of such sternness that he blinked and looked away.

When I brought food to the women, they set aside the henna and, except for Mesha who was too busy admiring her arms, devoted themselves to eating.

"How long will the henna last?" I asked.

"A few days," The Mother answered. "Then the color will fade. In a week it will mostly be gone." She tore a piece of bread in half, wrapped it around a hunk of cheese and stuffed it in her mouth.

We finished eating, and I took away the basket, leaving Abi and Hada to be adorned. I hadn't asked Ruth and Orpah to come with their paints, so why did I feel I had to give in to what they wanted? Would we have missed the flowers and vines winding up and down our arms? There was still much to do for tomorrow's feast, yet my serving women seemed to have forgotten, and I didn't have the mettle to deny them their pleasure.

I was removing butter from the churning skin when Orpah came and said with a smile, "Your turn, Naomi."

Reluctantly, I wrapped the butter in leaves and then went to have my arms decorated. I could have said no. I could have explained that we were much too busy to put aside what we were doing for the sake of decorated arms which were only going to be seen by ourselves anyway. But I didn't.

It was mid-afternoon when they finished. As they packed up the henna and wrapped bits of cloth around their brushes, Killion appeared.

"I'll walk you over the hill and see you to the village," he said.

His offer to walk with them, unaccompanied by a male relative of the girls, shocked me. Had I not taught him better?

"Your father needs you," I said. "Hada and Abi will walk to the top of the hill with them."

Killion's look held a spark of defiance, but the look I returned quieted his. I sighed. Only a few more months, then we'd take down our tents and go back to where my son wouldn't be tempted by Moabite women.

We adorned Mesha with what little we had – a couple of bangles belonging to me, a new white shawl, an amulet to wear around her neck – then left her alone in the back of the cooking tent while we finished preparing the food. The men had slaughtered one of the wethers, and I saw more than one person licking lips as his mouth watered at the aroma. There were also doves which Machlon had downed with his sling.

Two boys from the village arrived early in the afternoon to sit with the flock, allowing Uri and the mute to join the celebration. Shortly afterwards, our guests came, bringing their cups. The women gathered beneath the cedar and the men at the bottom of the north hill. Led by three musicians from the village and Uri with his pipe, the men marched with Arioch toward the women's tent. Arioch, scrubbed until his skin was pink and raw, walked in front, baring his large teeth in a grin.

I couldn't image Arioch's grin becoming bigger, yet it did when Hada held open the flap and Mesha appeared, her face covered. Arioch took her hand, walked her to their new tent, and lifted the flap. A cheer went up as they stepped over the threshold for at that instant, according to our tradition, they became husband and wife.

While Arioch and Mesha enjoyed the pleasures of newlyweds, I, and two women we'd hired from the village, served the men. Hada and Abi, after severe warnings not to spit, served the women. When we finished eating, the musicians placed themselves between the men still gathered at the foot of the north hill and the women beneath the cedar. As they played, the talk and laughter grew louder, and we danced. Even The Mother danced. Hoglah remained seated, but she clapped and sang with enthusiasm. Once, I glanced over at the men and saw them engaged in a lively dance with much laughing and tripping over each other's feet. Lechben wiggled his fat pouch in a poor attempt to keep time to the music.

Late in the afternoon, a man leading two laden donkeys descended the hill along with a second man carrying a falcon on his arm. I watched Achilla go to meet and accompany the new arrivals to where Elimelech had stepped away from the others.

"Wine," I heard Achilla say as he gestured to the jugs.

Elimelech thanked him and motioned for the man to bring the donkeys to where our nearly empty wine jugs stood. While the men gathered around, holding out their cups, I breathed a sigh of relief that Arioch was occupied and in no danger of becoming drunk,

The music had changed when I turned back to our women guests. Orpah, with half-closed eyes, performed her sinuous dance, undulating her hips and moving her arms like serpents. Did the tempting of Adam have something to do with a dance such as this? I looked first at Noa and then at Hoglah, expecting them to stop Orpah for the men were close enough to see. But both smiled indulgently, unconcerned at the unseemly display.

The men had moved from the hill to the open pasture to watch the falcon dive for pieces of meat, shouting and clapping at each successful attempt. Only Killion didn't watch. Oblivious to the cheering around him, he stared at Orpah.

"Damaris should be here," Abi said, appearing with a ewer of rose water. "Arioch was her favorite."

Quickly, I turned my eyes from Killion, not wanting Abi to see what I stared at and held out my cup for her to fill. "When we get back, you can tell her about the wedding. She'll like hearing you describe it."

"And she'll be glad to know about all the food. But Hada's bread isn't as good as hers."

"We musn't be hard on Hada. No one's bread is as good as Damaris'."

After filling mine, Abi filled her own cup. "I'll ask Damaris to teach me to make bread the way she does."

"That would be wonderful."

"And you promised to find a husband for me."

"I will, Abi. I will."

Afternoon turned to dusk; the food was eaten to the last crumb; the musicians played with less enthusiasm; the dancing slowed. We women collapsed to sit or lay on the grass where we talked of other weddings. Occasional bouts of laughter drew our attention to the men. As the angel of night spread her wings over us, we became quieter, each absorbed in her own thoughts. I watched the dark forms of our husbands and sons as they moved back and forth between the fire and the jugs of wine.

What had people in Bethlehem eaten today, I wondered. We'd feasted on meat, fresh greens, quails' eggs, delectable dishes made from cheese, nuts, fruit, and honey. If the rains failed again this year, some would be reduced to eating carob pods.

A fat, bright moon lit the way for our guests as they struck out over the hill with candles. We watched the specks of light disappear over the crest, then we did what we had to do before we could escape into the sweet solace of sleep.

When I went to relieve myself, I thought everyone else had retired but as I made my way through the copse of trees behind my tent, I recognized Machlon's voice as he mumbled something, slurring his words. Then I heard a giggle. Killion's. I felt my way to where the sounds came from.

"What have you done?" I hissed between clenched teeth when I found the dark forms of my sons sprawled on the ground next to the oak log. They sat up, Killion quickly, Machlon more slowly. They stank of wine.

"We were having fun like everyone else," Killion said. "Only Machlon here hasn't learned how much wine to drink. Or to *not* drink." He moved his head so that a beam of moonlight caught his smirk as he watched Machlon lie down again.

I imagined smoke coming from my ears, so angry was I. Machlon wasn't the only one who'd drunk too much. Killion had consumed enough to not be aware of my fury.

"Go to bed," I ordered. "Your father will deal with you tomorrow."

Killion rolled his shoulders and stretched his arms lazily. "We can sleep out here."

"Don't argue with me. Go to your tent."

Killion lumbered to a standing position. "Come on, Machlon."

"I can't."

Killion grabbed him by the shoulders and shook him. "Get up."

Machlon sat up and, with Killion's help, struggled to his feet.

"Go. To. Bed. Now," I repeated.

Killion made a sound as though about to say something, but, seeming to think twice, he quietly led his brother away.

Fuming, I went to my tent and lay down beside my snoring husband. Why hadn't he been watching our sons? This awful land had made them defiant and rebellious, and as though that weren't enough, Killion lusted after a Moabite girl. We had to return to Bethlehem straightaway.

Chapter 26

Killion managed a repentant look that lasted the entire following day. He performed his chores with a show of enthusiasm, including the extra ones Elimelech gave him, then asked for more. Our younger son couldn't do enough to make his angry parents happy.

Machlon spent the day looking miserable, grabbing his head between his hands and squeezing his temples, rubbing his eyes, groaning. I guessed he'd been up most of the night for the ground outside the men's tent stank with vomit. Neither Elimelech nor I showed sympathy.

My husband humiliated our sons further by calling everyone together. "No one is to give either of my sons so much as a taste of wine, barley beer, date wine, or anything else fermented. They can drink milk or water." He glared at every bondsman and servant until they nodded their agreement. Only Arioch and Mesha, in their tent where they'd be for the remainder of the week, didn't hear Elimelech's ultimatum.

As the afternoon drew to a close, Killion found me behind the cooking tent, emptying a basket of broad bean hulls. "Are you still angry?" He asked.

"Yes." I thumped the basket to rid it of the last hull.

"*Everyone* was drinking wine."

"No one else drank themselves silly."

"I'll never do it again. Machlon won't either."

"No, you won't." How do you keep nearly grown sons from doing things they shouldn't? It was impossible to watch them every moment.

"They gave us un-watered wine," Killion said.

"Who gave it to you?"

He shrugged. "I don't remember."

"We have to go," I said to Elimelech as I lay beside him that night, still angry with both him and my sons. Where was he when *they* were giving Machlon and Killion un-watered wine?

"Go?" He lay on his back, one bare arm resting on top of the blanket, the other beneath.

"Moab is corrupting our sons."

"The wine, you mean?"

"That, and other things."

"There's wine in Bethlehem. We drink it daily. It's served at every feast. At every celebration. They have to learn. From here on they won't go unobserved until proper behavior becomes a habit. My constant watching should be enough to make them mend their ways."

"You weren't watching them yesterday."

He rolled over to face me.

"You're right. I wasn't watching them. I thought I'd taught them better."

"It isn't just what happened yesterday."

"What else?" He draped his arm over me.

I pushed him away and sat up. "Killion lusts after Orpah like she's a ewe ripe for mating."

"He's eighteen, Naomi."

"Did you lust after girls when you were eighteen?" When he didn't answer immediately, I said, "Don't tell me. I'd rather not know."

He laughed. "At eighteen, I was too busy breeding sheep to lust after girls. Did I not hear that Orpah is to marry Gideon?"

"Yes, but they aren't married yet."

"Killion isn't going to do anything foolish. Nor will Orpah. But I'll talk to him."

I sighed. "At least Machlon knows he's to marry Galatia. There'll be no problem with him desiring Moabite girls."

Arioch and Mesha emerged from their week in the bridal tent, Mesha blushing, Arioch strutting like a grouse. Other than a few knowing smiles no one paid them much mind for, as always, there was much work to be done. The months of Tammuz, Av, and Elul passed in delightful tediousness. Birdsong filled the air as I worked in my garden, prepared food, and wove cloth, including a red piece for Hoglah. Our sons became a year older, and we were three months closer to the day we'd return to Bethlehem.

The olive harvest began. After filling our water jars, we sometimes lingered in the village to watch the workers. Some climbed the trees to pick the fruits, while others beat the branches with sticks and then collected olives from cloths spread on the ground. The entire village smelled of olive oil. Most villagers had only one tree and used mortar and pestle to press their olives, but those with numerous trees dumped their olives into vats and trod on them as they did their grapes.

A few weeks later, the aroma of fermenting grapes and the delectable perfume of spiced pomegranate wine replaced the smell of olive oil. I exchanged a few woven pieces for baskets of pomegranates and grapes.

My command of the Moabite tongue had greatly improved, making conversation with the villagers easy. At the bidding of The Mother, we visited Achilla's wives several times, and they returned the visits, bringing Ruth and Orpah. *Please, leave your daughters at home*, I wanted to say but never dared. Occasionally, I stopped in to see someone's new baby or sick aunt, sometimes to have a special treat someone offered me. One day after instructing a young woman how to tighten her weave, I returned to our encampment and realized that, for a little while, I'd forgotten the people in the village were Moabites.

Late in the summer, Hada and I made incisions in the mastic trees which grew on the south hill and collected the sap. From the yellow-white drops, we would make balm and store it as salve for cuts and bruises. Several of the trees looked as though someone else had recently incised the trunks. The villagers never wandered onto the south hill, so I wondered who had done this.

Each morning, Elimelech and Uri went from sheep to sheep smelling hooves for signs of infection. Hada accompanied them with a mixture of water, vinegar, and vitriol. When a sheep showed signs of the rot, she soaked their feet in the mixture.

"I feel sorry for you," I said to Blackfoot one day.

"And why do you feel sorry for our soon-to-be number one ram?" I hadn't heard Elimelech come up behind me. He pushed aside the thorn bushes that formed the gate and went in.

"Because of what you're doing to the poor lamb. He has to endure twice as much pushing, pinching, probing, and hoof smelling as the other sheep."

Elimelech, his hand resting on the lamb's back, looked sideways at me. "As you can see, his head now reaches half-way up my thigh. He's no longer a lamb. Thanks to your sneaking him grain while the other sheep were starving, Blackfoot has thrived."

"I seem to remember you, my naughty husband, doing the same."

Elimelech smiled and went back to his examination.

"What am I to call Blackfoot if I can't call him a lamb? He isn't a full-grown ram yet."

"Call him *Our number-one-ram-to-be.*"

Blackfoot was not only number one, but the only one, since Little Samson now belonged to Achilla, and poor Springer had been killed by wolves. Elimelech never mentioned either but I knew he still felt their loss.

The fire of summer died. As leaves turned orange and yellow, rattling in the wind and falling to crunch beneath feet, I slipped away twice to look for Kir's hiding tree. Once, I thought I'd found the tree but dug moss from a hollow in the trunk only to find rotted wood inside. Disappointed, I returned to camp with nothing more to show than dirty fingernails. I knew *what* Kir was doing – hiding silver – but not *why*.

Cool weather crept in, making us shiver and throw on our outer garments as soon as we awakened. Evenings, we drew close to the fire, holding out hands to the flames. Fogs rolled in. Sometimes, after returning from the village, I'd stand at the top of the hill and look into the blurry distance, marveling at my inability to see where the sky stopped, and the hills began.

Then it rained. God help us! It rained and rained. Even when we had a short reprieve from the showers, the wet grass soaked our feet and wetted the hems of our garments until we could wring water from the wool. Day and night, I dreamed of my dry home in Bethlehem.

Arioch and Kir erected a goat skin canopy over the bread oven to keep the downpours from extinguishing our fire. After doing their chores in the rain, the men huddled beneath the canopy to warm their hands and dry their clothes, getting in the way of those doing the cooking. Water rushed through the wadi at the bottom of the north hill. We no longer went to the village well because our cistern overflowed as did the watering ditch around which a sea of mud had formed. Instead of one black hoof, Black Foot now had four muddy legs.

As cool weather became bone-chilling cold, we slept beneath fleeces. Each evening as I lay shivering in my tent, desperately wanting winter to end, I counted the days until the planting of barley, then added the time needed for the crop to grow and for harvesting. I added a few more days for shearing. After that, we'd go home to be warm and dry again.

When I thought the weather couldn't become any colder, it did. I sat at my loom wrapped in blankets, feet bound in rags, and fingers so frigid with cold I was barely able to pass weft over warp. Nursing my own complaints, at first I failed to notice what went on around me –Abi's hostility; Hada's withdrawal; Uri's silence – but then I took note.

"Uri, what's wrong?" I asked when I took food to him one day. He huddled inside a three-sided hut the men had built for our shepherds.

"Nothing's wrong."

"You're cold and homesick like the rest of us."

He nodded as he took the basket of food. "I don't know how my mother fares. My brother will take good care of her, but . . .. Maybe something has happened. Maybe she's become ill. Maybe she ran out of food."

"I'm sure she's fine." I said this even though I couldn't deny those possibilities. "Tell me again, how many sheep do you have now?"

His face relaxed. "Four ewes and two lambs. Only one of my ewes died."

"After lambing season, Elimelech will give you another lamb as pay and a second lamb to replace the one that died. A couple of your ewes will probably drop twins, so you'll return to your mother with at least ten healthy sheep. Maybe more."

"Almost enough to call a flock." He looked happier as he handed me back the bit of cloth the bread had been wrapped in. "Someday, I'll have so many sheep that I, too, will hire a shepherd and stay home with my family."

"I can hardly wait to meet your children. Surely, you'll have a half-dozen."

He smiled at the idea.

Hada's sadness was more difficult to understand. Never one to talk much, she'd said little for weeks. She pounded mortar against pestle harder than necessary, frowned at the curds as she made cheese, turned stone-face when Abi annoyed her.

"Is everything all right?" I asked over and over.

Her face as rigid as the rockface of the south hill, she'd reply. "Yes, everything is good." Then she'd add something about the bread being almost ready, the cheese not curdling properly, or that more milk came from the goats than she'd thought possible.

One evening, after putting away the supper dishes I followed her when she wandered off, something she'd taken to doing lately. Sometimes she climbed halfway up the hill. Other evenings she walked to where the flock was. This time, she didn't go far – only to the rams' stall.

She pushed aside the thorn bushes and went inside. Blackfoot was alone in the pen for No Name had been put with the flock. I heard her murmuring.

"You have wonderful soft wool," she said, running her hand along Black Foot's back. "I hope it's a long, long time before someone sleeps on your fleece."

"Hada," I said.

She jumped.

"I didn't mean to startle you. Will you come out and talk?"

Reluctantly, she came.

"Walk with me," I said, looping my arm through hers.

I led her along the base of the south hill. We drew our cloaks closer for an icy wind chilled our bodies. "Have you become silent because you're homesick?"

"Yes, we had many friends. I'm sorry. I'll try not to think about them so much."

I guessed there was something else. "What is it that really bothers you?" She let out a single sob.

"Sit down." One hand pointing to a log, I put my other hand on her arm, urged her toward the log, and we sat huddled shoulder to shoulder against the cold. "Tell me."

"It's a selfish thing, and I'm ashamed."

"Whatever it is, I won't hold it against you." Could I keep that promise if she told me something awful?

"It's Mesha and Arioch." She wiped her sleeve across her eyes. "It's them. They're happy. They're a family with a tent of their own. They'll have children. It isn't that I don't want them to be happy." She sucked in a deep breath. "It's just . . .."

"Just what?" I asked when it seemed as though she wouldn't continue.

"No man will ever want me."

"Hada!"

"It's true. I'm too tall and ungainly. My face is like a block of clay with slits for eyes and brows as heavy as a man's. I walk like a cow and stumble over my own feet."

"Aaahh, Hada. That isn't true." I put my hand over hers. Which hand was colder, I couldn't say. "Slits for eyes? No, you have the kindest and most intelligent eyes of anyone in our little family here. And I've yet to see you stumbling over your own feet, and please, for the sake of our cheese . . .," I injected a playful tone into my voice, "don't stumble when you're carrying a skin-full of milk."

She allowed herself a small smile. "I don't want you to think I resent my sister's happiness. It's just that sometimes I'm disappointed that I don't have that to look forward to."

"No one can say what the future holds." I squeezed her hand and vowed to find her a husband. If we'd given Mesha a tent and furnishings for her marriage, then we could also offer an enticement to gain a husband for Hada. A couple lambs to start a flock, perhaps.

Kir was neither happier nor sadder than before. Still secretive, I'd learned nothing new about him despite being often in his company. When he wasn't working, he sat off to himself, carving combs and hairpins from bones. What he did with them, I couldn't say. At least he hadn't lured us to Moab to cut our throats and steal our riches.

Abi was easy enough to cheer up. She only needed a reminder of my promise to find her a husband. "It won't be long now, Abi," I'd say. "Spring will be here soon, and we'll be so busy planting and harvesting barley, and shearing sheep that before you know it, it will be time to pack our tents and go home. There are dozens of suitable young men in Bethlehem. We'll choose one for you right away."

Festus and Skinny, despite having been with us several months had little to say when I asked them about homesickness. They shrugged and said they'd be glad to go home, but meanwhile, they could bear it here because they liked knowing they could count on three good meals a day.

Unlike the rest, Mesha and Arioch were happy, unconcerned about the cold, the isolation, the distance from home. We all watched Mesha's stomach, hoping to see a bulge.

As for my sons, I worried about their unhappiness at being bound to a small encampment consisting of nothing more than eleven people, a flock of sheep and goats, and a few beasts of burden. Elimelech also worried. When they agreed to undergo a humiliating breath test upon their return, he allowed them to go to the village more often than I thought wise. Sometimes they met Gideon and Habish at the top of the hill, and the four of them hunted with the falcon. I had learned to tolerate Achilla's nephews, but I still didn't trust them.

Chapter 27

Spring came and, with it, lambing season. Elimelech was jubilant when an unusual number of ewes dropped triplets. "We'll go back to Bethlehem with a flock nearly as large as the one we left with," he repeated over and over as though we hadn't heard the first hundred times he made the pronouncement.

Since the ewes would only suckle two lambs at a time, triplets presented us with a problem, though a happy one. The men constructed a holding pen for the extra lambs, and we rolled up rags, dipped them in milk, and let the lambs suck. For those that showed a distaste for wool, we simply dipped our hands in the milk and let them suck our fingers and lick our palms. It was not an unpleasant job. The lambs waggled their tails while suckling, and we laughed. Once they'd gained control of their spindly legs, they sprang into the air like grasshoppers, and we laughed again.

As for the lambs that remained with their mothers, Elimelech, like a proud father, checked them several times a day. When they were a couple weeks old, he gathered the male lambs, walked among them, feeling, looking, smelling, trying to decide which three to choose as possible breeders. The rest would have their genitals banded. Of these, a few would grow up as wethers to be used for food; most would be fattened and taken to market.

The new flock of lambs wasn't the only thing we were happy about. There would also be another addition when we returned to Bethlehem, for a child grew in Mesha's belly.

◆ ◆ ◆

Each week, the barley grew higher in our little patch of a field, and my mood improved proportionately, for after the harvest we'd leave. With so much rain in Moab, how could the rains not have come on the other side of the Salt Sea such a short distance away?

But while my mood improved, my sons became restless. Sabbaths were especially hard for they hadn't the patience to while away the day resting.

One Sabbath, while Elimelech and I lounged on cushions in the shade of the cedar, Machlon leaned against the trunk throwing a pebble into the air, catching it, throwing it again. Killion roamed, kicking at clumps of dirt, picking up sticks and tossing them, plopping down on a cushion with a loud sigh only to get up again moments later.

"Could we not go to the village?" Killion finally asked.

"That isn't allowed," Elimelech answered.

Killion, aiming the stick at a limb, hit Machlon instead.

"You hit me." Machlon threw down the pebble. "That hurt."

"Sorry." Killion made a face expressing his regret then looked at his father. "Why can't we go to the village?"

I didn't give my husband time to answer. "You know why," I said. "We agreed you'd never go to the village again on the Sabbath."

Irritated, Elimelech sat up. "Why do you want to go to the village?"

If Killion noticed his father's irritation, he didn't show it. He sat down, leaned back on his elbows, and watched a hawk swooping past. "We could walk around," he said. "Look at people. See what they're up to."

"Surely you can cool your heels one day a week."

"It's hard sitting around doing nothing." Killion looked at his brother. "Isn't it, Machlon?"

Unlike Killion, Machlon recognized his father's irritation. "We could go for a walk on the south hill," he said to his brother.

Elimelech stood suddenly and gave the boys a stern look. "Gather everyone."

Except for Kir, who was nowhere to be seen, everyone seated themselves around Elimelech, stealing glances at each other, wondering why they'd been summoned.

"We've been here for the better part of a year," Elimelech said. "As soon as the barley is harvested, and the sheep relieved of their wool, we'll leave. This evening we'll pray for our safe exodus." He looked around at the place we'd called home for the past few months, "We're in the land of Chemosh, but Yahweh is still with us, and he knows all. We will *not* go walking in the village on our holy day, opening ourselves to temptation. Nor will we drink to excess. Ever." Machlon and Killion looked away. "Our flock has thrived," Elimelech continued. "We've worked hard. We've followed the laws. We've avoided Chemosh's attention." He spoke quietly as though he didn't want Chemosh to hear. "From here on out, we'll try doubly hard to follow the laws so that we won't anger Yahweh." He looked off to the side. "I want to go back. Only Yahweh knows how badly I want to." After a few moments, he turned his eyes back to his listeners. "Mark my word, for these next few weeks, the punishment will be severe for anyone who doesn't follow Moishe's law for I intend that we all return in good grace and good health."

I shuddered, remembering Dorcus' prediction. *Not all of you will return.*

Chapter 28

Three weeks later, grain heads of barley emerged from their shafts; the stalks turned a light-yellow hue with golden streaks; and the ear was dry enough to separate the grain. The men made their way down the rows, seizing a bunch of stalks with one hand, cutting them, and then leaving the stalks on the ground for gathering. Hada and Mesha collected the stalks and piled them beside the field for my sons to bind into sheaves. Abi and I brought food and water to the workers and vinegar for dipping bread for the weather had warmed.

The mood around our fire in the evening became light and jocular, even giddy, for though our field was small, the barley it produced promised to be enough to feed us for another year.

One day, as the harvesting drew to a close, Machlon came from the field to sharpen the shearing knives. Before he began, he brought a gourd of water to me. I drank and then went back to crossing weft over warp. I wanted to use up last year's wool before the new piled up.

"When will Galatia and I be married?" Machlon asked, sitting down beside me.

"When you are twenty."

"I'll be the first of my friends to marry."

"And Galatia will be the last of hers to marry. Her father had to be convinced to let her wait that long."

"Will the bride price be high?"

"Yes." Though my cousin Imla, Galatia's mother, was dear to me, Galatia's father was a greedy man.

"She's worth it," Machlon said. "She's prettier than Orpah."

"She's more industrious than Orpah."

He laughed. "Those two sisters are overly spoiled, I think. But it isn't their fault."

"It's Noa's for being lazy herself, and Achilla's for having too many servants."

Machlon touched the piece I was weaving, a small blue square using the softest wool I could find. "What's this going to be?"

"A swaddling blanket for Mesha's baby."

His fingers lingering on the blanket, his forehead creased. "Killion is bewitched by Orpah."

"He'll get over her soon enough. There are plenty of pretty girls in Bethlehem who also happen to be industrious."

"Do you know what Galatia reminds me of?" He leaned back on his arms and, smiling, answered his own question. "She reminds me of butterfly wings. Beautiful. Delicate. Orpah is more voluptuous."

"Machlon!"

"It's true."

"You shouldn't think those things."

"I do think those things. And Killion, for certain, does." Machlon shrugged. "Killion didn't stand a chance with Orpah anyway. Gideon claims he's going to marry her." He rose. "Shearing knives await my sharpening skills. Back to work for both of us."

That same day, Abi came to help me when she finished making cheese.

"I'm right tired of goat cheese," she said, grabbing the weft as I passed it through. "I smell it in my sleep."

"I'm sure you must." Her clothes reeked, not only of sour milk but of herbs worked into the cheese.

"Do you smell wool in your sleep?" she asked.

"I don't notice it."

"You said you'd find me a husband when we get back."

"Yes. I remember." How could I not? She brought up the subject at every opportunity.

"There are some fine-looking boys down in the village."

I almost dropped the thread. "Abi!"

"I don't mean I want to marry one of them. They're Moabites. I just look at them and think about what the boys I knew in Bethlehem must look like now. It's exciting that Mesha is having a baby, don't you think?"

"Yes, of course."

I worried about the baby. What if he came during our return through the desert or at some other dangerous time?

Others among us worried, too, but not about Mesha's baby. Beneath smiles and merriment, I noticed tightened shoulders, fidgety hands, and I knew what they were thinking. *What if the drought hasn't ended?* I got no further than that thought: *What if the drought hasn't ended?* I refused to think of remaining in Moab another year.

Chapter 29

In Bethlehem there were three threshing floors, but in Achilla's village only one. Achilla's *protection* didn't extend to securing us an advantageous place in line so we were the last to use the floor. Since our threshing sledge remained in Bethlehem, Elimelech had to resort to the more arduous method of walking the oxen over the grain. But soon it was done – chaff blown away, straw collected, and grain scooped up, cleaned, and heated to prevent sprouting. There was only one thing left to do before we departed.

For the first time we'd be shearing sheep without the help of Boaz's men. For as long as I'd known Elimelech, he and his cousin had worked together. Some years they'd do Elimelech's flock first, other years Boaz's. I felt a pang. Surely Boaz had lost most of his animals in the drought. Short on the heels of the sad thought, however, was the happy one that next year Elimelech and Boaz would once again shear together.

The men drove the sheep close to the watering ditch where they could be washed. Because the wool was still on the sheep, it dried quickly. Soon, the smell of shorn wool and men's sweat rose like a cloud around our encampment. By mid-afternoon of the first day there was enough wool to keep me busy for the next year. The rest we'd sell.

When I went to get water from the cistern, I laughed at the wool piling up. Elimelech, working nearby, gave me a puzzled look. "It's nothing," I said. "I was just thinking this new wool will make you a nice cloak with stripes of red and yellow."

He grimaced but then grinned, knowing I teased. He despised showy clothes.

◆ ◆ ◆

With everyone busy harvesting, winnowing, and then shearing, Elimelech hadn't been able to send a workman to the King's Highway to ask the caravaners about the weather on the other side of the Salt Sea. He decided to go himself, taking me and our sons. He'd sell our wool, ask caravaners about the rains, and then we'd return to pack and leave.

"The wool should fetch a good price," he said as we made our way out of the hills. Our sons, long-legged, full of youthful energy and impatience, strode ahead of us. In addition to the raw wool, I had brought a few woven pieces to sell.

I hooked my hand over his arm. "We probably would have had little wool had you decided to wait out the drought in Bethlehem."

"Less wool and little milk and cheese." A shadow crossed his face. "We've assumed the rains came this year. What if . . .."

"Don't." I tightened my grasp on his arm. "We'll find out soon enough. Let's think of pleasant things."

"What pleasant things would you like to think of?"

"Of this small journey we're taking. I'm glad to move about instead of sitting to weave or cook or kneeling to pull those never-ending weeds in the garden."

"You'll be glad enough to sit after we've traveled the King's Highway, crossed the desert, and then climbed into the Judean hills again. I wonder how Boaz has fared."

"It won't be fitting for you to compare flocks when we return; he'll have lost many sheep."

"No, it won't be fitting."

◆ ◆ ◆

The sun was setting when we reached Kir-Harseth. We found an inn, unrolled our mats, and immediately fell asleep. The following morning, we awoke with sore legs, ate what Abi had packed for us, and then set off for the market.

Elimelech took Machlon with him to sell the wool and sent Killion with me to find a place to spread a cloth where I could sell my woven goods along with the herbs I'd brought. We found a spot near the entrance, spread the cloth, and I sat down behind my goods.

"Look," Killion cried and held up a blue cloth to the first woman who passed. "The finest-woven wool you've ever seen."

Drawn by my son's smile and good looks, women stopped and looked while he courted them with compliments. *Your child is beautiful. So well-behaved. I can see from your dress that you're a fine woman. Such beautiful eyes you have.* Soon, everything was gone, and we were free to explore the market. I secured the silver from the sales in a packet beneath the folds of my robe and, arm in arm, Killion and I wandered through the aisles and lanes of the bazaar, looking, admiring, wondering.

When we tired, we went to the place we'd agreed to meet Elimelech and Machlon. We didn't have long to wait.

"There they are," Killion said, pointing.

Heads down, my husband and son trudged toward us. A few cubits away, they stopped and looked up. They didn't have to tell me what news they brought, for I saw the abominable tidings in their faces. The drought in Bethlehem persisted.

Chapter 30

Our bondsmen and serving women stood on the slope of the hill, watching us plod toward them. Later, I learned that Hada, collecting wild figs on the hill, had been the first to spot us and called out to the others. Even Uri came, leaving the mute alone to watch the sheep. They saw in our faces, just as I had in Elimelech's, that we would not be returning to Bethlehem. Not this year. In a silence as thick as death, they returned to their chores.

I went to the cistern and splashed water on my face. I'd restrained myself from crying in front of husband and sons; now I'd do the same in the presence of our servants. Later, I'd find a place to hide and shed tears, then I'd go on as I must.

But someone else sobbed. The sound came from the trees behind the oxen enclosure. Please, not my husband! I'd be undone if I found him crying for he was my rock. Skirting the stall fence, I found Uri hidden behind a tree, weeping.

"Uri," I said, going to him.

He wiped his eyes. "I'm twenty-one," he said. "Too old to cry."

"We all want to cry."

"Will my mother starve? People in Bethlehem must be starving to death." He gave me a heart-breaking look.

"The elders will have distributed grain, and they'll distribute more."

"And when it runs out?"

"There'll be enough for another year." I didn't know if that was true. If everyone had put aside a seventh of their harvest, and then shared a tenth of what they saved, it would be enough. But had everyone saved a seventh? And if they had, would they share according to the commandments? Greedy people existed along with the kind-hearted and law-abiding.

Uri was looking at me, waiting for assurance.

"Your mother is fine, Uri. She'll be overjoyed when you return, not only to see you, but at the number of sheep you have. She'll be proud."

His face relaxed.

"You're as bad as Elimelech," I said jokingly, trying to cheer him.

"How am I bad?" He looked both shocked and puzzled.

"You're as attentive to the sheep as he is. You worry about every tiny scratch, nicked ear, and dirty hoof. But that's good. You're going to have a fine flock when you return to Bethlehem."

"It's true. The sheep are my friends, and I take good care of them. And Elimelech is like a father. He's taught me everything I know."

We were again invited to the harvest festival in the village. This time, we would all go.

"Our bondsmen and serving women need something to look forward to," Elimelech said.

When the day came, as soon as animals were fed and watered, dung collected and laid out to dry, we set out for the village. Only Uri and the mute remained behind. We brought with us a stew of broad beans as well as goat cheese balls rolled in honey and pistachios.

At the top of the hill, we stopped and looked down to where the entire village appeared to be gathered in the commons, laughing, singing, beating drums. The stink of sacrifices floated from the altar up to where we stood.

Elimelech turned white. "I thought it was just a feast."

Abi piped up before I could respond. "Astarte has seen us already." She looked to where the figure atop her column stared in our direction. "We have to pretend we're not beholden to Yahweh or she might harm us."

"Look." Killion pointed. "They're moving toward Achilla's house. They've finished their ritual and are getting ready for feasting."

Elimelech looked unsure.

Killion, his excitement showing, had been leading our group and was a few steps ahead of us. "Last year we came later in the day and didn't see them making sacrifices," he said, looking at us over his shoulder. "But they're done with that now, and the fun is about to begin." Without waiting for a reply from his father, Killion started down, and we followed. I knew Killion's motivation for going had nothing to do with Yahweh or Astarte or any other god. He wanted to see Orpah.

◆ ◆ ◆

Hoglah and I sat together, listening to the younger women sing silly songs. "Your serving woman has become quite round in the face," Hoglah said, nodding at Mesha.

"She'll be having a little one soon."

"I look forward to the day our two girls will present us with grandsons."

Orpah and Ruth, wearing clothes made from the cloth I'd woven for them, sat with their friends on the other side of the roof, singing at the tops of their voices.

"Have you chosen their husbands?" I asked. Although, the girls were Noa's daughters, Hoglah seemed to be the one in charge.

"We're considering who their husbands should be," Hoglah replied. "The young men in the village don't have the wealth Achilla wants in sons-in-law."

Then who, I almost asked, *and what about Gideon?*

The musicians switched to a lively tune, and people jumped up to dance. Soon, there was so much clapping, stomping, and jumping, I feared the roof might collapse. Abi joined the dancing with enthusiasm, and I noticed for the first time her grace and agility. I'd thought her lank and clumsy, teetering like a stalk in the wind, but she was growing up to be sinuous and rhythmic. Her tight curls bounced and her long fingers wove gracefully as she moved to the beat of the drum.

I, too, joined in and, for most of the afternoon, forgot we were stranded in an enemy land for yet another year. Only, when I sat down, winded, my face flushed from dancing, did I remember.

The afternoon wore to an end, and we took our leave. Stepping to the rhythm of snares and tambourines we headed homeward, meaning to get there before darkness swallowed us.

As we began our climb over the hill, I noticed that not all of us stepped to the rhythm of snares and tambourines. Arioch trailed behind, stumbling. Killion, looking smug, walked beside him, attempting to support our bondsman, undoubtedly hoping no one would notice. Elimelech, deep in conversation with Kir, paid no attention. Mesha noticed, however. Theirs would not be a happy tent tonight. Wondering how my husband could have been so engrossed in having a good time that he failed to notice what members of his own party were doing, I vowed to tell him this time.

As to Killion's smugness, the reason became clear when Machlon came to walk with me.

"Killion won all the contests," he said. "Racing, wrestling, rock throwing. The only one he didn't win was with slings."

"Who won that one?" I knew the answer but asked anyway.

"I did. Gideon won nothing. He was pissed. Before we came, he was first at everything."

Machlon and Killion had shown up the nephews of the village chief. Tomorrow, after dealing with Arioch, Elimelech needed to warn our sons about making enemies of Gideon and Habish.

We breached the hill and started down the other side, the music from the village growing fainter until it died out altogether. As we neared our camp, Uri's clear voice rang out in the dusk.

Blessed are the hills, the trees, the grass.
Blessed are the bees, the birds, the sheep
Blessed are . . ..

He was happy. A few days earlier, he'd been in tears.

Happy are those who sing, who dance, who pray.
Happy are those who . . ..

What had changed his mood so quickly? The rest of us labored to not despair, yet Uri's voice rang with cheer.

Chapter 31

I looked up from where I'd been chipping away at a block of salt and saw Achilla, accompanied by his brother, Aaron, his cousin, Lechben, and his two nephews. Talking loudly and laughing, they headed toward the pasture where Elimelech was filing the hoof of one of the wethers. I set aside the salt and motioned for Abi to prepare refreshments. After her enthusiasm at joining their dances, I was confident she'd gotten over her urge to spit.

Bringing water and cups, I was short on the heels of Achilla's group and caught Elimelech's grimace at being interrupted.

"Shalom," Achilla said.

Without letting go of the hoof, Elimelech replied, "Shalom." Then he returned to his task. "A moment, and I'll be finished."

"I'll wait," Achilla said.

I filled a cup and held it out to him. "Let me offer you water."

As I poured water for the others, I saw my husband's brow crease when Achilla began to move through the flock. Aaron finished his water, handed back the cup, and then joined Achilla in assessing sheep while Gideon and Habish stood by looking bored. Cousin Lechben, whose stomach still mounded like a pregnant woman's, who still smelled of garlic, and whose eyes still roamed my body, crouched beneath a nearby elm. An unbridled wish that a limb would fall on him flashed through my mind.

His face dark, Elimelech finished with the hoof and stood up.

"You're staying another year," Achilla said, looking down at the lamb on whose back his hand rested. When Elimelech said nothing, he faced my husband. "Gideon told me."

"The drought continues in Judea," Elimelech said.

"You still need my protection."

The pitcher of water shook as my hands trembled.

"We agreed on ten lambs for protection," Achilla said.

"I gave you ten lambs." Elimelech crossed his arms.

"Those were for last year."

"I understood that I was to give you ten lambs. No time limit was mentioned."

Achilla moved to another lamb, pulled back her ears, and looked inside. "That's the way an agreement always is: for a year.

"That's right," Aaron said. "For a year."

Just give them the lambs, I pleaded silently.

"Have you no heart?" Elimelech asked.

"Would you have a heart if Moabites invaded your pastures in Judea?"

"No one was using this pasture," Elimelech countered. "It stood empty before we came."

"Ten lambs." Achilla wore his hyena smile.

"Choose, then." Elimelech's voice was bitter. He grabbed another sheep, imprisoned it between his legs, and lifted a front hoof, pretending to check it.

Unmoved by Elimelech's pain, Achilla walked about, examining lambs with Aaron's help.

I took more water to Lechben. Achilla's cousin reminded me of a slimy slug but giving him water gave me an excuse to remain. I stood as far away as I could when I handed him the cup and then took a step back. He gulped the water then held out the cup, his hand purposefully brushing mine when I took it.

I had become a different woman. Instead of slipping quietly away as the old Naomi would have, I glared at Lechben until he seemed to shrink. Finally, he shrugged, rose, and went to join Achilla and Aaron.

Ropes in hands, Habish and Gideon waited impatiently for Achilla to decide which lambs to take. Angry at the lot of them, I headed back, meeting Abi bringing a bowl of pistachios to our visitors – our precious pistachios that we now had to purchase because we had no trees. Sensing my anger, she said nothing as we passed. Achilla took our sheep and ate our pistachios. I'd have nothing else to do with them. I'd stay away from the village. We'd not go to another of their celebrations. And I'd never, never weave cloth for the women of that family. They could go naked before I'd lift one finger for them.

A few days later, Elimelech sent Festus and Skinny to watch the flock so Uri and the mute could join us for the evening meal. While waiting, Uri whittled holes in a piece of reed nearly as long as his arm and about half the size of his wrist.

"A new flute, Uri?" I asked as I set down a basket of bread.

"For Killion. He wants to learn to play."

"You're going to teach him?"

Uri raised his eyebrows. "I'm going to *try*. Killion can barely sing in tune, but maybe he'll be better with the flute."

"We'll hope so." I fanned away a fly. "You're happier now."

"Yes," he said and smiled down at the piece of wood."

Several days later, we were preparing the evening meal and the men finishing up their afternoon chores, when the mute came from the pasture and tried to tell Elimelech something. He grunted and made motions with his hands and then pointed to the flock which was nearby. Elimelech, failing to understand, asked him to repeat the motions. When the mute realized I stood nearby, he set out at a run toward the pasture.

After giving me a puzzled look, Elimelech followed. The mute had reached the flock by the time Elimelech caught up. I watched the distant form of my husband approach him and the mute walk away. After what appeared to be a short conversation with Uri, Elimelech wandered among the sheep, then walked the perimeter of the flock. I guessed he was searching the hillsides. He returned shaking his head.

"You didn't learn what the mute was trying to say?" I asked.

"No." He ran his tongue around the inside of his mouth as he was wont to do when he was puzzled about something. "He tries to tell me something, then suddenly he wants nothing to do with me. Strange."

"Did you ask Uri what he might have been trying to say?"

"Uri guessed it had to do with thinking they heard wolves earlier today. He decided later it was only dogs."

The memory of the carnage we'd experienced before crossing the desert still shook me, so I understood why the sound of wolves would worry the mute.

My sons had finished their dung duty and were squatting beside the fire. Looking thoughtful, Elimelech squatted beside them. I brought knife, bowl, and the cucumbers I'd been shredding for barley cakes and joined my family. The fire felt good. Although the days were warm, the weather cooled as evening drew near.

"The mute is probably seeing spirits," Machlon said to Elimelech and scoffed. "Right, Killion?"

Killion held out his hands to the fire and stared into the flames.

It was unlike Killion to say nothing. Did he know what the mute had been trying to tell us? But that made no sense. Killion loved being the conveyor of news.

The men, when they weren't engaged in work, often wandered the hills in search of wild wheat. They'd cut the stalks, bind them into a small bundle, and roast the bundle over a blazing fire until the chaff burned off. Then they rubbed the grain between their hands to peel away the husks. One day, when I wandered the south hill collecting greens, I encountered Kir carrying several bundles of wild wheat.

"You've found quite a lot," I said.

He nodded. "There are several stands there." He pointed to a place near the top of the southern row of hills. "You can see the Salt Sea from up there."

"We're that close?"

"On a clear day, you can see the Judean hills."

"Show me." I began walking in that direction.

It took us some time, but he led me to the top of the highest hill and, there, in the distance, appeared a blur of purple that was the sea, and beyond the sea, the faint outline of hills.

"Judea." Tears stung my eyes.

"Yes. Bethlehem is directly across from us. Maybe the dark spot there toward the middle."

I stared at a blur of violet, trying to make out the shape of a town but the blur remained nothing more than a blur. I imagined rooftops projecting above Bethlehem's walls, our roof taller than the others. I imagined the vineyards, the threshing floor, the columns to keep jackals away. Women and children would be collecting ripe figs in baskets or in their bunched-up tunics. Olives would be nearing ripeness.

Then I remembered. There would be neither figs nor olives. Not with the drought beginning its third year.

Not wanting Kir to see the tears that ran down my cheeks, I turned my back, pretended to look at something else, and wiped my eyes.

"I'm sorry," Kir said. "One longs for home."

I gave him a sharp look. I had never heard him mention *home*. Had he ever even had one? I suspected his mother had abandoned her malformed-faced baby in a dark corner of a village somewhere, and, somehow, he'd survived.

On the Sabbath, Elimelech decided the distance to the place Kir showed me fell within the two thousand cubits we were allowed to walk on the holy day, so we went together.

"What do you think they're doing now?" I asked as we looked across the blurry sea.

"Damaris is sleeping the afternoon away. Zacharias is on the roof swatting flies. He's wondering how long it will take, once the drought ends, for the vines to produce a new crop. Boaz is praying for his flock, asking that he have the greater number of sheep when we return. Boaz's wife is sick as usual. Your relatives are complaining about this and that. Our nieces and nephews, like our sons, are bored at not being allowed to do anything on the Sabbath."

I laughed. "At what age does boredom give way to relief that we've been assigned a day to rest?" I grabbed Elimelech's hand and pulled him down with me as I sank to the grass.

He leaned back on his elbows. "I hope that day comes soon for our boys. Their furtive looks in the direction of the village are wearing on my patience. I should make them work doubly hard before the Sabbath so they'll be glad to stay home."

"You call our encampment home?"

He took my hand and kissed it. "It's our home for as long as we're here." A shadow crossed his face, and he let go of my hand. "I want to go back, Naomi. You have no idea how badly I want to go back."

"I have a *very* good idea, for I have the same want."

"I miss everything. Our house. Our friends. Our kinsmen. Even the blasted field that requires constant work to keep the tares out. I miss the elders arguing at the town gate."

"Surely not that."

"Yes, even that." He lay back, pulled me down beside him, and we looked up at the sky. "You hated coming here. I hate being here as much as you hated coming, but I believed it was the only way to save our flock. Boaz has probably lost most of his sheep. I wish I could give him the lambs Achilla took from us."

"There'll be more in the spring. We'll be leaving after next year's barley harvest and you won't have to give any to Achilla. You can give them to Boaz instead."

"Yes. I'll never again give lambs to Achilla."

That evening, the mute came to collect food for himself and Uri. I gave him a basket filled with barley cakes, nuts, cheese, and olives, but instead of leaving, he tarried. Elimelech knelt around the fire with the other men, roasting wheat stalks. They were laughing at a crude story Arioch had just told about a frog and a snake. Even Kir smiled. Hada and I pretended to not hear, but Mesha, going back and forth as she brought out barley cakes and lentil stew, shook her head at her husband's tale. Abi was all ears. I saw her covert smile.

The mute tapped Elimelech on the shoulder, curled his forefinger, and beckoned him away from the fire.

They stopped near where I knelt to pick up cheese I'd spilled. Not realizing I was there, the mute bleated like a sheep and went through the same motions he had before in which he cupped one hand and poked the forefinger of the other up and down in his curled fist. Finally he moaned and, looking up, covered his head with his hands as though to protect himself from the sky falling.

When Elimelech didn't react, the mute tried again.

"I understand," Elimelech said, holding up his hand. "Go back to the flock."

His face dark as night, Elimelech returned to the fire and sat down beside Killion.

Killion's bundle of wheat had caught fire, yet he didn't notice. "Pay the mute no mind," he said in a soft voice. "The man is crazy."

The following evening, as we were setting out food, Elimelech drew me aside. "Serve the others," he said. "I'll be back soon."

Before I could protest that the others could wait for their master, he started toward the flock.

About to wash his hands, Killion stopped. "Where's Father going?"

"He said to begin our meal without him. Finish washing. The others are waiting."

"I'm done." His face rigid, Killion went to sit beside the fire, his eyes fixed on the diminishing form of his father heading toward the sheep..

Arioch, never aware of others' tension, plunged his hands in the basin. "Just look at that wife of mine," he said with a grin. "Her stomach is soon going to turn into a sideways mountain."

"Your son's going to be a big one," Mesha said, removing stew from the fire.

Arioch waved his wet hands at her. Drops landed on the flames, making the fire sputter. Killion's frown deepened.

"Stop raining on the fire, you ox," Mesha said.

"The rain's for good luck." Arioch grabbed her around the waist, pulled her to him, and kissed her on the cheek.

"If you make me spill this stew, you're in for it."

He let go. "Just don't spill my share."

"Stop annoying your wife and sit down and tell us a story," Machlon said.

The others had finished washing and were seated, waiting for food. "Story, story, story," they clamored.

"The one about Ehud hiding a sword under his clothes and stabbing the King of Moab until the dung came out," Machlon demanded.

Killion, usually the first to beg for a story, remained silent.

"What's wrong?" I whispered to him as I set down a plate of olives.

"Nothing."

"Are you sick?"

"No, I'm not sick."

"Ehud comes to the king and tells him he has a secret message . . ." Arioch began.

As he continued, the story drew laughter from everyone except Killion. Puzzling over Killion's dour expression and the mystery in the pasture, I said nothing about the inappropriateness of telling a story centered on dung during a meal.

I sat on the side of the fire that allowed me to see the flock, though the dimming light made it impossible to distinguish sheep from goats. A dark figure – the mute, I thought, because of his height - wandered along the southern side of the flock.

"And Ehud persuades the king to go together to the place where they relieve themselves, and . . . .." Arioch's voice had become boisterous, encouraged by the laughter.

Though deploring the tale because of its coarseness, at the same time I was glad to have the others distracted. I saw Elimelech's dark form edging around the northern edge of the flock. Then he slipped behind a row of trees skirting the bottom of the hill. I squinted, trying to find Uri among the sheep.

A sideways glance told me that Killion wasn't eating. "What's going on?" I asked.

He shook his head.

"You know what's happening, Killion. Tell me."

Tears filled his eyes. "I can't."

Chapter 32

Arioch's story ended. The king had been stabbed, his dung splattered on the floor, and Ehud and the Israelites rewarded with a victory. Night had descended, and everyone fell quiet. Machlon threw another stick on the fire, and flames leapt up to consume it. From the trees lining the wadi, came the *whooooooo* of an owl.

Then our peace was shattered. We looked up to see Elimelech, his face aflame, dragging Uri by the arm toward us. He shoved Uri to the ground where our shepherd curled like an unborn baby in his mother's womb.

"Bestiality," Elimelech cried out in a broken voice. "One of us turned heathen. An abomination."

Struck by thunder, we stared. Only Killion didn't stare. He closed his eyes and let his chin sink to his chest

Elimelech gasped and pressed his hand to his heart as though wounded. For a few moments, I thought my husband wouldn't breath again. Finally, he said, "Whoever lies with an animal shall be put to death."

"No!" I cried.

Elimelech looked at me, his eyes distraught. "Would you have Sodom and Gomorrah repeated on our family?"

Uri, his eyes wild with fright, vomited. My stomach heaved, and I ran behind our tent and retched until there was nothing left.

Trying to believe this was a nightmare, I returned to the others. The men had backed away from the firepit, their faces unreadable in the dark. While Uri lay in his own vomit, Hada and Mesha cried, shivering. Abi sat on the ground with her arms wrapped around her legs and her face propped on her knees. Her shoulders shook. I knelt and, hugging her to me, rocked her back and forth. Machlon came and put his arms around my shoulders.

"Someone must watch the flock," Elimelech said, his breathing labored.

"I'll go," Kir said, stepping forward.

Elimelech gave a nod and then looked at Uri cowering on the ground, sobbing. "You'll sleep in the men's tent, and Arioch will sleep at the door."

Hope shot through me. If Uri ran away he couldn't be punished. Arioch slept like a rock, so it would be easy to slip past him.

After a sleepless night and a thrown-together breakfast which was only nibbled at, everyone dragged off to do their work except for Elimelech. He called Killion and me into our tent.

"You knew what Uri was doing?" Elimelech asked Killion. The tent flap had been left open, allowing enough light to see the fear in Killion's eyes. Afraid for my son, I shook, twitching like a dying chicken.

Killion looked around the tent – everywhere except at his father. "Sometimes . . .. two or three times . . .. when I carried him food or went to talk to him or . . .. It looked like . . .." He sobbed. "What are you going to do?"

"You know the law."

"No," I cried. "You can't."

Misery mingled with hardness on Elimelech's face. He waved Killion away, then fell to his knees and covered his face with his hands.

I sank down beside him. "Elimelech, please. You can't." I kissed his feet. "Please, show compassion."

"It's the law," he said. "I have no choice."

There was barely a human sound in our encampment that day. A few whispers. Thuds of wood being thrown on a pile. The scrape of bowls being stacked. Arioch took Uri food but brought it back uneaten.

Elimelech left at the break of dawn to wander the hills only to return at sunset. He drew me aside. "I will take Uri to the nearest town occupied by the tribe of Reuben. The Levites there will decide."

"Please, Elimelech," I begged. "Can you not forgive him? He was lonely. He misses his mother. He misses the girl he was going to marry."

"It isn't for me to forgive." Elimelech's voice was hoarse, as though he'd spent the day shouting. "It's written in the Law."

"*The Law*. We follow the law, yet a drought has driven us from our home. Which law did we break to be punished like this?"

"The Law binds our people together and makes us separate from all others."

"If it makes us cruel, then why is being separate a good thing?"

Elimelech held up his palm. "Say no more, Naomi. "Tomorrow, Uri and I leave for the Land of Reuben."

Chapter 33

That night, I invoked any god who chose to listen, begging him to move Uri to run away. No god listened. When morning came, they set off, Elimelech ashen-faced, Uri barely able to walk. Uri forgot his sandals until Arioch ran after them and thrust them into his hands. Uri frowned at the shoes as though he didn't know what they were.

Even after they disappeared through the trees, we continued to watch.

Finally, we turned to our tasks. The wielding of Hada's pestle against mortar was a weak thump instead of a pound. Listlessly, Abi swung the goatskin to separate curds from whey. With the lethargy of her movements, I doubted they'd separate. Nor did I care. Mesha, suffering from morning sickness, or pretending to, for it was well past the time when she should have suffered from that malady, hid inside her tent. Listlessly, the men did what they usually did except for Killion and Machlon who were charged with taking turns shepherding the flock.

I sat in front of my loom, staring at the threads, occasionally running my fingers up and down the warp as I pictured the Levites wearing looks of righteous indignation while they listened to the charge against Uri. They'd be strutting in their fine linen garments embroidered with gold and embedded with twelve gemstones representing the twelve tribes of Israel. Their cropped hair would be topped by ornate headdresses. Clad in their finery, they'd judge a poor shepherd boy, homesick for his mother and his country. Would they cast lots to decide, or was it such a straightforward case they'd condemn Uri to death with barely a thought?

Or would Uri run away before they reached the Land of Reuben?

I marked off the days, counting, guessing how many would pass before I saw my husband again. Three days there and three back? If they walked fast. But how many for the Levites to convene, listen, and pass judgement?

On the third evening after Elimelech's and Uri's departure, I heard a noise behind my tent and found Killion sitting on the fallen oak, his face lit by a half-moon. I didn't need to see what he had in his hand, for the smell told me.

"Shame on you," I said. "Drinking to cover sorrow is cowardly." My words lacked sting, for I was weighted with dread.

"You're right, Mother. It isn't allowed. But tell me, what *is* right? We Israelites approve of killing, don't we? So, I guess that's *right*. We kill by the thousands, fighting our battles and taking revenge. Moishe ordered his troops to execute Midianite women and boys – more than 60,000 innocent women and boys he ordered to be killed; Samson slaughtered innocent Philistines; the stories go on and on. Or we kill individually. Ehud stabs the king while they're relieving themselves. Jephthah sacrifices his daughter. And now Uri. When has Uri ever harmed a single hair on someone's head?" With his last words, he stood and flung his cup into the trees, the cup shattering as it hit a trunk. He stared into the darkness for a few moments then broke into sobs. I put my arm around him and pulled him to me as I had when he was only a boy.

"Please tell me Uri will come back, Mother," he said finally, drawing away. He wiped his face with his forearm. "He's my friend."

"Uri is everyone's friend. I don't understand why things are the way they are, Killion. I don't understand."

Each day we did what we had to do, barely speaking. We retired early. I both hoped for and dreaded Elimelech's return. I tried to picture my husband returning through the copse of trees, Uri beside him, forgiven. Warned, but forgiven. Yet, an angry Yahweh didn't forgive. He killed people with floods, with fire and brimstone, with plagues. He allowed us, his chosen people, to be slaughtered by enemies, just as the gods of our enemies allowed them to be slaughtered by us. What was wrong with the gods that they allowed this?

Mornings, I awoke angry, unsure whom to direct my anger at. Uri, for what he did? The mute for making Elimelech aware of it? Elimelech for following the laws of Moishe? Yahweh for punishments that made no sense? Killion was right. Yahweh was a bloodthirsty god.

When Elimelech had been gone twelve days, I despaired. Then a tiny hope lodged in my breast. If it was taking such a long time to decide Uri's fate, maybe there was something about the laws Elimelech didn't know. Something that would allow Uri to come home.

Chapter 34

On the second day of the third week, Elimelech returned alone.

Each of us stopped what we were doing and watched him walk into the encampment, slow of step, shoulders stooped. My husband had become an old man. He stopped for a moment, his eyes moving over us without seeing us. Then he went to the cistern for water. I ran after him, getting there before he did, filled a gourd, and handed it to him. Sweeping his eyes over my face, he barely acknowledged my presence. After drinking, he handed back the gourd and, without a word, went to check on the animals in the stalls although I doubt he actually saw them.

When he started toward the flock, he stopped before he had gone far, turned his back to his sheep, and retreated to our tent where he stayed for the remainder of the day. The following morning, he set to work with as few words as possible. On the Sabbath, he said nothing at all. Machlon, hesitant and unsure, led the prayers. There were no lessons, no questions, no praise, no singing.

And so it went. My husband was broken. He had followed the law; yet he was broken.

One day, I filled a basket with herbs. Using the excuse that The Mother had a hard time finding these particular ones because they grew mostly on the southern hill, I went to the village, taking Abi with me.

Uninvited, I went to Achilla's house, begged to be admitted, and, leaving Abi in the courtyard, was shown to the roof. Hoglah was rubbing ointment on her ankles while Noa polished a bangle.

"Aaahh," Hoglah said, setting aside the bowl of ointment. She rose and kissed me on the cheek. "We were afraid you'd given up on us."

Noa also rose and kissed me. "We're glad to see you," she said.

They acted as if they *were* glad to see me, and I felt a fleeting relief from the tension of the past weeks.

"Sit down," Hoglah said, placing cushions near where she'd been sitting. She hobbled to the ladder-well and called down, "Sari, Bring refreshments. And tell The Mother we have a guest." Looking at my basket of herbs, she said, "You've been busy."

"I brought these for The Mother."

"She'll be delighted."

"You never told me whose mother she is."

"Why, Achilla's of course," Hoglah said as she sat down.

"And she's very angry with her son," Noa added. "As we all are. Because of the lambs."

Hoglah touched my hand. "We told him how much we abhorred his taking them."

I struggled to not cry at their kindness. The lambs were no longer important. I would have given a hundred lambs to have Uri back.

The Mother climbed from the ladder well. "You've made yourself scarce, lately," she said.

I held the basket out to her. "I thought you might like these."

"*Toda.*" She poked around, checking the greens. "Age is catching up. It's harder for me to walk into the woods to find them. I'd like to teach my granddaughters, but they're not interested." She gave a wave of dismissal.

I wondered what they *were* interested in. They danced. They flouted themselves about the town. Other than that . . ..

"My son won't be taking any more of your sheep," The Mother said. "We've set him straight." She made a motion indicating that Hoglah and Noa were part of the *we*.

I didn't know what to make of their banding together in our favor against Achilla, but whatever the reason, I was glad.

The servant brought quail eggs, figs, and water. We talked and ate. I might even have laughed at something. It was good to be in the company of other women again. Reluctantly, I took my leave when I deemed my visit had lasted long enough.

Instead of remaining in the courtyard where I left her, Abi had gone to the commons where she watched a group of children playing. Or so I thought. I soon realized that, instead of the children, she watched three young men who were repairing a door on one of the houses. That it took three to do a job easily done by one struck me as foolishness.

"Astarte doesn't look so scary now," she said as we started for our camp.

I looked up at the figure on the column. "No, she doesn't."

"Why don't the Israelites have a woman god to care about us?"

"I don't know."

"Yahweh could have a consort like Astarte. That would be good."

"I suppose. But we musn't talk like this."

Abi shrugged. "Damaris thinks it's all nonsense, and she's never got struck down for thinking that."

"Not yet."

Abi gave me a scared look. "You don't think . . ..?

"I don't know what to think, Abi, and so I must think what I've been told to think. Sometimes it's too painful to think at all. We just have to wait for the future to unfold, hoping that what it brings will be a blessing and not a curse."

Chapter 35

Had it not been for Mesha we would have drowned in our sadness. Her belly as round as a full moon, she'd arch her back, trying to ease her discomfort. "Ahhhh, me," she'd say, patting her stomach, "The little son is growing big as an ox, and he's weighing me down."

As we waited for the happy event, we went about the business of living. Machlon and Killion took turns replacing Uri, setting about their new job with gloomy faces. Soon, it became evident that the downturned mouths had to do with more than Uri's fate. They were bored. Machlon made an attempt to overcome the monotony by practicing with his sling and became so adept we had no end of doves for the stew pot.

Elimelech, still unsmiling and mostly silent, sent Kir to the market to sell our fattened lambs. He also instructed Kir to buy him a new pair of sandals for the straps on his old pair had worn almost completely through.

While Kir was gone, Elimelech decided to slaughter two goats and dry the meat to be eaten later. After slaughtering, he and Arioch cut around the hooves and neck to keep the skins whole, removed the skins, and gave them to Hada to make into water containers. She buried the hides, dug them up a week later, and rubbed off the hair with a stone. While she washed the skins, Abi and I went into the village to exchange herbs for pomegranate rinds to fill the skin when the openings were sewn up. After a week, the skin would be emptied, washed, and filled with dried black olives for a period and then emptied and washed again.

The planting and harvesting of barley was still months away, yet my husband planned. The vision of our return seemed to be his only joy now. "We're going back, drought or not," he said. "We'll save the dried goat meat for our journey. We'll have enough grain to see us through another year, and the sheep will be healthy enough to survive the trip."

I knew he'd change his mind if the drought continued. His depression would wear off, and he'd once again be the old Elimelech, worrying about his flock. Though healthy now, if the Judean hills were barren, our sheep couldn't survive with nothing to eat.

"The women of Achilla's family promised that Achilla will take no more of our lambs," I said, trying to cheer him up.

He looked at me in puzzlement. "Why?"

"Maybe because he realized what he did was wrong."

"Achilla admit he's wrong? Never. Either he lied to the women or he has another motive. Achilla is a greedy man."

Summer ended, my sons became another year older and, for the second time, leaves changed color, fell, and piled up, red, brown, yellow. I had become happily accustomed to the constant aroma of cedar and pine as well as the smell of wood smoke which drifted into our tents to infuse cushions and sleeping mats with its aroma. I had even grown to enjoy birds waking us in warm weather and the quiet that prevailed when the cold drove them away.

Bit by bit we forced ourselves to smile, to forget to listen for Uri's pipe, to stop remembering that the food we took to the watchers of the flock wasn't for him. Elimelech never referred to what happened in the land of Reuben. Only once, when Machlon absent-mindedly picked up a rock and threw it against a tree, did my husband's spirit awaken. "Never . . ..," he shouted at my son, ". . . never throw a rock in my presence. And that goes for all of you." He looked around at the surprised faces of those nearby. Then he stormed off, leaving our bondsmen and serving women staring after a master who had never before raised his voice to them.

The change in Elimelech wasn't entirely bad. Once playful and passionate, he became tender and sensitive, touching me at every opportunity. Around the fire, he insisted I sit next to him, our thighs touching. If I went to watch him at work, he'd come to stand beside me for a while, shoulder to shoulder. He held my hand when we went for walks. Nights, he pulled me close to him.

He was easier on our sons, too, allowing them to spend time with Gideon, Habish, and their friends. Some of that time they spent with the falcons. As for the rest I can't say what they did. I imagined they'd given up the jumping, throwing, running contests of boys and, instead, merely bragged about their prowess. I suppose they looked at the village girls. Thankfully, Killion no longer spoke about Orpah, although I wondered if the reason he remained quiet was to keep peace with me.

Cyrus, back from another of his expeditions, gave us the pleasure of his company several times, entertaining us, especially my sons, with descriptions of places we'd never go.

As for me, trips to the village well were my salvation. Sometimes, knowing we had neither orchard nor vineyard, someone gave me a small jug of oil or wine, or a basket of grapes or figs. I brought greens and herbs and let the women have their pick.

Time rolled on. Blackfoot, now in his second year, was ready to do his job with the ewes. Elimelech put him with the flock earlier than usual in order to hasten lambing season, claiming that older lambs would have a better chance of surviving the return trip. In the spring He reminded our sons to keep watch for the ewes whose tails were too heavy for Blackfoot to shove aside when he tried to penetrate.

During the month of Shebet, Hada woke me before dawn one morning.

"It's Mesha's time," she called through the tent opening.

I threw back the blankets and sat up. Elimelech stirred.

"I'm coming," I said to Hada. And to Elimelech, "Go back to sleep."

I threw my cloak over my tunic, slipped into my sandals, and went to Mesha's tent. A frightened Arioch stood outside shivering.

"She was screaming," he said as though he didn't know that's what women in childbirth did.

"Go find something to keep you busy," I said as I lifted the flap to go inside.

"What should I do?"

"Build a fire. Check the oxen. Dig a well. Just go. There's going to be a lot more screaming."

Baby Uriah was born toward nightfall. Still red from his mother's womb, we rubbed him with salt and swaddled his arms to his side. In the glow of an oil lamp, we marveled over the baby's mane of bright red hair.

"Like his father's," Mesha said, and we laughed.

Worn out but happy, she nursed her new son while Arioch hung over the pair, a proud father in awe. The wool cradle I'd woven hung in a corner of the tent. Arioch had attached the cradle to two forked sticks planted deep in the ground.

In the days that followed, we women argued over whose turn it was to loosen the swaddling, rub baby Uriah's skin with olive oil, or dust it with powdered myrtle leaves. Touching his soft, plump, skin allowed the sun to peak around the cloud hanging over us, and thus Mesha gracefully gave in to our claiming so much of her baby's care.

One morning, we woke to find the ground covered with white. We'd seen snow – silvery white jewels floating from the sky, melting before they hit the ground – but when we stepped outside our tents, the snow had piled as high as our ankles. Shrieks of both pleasure and pain filled the air as we waded through the icy white. We pulled dry logs from the bottom of the pile for a fire, and soon enough, we discovered that waterskins worn over our feet and tied about our ankles prevented feet from freezing. Other than tending the animals, the men did little work that morning. Instead, they played in the snow like children.

By mid-afternoon, the snow had disappeared, leaving soppy mud and the smell of wet earth. Elimelech, whom I'd never seen idle, lay inside our tent, covered in blankets, shivering. I brought him warm milk sweetened with honey. "I can't have you falling sick on me," I said.

"I have no intention of falling sick." He sat up and took the cup. "I'm just not accustomed to such cold." He drank and then handed the cup back.

"You've been working too hard." He'd awakened several nights complaining of leg cramps.

"We've all been working too hard. I've treated the men badly, driving them when I should have let them rest."

I squeezed his hand. "Don't be so hard on yourself."

"Am I too hard on our sons?"

"It isn't good for them to be lazy and spoiled."

"Like Achilla's daughters?" He gave me a wan smile.

"Yes, like them."

"They're pretty. Especially the younger one. I understand why Killion enjoys going to the village." Elimelech's eyes twinkled. I breathed a sigh of relief for it had been a long time since his eyes twinkled.

"We'll find Killion a proper wife in Bethlehem," I said. "As soon as we return, I'll make enquiries about suitable girls."

"Girls with no brothers and who have fields to inherit. It should be done soon. Killion is growing up fast that way."

"That way?"

"Lusting after women."

Elimelech looked pleased, as though it was good that his son behaved like one of his prized rams. He lay back and pulled me down beside him. We lay there, arms wrapped around each other. "Do you know why I wanted to marry you, Naomi?"

"No. Tell me."

"Because you laughed. It was time for me to choose a wife. Past time. You know how it is that I have to have everything ready and in order before I do something important. I went to your father's house. I'd seen you three girls. You, Imla, and Dorcus. Many times. At the well. At celebrations. You, singing and dancing. Imla and Dorcus, too. But I was too busy counting my sheep to pay attention." He stopped to chuckle. "Yes, even then, *especially* then, I did a lot of sheep counting as I struggled to make something of myself.

"The day I went to see your father about the possibility of a wife among his daughters, the three of you were cooking stew in the back yard. Dorcus was fussing at Imla. I think Imla had left out the salt. But you were laughing. Your father and I climbed to the roof with your laughter ringing in my ears, and I thought how pleasant it would be to hear your laughter until the end of my days."

I nestled closer to him. *Naomi* meant pleasant, and I *had* been the pleasant one, the happy one. But I'd been afraid no man would want me because of my height. "You must try harder than other girls," my mother told me repeatedly. "A good wife is meek and obedient, but you're taller than most women and might frighten a man into thinking you won't be humble. And if a prospective husband learns how outspoken you are, or how you question everything . . .." My mother always sighed and shook her head at that point.

"I don't think I've learned to be a meek and obedient wife."

Elimelech laughed. A thrill of pleasure ran through me at the hearty, robust laugh, the first one since his return from the Land of Reuben.

He drew back to look in my eyes. "Why do you think you should be meek and obedient?"

"Am I not supposed to be?"

"No."

Surprised, I sat up. "No?"

He threw back the covers, stood, and reached for his cloak. "It's disgraceful to lie in bed in the middle of the afternoon. A fine example I am." He threw his cloak around his shoulders.

I grabbed his ankle, so he couldn't walk away. "Why should I not be meek and obedient?"

"You're my partner, not my servant."

That night, we were about to retire to our tent when Elimelech glanced skyward. "Look, a falling star." His moved his arm in an arc, following the path of the star. "An omen," he said.

Chapter 36

The following morning, the weather warmed so Elimelech decided to go to the field to judge how much work needed to be done before barley could be planted. He also mentioned something about removing rocks. A minor rockslide had dumped a few dozen small boulders near the south hill where rows needed to be ploughed.

"Take Arioch and Festus to move the rocks." I was at the fire pit, boiling cochineal insects for dye.

"They're mending the stall for fattening lambs." He had a water skin draped over his shoulder. "As soon as the stall is finished, we'll all work on the field."

"Then why do *you* have to go? You could help with the stall and it would be finished that much sooner."

"You're being contrary this morning." He set the water skin down and knelt to retie his sandals. – his old sandals. The straps would wear completely through before he'd use the new ones Kir had bought him in Kir-Harseth. "I'm merely having a look to see how things stand in the field. When I finish looking, I'll help with the stall."

"Fine. Have a look. But don't move boulders."

"Yes, my queen." He stood, saluted, and, as he strode away, called over his shoulder, "There's a red streak on your brow."

"Before the day is over, I'll have red streaks in more places than just my brow."

He walked away, and I went back to stirring my red brew. Later, I'd send someone to make sure he wasn't lifting boulders. He needed to let the younger men do that job. Against my wishes, my husband hadn't eased up working even though he'd become pale, sniffled with a cold, and awakened at nights with leg cramps. I looked forward to the summer sun putting color in his face and a spring in his step.

Instead of sending someone else to check on Elimelech, I went myself and found him stooping over, pulling weeds on the opposite side of the field from where the boulders lay.

"Is something wrong?" he asked, straightening.

"Since you're not lifting boulders, there's nothing wrong. You said you would check the field and then come back to help with the stall."

"And so I shall." He lifted his hand toward the sky. "The sun here is warmer than in the shade where the men are working so I was tempted to pull a few weeds and feel its warmth on my back for a while longer. But I'm coming now. I'll get my water skin." He stood, nodded to where the skin lay on top of one of the boulders, and started toward it.

I turned and left.

As the sun approached the midpoint in the sky, I washed the red from my hands as best I could and went to join the others beneath the oak for a simple lunch of bread, honey, and labneh. Abi had taken a basket of food earlier to the mute and Machlon whose turn it was to guard the flock. Mesha leaned against a tree, nursing Uriah.

"Where's Elimelech?" I asked as I brought out cups.

"He went to the field," Killion answered, reaching for the bread.

"Again?"

"He went just once that I know of." He tore off a piece and crammed it in his mouth.

"That was earlier this morning," I said. "He was returning to help with the stall when I saw him last."

Killion shrugged. "Then he must have gone to check on Blackfoot's progress with the ewes."

Except for Kir, the others laughed and made comments about Blackfoot's virility.

Kir rose. "I'll look for him." He set off at a run toward the field.

Peeved with my husband for not coming back when he said he would, I looked toward the flock, but the sheep were too far away to see if Elimelech had gone there. I went to where Mesha had finished nursing. "Let me take him," I said. "You go and eat."

She handed the baby to me. "He's growing."

"Yes. He looks bigger every day." I gave his plump cheek a tweak.

"And well he should." Mesha closed her tunic, covering her exposed breast. "If he keeps eating like this he's going to be as big as Arioch."

"My son will be as big and strong as Samson himself," Arioch called from where he sat.

"As long as he's not as dumb," Killion said.

"Killion!" I warned. "We've heard that story one time too many."

Killion grinned. "Wouldn't you agree Samson was dumb to marry a Philistine woman and, at the wedding, tell the guests a riddle, betting they couldn't come up with the answer in three days? Then the dumb ox tells his bride the answer and she tells the Philistines."

"That's enough." As I held Uriah to my shoulder to burp him, I looked toward where Kir and Elimelech should be returning from the field.

"My son won't be stupid," Arioch said. "He's going to be smart like his mother."

"Smart like his mother and big and strong like his father. You have a winning combination there," Killion teased.

A shout came from the field. Then another. Then a "Nooooo."

We ran. All of us. Toward the field, for it was Kir's voice we'd heard. I ran, still holding Uriah until Mesha caught up and grabbed her baby from my arms.

Elimelech lay in the dirt of the field, his eyes lifeless. Kir knelt over him, rocking back and forth, keening.

I threw myself on my husband. "Wake up," I screamed and shook his shoulders. "Wake up. Wake up. Don't do this, Elimelech." Over and over, I shouted, "Don't leave me. Come back."

Someone pulled me away.

"He's already in Sheol," another whispered.

I lay on the ground wailing while they covered Elimelech with someone's cloak.

They carried me to my tent. Did they prop me up as I walked? Did they pick me up and carry me? Did they drag me? I don't know. How can I describe the darkness of that day, how I thought the world had ended, how time stopped, how the sun dared shine. I lay in a stupor while they dug a grave, hurrying to finish before nightfall.

The news blew on the wind, over the hill and down to the village. They came. Achilla and his family, his cousin, his brother, Gideon and Habish, women I'd stood at the well with, people I didn't know but who I'd observed wandering about the village. Someone led me out of my tent, and I sprinkled myrrh on my beloved's body. Then they brought rocks to cover his burial place while they lamented, their cries rising to shake the white moon.

"Where is Uri?" I asked, although I knew that he, too, had become still. We needed him. We needed his song. Then I became angry at Uri, for this was his fault. *He* had been the cause of my husband's death.

When they laid the last rock, the men shaved their heads and beards and wallowed in ashes. I, too, rubbed ashes on my body and tore at my hair and clothes.

Throughout all this, I heard – but didn't know I heard until later – Kir as he kept repeating, "He was gray and gasping for breath, and then he became still." Kir said it over and over as though trying to convince himself that his master had died. *He was gray and gasping for breath, and then he became still.*

He became still. He became still.

Chapter 37

When the seven prescribed days of mourning passed, my sons staggered to life like sick sheep regaining their footing. Wearing looks of surprise, pain, and confusion, they did what they had to do. I, however, remained lifeless. Even when I noticed what went on around me, I failed to make sense of it.

Mesha blossomed while the others blundered about. Only later did I realize that, instead of the pleasant piece of fluff I'd judged her to be, she proved the strongest among us. She took over, instructing Hada and Abi what to do. Her round face hovering over me, she fed me like a baby, putting food in my mouth and ordering me to chew. She brought water to bathe my hands and face. When she decided it was time to invite life back into my body, she made me walk in the hills with her to collect greens. She forced me to shell broad beans and pull weeds from the garden. Sometimes, she handed Uriah to me and asked me to swaddle him, or un-swaddle him, or burp him, or any of a dozen other things she thought of to keep me busy. I followed her orders. Doing what I was told was easier than protesting.

Sometimes I did something and had no recollection of having done it until someone told me later. When Mesha insisted I needed more saffron for dye, we went together to collect crocuses on the south hill. When we returned, I collapsed in front of our campfire, exhausted. During that time I was always exhausted. I closed my eyes, thinking only of the warmth of the fire. Then I smelled the hay-like fragrance of the saffron threads, opened my eyes, and wondered why there was a basket full of purple flowers in my lap.

"We gathered it," Mesha said when I questioned her.

One day she led me to my loom, made me sit, then set a basket of wool beside me.

"Uriah will be toddling soon," she said. "He needs a tunic."

The next day, I saw the partially woven piece and wondered who had done it.

I was vaguely aware of the field being plowed and barley planted.

But of one thing I was very aware. Elimelech had worn his old sandals to the field that day. His new ones lay just inside our tent opening. One day, Mesha tried to take them away, perhaps thinking that if she hid them, I'd forget. I protested with such vehemence that no one touched my husband's sandals. They continued to lay just inside our tent opening.

Nights, as I lay beneath Elimelech's cloak, I'd sometimes awaken, smell his sweat, and, for a few brief moments, think he lay beside me.

Day followed day; week followed week. New lambs were born. *A fine harvest of lambs*, Elimelech would have said. I cried over each lamb as though it were a child who would never know its father.

Little by little, I awoke from my torpor and became aware of the extra hours the men put in to make up for Elimelech's not being there. I saw how Machlon strove to step into the shoes of his father, and how Arioch and Kir tried to make that easier by asking Machlon questions they already knew the answers to; how they appeared to defer to his judgement even when they knew he'd made a bad choice. They'd look as though they were about to carry out Machlon's wishes, but then Kir would suggest another choice that might be considered. Thankfully, Machlon listened.

My heart opened to both bondsmen. Yes, even Kir. I'd almost forgotten about his mal-shaped face and beady eyes. I forgave him the hidden stash he'd crammed into the tree trunk and tried to convince myself that what he had there was nothing more than mementoes of a past life. Something of his mother's perhaps. How much he'd loved and revered my husband was abundantly evident.

One day, resting inside my tent, I heard Achilla's voice. "He's come for our sheep," I hissed at the walls of the tent and then realized how illogical the thought was. Even Achilla wouldn't be so cruel as to take advantage of us now. I opened the flap and looked out. Achilla, accompanied by Ruth, had brought two donkeys, one loaded with wineskins, the others with baskets. Arioch and Machlon were helping him untie the cords that bound the burdens to the animal.

When Machlon saw me watching, he said, "Achilla has brought us wine."

"And nuts, figs, and olives," Arioch added.

When I went to greet our visitors, Ruth knelt at my feet. "We can't make up for your loss, but please accept these gifts as tokens that we're thinking of you." She looked up at me, her eyes so full of sympathy that I relented in my harsh judgement of her idleness.

"Toda," I said. "But you don't have to kneel." I touched her on the shoulder and she rose.

"If you'll allow it, my two mothers would like to come soon. And my sister."

"They'll be very welcome." I longed to be surrounded by family and friends.

"My wives would also like for you to visit them whenever you wish," Achilla said. "They enjoy your company."

"Then I will come."

The ripening of barley was delayed for reasons I didn't try to understand. Machlon, following Kir's advice, decided to shear the sheep while waiting for the grain heads to emerge from their stalks. I couldn't sit inside my tent forever and leave the work to others so, when the wool lay in great piles waiting to be washed, I pushed up my sleeves and went to help. Even though the sheep had been washed before shearing, the wool needed a second washing to be thoroughly cleansed of dirt, dung, and tares.

At the end of the third day of wool washing, after the dishes from our evening meal had been scrubbed, I went to my tent early. Later, when I thought everyone had drifted away to their own tents, I started for the trees to relieve myself and heard my sons arguing.

"I'm not a shepherd," Killion said vehemently. "I can't stand another day of sitting in the accursed pasture, doing nothing."

"You call taking care of our sheep *doing nothing?*" Machlon snapped. "The sheep are our wealth."

"*Your* wealth. You forget, I'm the second son."

"And *you* forget that you get a share of them."

"A share. Find someone else to care for your sheep. I won't stay out there another day with no one to talk to and nothing to do but sit and pace and then sit and pace some more."

"No one to talk to? Arioch has been out every afternoon, and the two of you appear to enjoy more merriment than the rest of us put together. Even here, around our campfire, we can hear you laughing and being boisterous out there."

"Arioch's company for a sliver of the day counts for next to nothing. Find someone else to take care of your sheep. Hire a shepherd. I give you two days. After that, I'll leave them out there alone with the mute."

I was about to step in, but Killion wasn't finished.

"You think you're going back to Bethlehem and marry Galatia, but you know very well you aren't."

"I am," Machlon said, his voice rising. "We're going back, and I'll marry Galatia."

"Did you not hear what Cyrus said when he came back from his last trip? The rains didn't come. For the third year, there'll be no harvest in Judea. Go back, and you'll lose the flock." Killion's voice was spiteful. "You'll destroy Father's whole reason for coming here, losing everything we've worked for. There wasn't enough forage when we left: there'll be even less now."

I sank to my knees in misery.

"And Galatia is already married." Killion continued. "You know her parents insisted she marry at sixteen, otherwise her ass of a father thinks her bride price will go down. Nor will he risk you not coming back at all and Galatia being too old to find another husband. Be assured, she's married by now, brother."

The words stabbed my heart for Killion was right. Galatia would be married. I heard the crunch of leaves as Killion passed through the trees on the way to his tent. A single sob came from Machlon. My son, my sweet baby boy, was in pain. He'd lost both his father and the woman he was to marry. I rose, intending to go to him, but I heard the crunch of pinecones as he left in the opposite direction from his brother.

Chapter 38

Every tree limb low enough to be reached was covered with fleeces. The loose wool, shorn by the least experienced shearers, was spread on cloths making our camp look almost as it had when the snow came. It *would* look like snow if the wind scattered the loose wool so, as I picked dead insects from what would eventually become clothes for someone, I prayed that the day remain windless. As for the insects, wind or no, they persisted in dying atop the springy fibers. I flicked away the greenish carapace of a beetle, a dead fly's wings, a brittle moth.

With every motion of my fingers, I agonized over my sons' argument and the reasons for it. The drought. Galatia's impatient parents. Our being here when we should have been at home.

And I was angry with my husband. He'd left me alone to deal with my sons. They needed their father's guidance, yet he'd gone. Yes, as illogical as it was, I was angry with Elimelech. I needed him. His sons needed him.

Machlon, his hands and arms bloody from butchering a wether, came to the cistern near where I worked. He filled a basin, immersed his hands, and then splashed water over his arms. After drying hands and arms on a scrap of cloth, he gave me a brief look then walked away

"Machlon," I called, stopping him. "Come with me."

I brushed my hands together, ridding them of flecks of dead insects, and then led him to the fallen oak. For the first time in weeks I took close notice of my son's face. How had I failed to see how exhausted, how troubled, he was? Not yet twenty-one, he had become head of the household and was trying to measure up to his father.

"Killion . . ..," I began.

"He's unhappy." Machlon closed his eyes.

"We're all unhappy. Can you not find a shepherd from the village?"

"I'll look for someone." Opening his eyes, he swallowed. "Galatia . . .."

"I know." My son was heart-broken. The bride-daughter I expected to welcome into my home would be married to someone else.

"Killion wants to stay here," Machlon said at length.

"Stay here!" I looked at him in disbelief. "What is Killion thinking? That's impossible."

"He thinks he can marry Orpah and inherit half her father's flock and half his field."

"Israelites are forbidden to marry Moabites."

"Israelite women are forbidden to marry Moabite men. Israelite men may marry Moabite women if the women convert."

"Surely, you're not on his side." I said it with such force that Machlon drew back. "*You* don't want to stay here."

"No, mother, I don't. But my hot-bloodied brother has lusted after Orpah since the first time he saw her. And her father is rich. Killion sees her as a prize."

"Women are not prizes." Women had often been prizes, but I could no longer accept things as they had been. "Your father never treated me as such."

"I'm sorry. I didn't . . .. I just meant . . .." Machlon squeezed my hand. "Had you been a prize, Mother, you'd have been the most wonderful prize of all. Father was blessed to have you." A lump formed in my throat.

Machlon let go of my hand and looked away. "Killion, will soon turn twenty, and he wants what men want: riches and a beautiful woman. My arguments against this are as powerless as a tear-drop falling on a boulder."

"Orpah is going to marry Gideon."

"I hope so."

"Find a shepherd, Machlon. That should make Killion a little happier."

He nodded. "I will."

I found Killion sitting on a rock in the pasture, sulking.

When he saw me coming, he jumped up. "Mother, why are you here?"

"To talk to you."

A leery look crossed his face. "I don't think you intend idle conversation."

"You're right." I took in his full beard, the well-developed muscles, the determined face. He was no longer a boy.

"Machlon will hire a shepherd," I began.

A master at reading my thoughts, Killion waited, for he knew there was more.

"We *will* go back to Bethlehem," I said. "All of us." I waited for a retort but he only looked at me.

"There are beautiful girls in Bethlehem whose fathers have no sons. You'll inherit your share of your father's sheep as well as those of another man along with his field."

"Can you name these girls?" His voice was bitter.

Often, in my grief, I could barely remember what I'd done a few moments before. Even had I remembered who these girls were, things might have changed – brothers born, girls promised as brides, fathers ruined.

"Well, mother, have you thought of any suitable girls?" He raised his eyebrows.

"They're there. Gideon is going to marry Orpah. Meanwhile, your brother needs your support. He'll free you of your duties with the flock as soon as he finds a shepherd."

Cyrus came that afternoon. He'd just returned from the land of two rivers where he'd sold Achilla's grain reserve. "You've lost a good man, Naomi," he said. "I've seen few his equal." Then, after giving Machlon a hug, he pushed him to arms' length, and said, "I'm sorry about your father, but you'll measure up."

"Come and sit," I said, my voice breaking. "Tell us about your travels."

We sat beneath the cedar, and Hada brought water.

"The north countries will have a shortfall in their grain harvest this year." Cyrus took a cup from Hada, gulped down the water, and held out the cup for more. "The rains were nothing more than pitiful sprinklings. Another year of the same and their flocks will be diminished. We'll be able to sell them lambs at a good price."

"Speaking of flocks," Machlon said. "We need a shepherd. Do you know of one?"

Cyrus set the cup down. "I'll find someone." He rubbed his chin. "Achilla would like to offer you a means of disposing of your wool."

I shot a look at Machlon whose eyes had taken on a look of suspicion.

"I take Achilla's wool to Egypt where he can get a better price than on the King's Highway," Cyrus said. "You already know that, but maybe not that the villagers also entrust their wool to him. He offers to include yours as well."

"He gets a commission from the sale?" I asked.

Cyrus looked at me in surprise. "Yes. He gets a commission."

"I'm sure Machlon will think on it. You'll let him know about the shepherd?"

Cyrus remained with us for the evening meal. Machlon sent Festus to the pasture to replace Killion so he could join us. For the first time since Elimelech's death, someone laughed. And then someone began to sing. Arioch, I think. My sons and Cyrus joined in. It was a bittersweet moment.

When Cyrus departed, I watched him disappear over the hill then I turned back to our dying campfire. The others, except for Kir, had gone to ready themselves for sleep.

Nervously, Kir rubbed one hand along a thigh.

"Did you want something?" I asked.

"I can be of help checking the stores," he said. "I can measure what we have enough of and what we need more of."

I looked at him dumbly. How strange that Kir would offer to do this. Checking stores was women's work. Could he not see that I, once again, busied myself fulfilling my responsibilities. In any case, Hada would have checked the stores had I failed to.

"Thank you for your offer," I said finally, ". . . but you're already doing more than your share of work. Hada and I will take care of it."

He rubbed his chin.

"Is there something you want to tell me, Kir?"

"Only that . . .." He fidgeted. "Only that I'll do whatever you ask and help you any way I can." He said it rapidly, and I knew this was not what he really wanted to say. There was something else.

Chapter 39

The sun not yet risen, Machlon came to where I fanned embers in the bread oven. They caught. I threw on kindling, and we held out our hands to warm them. From nearby, came the sound of Hada's pestle.

"What excuse do I offer Achilla for declining his offer to sell our wool?" Machlon asked.

"Say you've never been solely responsible for the sale, and before you forget what your father taught you, you want to have the experience of taking it to market yourself."

Machlon nodded. "The barley will be ready by the beginning of next week. I'll take the wool to Kir-Harseth tomorrow, sell it, and be back in time for the harvest."

Killion could convince a fish it was in his best interest to swim into a fisherman's net, so Machlon took him along to help sell the wool. Festus accompanied them.

They returned late on the fourth day. Killion greeted me with a smile and a kiss on the cheek and then, light of step, went to take care of the donkeys.

"Did you get a good price?" I asked Machlon.

He nodded without smiling.

I set aside the almonds I'd been shelling. "What's wrong?"

"The rains failed to come in Judea. Neither the lesser nor the greater rains came. All the caravaners reported the same."

My heart didn't stop. No chill ran through me. No misery. Just a cold,

cold determination. We'd return despite the drought. We'd have enough barley from this year's harvest to see us through until next year. We'd sell off most of the flock since they couldn't survive in Judea. With the silver from selling wool and sheep, we'd survive.

Machlon looked at me in puzzlement. "I thought you'd be upset."

"I'm sad for the people in Bethlehem. But we'll return despite the drought."

"I don't think . . .."

"We're going back, Machlon. Go see to the barley."

The men began harvesting. Content that we'd be going home soon, I took a break from stringing warp to play with Baby Uriah. Rare moments of contentment penetrated my darkness when I bounced and tickled him for it was then that I thought of my grandchildren. The first grandson would be named Elimelech, the second, Abaddon, for my father. I didn't care what the others were named, only that they *were*. Then I reminded myself: it wouldn't be I who named them. Their parents had that privilege. But no matter; I'd rejoice in grandchildren whatever their names.

As Uriah babbled on my lap, I looked up to see a lanky youth, taller than anyone I'd ever seen, coming down the hill.

"Cyrus sent me," he said when he came to where I was.

"You're a shepherd?"

"I've cared for flocks since I was ten."

"Achilla's flocks?"

He shrugged. "My father's, but it's all the same. Everyone in the village herds their sheep with Achilla's. I'm good with dogs, and I'm not afraid of jackals."

"What's your name?"

"They call me *Tall Boy.*"

"Well, then, Tall Boy, I'll take you to the pasture. Machlon is busy harvesting. He can greet you later."

The flock grazed near the encampment so we didn't have far to go. I sent

Killion from the pasture to help in the field, introduced Tall Boy to the mute, and then left.

◆ ◆ ◆

Achilla's wives and daughters came in the afternoon, bringing dates and pomegranates. The dates, Noa told me, had come from the market on the King's Highway for there were no date trees in the mountains of Moab. I was reluctant to take them. Fruit from someone's own trees was one thing, but to accept a bought gift was another.

As their visit drew to an end, they invited us to celebrate the harvest festival with them.

"We won't be celebrating this year." Had they forgotten that only a few short months ago my husband walked about, vibrant and alive, but now he'd gone? Did they not know we'd be leaving after the harvest?

Killion appeared, carrying a scythe. "I see we have company," he said, glowing from ear to ear. Orpah glowed, too. Had it been night, we'd have had no need of an oil lamp with such brightness between the two.

Killion untethered their donkey and saw them to the foot of the hill then, instead of hurrying back to help in the field, he watched until they disappeared over the crest.

"Leave that girl alone," I snapped when he came in at the end of the day.

"They chose to visit us. I had no part in that."

"You should have stayed in the field. I know how to untether donkeys. She's a Moabitess, Killion."

"What's wrong with a Moabitess?"

"They're our enemies."

"Yet, we came to live among them. We drink water from their well. We celebrate with them. We visit one another. They look and dress as we do. They live in houses like ours and herd their sheep as we do. They plow their fields and harvest their crops in the same manner. They mourned when my father died. Is there a law that says how many years we're required to be enemies?"

"Honor thy parents," I said when I could think of nothing else to say.

"Does that mean I let you choose every twist and turn in my life?" He shook his head and walked away.

Frustrated, I went to see to the preparation of the evening meal. Hada jumped when I entered the cooking tent.

"I didn't mean to startle you," I said. "Is everything alright?"

"The levels in the wine jugs seem to recede faster than we're drinking it."

"How can that be when Achilla brought us more?"

She looked away, as though embarrassed to tell me what I should have observed myself.

"There's something I have to see to," I said and strode away in search of Kir.

I found him in the field counting the sheaves. "You wanted to tell me something the other day," I said.

He kept his eyes on the stack of sheaves.

"Kir, look at me."

Reluctantly, he met my eyes.

"You offered to help check the stores. It was the wine you wanted me to check, wasn't it?"

He moved restlessly, putting his weight on first one leg and then the other. I saw how he both wanted to tell and to not tell.

"Kir, I need to know."

"I hate to cause you grief."

"A little grief now is better than much grief later. Those nights when Arioch went to join Killion in the pasture, did he take wine with him?"

He nodded. "I threatened Arioch. Or tried. But my word means nothing. We can't do without Arioch, and he knows it. He has the strength of two men, and he lends an air of cheer to everything we do which makes the work go faster. As for Killion, he might not like shepherding, but I find no other fault with him. He wants to do what would have made his father happy."

"At least the penalty for stealing wine isn't being stoned to death." I started to walk away but stopped. "Would you have told this to Elimelech were he alive? Without his asking?"

Kir nodded.

"Then treat me as you would have treated my husband. Machlon is young. He can't be expected to control his brother."

"Men drink wine, Mother," Killion argued when I confronted him.

"Men will no longer drink wine in *this* camp," I snapped. "The jars have been sealed."

He looked at me in disbelief. "How often have you known me to drink to excess? But don't answer that. I'll answer for you. Once. Only once. At Arioch's wedding." His face softened. "I'm sorry, Mother. I didn't know how else to deal with my grief. I've upset you. Please, forgive me. I promise . . .."

"The jars have been sealed," I repeated. "And they'll remain that way." He wasn't going to beguile me this time.

"As you say."

His giving in was too easy. I should have taken note.

Chapter 40

"We need to make plans for leaving Moab," I said to Machlon as he stored the scythes after the last sheaf of barley had been bundled.

"We have to thresh, winnow, and then heat the grain for storage. After that, we can make plans."

"Our turn at the threshing floor is still a few days away. We can discuss this now since you're doing nothing but waiting."

"There's plenty of time later."

"Not if we're to leave straightaway. Come. Let's talk." I took him by the hand and led him toward the wadi, away from where the women prepared the evening meal.

"We can't go home yet," he said.

I dropped his hand. "Why not?"

"The weather. When we came, it was *before* the barley harvest. This year, we're having a late harvest. By the time we finish the desert will be scorching. Waiting for cooler weather has a double advantage. The trip will be easier, and the sheep will have had more time to fatten here in Moab."

Though sorely disappointed, I didn't argue for what he said made sense.

That night, the agitated voices of my sons awakened me. Wrapping Elimelech's cloak around me, I crawled to the tent opening, and eased open the flap. In the glow of a full moon, they huddled beside the cold firepit.

"You're head of the family now," Killion said. "You get to make those decisions."

"But mother . . .." Machlon's voice was low, indistinct.

"Mother will love them when they're part of the family."

Them? I was puzzled.

"Par . . . of . . . family," Machlon repeated dumbly, stumbling over his words.

They'd been drinking! I'd checked the wine jugs daily, and no one had toyed with the seals so where . . .?

"Brother, you can't hold your beer, can you?" Killion said. "I'll walk you to the tent. We can talk about this tomorrow when you're sober."

Beer! They'd have gotten it from Gideon and Habish. I felt too sick at heart to go after my sons. I, too, would wait until tomorrow.

Tomorrow. My last thought before falling asleep was that there had been too many *tomorrows* in this accursed place, and my first thought upon waking was that I should be ashamed. Overcome with grief, I'd left my sons to deal with theirs alone, and they'd chosen badly. I had to help them find another way.

At breakfast, Machlon refused food.

"Headache," he mumbled. "The weather's turned too soon hot." He ran to the trees to throw up.

Killion ate quickly then went to load sheaves on the oxen for our turn at the threshing floor would come around midday. I was unable to catch him alone that morning. Not only did he do his own chores, but those of his brother as well. Killion had the talent for angering me greatly and then warming my heart even more.

Three days later, the threshing was finished, and I cornered Killion as he put down fresh hay for the oxen.

"Walk in the trees with me," I said.

He gave me a wary look but followed without protest. Rarely did Killion remain silent, but from the covert looks he cast in my direction I knew he'd noticed my set jaw. We were well into the copse before I stopped and faced him.

"I hardly know what to say," I began. "We sealed the wine containers, yet you find a way to drink. I suppose those ruffians from the village gave it to you?"

Avoiding my eyes, Killion picked up a pinecone and threw it.

"And you're trying to convince your brother to let you marry Orpah."

He looked at me in surprise.

"Don't pretend it isn't so."

He straightened. "Yes, mother, it's so. I want to marry Orpah."

Hearing it from his lips twisted the knife in my belly. "You can't marry a Moabitess."

"An Israelite man can marry a Moabite woman as long as she converts."

I was too wounded to respond.

"Machlon has no problem with this," he said. "Mother, I love her."

"Love! You know nothing of love. You're only nineteen."

"Soon I'll be twenty. You married at sixteen and loved my father."

"A woman marries when she's young. A man establishes himself first."

"And how am I do that? Next week, next year, or ten years from now, I'll still be the second son and, without marriage, I'll have no more than I have now. If I marry Orpah, Achilla will give me sheep."

"That's the reason you want to marry her?"

"I love her, Mother" He fell at my feet, kissing them. "Our lives have been turned upside down. Have you not noticed that Machlon and I suffer the loss of our father? And I've lost something else. A short time ago, I had a brother. Now my brother is head of our household. He's part brother, part master." He looked up with pleading eyes, guile replaced by sincerity. "It's like I'm adrift on the Great Sea, with no harbor in sight. We came here, planning to return. We didn't. A second year, we stayed. Now again, we won't go because the drought continues. There's no certainty about anything. No roots to cling to. I need Orpah."

"You barely know her."

"As well as father knew you. She's beautiful. She's funny. She loves me."

"How do you know?"

He sat back on his heels, the muscles of his face soft. "I know from the way she looks at me. From the way she talks to me."

"I thought she was to marry Gideon."

"She despises Gideon."

"And Achilla? The Mothers? What do they think?"

He rose, his eyes alight with impudence. "They think it's good that we have more sheep than Gideon. And despite my distaste for shepherding, they know I'm more industrious than Gideon."

My son had chosen to ignore Orpah's lack of industry. "Is she ready to assume the duties of a wife? We don't have servants to wait on her."

"Both she and Ruth want purpose in their lives."

He knew these girls better than I'd thought. His trips to the village, the evenings at the top of the hill with the falcons – had Orpah and Ruth been there, too? I asked as much.

He hesitated, then answered, "Sometimes. But there was always someone with them. The Mother, or a servant. Achilla's daughters aren't loose women."

Something inside me was crumbling. It was as though I crossed a stream on a log and in the middle realized the log was about to break apart, and that there was nothing I could do to keep from falling in the water. Though part of me still fought it, I knew I was giving in to Killion's desire. But there was more to come.

I asked Machlon to go with me to deliver food to the shepherds. We left Abi pouting because I'd robbed her of her daily trip to the pasture. She'd begun to think taking food to Tall Boy and the mute was her privilege.

"I spoke with Killion," I said when we were halfway there.

Machlon shot me a sideways glance.

"How often have you drunk too much?" I asked.

"Only twice have you seen me sick."

"Perhaps I haven't been observant enough. Gideon and Habish bring beer when you meet on the hill?"

"And when we see them in the village. I don't like it, but they make fun of me if I don't drink with them. *The rich and proper Israelite,* they taunt. Then they laugh about Moishe being afraid to pass through their land and having to go the long way around. I drink their beer to shut them up. What am I supposed to do, Mother? We have no other friends."

"I'm sorry, Machlon. Truly I am. But promise me you'll do no more than taste and sip in the future." He'd be twenty-one in another week, a grown man by any country's standards, and able to do what he wanted. "The laws say . . .."

"I know what the laws say. I'll taste and sip, as you say. Is that all you wanted to speak to me about?"

"No."

"I guessed as much." He kicked a dried turd from his path. "Killion loves her. He's determined."

"And you agree to this marriage?"

"There won't be peace in our family until it happens. And Achilla wants it."

I stopped. "How do you know?"

He'd taken a step or two beyond me but turned around. "He's referred to it often enough."

"I thought Gideon was to marry Orpah."

"Achilla sees that Killion has more to offer." He shrugged. "Gideon will be angry, but he'll get over it."

I was barely able to lift my feet as we resumed walking.

"I'm sorry, Mother," Machlon said. "You didn't ask to come to Moab, nor did you have any control over the drought that drove us here. You had nothing to do with Uri, or what he did, or with his death. Or with Father's death. And now this. You deserve better. But know this: you're the best mother possible, and both Killion and I love you." He took my hand.

"What must be, must be," I managed to say.

"Oh, Mother. . ... There's more. . ... I'm to marry Ruth. Achilla has decided his daughters must marry together."

Chapter 41

I visited Achilla's household and professed happiness over the union of our families. A few days later, Hoglah and Noa, along with The Mother, and my future bride-daughters came, and we began planning the festivities which would take place when the leaves began to change color.

Achilla purchased tents for the two couples and sent servants to help erect them. Furnishings began to arrive from the village – rugs, pillows, a low table for each tent. Achilla promised to send men to build a house when the spring rains were over. I didn't argue with him, or tell him we were returning to Bethlehem, taking his daughters with us. Or not taking them, if they chose not to go.

While keeping these thoughts to myself, I discovered there were two of me: one that ooohed and ahhhhed over the gifts, the plans for the feast, the beauty of Orpah and Ruth, while the other me crouched deep inside, resentful of what I'd lost and was about to lose – husband, sons, home, friends, kin, and the right to hold up my head unashamed.

In addition to the tents and furnishings, Achilla agreed to give as dowry for each of his daughters, ten sheep, ten jugs of olive oil, and ten of wine. We had little to give as presents to his family. "Woven goods," suggested The Mother.

I set to work, but not happily. Abi helped me weave while Hada and Mesha spun wool every moment they could spare from other duties. Uriah had begun to toddle about so Mesha kept dropping her spindle to run after her son. Our hands and arms were streaked with red, indigo, and umber. The area stank from dyes.

"How is Gideon taking this?" I asked Machlon when he passed my loom one morning.

He dropped the hoe he carried and sank down beside me. "Achilla plans to send Gideon and Habish to Egypt with Cyrus to sell the village's olive oil, and The Mother is looking for wives for them in another village."

I hoped they'd be in Egypt a very long time.

Meanwhile, Abi sulked. She had little fits of anger. She took up Damaris' habit of spitting when something didn't please her. When I stationed her behind my loom to help, she wore the look of a viper and complained. She studied her fingernails and frowned when I tried to talk to her.

"Why are you being difficult?" I asked finally. Half a saffron-colored piece was formed on the loom between us.

She examined her thumbnail then stuck it in her mouth, bit off the end, and spit it out. "I should be getting married," she said. "You promised when we got back to Bethlehem you'd find a husband for me, but we haven't gone back. I don't even know if we *are* going back. And sometimes you don't let me carry the food to Tall Boy and the mute."

I blew out an irritated huff. "We barely have time to finish the weaving, but I promise, as soon as we're done you can be the one to take food to the shepherds again. We *are* going back to Bethlehem, and I *will* find you a husband."

She contorted her face as though she didn't believe me. I hadn't meant to deceive her when we'd promised to return after the first year. Or after the second year. Had I known we'd still be here, I'd never have made those promises.

My fingers became raw from handling the wool, and my back ached from long hours at the loom, but the results of my labor were gifts for each person in Achilla's family. Robin's egg blue for Ruth. Bright yellow for Noa. White with blue borders for Orpah. yellow for Achilla, and a brighter yellow for Hoglah. And for The Mother, a striped piece using all the colors.

My sons and I delivered them two weeks before the wedding. After bestowing our gifts, we drank spiced pomegranate wine on the roof with Achilla and the women. When we descended the ladder to leave, we found Gideon and Habish at the bottom scowling at us.

"Greetings," Killion said with a smile. He smiled constantly now.

The nephews swept their gazes between Killion and Machlon. Then, as one, they turned their backs to us and stood with arms crossed.

"Come," Machlon said motioning us forward. "They're not in a friendly mood today."

"No, we're not in a friendly mood," Habish snarled. "Accursed Israelites."

"*You shall be cursed, thus sayeth the Lord,*" Gideon shouted as we walked away. Then he erupted into wild laughter.

I stepped between my sons, put my hands on their arms, and urged them to move faster.

Achilla sent his servants to ready the food for the wedding feast, for we'd told him that our bondsmen and serving women were our only family and that they must come with us when it was time.

Machlon and Killion led the procession over the hill and down into the village where we were met by the villagers. Clapping and singing, they followed. Some had brought instruments. They merrily beat drums, slapped tambourines, and plucked lyres, while shouting obscene remarks about the marriage bed, regaling the crowd with laughter. Achilla's kin had crowded onto his roof and shouted gayly to the crowd below as we arrived.

We waited in front of the entrance, the revelry increasing with calls demanding that Achilla present his daughters. He finally stepped out and, holding up his hands to quiet the crowd, bowed his head in greeting to his new sons-in-law. Then he spread his arms wide. "My daughters," he proclaimed.

He moved aside and, the crowd roaring its approval, Orpah and Ruth stepped forth, veiled, adorned with jewelry, hands covered with designs from henna. Led by the bridal pairs, the merry crowd paraded away, singing and dancing through the streets, over the hill, and down to our camp.

I set aside my sadness. A mother likes to see her children happy, and

Killion was indeed happy. What could I do other than be glad for him?

And Machlon? I couldn't read the look on his face. Was it contentment? Nervousness?

When we reached our encampment, my sons led Achilla's daughters into their tents, and thus were they married.

We feasted for three days, servants running back and forth to the village to bring more food and wine, for the attendees ate and drank far more than expected.

The two newly-married couples must have slipped from their tents to relieve themselves from time to time, but I never saw them. We left plates of food in front of the door flaps. When the food disappeared, we left more.

Only Aaron, Achilla's brother and father of Gideon and Habish, didn't share the joy. He sat off to the side, sulking. He'd thought *his* sons, not mine, would marry Achilla's daughters. Meanwhile, I entertained the impossible hope that Gideon and Habish would remain in Egypt.

Chapter 42

The newly-weds emerged from their tents after seven days, my bride-daughters blushing, my sons puffed up. Having been raised to be idle, neither Ruth nor Orpah offered to help prepare breakfast. Instead, they settled beneath the cedar tree, chatting and laughing, undoubtedly comparing their week in the bridal tents while the rest of us served the men. When my bride-daughters saw that the men had finished, they ran to wash their hands and join the women for our meal.

It was lambing season. While we women ate our breakfast, Machlon, Killion, and Kir went to check on newborns and rescue any lambs unable to suckle because of being the weaker in a set of triplets. I had doubts that my sons were ready to step into their father's shoes when it came to the sheep. Elimelech had been the best breeder in Bethlehem. Now, the future of our flock lay in the hands of my inexperienced sons, both giddy from their week of pleasure. At least Kir was with them. I'd accused Elimelech of depending too much on his bondsman, of listening to his advice. Now I expected Machlon to do the same.

While I worried about the sheep, Mesha did what I should have been doing., engaging Ruth and Orpah in conversation. She chatted about her son who sat in her lap, grabbing food from her hand, making everyone laugh. She described the huge honeycomb we found on the south hill, then rattled on about new lambs and noisy birds. I gave secret thanks for my silly, talkative serving woman.

Then Ruth said something to me and waited for a response.

"Please forgive me," I said. "But I was thinking of the new lambs. Later, we can take a walk to the pasture if you like."

"Oh, can we?" Orpah looked excited.

"I'd like to do that," Ruth said.

"Tell me what you were saying that I was so rudely ignoring."

"I was saying that Orpah and I were never expected to do what other women do, and that we're both eager to learn . . . .." Ruth looked at Orpah who nodded in agreement. "We want to be good wives. We beg you to teach us."

"You will be good wives. I can see that. And of course, I'll teach you. Shall we begin with cleaning the breakfast dishes?"

And so, we began. By the time the men came for the midday meal, my bride daughters were weary to the bone. That afternoon after we went to look at the new lambs, I suggested they rest. Soon enough, they'd become accustomed to work, and I didn't want to overtire them for perhaps they already carried my grandsons.

That year many ewes threw triplets. The job of feeding the extra lambs was a task for which I was grateful. If they all survived, our flock would be what it had been before leaving Bethlehem. Elimelech would have been proud.

Both girls – I shouldn't have called Ruth and Orpah girls, but I did for they were so young – cried over the binding of the ram lambs. Despite their father owning a large flock, they'd never seen testicles being bound.

"It's cruel," Orpah stormed at Killion. "Why must you do that?"

"Every sheep owner does. We want to control which rams impregnate the ewes. This way we get to pick the best breeder."

"Blackfoot is father of the entire flock?" Ruth asked.

"Mostly. The sweeper takes care of the ones Blackfoot misses."

I thought of Little Samson seeding Achilla's flock. Then I thought Of Uri. And of Elimelech, for he never left my mind. How long did one hurt from such a loss?

It was good that my bride daughters came to me knowing little. Teaching them to weave, garden, and bake bread gave us something to talk about. Orpah especially liked preparing food for her husband, thus Killion was the recipient of many treats. But she hated pounding grain. Hada, who had taken a liking to her, would, after a few tries on Orpah's part take over, saying that so long as Orpah knew how to do it, that was fine. She'd probably never have to grind grain on a daily basis.

Both Orpah and Ruth knew the basics of weaving, but neither had practiced enough to be proficient. Their pieces turned out loose and irregular. They showed distaste for dying, complaining of the stink. When they couldn't wash the dye from their hands, they tried to hide them from their husbands. Killion laughingly forced Orpah's hands from where she stuck them in the folds of her tunic, made some silly comment, and then kissed them.

Machlon's and Ruth's relationship was a quieter one, but there was an ease in my son's eyes. Ruth quietly took care of his needs, seeing that he had food, bringing him water when he worked, dusting off his sandals. She also monitored the wine he drank. I wondered why she thought to do that.

The time soon came when I had to explain to Ruth and Orpah that they must separate themselves from their husbands for seven days, that their husbands could neither touch them nor sit where their bleeding wives had sat. I was disappointed for I'd hoped at least one of them would be carrying my grandchild. The attention they heaped on Uriah made me believe that was a sign they were with child. But I was to be disappointed over and over.

Weeks passed. My sons were happy. Sometimes at the end of a day, Killion and Orpah wandered into the trees where I'd hear them laughing.

"You're happy," I said to Machlon one evening when Killion and Orpah had disappeared. Machlon sat against the cedar tree, his feet outstretched, a look of contentment on his face.

"Yes, Mother. I'm happy. I hope Galatia is happy, too. Do you think she is?"

"I'm sure of it. Her mother would find someone to make her happy."

"I'm glad."

I searched his face.

"Ruth is a fine woman," he said.

"Yes."

"Trust her if ever the need arises."

"Of course, I'll trust her." I had no idea why my son would make such a strange statement.

"She shouldn't be blamed because her mother taught her nothing," Machlon said.

"I don't blame her. She learns willingly and never complains." Then I admitted what I never thought I'd admit about Moabite bride-daughters: "My life isn't so lonely with them here."

The sound of a broken chord from a harp rippled through the air. And then another and another, followed by the plucking of a tune. I looked around trying to discover where the music came from.

"It's Ruth," Machlon said with a smile. "Over there." He nodded to where Ruth's dark form reclined against a tree.

"I didn't know . . . .."

"You've kept her too busy. She's had little energy left for playing the harp. Killion and I used to sit on the ground outside her house and listen when she played on the roof." He threw me a quick glance. "Not often, since you and father conspired to keep us away from the village as much as possible."

I smiled. "A lot of good it did."

Arioch, about to bank the fire, sat back on his heels, and listened. Mesha came from the tent where she'd put Uriah down for the night and sat cross-legged beside Arioch, her hand on his thigh as she inclined her head toward where the music came from. Hada, returning after relieving herself, stopped and tilted her head in the same direction. Even Abi, about to go into the tent for the night, stopped to hear.

As he often did, Kir sat off by himself. If he enjoyed the music, he gave no indication.

"She's an artist," I said when the last note died away. I forgave Ruth her clumsiness at the loom in the face of such ability.

"She'll teach our children to play," Machlon said. "And our children will teach their children. We'll be a family of harp players."

From then on, Ruth played for us most nights as we settled down, at peace with the world as we hadn't been since Uri left.

Chapter 43

When I went with Ruth and Orpah to visit Hoglah and Noa each week, I sensed a new found pride as they described what they'd learned and done. Orpah chattered at length about the dishes she prepared, how she cleared weeds from the sprouting beans, how she'd mastered making goat cheese. Ruth added those things Orpah left out, especially how we fed the lambs by hand. I was proud of my daughters. Even their weaving was improving, though they'd never be experts.

As another season of barley planting neared, the men worked long and hard, clearing and re-clearing the field. One day, Ruth, Orpah, and I went to watch the sheep so Tall Boy and the mute could help with a final clearing for on the morrow planting would begin. Since neither I nor my daughters could wield a sling, we hoped the donkeys grazing with the flock would frighten away any jackals tempted to make a meal of our lambs.

We spread a blanket on the ground, took out the bundle of wool we'd brought, and began spindling. With the warm sun on our backs, we spun in a leisurely fashion. Ruth and Orpah fell into a conversation about how one of their neighbors dyed all of her wool the same two colors – an awful umber and a muddy yellow. The neighbor wove the two colors in varying width stripes, sometimes the yellow wide and the umber narrow, sometimes the opposite, but no matter the arrangement of stripes, the cloth always came out looking like a plowed mud field. Laughing, they told me how the neighbor's husband finally refused to wear clothes from her cloth, insisting that he preferred the natural wool color like most people's clothes. The day wore on with other stories. I began to feel at ease with the world.

Mid-afternoon, one of the dogs began barking wildly. We sprang up and looked to where the dog jumped around, snarling and growling, his eyes intent on something. A lion? A jackal? But he seemed to be barking at something on the ground. A snake? The dog ran a few paces toward us then turned and ran back to yelp at the ground. While we stood there, afraid to move, the dog repeated his actions as though he wanted us to come see.

"It's a snake," Orpah said, her arms clutched tightly to her chest. "

"If it were a snake wouldn't it have already slithered away?" Ruth looked at me for confirmation.

"I believe so." I took a few steps toward the agitated dog, Ruth and Orpah at my heels.

Now that the dog had our attention, he began running short circuits between us and whatever it was he saw. We edged closer, the tall grass concealing the object of the dog's attention. I was terrified of what might be coiled or crouched with fangs bared.

Then reason took hold. Whatever it was hadn't harmed the dog, and there was a ewe standing nearby. Had it been something dreadful, the ewe would have fled. I went bravely forward, and there it was: a hole. A gaping sinkhole. Inside were two lambs too scared to bleat. When I let out an audible sigh of relief that today we'd live, that there was no lion to eat us, no snake to poison us, the lambs opened their mouths and bleated. The ewe, who had come to stand at the edge of the hole, answered her babes with a loud bray.

I knelt beside the hole "We have to get them out."

Orpah knelt beside me while Ruth lay down on her stomach and tried to reach for one of the lambs, but the hole was too deep.

We stared at them for a few moments. Now that he'd succeeded in bringing us over to take care of the problem, the dog settled on his haunches to watch. I pushed the ewe away.

"Not you, too," I said. "Getting two lambs out is going to be difficult enough."

"One of us has to get in the hole," Ruth said. "I'll do it."

Before I could protest, she slid into the shoulder-deep hole.

"Ugh," she said, looking down at her feet which had sunk into the mud at the bottom. She pulled each foot up with a sucking sound, but as soon as she put one foot down to pick up the other, the first foot sank into the mud again.

Orpah laughed.

"If you think it's so funny, then you crawl in too." Ruth said.

"Oh, I think muddy holes suit you much better than me." Orpah's eyes danced. "Hand up the lambs so we can get you out."

Ruth rolled her eyes as she grabbed one of the lambs. I crouched down ready to take it but her lack of strength allowed her to lift it only halfway.

"It's going to take two people," I said.

"You'll to have to join me in the hole, sister." Ruth's eyes danced as Orpah's had done earlier.

Orpah let out a huff, turned around so that she could slide in backwards, and then let herself down. "Ugh, ugh, ugh," she said as her feet sank into the mud.

Ruth laughed.

I wanted to laugh, too, but getting the lambs out was uppermost in my mind. "I'm ready if you can lift them." I braced myself.

Together, the two girls lifted the first lamb. Wrapping my arms around her wooly body, I heaved her out. The lamb wasn't so heavy, but then I realized my arms had grown strong after pulling buckets of water from the well for many, many years while those of my bride daughters had not. I set the lamb down. She ran to her mother who sniffed suspiciously at her mud-covered offspring.

After rescuing the second lamb, I reached down to help first Orpah and then Ruth from the hole. Ruth pushed Orpah from behind, helping her up, then, together, Orpah and I dragged Ruth out. They were covered in mud from head to toe.

"You're a mud baby," Orpah taunted. Even Ruth's face was smeared with mud.

"You're not so pretty yourself," Ruth shot back. "What do you think of your two bride daughters now, Naomi? Are we not the most beautiful women in the land?"

"You're streaked with mud, too, Naomi," Orpah said. "We're all mud babies."

My tunic was covered, my hands caked, my face smeared.

We laughed. We laughed until tears ran from our eyes. Then we laughed some more.

When Tall Boy and the mute returned to take over the flock, they stared at us in disbelief. We related what happened, then returned to the camp and told the story again, each time laughing.

"Goodnight, my daughters," I said to them that evening when it came time to sleep. I hugged each, and each hugged me back. A warm, true hug.

There are tears that come with pain, and tears that come with relief. I cried when I went to bed for I couldn't remember the last time I'd laughed. The wound left by my beloved's death would never heal, but I'd learn to live around the scar. I felt like me again – me, Naomi, a living person. I wiped away my tears and smiled into the darkness.

Chapter 44

The barley peeped from the ground, tiny dots of green, evenly spaced. The rains fell, and the dots grew fuller. Then came the sheaths followed by the first leaves. Soon, other leaves grew through the curled up bases of the older ones.

When the barley had almost matured, Cyrus came. Still smelling of the dust of the road and the sweat of travel, he clasped my hand in both of his. "It's good to see you, Naomi."

"The drought in Judea, is it over?"

He nodded. "The rains came. Their harvest will be plentiful."

The words I'd waited so long to hear brought a joy I can't describe. My lungs expanded, my shoulders relaxed, and I seemed to grow taller.

Recognizing my happiness and relief, Cyrus' eyes went soft but there was also was a look of wariness in them. I was too happy to wonder what unspoken doubts filled his mind.

"How are things here?" He raised his eyebrows, and I understood he wanted to hear if grandchildren were on the way.

"Good," I answered but gave a slight shake of the head. Before too much longer, I hoped to announce the happiness of an expected increase our family, for I felt certain it would happen very soon.

He walked with me to the shade of the cedar. My serving women greeted him enthusiastically and my bride-daughters even more so. While Ruth and Orpah plied him with questions about his journey, Hada and Abi ran to bring cushions, water, and refreshments. With Uriah propped on her hip, Mesha remained for Cyrus had begun playing with the child's toes as he answered my bride-daughters' questions. *Yes, a good price for everything. No, there were no disasters on the trip. Yes, I brought frankincense for Noa and bangles for you. No, I saw no sites I haven't seen before. Nothing to amaze you.*

"The men are battling weeds in the barley field," I said. "Can you stay until they're done? They'll want to see you."

While we waited for the men, he talked about trading olive oil and wine in Egypt and bringing back linen which he'd sold for a good price to the Philistines. On the return trip from Egypt, his caravan had journeyed along the Way by the Sea before cutting across the northern end of Judea and crossing the Jordan to arrive at the King's Highway. While traveling on the Way by the Sea, he'd sent a runner into the hills of Judea to see if stories of the drought being over were true. When the runner returned, he described grass growing in abundance on the hillsides, wildflowers about to bloom, barley greening in the fields.

Happiness tingled down my spine. Even my toes were happy. Machlon and Killion, as sons of a former elder, and who themselves would be important men in the community someday, would remind our friends and neighbors in Bethlehem that, according to the law, Israelite men were allowed to marry Moabite women as long as they converted. I no longer thought of my sons leaving their brides behind and taking proper Israelite wives for I had grown to love my bride-daughters. Besides, how was one to tell they were Moabites and not Israelites? They looked and dressed the same. They'd learned to speak as we did. When they came to us, they'd left behind their idols, renounced their god, and acknowledged ours. I wanted them with me. I wanted their children in my lap.

"We'll return to Bethlehem as soon as we've harvested the barley and sheared the sheep," I said.

Cyrus gave me a troubled look. "Does Achilla know?"

It occurred to me then that Achilla *didn't* know. To avoid trouble about taking his daughters away, my sons wouldn't have told him. "Please, don't say anything," I begged. Then another thought struck me. Was our return to Bethlehem only *my* plan and not that of my sons?

That evening, Cyrus remained to sup with us. No one noticed my agitation as they listened to his adventures in Egypt and the plans for his next trip. He stayed late, so I couldn't talk to my sons. Nor did we talk the following day, for disaster struck.

Chapter 45

Except for Kir, who had been given the task of cleaning the grain cellar, the men went early the next morning to continue the Battle of the Weeds. Kir was to remove last year's grain, give the cellar a good cleaning, and then put the grain back. He'd been working only a short while when he came to me ashen-faced.

I had placed a tripod over the firepit and was about to hang the couscous pot. "What's wrong," I asked.

He swallowed several times as though there was something in his mouth that wouldn't go down.

"Kir?"

Hada, who had brought salt for the pot, dumped it in, brushed her hands to rid them of the remaining salt, and waited to hear what Kir had to say.

"The grain." Kir's voice was breathless. "It's rotted."

"No!" I set the pot down on the ground.

"Water leaked into the bottom of the cellar, and the jars became damp." He had a helpless look in his eyes. "I smelled the rot as soon as I removed the jars."

"But we've taken grain from them every day."

"The top layer in each jar is fine, but it's rotten beneath."

Hada and I ran to the cellar. Kir followed more slowly. There was a pitifully small pile of good grain on a cloth spread next to the cellar, while the grain remaining in the jars was a sodden black mess smelling of mold and rot. Speechless, we stared.

"There'll be more grain when we harvest." Hada said finally.

"This . . .," I motioned to the pile of dry grain, ". . . won't last until then."

The other women, sensing that something was wrong, had run over. Mesha and my bride daughters stared at the rotted grain. Abi, an expression of horror on her face, clutched at her throat.

"Bring jugs," I said. "Fill them with the good barley. If any is damp, even the slightest bit, leave it on the blanket to dry."

The women hurried to do as they were bid.

Kir, his shoulders slumped, repeated what I'd said. "This won't last until the harvest."

"We'll eat less bread." I was shaken. What if this had happened earlier? What if this had happened shortly after the barley harvest last year? Had it been so, we would have been forced to use our silver to buy grain to get through the winter. Silver spent on grain was less silver for the expenses of returning to Bethlehem. Less for the extra donkeys we'd need. Less for. ... I couldn't even remember what we needed for the journey.

"It's my fault," Kir said.

"How is it your fault?"

"I knew the ground in Moab was like this. That after an especially wet season the rains would build up in the earth. We should have made the walls thicker."

"Kir, are you a Moabite?" I recognized the demand in my voice, but I'd wanted to ask the question for a long time.

He gave me a sharp look. "No. Why do you ask?"

"You spoke the language when we came. You knew where the country lay in relation to Judea. You know about the ground here."

"I don't want to talk about what I am, or who I was." Frowning, he pressed his lips together.

The women returned with jars and began filling them, so I had no chance to respond. "Cover this," I said instead, motioning to the cellar. "We no longer need a place to store grain. As soon as the last ear of barley is winnowed and the last sheep is shorn, we're returning to Bethlehem."

I knelt next to Ruth, scooped grain with my hands, and piled it into a jar.

"My father will give us grain." Ruth spoke softly so the others wouldn't hear.

I considered my words before I replied in a voice equally soft. "I don't want to be a burden to your father."

"We'd be no burden."

"Nor do I want to feel like a beggar. Nor would Machlon. He's only recently become head of our family, and, surely, he doesn't want to feel as though he's failed."

She nodded, scooped up a double handful, and dumped it in the jar. "We don't need so much bread anyway. We have plenty of other food."

We *didn't* have plenty. We had only those things made from milk. Butter, cheese, labneh, along with wild greens. Other food – olives, almonds, wine – we had to buy or accept as gifts when people were moved to offer them. For now, we'd have to live on what our sheep and goats provided and the greens we could collect in the hills.

The same day as the grain disaster, I noticed the eyes of my women following Abi. At first I paid no attention, but after the midday meal when she started toward the flock with food for Tall Boy and the mute, a breeze blew her tunic tight against her body, and I saw. Since the arrival of Tall Boy, she'd begged to be the one to take food to the shepherds, and her returns had been more and more delayed. Now, I knew why. Furious, I set aside the dishes I'd been about to put away and followed.

"Abi," I called when we were well away from the others.

When she turned and saw my face, she seemed to shrink.

"I see what you've done," I said, catching up with her. My voice was as cold as the snow in winter.

She looked down.

"You've sinned grievously." I felt Elimelech's spirit rising in me, his abhorrence for shame, his intolerance for breaking the law.

"Please, please," she said. Her voice shook with fright. "I didn't mean for it to happen; it just did."

"It didn't just happen. It happened because you let it."

She broke out sobbing. "What are you going to do with me?"

What *was* I going to do with her? Uri's fate still haunted me. Law or no, had I been the one deciding his punishment our shepherd would still be with us. I loved my husband; I loved everything about him except for one thing: I could not abide his cruel god.

"Will he marry you?" I asked.

She shrugged.

"Does he even know?" But of course he knows, I thought. How could he not? Her rounding stomach wouldn't have been hidden from him. "Come." I took her by the arm and dragged her to where Tall Boy was.

"You'll marry her," I said when we stood before him.

White-faced, he stuttered something.

"I hope what you just uttered was agreement. My son will require that you marry." Then I invoked the names of Achilla, his nephews, his brother. I hated using Achilla's power, but if I had to, I would.

Tall Boy nodded, and Abi gave a sigh of relief.

Bad things come in threes. After our evening meal, I went to relieve myself with the expectation of going early to bed. As I passed through the copse behind our tents, Machlon and Killion, hidden in the trees, spoke in low voices.

"We've discussed it over and over." Killion said. "We'll never have to worry about droughts if we stay here. If we go back we'll lose sheep along the way. Have you forgotten the desert on the other side of the Jordan? Or the buzzards waiting for our sheep to drop dead?"

I staggered under the weight of Killion's words.

Machlon muttered something I couldn't make out.

"You're thinking only of yourself." Vexation colored Killion's words. "When we get back, you'll have a large field and a large flock. I'll have a small flock and no field."

"I'll split the field and the flock with you," Machlon said. "You can have half of everything."

Killion laughed. A jeering, frustrated laugh." Am I to know that for sure?"

"Have I ever lied to you?"

I barely breathed as anger, hurt, and disappointment built toward my younger son.

"No," Killion said finally. "You've never lied to me. But brother, you know the elders will insist we abide by the laws." His voice softened to a plead as he said, "Not just I, but both of us will have more if we stay here. Achilla's servants will help build a house for each of us. When the time comes, we'll have Achilla's flock."

"If we go back, I'll give you Uri's sheep."

"He had how many? Five? Six?" The bitterness had returned to Killion's voice.

"And all the lambs from them," Machlon said.

"Achilla has nearly a hundred sheep."

I could stand it no longer.

"What are you asking?" I hissed at Killion as I made my way toward them, nearly tripping over a fallen limb. "We are Israelites. We cannot remain here."

Machlon jumped up and hugged me to him. "Mother, don't fret. Things will work out. Go to bed and leave this to me. Come, I'll walk you to your tent." Casting a look at his brother, Machlon led me away.

I went to bed, not to sleep, but to toss and turn while missing Elimelech more than ever. The warmth of his body next to mine; his calloused hands on my thigh; the smell of sheep and grain on his clothes. I needed him. Oh, how I needed him here to be strong with our sons! Killion had persuaded Machlon to give his blessing to a marriage with Orpah, then he'd persuaded Machlon to marry Ruth. Would he also succeed in persuading Machlon to remain in Moab?

Chapter 46

After a fitful night, I rose, pulled on my outer garment, and dragged myself toward the cooking tent. Their backs to me, Arioch piled wood on the flames in the bread oven while Hada and Mesha, with Uriah on her lap, rolled dough.

"We've been cursed," Arioch muttered, unaware that I'd come from my tent.

"Take the baby," Mesha said, and held Uriah out to Arioch. "He keeps trying to play with the dough. He has it all over his face."

"Did you hear me?" Arioch asked as he took his son and brushed flour from one of the baby's cheeks. "We've been cursed. First Uri. Then Elimelech. Yesterday, the grain. Now, Abi. Chemosh isn't pleased to have Yahweh worshippers in his land. Or else Yahweh isn't pleased with us for being here."

"Shhhh, don't speak so loudly," Mesha said. "We'll talk about this later."

I slipped past, behind their backs. Maybe because Uriah put up a fuss at not being allowed to play with the dough balls they didn't hear me. In a sour mood, I piled olives in a dish. My twenty-one-year old son was in charge of my life, but sweet, thoughtful, and well-meaning as he was, Machlon let his younger brother bully him. At least Machlon's kind wife had never presumed to replace me as head of our home.

That day, I worked until I could barely stand. Late in the afternoon when I went to the cistern, scratched, dirty, and tired, Machlon came and asked about living arrangements for Abi and Tall Boy. "Ask your brother," I said bitterly.

Machlon gave me a puzzled look.

"Go," I said and waved him away. "When you tell me we're returning to Bethlehem, I'll talk to you again. Until then, don't bother me."

The sun still hovered above the hills when we finished our evening meal. Machlon and Killion, the air between them tense, lingered at the fire, while Kir went to see to the oxen. Arioch set Uriah on his shoulder and followed, intending to show his son the animals. Festus and Skinny wandered off. Overcome with bitterness, I didn't help clear away the dishes. Instead, I sat idly watching the flames die.

Ruth and Orpah, trying to cheer their husbands, stroked their hands, teased them, chatted about this, that, and nothing. I had relaxed my rule about wine and, once again, we served a cup with the evening meal. The other dishes had been taken away, but Killion still had his cup. Summoning his winsome smile, he held the cup out to Orpah and said, "One more, sweet wife."

"Yes, my handsome husband." Orpah gave him a flirtatious smile as she rose. "Shall I fill your cup too, Machlon?"

"Thank you," he said and handed her his.

I rose and followed Orpah into the cooking tent as did Ruth. Orpah set down the cups and picked up the wine ewer.

"They've had enough," Ruth said.

"They're in such an unhappy mood this evening. They need cheering."

"Machlon doesn't hold his wine well," Ruth persisted. "He shouldn't have any more."

"You're deciding how much wine your husband is allowed to drink?"

"Yes."

Orpah looked at me to settle the issue.

"If Ruth played her harp that might put them in a better mood," I said. I didn't want to take sides with my bride daughters lest I become a subject of argument between them, but in my heart I thanked Ruth many times over.

Reluctantly, Orpah put aside the wine pitcher. "Very well. We can sing."

When we returned to the fire, Killion, his eyes alight, seemed to have forgotten that Orpah was to bring him wine. "Look!" he said, pointing to the crest of the hill where a falcon swooped down, soared upwards, then down again, a black shape against the darkening sky. Another falcon joined the first as human figures appeared on the crest. "Gideon and Habish have come with their birds." He jumped up. "Let's go hear about their adventures. Come, Machlon." He started for the hill.

Orpah held out her hand as though to stop her husband, but he didn't notice.

"It might be better to hear about their adventures another time," Machlon called after his brother.

"Why not now?" Killion spun around.

"The light will soon be gone." Machlon had risen, too, as though by standing he had a better vantage point for arguing with his brother.

Killion shrugged. "We have whatever time is left. Come on."

"Don't go," Orpah said.

Killion gave her a look of disbelief. "You really mind that I spend a brief time watching falcons?"

"It's nearly dark. They won't fly the birds when the light is gone." Orpah was clasping and unclasping her hands. She looked to me as though hoping I'd intercede. Not wanting to come between husband and wife I held my tongue, though with great difficulty.

"It isn't about watching the falcons," Orpah said to Killion when she saw that I intended to say nothing.

"Then what is it?"

"Gideon said he would kill anyone who married me."

"Gideon pretends to be a bully, but he's all talk."

"No, Killion," Ruth said. "Orpah is right. Gideon is mean and vengeful."

Killion squared his shoulders. "Gideon isn't going to kill me up there on the hill in plain sight. Besides, Achilla would punish him severely."

"What my father does to Gideon for killing you is of no consequence to me." Orpah's voice had risen. ". . . for you'll be dead, and I won't have a husband. But if you don't care how I feel, then go ahead. Go watch his falcons." She turned away in fury and stormed into their tent.

"Let's not go, brother," Machlon said.

"They've come to offer peace. Why else would they be here?" Killion headed for the hill..

Ruth jumped up and put her hand on Machlon's arm. "Stay," she said.

"I can't let my brother go alone." Machlon kissed her on the cheek, then followed his brother.

❖ ❖ ❖

The moon moved across the sky, and still my sons stayed on the hill. A fire burned on the crest, and we heard laughter which became rowdier as the evening wore on. There would be drink. Tomorrow, Machlon would be sick and suffer a headache, while Killion would laugh at him for lacking tolerance. None of this I liked, nor would I like it any better tomorrow, but I accepted that my sons were making peace with Achilla's nephews. Their journey would have tamed Gideon's and Habish's anger, and they'd have recognized that Orpah and Ruth would not be theirs. I resigned myself to one night of indiscretion with wine, or barley beer, or whatever they drank.

I explained this to Ruth who had remained sitting beside the firepit.

"I pray that you're right about this." She picked up a stick to poke at the embers. "Machlon told me about Galatia," she said after we'd sat in silence for a few moments.

"He's happy with you."

"And I with him." Sparks flew as she jiggled burnt logs. "I'm so sorry, Naomi, that you lost Elimelech. He was a fine man. Machlon is a fine man, too. He's young, but one day he'll be wise. He's learning his way." She threw aside the stick and sighed. "I can say that about myself, too." She gave a little laugh. "I'm young, but one day I'll be wise like you. Or I hope I will be. There's even more for me to learn than there is for Machlon, but with your help, I will. Orpah and I were idle, silly girls before. I like having purpose in my life."

I squeezed her hand, pleased with what she said, and even more pleased that soon, very soon, I hoped, she'd have even more purpose in her life when she presented Machlon with a child and me with a grandchild.

Chapter 47

Despite my resolve to lie awake until my sons returned, I fell into a deep sleep only to be awakened by the morning chorus of birds. Then a harrowing sound drowned out the birdsong. I ran out of my tent, barefoot and wearing only my tunic. Everyone else had done the same. Orpah, bleary eyed and confused, looked toward the top of the hill. My eyes followed hers. Against the gray light of dawn, Ruth's dark form knelt over something on the ground as she keened.

We dashed up the hill to find Ruth stretched over the body of Machlon. Killion lay nearby, motionless, his blank eyes staring at the sky. Gideon, Habish, and three of their friends lay or sat on the ground nearby, blinking their eyes as though trying to awake from a dream.

"He's dead. He's dead," Ruth screamed.

"Dead?" Orpah repeated, refusing to understand.

In those brief moments, I ceased to be a living woman. I became a clay figure, hollow, unable to move. Something beat inside me, but it wasn't my heart for I no longer had one. As though I watched the scene from outside my body, I saw Orpah trying to shake Killion back to life; Kir feeling the pulses of my two sons and shaking his head; Arioch stepping up as though to help but then doing nothing; my serving women hanging back gasping, moaning; Gideon, Habish, and their friends stumbling to their feet. I was aware of the burned out campfire, the empty ewers lying on the ground, the smell of sour barley beer. I was aware of all this, but I was dead inside.

Ruth, who had never raised her voice, threw herself on Gideon, beating his chest and screaming that he'd murdered her husband.

Blackness engulfed me.

Later – Was it a day? A week? Or only part of a morning? – I revived inside my tent; Elimelech's cloak lay over me.

A person knelt beside me, fanning my face. Someone opened the tent flap, let it drop again, then came to where I lay. Two dark forms loomed over me, half-seen from beneath partially closed lids.

I succumbed to darkness again.

When I revived a second time, someone was wiping a wet cloth across my face. Brushing away the hand that held the cloth, I sat up, listened to voices from outside, then crawled from my mat. Hada and Mesha moved aside as I crept on all fours to the tent opening then through it. Arioch and Festus, shovels in their hands were on their way to somewhere. They stopped, stared at me, and then, looking down at their feet, continued on. Ruth and Orpah clung together in front of Ruth's tent, weeping.

"What did they do to my sons?" I demanded of Kir who had also appeared with a shovel.

"Poison parsley," he said. "Hemlock. They made it into a tea and mixed it with the beer they gave Machlon and Killion."

"How do you know this?" My words sounded as hard as the iron forged by the Philistines.

Kir nodded to where one of Gideon's friends lay in a heap, alive, but battered. "Arioch forced it out of him."

I went to Ruth and Orpah and went through the motions of comforting them, all the while aware that, nearby, the angel of death watched and waited, hidden behind a tree or stone, or in the tall grass growing beside the wadi, or in the copse behind our tents. Stepping away from my bride-daughters, I held out my arms, welcoming death.

Before night fell, we buried my sons.

Achilla came. And his wives and The Mother. No one else. I went through the motions, doing what I was supposed to do, saying what I was supposed to say, moving from one place to another when someone steered me. I couldn't bear my own pain, much less that of Ruth and Orpah. I left them to be consoled by their mothers. When the burial ended, I was put to bed like a baby.

Chapter 48

I wakened to the sound of bleating. Awakened? Had I slept? I thought not, but I must have for when I looked through the tent opening night had passed. Or was it still yesterday?

Confused, I crawled out of the tent. The sheep weren't in the pasture, yet I heard them. Then I looked toward the hill and saw strange shepherds herding Elimelech's sheep toward the crest; some were already disappearing over the top.

"Achilla is taking them," Abi said, rushing up to me, breathless, as though she'd bolted from the far side of the pasture. She clasped a parcel to her breast. "You have to leave. Chemosh has cursed this place." She started toward the hill where Tall Boy waited.

"Where are you going?" Ruth cried, for she and Orpah had also come out of their tents.

"A curse," Abi shouted and kept running.

Orpah ran after her and grabbed her arm. "You're leaving?"

"Everyone has gone." Abi's eyes looked like those of a frightened animal. "Arioch, Mesha, and Hada went last night. Skinny and Festus, too. And Kir. When the last rock was placed on your husbands' graves, he disappeared into the night. Even the mute has run away. They . . .." she nodded to the shepherds driving the sheep over the hill, ". . . say the people from the village won't come because they're afraid." She yanked her arm from Orpah's grasp. "You have to leave. This place has been cursed. First Uri, then Elimelech, then the grain, and yesterday her sons." She pointed at me as though afraid to say my name. "And now Achilla's taking the sheep." She backed away, slowly at first, but then twisted around and ran.

I gathered up my tunic, exposing my bare legs and ran toward the flock, stones and briars cutting into my feet. When I caught up, the sheep had started down the other side of the hill. The shepherds looked up at the wild woman running after the flock, but I ignored them for I'd seen Achilla watching from half-way down.

"What are you doing?" I screamed at him.

"Moving the sheep to join mine."

"You can't do that."

He smiled his hyena smile.

"Bring them back," I shouted even though I stood only an arm's length away. "You can't take my sheep."

"The sheep belong to my daughters, and since they can't care for sheep that task falls to me."

"The sheep are Elimelech's. They're mine." I was no longer shouting but pleading. Elimelech's lifework was being herded down the hill to someone else's pasture.

"You're wrong, Naomi. The sheep belong to my daughters."

I fell to my knees. "Please. This flock was Elimelech's life."

"Elimelech is dead."

I lay face down on the cold ground and broke into a howl. A moment later, I felt Achilla's hand on my shoulder.

"Naomi, you need my help, and I give it to you willingly. Come, you have to bear up."

I curled into a ball, arms wrapped around my head to cover my ears.

"For now, you'll live with us," Achilla said. "Later we'll talk about Lechben."

"Lechben?" I asked, confused.

"My cousin has agreed to take you as a second wife."

"How dare you?" I jumped to my feet.

My bride daughters had joined us. Ruth took my hands in hers.

"What did you say to her?" Orpah demanded of her father.

"That I'd take care of her."

"And what else?" Orpah glared at him.

"Why are you taking the sheep?" Ruth asked before Achilla could answer.

"Someone has to tend them."

"We could have," Ruth said.

"Women can't care for a flock."

"We can." Ruth stood tall. "We can do many things you think we can't."

"What else did you say to Naomi?" Orpah asked again.

Achilla turned as though to walk back to the village. "You've just lost your husbands so I will forgive you, my daughters, for questioning your father and for your lack of respect. Tomorrow, you'll think better of what you say. As for Naomi . . . .."

Achilla gave me a look of such disdain that I understood clearly what I had become: a widow with no sons and no property. A nobody.

"Lechben agrees to take Naomi as a wife," Achilla said. Arms folded, he took a long breath, blew it out, and, after giving his daughters a hard look, dropped his arms and started down the hill.

"Never," Orpah shouted to his back as he strode away.

"Her sons have been dead for less than two days and you're speaking of marrying her to your ugly cousin?" Ruth called after him.

Achilla, sounding tired, turned around. "If she objects, she can live with us."

"And what about Gideon?" Orpah's voice broke. "He killed my husband and my sister's husband. What are you going to do?"

For a few moments Achilla was silent. "We'll see," he said finally. "Go back and pack your things. I'll come in the afternoon for you."

We trudged back to our encampment. There was no fire in the pit, no voices, no cries from Uriah. The stalls were empty. No animals remained in the pasture. Missing was the smell of baking bread. Of men's sweat. There was only the sound of tent openings flapping in the breeze. Even the birds had fallen silent.

I directed Ruth and Orpah to go to their tents, pack their things, and ready themselves to return to their home. Instead, they huddled in Ruth's tent, crying. I let them be and went to the cooking tent to gather food. The angel of death would have to follow me to Bethlehem. Die though I would, I refused to die in this accursed place. If death caught up with me on the journey, at least my feet would be headed in the right direction. Moab would lie behind me.

Inside the tent, jars were overturned and coverings left off those that still stood upright. Some jugs stood empty while the levels of food in the others had been greatly reduced. Our bondsmen had helped themselves. Even Kir, whom I had finally decided to trust – at least a little – had gone. I'd been right in the beginning. He was not to be depended on.

I began filling a goatskin, cramming in olives, dried cheese, nuts. I had filled two skins and had begun to fill a third when Ruth and Orpah came to me, their eyes swollen.

"We don't need to carry food. My family has enough," Orpah said. Her beautiful bronze-colored hair lay like a pile of hay disarranged by the wind.

Ruth stared at the skins.

"I'm returning to Bethlehem," I said, answering her unasked question. "To my home."

"But how will you get there?" Orpah's surprise showed through her agony.

"The same way I came."

"You can't," Ruth said. "It's dangerous even for a man traveling alone."

"Nothing can happen that's worse than what has already befallen me."

The three of us looked at each other in silence, each engulfed in her own pain but also acknowledging the pain of each other. Words don't always have to be spoken, for sometimes we hear each other's thoughts.

In the afternoon, Achilla, came with The Mother and Hoglah. In addition to the donkey Hoglah road, Achilla's bondsman led three others. "It's time," Achilla said.

My bride daughters and I were seated beneath the cedar, holding each other's hands, speaking of my sons, their husbands, reliving how we found them, unable to believe their deaths had really happened. None of us had packed our belongings.

"I'm not ready," I said to Achilla and gave Ruth and Orpah a look hoping they understood they weren't to reveal my intentions.

Achilla frowned. "You need bring nothing other than your clothes."

"I must have a day to mourn in this place where we've lived for the past ten seasons." I was surprised at the calmness with which I spoke even though my every sinew vibrated with grief and nervousness.

"You can't be alone," Hoglah said.

Ruth rose. "She won't be alone. Orpah and I are staying, too." Ruth, always obedient and eager to please, spoke as though in charge. "Leave the donkeys here. We'll tie them at the doors of our tents to protect us from wild animals."

"Yes, we'll be fine." Orpah gave her father an appealing look. "We'll load the donkeys in the morning and go home without you coming for us. You can indulge us in this."

Grateful to my bride-daughters, I said to Achilla, "One day is all I ask."

He hesitated, and for a few moments I pictured myself imprisoned in his house, watched, unable to get away, forced into a marriage with Lechben. Finally, Achilla let out a long sigh. "I'll come for you tomorrow before the sun crosses halfway to midday."

"We can walk on our own," I said.

"No, I'll come for you. I want the villagers to see that I welcome you to my house."

I knew what he really wanted the villagers to see was that I accepted his dominance.

Chapter 49

There wasn't much to pack – my second set of clothes, what food I could carry, my sleeping mat, cloth for my shroud. Ruth and Orpah didn't leave my side, hanging over me listless and tearful. I was beating my mat, ridding it of insect wings and shriveled leaves when Ruth said suddenly, "I'm going with you."

I laid aside the mat and took her hand. "Your kindness is a gift I'll never forget, but you can't come."

"I'm going with you, too," Orpah said.

Still holding Ruth's hand, I took Orpah's. "I love you, my daughters, and, because I do, I won't allow you to come. There are a hundred reasons why." After giving their hands a squeeze, I let go. "I'm going to walk out there." I pointed to the pasture. "For a little while, I want to be alone to roam among the ghosts."

Though the sky cried, I walked for most of the afternoon. Soaked with rain, I went from one end of the pasture to the other, pulling tufts of wool from bushes and tucking them in my bosom, walking through tall grass where the sheep hadn't grazed for a few weeks and through cropped grass where they had. The sheep had been Elimelech's pride and my sons' inheritance.

The rain had stopped by the time I returned to our encampment, chilled to the bone and smelling of the wet wool tucked inside my clothes. Orpah had dragged her mat outside the tent and fallen asleep, copper hair blown across her face, and a dead leaf poised on one shoulder.

Ruth, huddled in her cape, sat beside the cold firepit.

"I'm going with you," she said when I sat down beside her. She whispered so as not to awaken Orpah.

I shook my head.

"I *am* going with you. Wherever your home is, that's my home too."

"Ruth, you can't. Even if we managed to get to Bethlehem alive, the people there wouldn't accept you."

"Because I'm a Moabite?"

"Yes."

"They'll accept me when they know I've chosen their Yahweh. I'll love your relatives as my own. They, and your neighbors will know me as your bride daughter and soon forget where I came from."

I shook my head again. She was being foolish.

"I will stay with you, Naomi, for as long as you live. I'll be with you when you close your eyes for the last time which won't be for a long time yet."

"It will be soon."

"Then, I'll be with you. Come." She stood and, grabbing me by the hand, helped me to my feet and led me into the cooking tent. She examined the food I'd packed for my journey.

"You haven't packed very well, Mother." She gave me a chiding smile. "This . . ." she swept her hand in a half-arc motioning to the skins, ". . . isn't the way you've taught me to do things. You rest while I put order to your disarray and pack more. I'm young and strong and can carry more than what you've set aside."

I sank to the ground and watched while she filled goat skins. Lacking the energy to stop her or argue further, I let her give way to her imaginings. On the morrow, I would leave while she still slept.

There remained one last thing to do. Late in the afternoon, while Ruth and Orpah packed their belongings for a journey they wouldn't make, I took a shovel from the storage tent, went to the empty ox stall, and shoved aside the rocks beneath which Elimelech hid the silver. When I didn't have to dig deep for the goatskin, I was puzzled. I was even more puzzled when I picked up the bag to find it weighed nearly nothing. Thinking there had to be another, I dug deeper but found no other.

Inside the bag there was only a few shekels' weight of silver. A moan, loud enough to wake the gods, escaped my lips. Covering my face with my hands, I sobbed. The Yahweh who opened up the Red Sea for the Israelites, filled the air with manna, and tumbled the walls of Jericho had chosen to lay low a poor woman who had lost everything? Why? I screamed the word over and over. "Why? Why? Why?"

Ruth and Orpah ran to me.

"This is all there is," I exclaimed, opening my hand to reveal the puny amount of silver.

Ruth picked up the empty skin and looked inside.

"The silver was part of the bride price," Orpah said, her voice breaking.

Ruth and I looked at her in disbelief. "The bride price?" I repeated dumbly.

"How did you know?" Ruth asked.

"I overheard them haggling. I wanted to marry Killion so very much, I didn't consider what it was costing you."

Bursting into tears, Orpah fled to her tent.

"I'm sorry," Ruth said. Then she brightened. "I have bangles and amulets. We'll sell them in the first market we come to. They won't bring much, but at least we'll have a little for food. I'll gather them now." Then she, too, ran to her tent.

Chapter 50

Before the sun rose the following morning, I went to the trees to relieve myself, the paltry amount of silver already tied around my waist beneath my tunic. Then, despite being alone and lacking silver for the journey, I'd shoulder my pack and leave before my bride-daughters awoke. There would be no good-byes.

Though there could be no shadows without the sun, around me the tree trunks rose as though they themselves were shadows. One separated itself from the others and glided toward me. I almost cried out for the men before I remembered they'd gone. The shadow came closer. It was Death. The world spun, and I toppled.

From the blackness, a face emerged, blurred and floating above me. A warm hand supported my neck, and someone's breath brushed my forehead as the person spoke my name. "Naomi. Naomi."

"Kir," I said, ". . . I thought you'd gone."

"I went to do what I had to do. Let me help you up." He stood, grabbed my hand, and pulled me to my feet. Then he picked up a bundle which he must have thrown to the ground when I fainted. "I guessed you'd be leaving, but a woman can't travel alone."

"If I die along the way, at least I'll know where I was headed."

"Dying isn't the worst thing that can happen to a woman. I brought you these."

He held out the bundle. When I didn't take it, he opened it himself. Inside were two long, narrow scarves like those worn by men of the desert.

"You must become a man for your journey." He held the scarves out to me, and I took them. "As a man of the desert, you can hide your face and lack of a beard."

"Thank you," I murmured, stricken at how I'd again misjudged Kir.

"Everything is arranged. We have to get to the King's Highway by nightfall. I've made arrangements with a caravan that leaves early tomorrow. You'll give the caravan master silver, and he'll protect you for most of the way. After the caravan fords the Jordan, it will cross the hills of Judea and then follow the Way by the Sea toward Egypt. When you come to the path that leads into the Judean hills and to Bethlehem, the master will point it out to you. From there, you'll have to go alone."

"There is no silver." A thousand daggers stabbed my heart as I showed him what little there was in the bag. "This is all."

He stared at the pittance in my palm. "Come," he said finally and started toward the south hill.

When I didn't follow, he turned back and beckoned. "Come. I don't want to leave you here alone."

We went part way up the hill and into the trees, the fallen limbs smelling of wood rot and the moss stinking of mildew from the seasonal rains. I followed Kir to the spot where I'd seen him hiding something in a trunk – the place I'd never been able to find but which I now recognized. He removed loose bark from the hollow and pulled out a skin.

"It isn't much," he said and held it out to me.

I took the skin and looked inside. "Where did you get this silver?"

"I sold the clothes you wove for me, and mastic gum, and things I carved from bone. Elimelech knew I did this."

"Why would you give me your silver?"

"Except for Elimelech, no man ever trusted me." He motioned to his face. "People think my heart is as misshapen as my face. And no woman ever treated me as kindly as you."

I hadn't treated him kindly. I had distrusted him, ignored him, thought the worst of him. Yet, he was offering me his silver so I could return to my home. Overwhelmed with guilt, I tried to hand back the silver but he stuck his hands in his agora.

"I can't take your silver," I said. What would this refusal, this act of being fair cost me?

"You must take it. Elimelech trusted me to do his business, and I'm doing that now. Your husband would insist you take this and return to Bethlehem."

"Tell me, Kir. Who are you?"

"Not now. We have to hurry if we're to get to the Highway by nightfall. I'll tell you on the way."

Anxious to be off before Ruth and Orpah awoke, I ran to my tent and changed into Elimelech's clothes. As I was about to wind the scarf into a turban and face covering, Ruth came.

"What are you doing?" she asked, staring at the scarf.

"Dressing as a desert man."

"Then I will, too."

"No, Ruth. You're not coming."

"I'll wear Machlon's clothes."

"There's nothing for you in Bethlehem. Do you think I have another son in my womb to marry you? Or that you'd wait that long if I did? You'll return to your family. This is a bitter potion we both must swallow."

"*You* are my family." She gave me a sideways look and left.

I wound the scarf around my head and face like the desert dwellers and emerged from my tent as a man. Kir was at the cistern filling water skins. Quickly, because we needed to leave before either of us expended too many more breaths, I ran to the cooking tent and grabbed the skins filled with food. Then we set out.

"Wait," I heard Ruth call as Kir and I made our way through the trees behind our tents. I turned to see her scurrying toward us dressed in Killion's clothes. Orpah stood in her tent opening looking dazed.

"Machlon's clothes were too long, so I took Killion's," Ruth said as she hurried to join us. The tunic came to her feet and the cloak dragged on the ground. She'd tied the agora around her waist but hadn't knotted it properly. Under one arm, she held her rolled sleeping mat and a bundle that I assumed were her woman clothes. A corner of her harp peaked from the bundle.

Dangling from her free hand were scarves to be used as a turban and a lower face wrapping.

"Please," I said. "I can't waste time with arguments. You have a home here. You and Orpah will have other husbands someday, and babies. You'll remember me, and I'll remember you with love, but you must stay."

Ruth said nothing, but Orpah rushed over and enveloped me in a hug. After hugging her back, I pushed her away. "Goodbye, my Daughter." I turned to hug Ruth but she stepped aside.

"We have to go," Kir said.

Fighting tears, I turned away from my bride-daughters and followed Kir. We'd gone only partway through the copse when I realized that Ruth followed. Before I could chastise her, she said, "I'll follow even if it has to be from behind. Wherever you go, I'll follow."

Part III

The Return

Chapter 51

"You'll walk at the end," the head of the caravan, the madouga, said, accepting the bag of silver. Kir had instructed me to pay half in the beginning and the rest when we arrived at the path leading into the hills of Judea. The madouga ran his gaze over our dirty clothes and then held the bag at arm's length, judging the weight. He frowned. "It's hardly enough. Even when you pay the other half, it isn't enough."

"It's all we have," I said in a low voice, mimicking a man. It was indeed all. The second bag contained, not silver, but the bangles and jewelry Ruth had brought. "I'll give you the rest when we get there."

He blew out an irritated huff. "Then stand aside and wait for the end of the caravan." The madouga raised his staff and jerked the rope halter of the lead camel. The beast grudgingly lurched forward, forcing the camels linked to him by their nose rings to follow. The madouga fell into step beside his animal while, behind him, the caravaners shouted and banged on pots to entice their animals to move forward.

As we waited for the end of the column, we checked our turbans and drew our cloaks tightly around us. Only moments before, the sun had risen out of the desert to the east and hadn't yet warmed the air. The stench of sweat, urine, and animal droppings billowed around us, along with the foul breaths of camels and the stinking belches of oxen and donkeys. Strings of camels piled high with spices, oxcarts loaded with grain or salt, and mules bearing olive oil, wine, and all manner of foodstuffs passed us by. Some animals transported goods hidden in linen or sackcloth. I imagined these to be gold, ivory, and precious stones – things people coveted but none of which could buy back what I'd lost.

Two braces of oxen, straining at a cart loaded with acacia wood, brought up the rear of the caravan. I nudged Ruth, and we went to walk behind the cart, dipping our heads so that only our eyes and foreheads were visible. Slung over our shoulders were our only possessions.

And so our journey began. Day after day, we walked in a trance, Ruth and I inhabiting our separate worlds of misery. To keep away the pain that came with thought, I counted steps. When I reached the highest number I could count to, I began again, counting, counting, from morning 'til night. We spoke to no one, ate and slept apart from the others, and, in fear of revealing that we were women, whispered when we spoke to each other. At first, the oxcart driver attempted to converse but we cast our eyes down and shrugged until he gave up. We closed our eyes when the men relieved themselves in front of us. As for ourselves, mostly we let our urine run down our legs for there was little opportunity for privacy. Soon, we began to stink.

When we came to the end of the King's Highway, we turned west and crossed the Jordan, coming once again to the oasis. In a moment of forgetfulness, I thought I saw Killion running to greet the caravan in the place where falcons rode in cages perched atop donkeys. Machlon ran behind him, more slowly, but just as curious. I blinked, and they were gone.

After resting a day at the oasis, we traveled on. Just as Mesha had once done, Ruth fed me like a baby, putting food in my mouth and commanding me to chew. She forced me to lie down at night and to get up in the morning. My grief had numbed me to everything; hers had been pushed aside as she strove to take me home.

We crossed the desert between the oasis and the hill country of Judea. As before, our sweat-dampened clothes clung to us, and our scalps itched with an intensity that nearly crazed us for we never removed our turbans. I had begun to hobble, for my left hip pained me. On and on we went, my limbs wooden, my mind numb.

Yet sometimes something *did* prick at my conscious – something I didn't want to acknowledge. Prick, prick, prick like a needle, the buried thought harassed me. Wanting only to be aware of the steps that brought me closer to home each day, I tried to close the door of my mind to whatever thought it was that tried to penetrate the barrier of my consciousness.

When we came to the Judean hills, we didn't turn south to wend through them as we had on our journey to Moab but crossed them to arrive at the Way by the Sea.

"Some call it the *Way of the Philistines*," the ox-cart driver told us in a renewed attempt at conversation. "And the Egyptians say *The Way of Horus*."

We lowered our eyes and shrugged.

Sometimes we traveled close enough to the sea to smell the salt air and catch glimpses of the waves. Other times the path led us away then, after part of a day, brought us back again. With each step, whether near the water or far from it, we were one step closer to Bethlehem, and I began to awaken from my long, miserable sleep.

With the awakening came pain so unbearable I can't speak of it.

Soon we began to hope that at any moment the madouga would summon us and point to the path that led homeward. One morning, afraid he might have forgotten, we went to the front of the long stream of animals and people.

"When will we arrive at the path to Bethlehem?" I asked.

"Soon," he said and waved us away.

Every day, the caravaners sang. On the third day along the Way by the Sea, they began singing as soon as we set out, their voices louder and more animated than before. "Egypt isn't so far away now," the driver of the oxcart said. "The singing will make the camels move faster."

That same day, the sun had barely risen above the hills when a boy came running to us. "You're to go to the front," he said.

"The path is ahead," the madouga said when we arrived breathless at his side. "From there, it's a long day's walk to your destination." Then he noticed how I hobbled with my sore hip and swollen ankles. "Or perhaps two days." He held out his hand.

Still walking, I reached inside my tunic, undid the cord, and withdrew the bag containing Ruth's jewelry.

Again the madouga tested the weight of the bag in his palm, then, with a sniff, tucked it into his agora and walked on in silence. A short while later, he raised his stick and motioned to a path jutting off to the left. "There," he said.

We hurried toward the path that led into the Judean hills, but not so fast that we failed to hear the boy who had come for us speaking to his master.

"Two nobodies," the boy said. "They couldn't even pay properly for your protection."

"Yes, nobodies," The madouga replied. "We'll never hear of them again."

◆　◆　◆

We climbed the path for about the length of two fields before pausing to look down at the stream of men and animals moving toward Egypt. The clack and jingle of cowrie shells and silver ornaments strung around the necks of camels had grown faint as had the mooing of oxen, the clop, clop of hooves, the singing.

"We're in your land now?" Ruth asked.

"Yes. We're in Judea."

How is it that a heavy heart can feel lighter and, at the same time, heavier? I was almost home, but I'd returned without the three people I loved beyond all imagining.

We resumed our climb surrounded by the raw nut smell of barley, for it was the time of the barley harvest. We spoke little other than to ask directions and stopped only once during the morning to refill our water skins. When the sun sat in the middle of the sky, we paused to eat, carefully dividing our remaining dates and parched grain into two small piles, one of which we rewrapped for the following day. When we'd consumed that last pile, we'd be beggars, at the mercy of my family or whoever deigned to share with us.

That evening, we settled into a thicket, too tired to worry if the bushes were enough to protect us from jackals or lions. The first rays of sun woke us, and, after a breakfast of dates, we set out, again stopping only to draw water from a village well and, for a brief while in mid-afternoon, to rest beside a wadi coursing with the latter rains.

We removed our turbans, waded in, and washed our stinking, matted hair. When we climbed out of the water, Ruth stared at my hair, then quickly turned her eyes away. I pulled my wet locks forward to see why she stared and found my hair streaked with gray. I had become an old woman.

Once again we set out, consuming the last of our dates and parched grain while walking. As the sun began to slide behind the hills, we came to the promontory where Elimelech and I had paused for a last look at our home.

"There," I said, and pointed. "Bethlehem." Like a dream, the village perched on the hill. Drinking in the sight of the town walls and the roofs rising above, I breathed in a long, tired breath as I removed the turban and shook my hair loose.

While Ruth removed her turban and opened her tunic to unbind her breasts, I dropped onto a rock, gazed across the fields, now emptied of workers and animals, my eyes feasting on the terraces planted with grape vines, the nearby watch towers, the patches girded with olive trees. Figs and pomegranates grew closer to the walls. The rocky slopes unsuitable to serve as fields or orchards were pockmarked with water cisterns carved into the rock. These things were barely visible, some not visible at all in the shrinking light, but I didn't need light to see them.

Unable to tear myself away, I watched while darkness swallowed the fields and the town flattened into a ragged black shape in front of a rose-colored sliver of sky. Such was my sorrow that, had I any tears left, I could have turned the Jordan into a raging torrent, but I was as dry as the great desert.

"We'll sleep here," I said in a broken voice.

Ruth laid a hand on my shoulder. "Naomi . . .."

"Don't call me that." I brushed away her hand. "I'm no longer that woman. Call me Mara. I've drunk from the cup of bitterness as no woman should ever have to."

I was ashamed of my abruptness, but I could no longer restrain myself. When the sun rose, I would return to my home without my beloved, without my sons, bringing nothing, for I had nothing other than a bride-daughter who would not be welcome.

Moonlight reflected off a rock and, in its dim glow, I watched Ruth as she spread her mat and lay down. I spread mine next to hers, touching her shoulder when I lay down, leaving my fingers to linger there – a petition for forgiveness. She squeezed my fingers, accepting my apology. I would never have reached Bethlehem without her. Somewhere along the way, in my misery I would have ceased to live.

Chapter 52

Armed with scythes, reapers headed toward the fields of ripe grain without glancing at two women making their way toward the town. We pushed our way through the town gate, a weak incoming tide against the stronger undertow of workers.

Ruth had said little from the time we awoke. Head down, brow creased, she followed me to the well. When I first stood among strangers at *her* village well, I had been the same – uncertain, nervous, afraid.

The men and boys had already watered their livestock, leaving the women to draw water. I stopped a short distance from the well, searching among the chattering, happy women for familiar faces. Someone glanced in my direction. Still looking at me, she nudged the woman next to her, and they both stared. Then an older woman looked up.

Damaris! My heart leapt. Damaris was alive!

"Naomi?" She set her jug down. "Naomi?" She called louder, and heads turned.

She rushed over and enfolded me in her arms. Others crowded around. I hadn't seen Dorcus in the line of women, but she was suddenly there. Hugging me. Crying. I wondered where Imla was. Damaris had grabbed my sleeve and wouldn't let go.

"Naomi." Dorcus clasped my arm. "We didn't know what . . .."

"Call me Mara," I said. "All that's left of me is bitterness."

"The others?"

"They're dead." I put my hands over my mouth for saying the words scorched my tongue.

"Elimelech?" someone asked.

"Dead," I said through my hands.

Damaris began to keen.

"Your sons?" someone else asked.

"They, too, are dead. Our bondsmen and serving women ran away because we were cursed."

There was a chorus of *no's*. Shaking of heads. Wrinkling of brows. Damaris keening louder. No one seemed to notice Ruth.

"Come," Dorcus said. "Come to my home."

She put her hand on my shoulder to guide me away.

"Wait." I took Ruth by the hand and pulled her forward. "This is my bride-daughter, Ruth. She married my Machlon."

Dorcus dropped her hand from my shoulder; Damaris stopped keening; the other women fell silent. I didn't fail to notice those who took a step back.

"Yes, Ruth is a Moabitess, but she's my daughter, and I hope you will welcome her as such."

Ignoring the quiet that had fallen over the group, I turned to Damaris. "Do I still have a home?"

She nodded.

"Sister, you'll forgive me," I said to Dorcus. ". . . but I've waited for many seasons to return to my home, and I want to go there now. It would please me if you came, too."

She cast a quick glance at Ruth, then a questioning one at me.

"Ruth is my daughter," I repeated.

I had dreamed of the moment I'd come home, imagining myself walking through the creaky front gate, climbing the ladder to the next floor and then to the roof. I had longed for Damaris' bread baked in my own oven. I'd imagined stringing warp on my loom and Imla helping me weave. But my dreams had included Elimelech and my sons. Now, only Damaris with her water jar, and Ruth and Dorcus were with me. Women from the well had trailed behind, some glad to see me, others curious, but they'd stopped at our front gate, understanding my need to enter my home without a crowd.

Things were as I remembered, yet not as I remembered. The stalls contained nothing more than stale hay. A few empty jars stood in one corner of the storage room. The bread oven was cold. No baskets of wool lined the room where I did the weaving. But there was something new in the room! Against the wall opposite the small window, a ray of light fell on the crossbeam of a new loom.

"Oh, Zacharias." I brought my hands to my cheeks. I hadn't asked about him earlier because I knew the answer without asking.

And Damaris knew my question without asking. "Last year," she said hoarsely. "He breathed his last during the time of shearing. My nephew has stayed with me. Matthias and I have done the best we could."

I pressed Damaris' hand to my cheek.

Dorcus looked at my limp food bag and asked, "Have you eaten today?"

I shook my head.

"We have a few dried fruits and nuts," Damaris said. "Come, rest on the next floor. I'll bring you food and water."

"This is our first harvest in three years," Dorcus said, ignoring Damaris. "The grain containers have been empty for some time, but I'll bring whatever I can spare. Ruth can come and help."

"Ruth has taken care of me during this long journey," I said. "If anyone is to help, it will be me."

Dorcus looked taken aback. "So be it." She gave Ruth a weak smile. "Both of you go and rest.'

"A Moabitess!" Dorcus whispered as she left. "How could you have brought her here? She doesn't belong. The Moabites are our enemies."

"She belongs where I belong," I said with force. Dorcus no longer intimidated me. "If my daughter isn't welcome here, then I'm also unwelcome."

While Damaris went to fetch what food we had, Ruth and I climbed to the living floor. I was ashamed for my daughter to see that we possessed nothing other than one low table, a few cushions which we hadn't taken with us, and a couple of old oil lamps, cracked and chipped.

"You left a life of ease to come here to nothing," I said as we sank down on the cushions. I could barely walk. But I was home.

"I don't care for a life of ease," Ruth said.

Imla was the first to come. I heard her crying out, "Naomi, Naomi," as she ran through the corridor toward the ladder. She arrived out of breath, flung herself into my arms, and cried in joy and then in grief. When she finally contained herself, she drew Ruth to her and kissed her on both cheeks. "Welcome to Bethlehem," she said.

All day, people came. How many lonely moments had I spent during the past seasons longing for company? Yet I saw the questions in their eyes, the ones they wouldn't ask. Later, they would. A question tomorrow, another next week, a few more later, until the whole town knew all that happened. They'd pass judgement, feel sorry for me, predict Ruth's hopeless future. In the eyes of a few, I caught glimmers of condemnation at the poor decision that took my family away. None seemed interested in what I'd seen, or how big the world was, or how things might be different in other places.

"My bride daughter, Machlon's wife," I said each time I introduced Ruth. "She gave up everything to bring me safely back."

They looked at Ruth from the corners of their eyes, or with raised brows. A few stepped away. Others ran their gaze over her from head to toe as though they thought a Moabite would look different than an Israelite. Only Imla treated her with honor.

A few brought food – dried fruit, cheese, nuts. Despite their grain cellars being empty, they were full of happy anticipation for Yahweh had succumbed and made the rains come. They could afford to be generous because soon the perfume of baking bread would fill their homes. And after the barley, would come the wheat.

At midday, my brothers left the fields to see if it was really me and to reprimand me for leaving Bethlehem in the first place.

"No good was bound to come of it," one said. "

"Elimelech should have listened to us," Dorcus's husband said.

They stole glances at Ruth, but when I introduced her, they offered no greeting, no welcome, but plied me with questions on how I planned to survive.

"I suppose you'll have to live with one of us," Dorcas's husband said. "But we can't have a Moabitess in the house."

"Where I go, she goes," I said.

He scratched his head. "She could . . . uh . . .., well, she could join the servants." He said this in Ruth's hearing.

"Thank you for your offer, but Ruth and I will live in *my* home."

They left with raised eyebrows, cutting their eyes at each other.

Later, Imla returned. "Our brothers tell me you plan to remain in your home. But how will you live? Will you sell your field?"

I nodded. Selling Elimelech's field would be like tearing away my flesh, but it had to be done.

"If I had grain, I'd give it to you gladly," Imla said. "We scraped the last few kernels from the floor of the cellar weeks ago, but soon we'll have plenty. Some of it will be yours."

I had left Bethlehem rich, but returned a beggar. "I'll go and glean."

Ruth, who had been sitting quietly to the side, stirred. "No," she said. "*I* will go and glean. You'll stay home and recover."

Imla looked at my swollen feet. "She's right, Naomi. You're likely to cripple yourself forever if you don't stay off your feet for a few days."

"My feet will be better tomorrow." I was no longer the wife of a rich man, and I had to act accordingly even with swollen and bleeding feet. I would not lie around waiting for the dogs to lick my wounds.

Chapter 53

Dizzy from too much sleep and wobbling because of sore feet, I limped out of my sleeping chamber the next morning, grabbed the roof support near the ladder well to steady myself, and stood in the shaft of sunshine beaming through the roof opening. Seldom in my life had the sun risen before me.

"Sit down. Sit down," Damaris said, coming up the ladder. She carried a flagon and a cup. "You need water."

I sank onto a cushion. "You went to the well without my help."

"These three years past, I've gone to the well without your help." She filled the cup and handed it to me. "Drink."

I drank. Water of Bethlehem; how sweet the taste. She poured more. After three cupfuls, I handed the cup back and asked, "Where's Ruth?"

"Gleaning."

"Gleaning! She doesn't know how. Her father was a rich man. They had servants to do everything."

"I told her all she needs to know."

"Will they leave grain for a Moabitess?"

"There's been too much hunger for harvesters to worry about who gleans."

After a breakfast of dried apricots and figs, I regained steadiness, but my feet felt even more sore than yesterday. Damaris brought salve and a basin of water.

"Tell me about Arioch and Abi," she said as she began washing my feet.

From the way she kept her eyes lowered, I knew she dreaded to hear. I told her how Arioch had married Mesha, and about their child, and that Abi had found true love – a small lie to make Damaris happy.

"And Uri?"

"Uri died." I swallowed. "An unfortunate accident."

"I always knew he'd have an accident the way that boy scrambled around the rocks." Her voice was choked. "I never saw him do this, but I heard from the other shepherds. And Kir?"

"I misjudged Kir," I said softly. "Elimelech was right. Kir was the best of the lot."

"What happened to him?" Forgetting my feet, she sat back on her heels.

"He's gone in search of his brother."

"His brother?"

"Kir was born into the tribe of Reuben. His unmarried mother left him in the streets to die when he was born. His grandmother saved him, thinking his malformed face would straighten as he grew and that she would be able to get money from the father who had no other sons. At first, she kept him hidden from his father." I swished my feet in the water before continuing; already they felt better. "A year or so later, Kir's mother had another son from the same man. When Kir's father saw Kir for the first time, he beat both the grandmother and Kir, and he threatened to sell them as slaves."

Damaris breathed out a long *Nooooo*.

"When the younger son was old enough, the man sold Kir and his brother to the head of a caravan. The two boys took care of the animals. As they became older, they plotted their escape."

"They ran away?"

"Kir escaped, but something went wrong and his brother didn't. For years Kir has questioned every caravanner he's encountered, trying to find his brother. Do you remember how Kir never wore the new clothes I made for him?"

"I do."

"He sold them and saved the silver. He hoped if he found his brother he could buy his freedom."

"He'd never have saved enough."

"Kir gave me what little he had."

Her downturned mouth set tight, Damaris focused her attention on my feet, rubbing in the last bit of salve, and then wrapping a towel around them. When she finished, she sat back on her heels. "You're the mistress, but right now I'm giving orders. You'll do no work, but rest today, and tomorrow, and for many days after." Then she smiled and said, "Blessings on Kir."

"It's your turn, Damaris. Tell me all that's happened since we left."

She told me of marriages, births, arguments between neighbors, rifts in families, the plight of beggars of which there had been more and more. She told me of deaths. A neighbor's husband. Her cousin. The old priest. Boaz's wife.

"So Lailah died." I wasn't surprised. Only sad. Boaz's wife had always been sickly, keeping mainly to her bed. "When?"

"Shortly after you left. The poor man has been alone these three years."

Late in the morning, a messenger came from the new priest, bidding me come.

"She can't walk," Damaris said to the boy before I could respond. I was still seated on the same cushion I'd been sitting on all morning.

"Priest Ulich insists she come."

"Did you not hear me?" Damaris propped her hands on her hips. "She can't walk. Tell that to the priest: She. Can't. Walk. Now, off with you."

The boy looked at me, waiting for me to refute my serving woman.

"Off, off," Damaris said again, waving him away with the back of her hand.

He turned and left.

Despite the pains in my hips and feet and the weather being too warm, at midday I climbed to the roof. I wanted to see the harvesting. Damaris brought dried figs and labneh for our meal.

"Where did the labneh come from?" I asked. Labneh hadn't been among the gifts people brought the previous day.

"Boaz. He sent it this morning."

So Boaz had heard of my return. "How did Boaz's flock fare in the drought?" I wanted to hear that some wondrous miracle had occurred to keep his sheep alive and healthy.

"Like everyone, he lost most of his animals."

He would have little labneh to spare, yet he had sent it. "When I can walk again, and when he isn't in the fields or at the threshing floor, I'll go and express my regret for the loss of his wife and thank him for the labneh."

I finished eating, rose, and hobbled over to the parapet to look out over the fields, now empty of harvesters for they were having their meal and resting. I stood there for only a short while before they emerged from beneath the few scattered trees, carrying their sickles. Soon the fields were alive with activity. Behind the reapers, came the gatherers, collecting the harvested stalks in the laps of their garments, and behind the gatherers, came the gleaners.

I searched the fields, wondering to which Ruth had gone. Not being accustomed to this type work, she was surely exhausted, yet I hoped she'd bring home enough grain for one loaf. My stomach rumbled, and my mouth watered at the thought. The bread we'd bake this evening would have a special taste, the longed for taste of my own bread oven and of Damaris' hands.

Though I dreamed of bread and a satisfied stomach, a knife ripped through my heart. My husband wasn't out there. His field lay barren, filled with weeds. My sons would never walk that field with their children hanging onto them, their wives watching from the roof. I'd never feel the warmth of a grandchild sitting on my lap.

Though I'd slept for so many hours during the night, I slept again in the afternoon. When I awoke to someone shaking me and telling me to wake up, I sat up confused, not knowing where I was.

"Wake up. Wake up. The priest is here." Damaris said..

"The priest?" I didn't understand.

"You didn't go to him, so he's come to you. He's waiting on the roof. Here . . .." She held my outer garment for me to slip into.

Reluctantly, I rose and let Damaris fasten the shoulder while I wondered what the priest wanted and why he came to me after I refused to go to him.

I found him leaning on the parapet watching the harvesters. He straightened and turned to face me when I stepped from the ladder well. Unaffected by the deprivations of three years of drought, he stood before me, fat-bellied and triple-chinned.

"Where is the Moabitess?" he asked.

I lifted my hand toward the fields. "She's gleaning so that we can eat."

"She's your servant."

"She's my daughter."

He gave me a hard look. "You went to live in the land of our enemies, and now you've brought one that you say isn't your servant to live among us. This is a bad example for your neighbors."

"I believe it's a good example."

"You're refuting me, the priest?"

"The Moabites eat, drink, and breathe, as we do. They laugh and cry. They love their children. They grieve their dead. If they're so like us, why should they be our enemies because of something that happened two hundred years ago?"

"They refused Moishe passage through their land."

"Two hundred years ago, and perhaps with good reason. How many tribes had the Israelites had made war on? How many people had they destroyed?"

"You're a woman; that isn't for you to judge. The Moabites are idolaters."

"As are some Israelites. Is your Yahweh any better than Chemosh?"

His mouth fell open. Then he sputtered until he finally managed to say, "You! You've become one of them. A Baal worshipper."

"No, I'm not a Baal worshipper." I sat down on a cushion and covered my feet with the edge of my garment. "I know of no god that I want to worship."

He gasped.

"Your god starved the people of this land for ten seasons. To what purpose? Does he love death more than he loves the lives of those who are supposed to be his people? I speak not only of the drought, and of other droughts and plagues. But of war and battles. How many have we Israelites killed? How many have the people of other gods killed? Is there no god in the universe that asks us to love each other?"

The priest's lips quivered.

"I bring a harmless, Moabite girl home with me, one to whom I owe my life, yet you reprimand me."

"You will regret your words." His face aflame, he took a step toward me. "I give you a few days to recover, but then you will amend what you have said and present a sacrifice."

"A sacrifice! I have sacrificed my husband. I have sacrificed my sons. I have sacrificed everything we had. What more can your terrible god want? Yahweh will get nothing more from me." I wasn't afraid. Yahweh, or any god, could strike me dead. I cared not.

Words choked in the throat of the priest. Finally, he gave up trying to find a suitable reply to my heresy. Nostrils flared and nose in the air, he left.

The aroma of the incense he wore had barely faded when I realized I was wrong about not caring. A tiny shred of care appeared like a torn flower petal bobbing on a wave, appearing, disappearing, and then appearing again to finally remain in constant view. I cared, for I had a daughter. I understood now what had needled me during my return. I couldn't die, for I had Ruth, whom I loved and for whom I was responsible.

"What have you done?" Dorcus screeched as her head emerged from the ladder well. "You've enraged the priest. He'll curse you. Maybe he'll curse your entire family. All of us." Her eyes full of fire and fury, she climbed onto the roof, came to where I sat, and loomed over me.

I drew myself up. "What I've done is nothing to you."

"Nothing to me! Everyone is talking about what you've become."

"And what have I become, Dorcus?"

"You're no longer high and mighty, married to a rich man. You're nothing but a . . . ., but a . . . .. You're nothing but a penniless widow with no sons. You don't own a single animal. Your husband's field lays fallow. Your storage cellar is empty. The rest of us will have to sacrifice so you can live. You and that girl you call your daughter. Yet you insult the priest."

"Don't sacrifice for me, Dorcus. I'll live without your help. And I *will* live, for there's something I must do." Though how I'd do it, I didn't know.

Chapter 54

Before the sun set, Damaris and I built a fire in the bread oven, impatience and hope nearly exploding within us as we awaited Ruth's return. Finally, we heard the front gate scrape open and then close.

"She's back," Damaris said, jumping up. Faster than I'd ever seen Damaris move, she scurried away to meet Ruth.

I closed my eyes and breathed deeply, relieved that Ruth was safely back.

"Wait until you see what she's brought," Damaris called from the corridor.

When they came to where I sat beside the oven, their faces were wreathed in smiles.

"Look." Damaris held out a basket filled to the brim with grain while Ruth held a cloth bundle.

"Parched grain," Ruth said, folding back a corner of the cloth to show me.

"All that?" I asked in disbelief.

"Yes." Ruth looked tired but happy.

"How . . .?" I held up my hands in a question.

"When the owner of the field came to greet his workers, he asked if I was the Moabitess who returned with Naomi. When I replied that I was, he told his workers to leave extra grain for me. Then he gave me water and invited me to share their bread and parched grain. They even let me dip bread in their vinegar." Her face was full of wonder. "He said I should come to his field for the remainder of the harvest."

"Whose field was it?" I, too, was in wonder at the kindness of this unknown benefactor.

"His name is Boaz."

◆ ◆ ◆

During those long, long days while Ruth gleaned, I recovered, often falling asleep several times throughout the day. My body was weighted with an exhaustion of such intensity that sometimes I found it difficult to sit up and eat. My nights weren't restful. I awoke from dreams to find myself drenched in sweat. Not only at nights did the ghosts appear, but during the day I'd look toward the ladder well and see Killion's bright smile popping into view, his eyes full of mischief or excitement at some wonder he'd encountered. Sometimes I'd see Machlon's quieter smile and know he was coming to tell me he'd engaged all day in men's work and done a fine job. Noise in the corridor always set my heart racing. It was Elimelech returning from the fields or the shearing pens, or from checking the vineyard. The ghosts came and went – the ghosts of my sons at all the ages they'd ever been, the ghost of my husband, always strong and handsome.

Only when Ruth returned, did the ghosts vanish. Each day, she brought her basket filled to overflowing. When parched grain was left over from the workers' lunches she brought that, too, saying Boaz had given it to her.

"What else has he said to you?" I asked.

"That he heard about the way I left my mother and father and the land of my birth to come here with you. That he understood living among strangers must be hard."

Though he was my husband's cousin and we'd been friends for many years, Boaz never visited during this time. He sent things: sometimes labneh, sometimes cheese or olives. I guessed the reason he didn't come. If he showed my Moabite daughter such favor in his field and also visited my home, people would remember the story of how the young men with Moishe fornicated with Moabite women.

◆ ◆ ◆

The barley was harvested, the grain winnowed, heated, and stored. The wheat harvest began soon after. Throughout both harvests, Ruth went to Boaz's field, returning each day with basketfuls of grain.

As the wheat harvest drew to a close, I sent Damaris' nephew to Boaz's field to quietly find out when they'd finish in the field and for which day Boaz had reserved the harvesting floor. On the morning of that day, I instructed Ruth to return in the middle of the afternoon.

"I'll explain when you come in from the field." I said before she asked me the question her eyes told me she wanted to ask: *Why?*

While Damaris washed Ruth's good set of clothes and laid them out to dry, I went to Imla.

"Do you have perfume?" I asked, after refusing her offer of food and drink.

"A little." She was puzzled at my abrupt request.

I answered the question in Imla's eyes. She said nothing for a few moments as she considered my plan, but then she nodded and said, "I'll give you what I have." Her face broke out in a big smile. "I can't guess how this will turn out. Ruth is, after all, a Moabitess. But how wonderful it would be if . . .." She rubbed her hands together in delight. "I'll get the perfume."

She hurried to her sleeping chamber and returned with a small amphora. "Here," she said, thrusting the vessel at me. "I bless this perfume with all my good wishes."

Ruth returned mid-afternoon as I had asked. I took the basket of grain from her and, with my other hand, took her by the wrist. "Come." I pulled her toward the end of the corridor where Damaris had placed a large basin and a small basin, both filled with warm water. "I'll explain as you bathe."

Ruth threw questioning glances at both Damaris and me as we helped her out of her clothes. I pointed to the stool where she should sit while bathing and handed her soap and a cloth while Damaris went to wash dirt from her sandals.

"Everyone will be sleeping at the threshing floor tonight," I said to Ruth. "Boaz is Elimelech's cousin. Do you like him?"

"I like him very much." Ruth dipped the cloth in the water then held it dripping over the vessel, waiting for me to go on.

I motioned to the cloth, indicating that she should be using it. She wrung it out and wiped her face.

"Boaz is much older than you," I said.

"Why do you point out what I can see?" She looked puzzled.

"Boaz's wife died three years ago, and he has no heirs. Their babies all died in the womb."

My daughter became very still.

"Would you mind so much being married to an older man?"

"I loved Machlon," she said, her eyes tearing. "He was sweet, and kind, and . . . .." She pressed her lips together in an effort to control her grief."

I fought to keep my heart from ripping apart anew. "We're going to bury these thoughts of Machlon for a brief while, Ruth. Our survival – yours and mine – would be Machlon's greatest wish now."

She nodded, took a deep breath, and said, "Boaz is such a marvelous man that I'd lie down in the dirt and let him walk over me if he asked."

I gave a little laugh. "He wouldn't be so marvelous if he asked that of you."

She smiled. "True. I would gladly marry him, but he won't marry me. Have you forgotten who I am?"

"No, I haven't forgotten who you are." I gave her a little pinch on the cheek. "You are the best bride-daughter a mother could have. So wash yourself, and then I'll tell you what to do."

While Ruth scrubbed her nails, Damaris returned with a jar of oil and Ruth's worn, torn, but now clean, sandals. "Put your feet in the water so the dirt will soak away." Damaris kneeled beside the vessel as Ruth put her feet in. "Hand me your cloth."

Damaris scrubbed vigorously, bringing a little sound from Ruth's mouth. "Your feet have dirt on them from two countries, two highways, a desert, the Judean Hills, and Boaz's field. So, be patient."

"My feet aren't *that* dirty," Ruth protested. "I've washed them every day."

"So you have." Damaris scrubbed harder. Finally, she finished.

"You haven't told me what I'm to do," Ruth said, trying to cover her nakedness with her arms.

"First, your hair needs tending." I lifted a mass of her dark locks, then watched them fall back down her back. The same wind that separated grain from chaff, blew hair into tangles despite shawls. "You won't feel like attending to what I say while I'm pulling at these snarls." I reached for the smaller vessel of water, and poured it bit by bit over her hair as I worked up a lather with our last bit of soap. I washed away the lather with the remainder of the water, toweled her hair with a bit of cloth, and began combing away the snarls and tangles. Finally, I set aside the comb and picked up the container of oil. Damaris had mixed mint into the oil, so it gave off a pleasing scent.

"Tonight Boaz will be threshing," I said, rubbing oil onto Ruth's back. "There will be food and laughter. Everyone will be merry. They'll tell funny stories and sing. They may even wiggle their bottoms while they're winnowing, pretending to dance." I rubbed the last of the oil on her shoulders and arms, then took the amphora of perfume from Damaris, and scented Ruth's wrists, ankles, and neck while Damaris went to bring Ruth's garments which had been drying on the fig tree.

"Stand up," I said finally. Ruth stood, and I helped her slip into the clean tunic, smoothing it around her hips. Then I reached for her outer garment. These were the clothes I'd woven for her – the light blue tunic, the dark indigo outer garment. They were finely woven, and expensively dyed. Boaz would see that Ruth had not been a beggar, but rather the daughter of a successful man. I arranged the outer garment over one shoulder, and Damaris fastened it with a fibula.

"Don't let Boaz know you're there until he's had plenty to eat and drink," I said. "Then show yourself so he can see how beautiful you are. But keep your distance. When he slips away to sleep, watch where he lies and then go and lie at his feet."

"At his feet?" She looked troubled.

I draped her white shawl over her head and arranged it evenly over her shoulders. "Slip your feet beneath his cloak."

Ruth blushed. "I must do this?"

"It will tell him you're available for marriage. Then wait and see what he says."

She frowned. "I'm to lie with him under his cloak?"

"Boaz is an honorable man."

A tiny seed of doubt surfaced. How many people had I misjudged? All that I knew about Uri had been good, yet he'd sinned abominably. And Kir had turned out to be everything I thought he wasn't. I steadied my breath. No, I would not believe I could be wrong about Boaz.

Damaris handed Ruth her still-wet sandals. After Ruth had put them on, I drew her to me and kissed her on the forehead. "Go with my love," I said.

She nodded and left us without looking back, disappearing through the front gate, her white shawl floating behind her.

"Boaz is a man like any other," Damaris said, looking askance at me. "He hasn't had a woman since his wife died."

Chapter 55

From the roof, I watched the threshing floor fade into a dark island amid a gray sea of fields as the sun set. Dark mounds of sheaved wheat lay piled beside the floor, awaiting tomorrow's winnowing. Earlier, I'd watched oxen tread the first of the harvest, dragging the threshing sledge over the unloosed bundles. Then the winnowers had tossed the stalks in the air so the west wind blowing in from the Great Sea could do its job. What I saw only in my imagination was the grain falling to the floor, the stalks landing on top of the grain, and the chaff blowing away. Workers had collected the stalks and piled them in carts. Later, the stalks would be dried and used as fodder. Last of all, the workers scooped up grain and loaded it into large baskets which they set aside to await the final cleaning. The following day, when all the wheat had been winnowed, women would sift the kernels through huge, round traylike sieves to separate out coarse chaff, dung, and small stones.

Pinpoints of light began to appear as lamps were lit, the lights flickering as workers crossed back and forth in front of them, finishing their work. Flames from several small fires licked the air. Workers would be huddled around the fires, parching grain. Soon, the aroma floated up to where I stood, along with song and laughter. The merriment would continue far into the night, until finally, exhausted, the workers would spread out to sleep, positioning themselves beside both the threshed grain and the un-threshed to protect it from thieves. This was when Ruth needed to be alert as to where Boaz chose to sleep.

"You must go to bed," Damaris said, coming to lean on the parapet beside me.

"I won't be able to sleep."

"I brought something to help." She handed me a cup. "Warm wine with honey."

I took a swallow, and then several more. The warmth running down my throat unloosed my tight muscles. "Where did you get the wine?"

She looked toward the dark island of the threshing floor where the workers had burst into a silly song about three donkeys.

"Damaris?"

"When you left three years ago, I dug a hole in the rams' stall," she said, still looking toward the threshing floor. "I buried a jug of wine. If thieves broke in, I wanted to make sure we still had something to celebrate with when you returned." Her voice breaking, she added gruffly, "You must go to bed." She turned to face me. "No arguing."

I lay down knowing I wouldn't sleep. How could I when my mind was a battlefield? Boaz was too old for my daughter. No, he wasn't too old. He'd make a fine husband for her and she a fine wife for him.

He would be honorable when he found Ruth sleeping at his feet. He wouldn't be honorable for he was a man, unsatisfied by a woman for a long time.

If someone saw Ruth do as I'd instructed, gossip would wing its way around Bethlehem with the speed of a swooping falcon. Ruth, the Moabite seductress, they'd call her. *What else can one expect of Moabite women?*

Maybe Boaz would reject her because she was a Moabitess. Or take advantage of her because she was a Moabitess.

I tossed and turned. The words of a song drifted to where I lay, funneling their way down the ladder well. I heard laughter. Then I drifted into the land that lay between waking and sleeping. My breathing slowed. Visions of sleeping workers filled my dream. Of Ruth watching Boaz to see where he would recline. *Half-concealed behind a pile of chaff, she watches, while around her, women joke, eye the men, try to hold their eyes open a little longer. Many are beginning to nod. Not Ruth. She leans forward and twists her head so that her gaze can follow Boaz as he walks away from the floor. He must be going to relieve himself, for he walks a little way into the surrounding field. Ruth's heart pounds. Will he return? Or has he found a place to sleep out of her sight?*

I awoke with a jerk, listening for sounds from the fields but hearing nothing more than cicadas snapping their wings. My eyelids were heavy, so heavy . . . .

Boaz returns to the threshing floor, picks up the last oil lamp that is still burning and walks a circuit, checking the workers, softly conversing with a few who haven't fallen asleep. After a second look around to ensure all is well, he goes to a stack of sheaves, sets the lamp down, and unrolls his mat. The planes of his face show in the circle of light as he places one of the sheaves as a pillow. Before he extinguishes the lamp, Ruth measures with her eyes the distance between her and him. Nineteen or twenty steps perhaps. She also notes the obstacles. A pile of winnowing forks lies halfway between her and Boaz. Boaz wraps himself in his cloak and pinches out the flame.

"Don't fall asleep, Ruth. You won't wake up if you fall asleep," I called out in the darkness, awakening from my dream. I sat up, sweating. Then I whispered, "Don't fall asleep, Ruth." I lay back down and felt myself drifting once again into the sleep which Ruth must renounce.

Ruth sits up, listens. Around her: snores, the cicadas, a breeze rattling the sheaves. Warily, she rises, takes careful steps toward where she knows the pile of winnowing forks to be. Eight steps. Nine. Then she puts out her right foot, feeling with her toes for the forks. She feels nothing other than grass and chaff. Another careful step forward, this time with her left foot. She feels the forks. Her toe causes one to move, making a scraping noise. She turns to stone, but then realizes that everyone sleeps in such exhaustion they won't hear the scratch of one wooden handle against another. She moves around the pile of forks and counts out another ten steps, slowly, cautiously.

Moonglow bathes the forehead and cheeks of Boaz's handsome face and illumines one shoulder, for he sleeps on his side, his head resting on the sheaf. Thrusting aside her doubts, for she trusts her mother-in-law, Ruth lies down at Boaz's feet, carefully, so as not to awaken him. His cloak has slid from his shoulders to cover only the lower part of his body so it's easy for her to arrange a bit of the garment over her feet.

Boaz awakens, sits up for a few moments as though trying to remember where he is. Then he looks toward his feet, reaching out his hand at the same time.

◆ ◆ ◆

Someone was shaking me by my shoulders. "Wake up, Mother," the voice said.

I sat up abruptly. The black of night had thinned enough for me to see Ruth. She smelled of the threshing floor.

"I did as you instructed," she said.

I clasped her by the arm. "Tell me what happened."

"He said good things about me."

"What good things?"

"That I was courageous. But come down to where Damaris is lighting the oven. We'll be warm while I tell you everything."

She helped me to my feet, and we joined Damaris beside the oven where flames had already begun to crackle. Ruth's shawl lay on the ground, piled high with wheat.

Damaris had taken up her mortar and pestle and was pounding kernels into flour. "Enough to feed us all week," she said, nodding to the pile.

"Boaz gave you all this?" I asked Ruth, wondering if it was a gift to a bride-to-be or a consolation gift. "You've kept me wondering too long." I sank to the bench and pulled her down beside me.

Damaris stopped the whop whop of the pestle.

"I did as you said," Ruth began. "I took note of where Boaz lay down beside a stack of sheaves. When everyone was asleep, I crept over and curled up at his feet. In the middle of the night, he woke and realized someone was there. I was afraid. . . .." She shivered and hugged herself. "I feared he'd shout and wake everyone up. But he didn't." She let out a sigh of relief. "He asked who lay at his feet, and I told him."

"What did he say then?"

"I can't remember exactly. Something like, bless you or . . . .." She shrugged. "He asked if I wouldn't prefer a younger man."

My heart sank.

"I told him I wanted a man as kind as he, and that I loved him already for his goodness. He didn't say anything for a little while. Then he said it would be an honor to call me his wife, but first he had to ensure that someone closer than he didn't wish to redeem me."

"Josea," I said. "A first cousin to Elimelech."

"Then we went to sleep, but he woke me before the others awoke and sent me home. He said he'd take care of what had to be done." She looked at me for an explanation.

"Did he say when?"

"Right away, I think."

Damaris had laid the pestle in her lap, dropping all pretense of making flour.

"Where are the clothes I wore when I came?" I asked Damaris.

"When you came? Why, you have them on." She motioned to my clothes.

"No, the man clothes."

"In the storage room where we keep the rags." She gave me an odd look.

I rose abruptly and went to the storage room.

No one noticed the strange man among the throng of field hands walking toward the town gate as they headed for the fields. Outside the gate, I settled in a spot beside the wall where I thought Boaz would assemble a quorum. Two traders had set up nearby, hoping to entice workers to spend part of their earnings on trinkets. Grain merchants had already made their way to our gates, prepared to buy. Three had stationed themselves outside the walls with their pack animals and bondsmen. With all this, no one would pay attention to a stranger haunched down wearing a scarf that hid most of his face.

Boaz soon came and stood a short distance from where I stooped, holding his hand over his eyes to shade them from the rising sun. A streak of gray had formed at each of his temples, but he was still handsome and fit. He grabbed a passing elder by the arm. "Step aside, old friend," he said, and motioned to a bench. "Take a seat. We have some business to take care of."

"Now?" The man gave Boaz an annoyed look. "It's my turn at the threshing floor this afternoon. I have to finish harvesting."

"This won't take long. Your head man knows what to do. Please." Again, Boaz motioned to the bench.

With an irritated look, the man went to stand beside the bench, crossing his arms and huffing impatiently. Boaz stopped another elder, and then another. Josea, the cousin, also caught in Boaz's web, came to stand with the elders. Soon, Boaz had a quorum of ten men, some sitting, some standing, but all impatient to be in their fields or at the threshing floor.

I had become uncomfortable sitting on my haunches. My ankles burned from the unaccustomed position, and, in nervous anticipation of what was to happen, I felt as though a colony of ants crawled beneath my skin.

Boaz turned to the elders. "This piece of business involves the sale of a field."

The elders' talk stopped, and they focused on Boaz. The mention of a field for sale had caught their attention. Most probably had no interest in purchasing a field, nor, after the drought, the means, but land ownership provided the same attraction for them as finding mates for children provided their wives.

"Thank you," Boaz said. "We're all busy, but we can do this quickly. Please witness." He turned to Josea. "The piece of property that belonged to Elimelech is being sold by Naomi, who, as you've heard, has returned from Moab. If you want to buy it you have first redeemer rights according to our laws for you are closest in kin. If you intend to do this, make it known in the presence of those sitting here." He swept his hand around, indicating the men present.

I held my breath. Josea was ten years younger than Boaz, making him age-wise a more suitable match for Ruth, but what more did I know of him? I knew Boaz to be kind, loyal, and someone whom Ruth could love.

"If you don't want to buy the land, then say so, for I'm next in line after you." Boaz folded his arms and waited.

Heads turned toward Josea who, looking pleased, shifted from foot to foot. "I have to think on this." He said this although he looked as though his mind had already been made up.

"Well, think on it fast," one of the elders said. "My grain is about to go to the threshing floor."

"And mine to the other threshing floor," said another. He snapped his fingers. "Come on, Josea, we see on your face that you want to buy the field. You look like someone just handed you a bag of silver."

"Yes, I want to buy the field," Josea said and grinned.

No, no, no. I searched Boaz's face, but he kept his expression as still as a day without a breeze.

"You realize," Boaz said. ". . . when you buy the field from Naomi, you also get Ruth the Moabitess, Machlon's widow. As the redeemer, it's your responsibility to have children with her to carry on Machlon's inheritance."

"I can't do that." Josea looked alarmed. "I'd jeopardize my own family's inheritance."

"But you must." Boaz looked sternly at Josea. "It's the law."

"She's a Moabitess. The law doesn't apply."

The others, very quiet now, swiveled their eyes between the two men.

"The law applies." Boaz kept his stern look fixed on Josea.

Josea looked around at the elders. "Is that true?"

"When she married Machlon, she had to convert and agree to worship Yahweh instead of Chemosh," one said. "That means the law applies."

Several nodded.

The first elder Boaz had stopped stood up. "Josea, either buy the field and marry Ruth, or don't buy the field and let Boaz buy it and marry Ruth. Whichever it is, my crop awaits. Give us your answer."

"No." Josea shook his head. "No, I won't marry a Moabitess. Boaz can buy the field and marry the slut." Josea stooped down, untied his shoe, and handed it to Boaz. "Here, I give you my shoe, signifying that I forfeit the right to act as redeemer."

Something *did* show in Boaz's face as he accepted the shoe. Happiness? Relief? Pleasure? Whatever the emotion, I knew it was good.

Boaz stared at the shoe for a few moments as though reading his future in its sole. At length, he lifted his face to the others. "You who are gathered here see that I have bought from Naomi everything that belonged to Elimelech and his sons. I will take Ruth as my wife and keep the name and memory of Machlon alive. You are the witnesses to what has happened here today." He took a step toward Josea, his eyes hard. "Ruth is an honorable woman. You will treat her with respect, and the word you just called her will never again come from your lips in reference to my wife."

Afraid that someone would see the tears of relief that sprang to my eyes, I pretended to dislodge something caught between my foot and the sole of my sandal. When I stood, the elders were dispersing, but I noticed for the first time that others had gathered to hear.

"We are witnesses, too," one called out. "We wish you much happiness, Boaz."

"And many children with Ruth," another shouted.

I left Boaz smiling as I hurried away to unwrap the pure white wool I'd saved for my sons' brides. On that day, I began weaving Ruth's wedding garments.

Chapter 56

Ruth and Boaz celebrated their nuptials during the Festival of First Fruits. The air was filled with the scent of newly made fig cakes, the perfume of honied fruit, and the aroma of freshly baked bread. Wine was drunk in great quantities. Days and evenings were filled with merriment, every song sung a hundred times over, every poem recited as often, every story retold with fresh embellishments. The air scintillated with excitement, for the wedding of Ruth and Boaz represented more than just a wedding. It was the end of a terrible drought and brought hopes for a bright future for everyone. Bethlehem was a joyful place indeed.

And I danced.

Yes, I danced. My feet had healed though my heart never would. Not completely. Yet, the pain had moved aside to allow a bit of happiness to creep in.

As he welcomed his new bride into his life, Boaz showed as much liveliness as a man half his age. There was something wonderful between them. Everyone noticed the way they looked at each other, the stolen touches that passed between them that no one was supposed to see but that everyone did.

My daughter and her husband begged me to live with them but I chose to continue in my own home for a while longer, although it was true, as many claimed, that I often spent the greater part of my days in their home, only returning to my own to sleep. Damaris and I always had our evening meal with them.

"I waited so long to return and wanted it so much," I explained to Ruth and Boaz. "You must indulge me while I deal with the ghosts. They haven't finished with me yet nor I with them."

Until the angel of death chased me down, Elimelech would walk beside me every day, still handsome, still good-humored. As would my sons. There'd always be Machlon's sweetness and Killion's smile which rivaled that of my husband, or perhaps even surpassed it. Sometimes, when I sat on the roof spinning, I'd hear Killion taunting Machlon to some mischief and Machlon resisting until, finally giving in, he'd laugh. Then the two of them would scamper off to indulge in whatever Killion had dreamed up. Once, I imagined I heard Machlon climbing the ladder. He's bringing me flowers, I thought. When he was too little to understand how quickly flowers withered, he sometimes gathered them as a gift for me. The most painful times were when I went to the parapet to look out over the fields and thought I saw Elimelech returning only to remember he'd never return.

I saw the others, too. Abi was often at the oven, her shadow arguing with Damaris, or she'd be swinging a skin back and forth, churning. Arioch, with his lion's mane would amble down the corridor, returning oxen to their stall, or putting away tools. Mostly though, I saw Arioch climbing out of the stairwell hungry as a lion. Kir, whose face had become both dear and beautiful to me despite its shape, was as quiet in spirit as he had been in body. I didn't think of Hada and Mesha as often as the others, for they had never lived with us before our ill-fated journey. But sometimes, I imagined them there, too.

I tried not to think of Uri, for that memory was too painful.

I blamed no one for Uri's death. Not Elimelech who believed with all his heart in following the laws. Not Moishe who had transcribed the laws. Least of all did I blame Uri. He was a young man, taken away from his home to be transplanted among strangers in a foreign land, bringing with him the passions and urges of a young man, the loneliness, the hopes. Was what he did so terrible that he deserved to die a horrendous death?

There were many things I didn't understand, but one that I did: what I knew and understood amounted to no more than one tiny grain of sand on a gigantic beach filled with endless sand. Whether or not the laws my husband so insistently followed were good or not was one of the things I didn't know.

It seemed that there should be something more to go with these laws, some other requirement. I was thinking this one day when Damaris asked me how we had spoken with the Moabites.

"We learned their language," I said. "It isn't so different from ours. Cyrus explained that our two languages are like cousins."

"Maybe many years ago the Moabites *were* our cousins."

"If the Israelites and the Moabites were cousins then why do we have two different gods?" I asked.

"Maybe we don't."

"Could it be that we have different names for the same god?"

"And the others, the Jebusites, and the . . . .." Damaris gave a little wave. "I can't even name everyone we've fought with. Maybe we were all cousins once, and maybe we each have a different name for the same god just like we have a different name for a fig."

"Yet we fight with each other. Sometimes we humans are worse than wolves." I thought of the attack that had left Springer dead. "Wolves kill for food, but we kill for greed and revenge, our awfulness encouraged by the gods."

Damaris raised her eyebrows. "Encouraged by the gods?"

"Doesn't Yahweh instruct us to kill our enemies? How many times have our prophets and leaders told us to . . . .."

"Maybe those that talk with Yahweh don't hear so good."

Damaris' answer left me breathless. Her heresy equaled mine.

We sat silent for a little while, then I asked, "Why isn't there a law saying we should love each other instead of fighting and quarreling?"

She shrugged her shoulders. "Seems like we need one. But is such a law possible?"

"I think not." No law could make me love Achilla and his two nephews. "Yahweh can send good weather and bad, blessings and destruction, but He can't force us to love." This notion was one of the moment, uttered without contemplation, but then a thought struck me. While walking the Way by the Sea, one day we'd seen waves large enough to knock a man down. The idea that Yahweh couldn't force us to love each other, and that humans themselves bore this responsibility struck me with the force of one of those gigantic waves.

"Why are you smiling?" Damaris asked.

"Boaz went beyond what the law required in regard to leaving grain for the gleaners and look what wonderful thing happened as a result. What if everyone acted with love and respect toward other humans as he did?"

"Hmmmph, there'd be lots more weddings and babies, wouldn't there?" I laughed.

Peace was made between me and the priest when Boaz provided sacrifices in my name. As for making peace with Yahweh, that was a journey I was still on. Perhaps it was simply a matter of my admitting that I wasn't meant to understand everything and having faith that my feet were set in the right direction..

The day came when I knew I had to stop dwelling on the dead and resurrect the shattered shreds of the Naomi that had been. More and more, my thoughts had been on Ruth and Boaz. I worried about Ruth. She tried hard but growing up without learning the house-keeping skills most girls do, I was concerned she wouldn't make Boaz happy, though the constant smile on his face told me otherwise. Still, I worried.

"Don't be a meddlesome mother-in-law," Damaris said when I criticized the way Ruth dried apricots. "Spoiled apricots aren't going to ruin a marriage, especially with what they're looking forward to."

"You're right," I said and laughed. Laughing had become easier, especially with a baby on the way.

"Anyway, you'll be needed there full-time any day now."

"And you, too, Damaris."

"Pish, nobody is going to need me. Lately, I'm about as useful as a toad."

"At least you're prettier than a toad."

"I haven't been pretty in fifty years."

And so I draw near the end of my story. In the telling, I find that some of the bitterness I expressed in the beginning has faded. The hurt and pain of having my family taken from me will always haunt me, but bitterness is a useless and self-defeating emotion. And since not one single person has called me *Mara,* despite my insistence, it appears I will be remembered as *Naomi.* Especially when a certain event, anticipated with much happiness, takes place. I await this with such eagerness that perhaps even I will forget that I once asked to be called "Mara."

Fulfilment

Chapter 57

"Naomi, Naomi!"

A woman is calling for me from the corridor. Damaris and I, in the middle of eating our breakfast, stop and look at each other. Her eyes light up, and I know mine have done the same for the person below has surely been sent by Boaz.

"It's time," I say.

"It's time," the woman calls out, as though I hadn't already announced that fact to Damaris. "Hurry."

We drop our bread and honey and rush down the ladder.

"It's happening fast," the woman says. "Maybe even while we're talking, the baby has come."

"Why didn't you call me when it started?" I scold, slipping into my sandals.

"Ruth insisted you get a full night's sleep because you'll be much needed later."

As fast as we can go, I in the lead, we hurry around two corners, up one hill, down another, and into the corridor of Boaz's home. We climb the ladder to find several women milling around, smiles engulfing their faces.

Boaz comes out of the bedchamber, his happiness bright enough to light the sky. "A son, Naomi. It's a son. A beautiful, perfect son. And Ruth is doing magnificently well." He grabs me by the shoulders and plants a kiss on my forehead. "My son's grandmother, go and see."

Two women are with mother and child. One holds a bowl of bloody water. It's easy to see she's too drawn to the sight of Boaz's healthy son and his *magnificently well* wife to leave. The other woman is gathering up bits of soiled cloth.

Ruth looks up from where she cuddles the baby to her breast. "Grandmother, come and meet your grandchild." Though tired, her eyes sparkle. "This is Obed," she says as she places the baby in my arms. "Your first grandson."

Boaz has returned with a cup of wine for his wife. "Is he not marvelous?"

"He is marvelous indeed," I say as I cuddle my tiny Obed. "Beyond all things on earth, he's marvelous."

A Prayer for my Sweet Grandson

Sweet, perfect boy, I adore your soft skin, chubby legs, and dimpled chin; the lock of dark hair curling against your forehead; your sweet baby smell; the tiny pink nails adorning your fingers and toes.

I press you to my heart which overflows with joy, with gratitude, with hope.

Your baby cry heals. The rips and tears in my soul are mended, the scars smoothed.

I have wishes for you, little one:

I wish that the world you live in will be gracious and loving.

That we treat others as we'd like to be treated ourselves.

That the things dividing us be forgiven and forgotten, our humanity forged into one. That Moabites and Israelites be friends. That *everyone* be friends.

Were I able, I'd build this world for you. A kind world. A wonderful world. But I'm an old woman. I pray that you, my Obed, whose name means "to serve," will be the beginning of how things should be.

Obed had Jesse.

Jesse had David, who became king.

David's descendent had the one who taught us:

Love they neighbor as thyself, love your enemies,

And Do unto others as you would have them do unto you.

Notes on *The Book of Ruth* and the Writing of this Novel

Naomi's story fascinated me for years before I finally put pen to paper (Metaphorically speaking. I am *not* one of those writers who composes in longhand before going to the computer!) In the beginning, what made me want to write her story, I can't say. Because it was my favorite story in the Bible? Or that it treats problems we're still stuck with: immigration, refugees, minorities, the status of women? Sometimes, I thought my interest had to do with Naomi being a woman who embodied a trait my grandmother advocated: *If you want to do something, don't make excuses; stop thinking about how, why, and when, just DO it!* In the end, this is what Naomi did. She was a strong woman.

Only while writing the book, did I realize what the real appeal of the story is. *The Book of Ruth* is a harbinger of the liberating breakthrough made in the New Testament which calls for an expansion of conscious love going beyond the restrictive laws of the Torah. Boaz was an embodiment of this kind of love. It's high time the rest of us followed suit.

The authorship of *Book of Ruth* (the only book in the Bible named for a Gentile) is contested. Some credit the prophet Samuel. Others claim it was written by a woman. No matter who the author is, it's a beautiful, heart-breaking, but ultimately wonderful story.

In *The Red Tent*, Anita Diamant changes the seven years stated in the Bible to seven months that Jacob was required to work in order to wed Rachel. (Plus another seven, making it a very long wait!) Considering the various issues with

Bible translations, seven months seems (to me) much more likely than seven years. Emulating Diamant's opting to be liberal in the interpretation of time, I changed the ten years Naomi remained in Moab to ten seasons. Also, I purposefully used a couple of anachronisms. The names for Jewish months hadn't been established during this time period. Nevertheless, I used them to help delineate the passage of the year. The Spring of Elisha wasn't so named until nearly a hundred years after Naomi's journey to Moab.

I apologize for whatever mistakes I've made in the writing of this book, historical, interpretational, or otherwise. Some will censure me for the opening of Naomi's mind. I do not apologize for that. Real faith and understanding come only after questions. Otherwise, we're not the logical creatures created in God's image as claimed in Genesis.

Glossary

Agora- a belt or waistband

Astarte- Chemosh's consort

Baal- god of the Canaanites

Bet Lehem- Bethlehem

Bondsman

Chemosh- god of the Moabites

Halil-

Kashrut-dietary laws of the Israelites

Labneh- yogurt

Mara- bitterness

Madouga- head of a caravan

Sheol- a place of darkness where the spirits of the dead go

Shofkha- penis

Tekhelet- a blue-violent or turquoise dye highly prized by ancient
    Mediterranean civilizations

Toda- thank you

Wether-a castrated male sheep

Yahweh- God of the Israelites

Zvena- whore

Acknowledgements

I could not have written this book without the help of quite a few people. Many, many thanks to Mary Powell, Bonnie Laudan, and Julia Pezzi for the time they spent reading, editing, and making invaluable suggestions. Your generosity and friendship is an inestimable gift.

When I began writing *A Woman of Valor*, I knew little of sheep. Nancy Cirigliano graciously spent a day answering my questions and providing information on things I didn't even have the background to ask about. I'm sure I've made mistakes on sheep and shepherding, but without Nancy's help I was at sea on the subject. And thank you to Jane Dreidame for introducing me to Nancy.

I am not a biblical scholar, but I spent time in libraries, bought books, and did marathons on the internet. After months of research, there were still many unanswered questions concerning life during the period of the Judges. Rabbi Uriel Smith, scholar and author, was kind enough to spend the larger part of a day with me and my unanswered questions. The hardest part of research, I found, was when to decide that no one knew the answer, leaving me free to make something up. Rabbi Smith was a huge help with this. Rabbi Smith, who struck me as a very special man, died four months prior to the publication of this book. Thank you, Sandy (Dr. Sandford Archer), for arranging for me to meet Rabbi Smith.

My writing group, Bluegrass Novelists, was with me every step of the way. My eternal gratitude to Jesse Siskin, Mary Morton, and Joy Welch. I couldn't have done it without you. You're my bread and butter, my rock, my balance when it comes to writing!

My Midsouth Writers Group was a blessing! I'll be forever grateful to Dianne Bellis, Nell Campbell, Lisa Haneberg, Krista Lea, Jennifer Caroland

Shaw, Adrielle Stapleton, and Nancy Walker. I look forward to wending my way through many more books (both mine and yours) with you!

Last but not least, I have the good fortune to have one of the best cover designers available. Thank you Nat Jones!

The Lady

By Judy Higgins

A Mystery About Unrequited Love

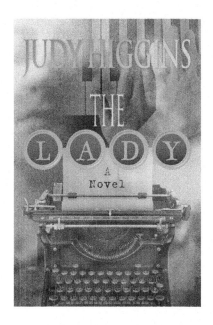

A Finalist in the Amazon Breakthrough Novel Contest

This isn't a good book; this is a GREAT book! ABNA Expert Reviewer

. . . a uniquely crafted novel with expert plotting and effortless pacing. Publisher's Weekly Reviewer.

Made in the USA
Monee, IL
21 October 2020